The Lunch

A Novel

A story of true love that transcends both space and time

by Robert Buchanan

Collaborator - Karen Sharon
Edited by Catherine Gigante-Brown
Cover Art by Robert Santora, Santora Design
Cover photo "The Rose" by Bob Buchanan
Author photo by Steve Morton

Published by Volossal Publishing
www.volossal.com

This book is a work of fiction and although it may read as true, it is not.

The events described herein are for the reader's entertainment, they having nothing to do with facts. As you read, you should know that absolutely no research went into keeping the past life events factual, as they are a figment of my overactive imagination.

Table of Contents

I05563641

Chapter One
Birds on Film

First, I'd like to apologize in advance for the rawness of this book—I'm a photographer, not a writer. I took the copy from the journal I'd been writing since this thing began, as I tried to get my head around what was going on. While I'm still not sure exactly what happened, I thought my experiences might help someone else who was going through something similar. For what it's worth, here goes...

    - J.S.

I was talking to Rocky at the local deli when my cell phone rang. At the time, I had no idea what a stream of life-changing events this call would unleash upon me. Innocently, I flipped open my phone. "Good morning," I answered cheerfully.

A sweet, familiar voice greeted me. "Morning, Jarred. It's Sherry. I'm just confirming our lunch today."

"How could I possibly forget? I'm looking forward to it," I said with a smile which I think showed in my voice.

"Me too!" she responded. "Listen, would you mind picking me up outside of the office? I don't want anyone knowing my business." I agreed to her request. "See you at 12:30," Sherry replied. I detected an odd tone in her voice, one I'd never heard before, but shrugged it off.

"No problem," I responded. "See you then."

"Looking forward to it, Jarred," Sherry said, ending the call.

First, a bit of backstory. Sherry was the sculptor in an artistic group I belonged to—Brush, Chisel & Lens. I thought it was a pretty catchy name for our little collective which included an artist, sculptor and photographer. (I was the latter.) Sherry and I first met when she began working for one of my clients, and we've been friends as well as business associates ever since. Smart, talented and witty, I liked her from the very first time I met her.

The lunch Sherry called to confirm was planned at Sunset Cove, a restaurant not far from her office. Situated on the Hudson River, on a perfect spring day like that one, Sunset Cove was a perfect place for a creative brainstorming session. Not only was the view great but the tables were spaced wide apart. It was beautifully-appointed without being stuffy, plus the food is excellent.

After hanging up with Sherry, I couldn't help but feel a little uneasy. There was something different about her this morning. Did I detect a slight nervousness in her voice? Or maybe it was me, a touch of spring fever that warm, sunny day was having on me. What I *didn't* miss was Sherry's desire to keep our meeting private. It wasn't unusual for us to get together for lunch, coffee or work sessions, but why was this so different? I slipped my cell phone back in my pocket.

Standing at the counter in Rocky's Deli, my attention shifted from my upcoming appointment with Sherry when I noticed a woman standing beside me, patiently waiting for her egg sandwich. An attractive lady with blonde hair and brown eyes, about five foot, five inches in height, she admired a photograph of a hot dog that hung on the wall.

"Wow! I love that picture," she said to no one in particular. "It looks so good, I should have ordered one for breakfast." Then she asked Rocky, "Where did you get it?"

Never one to pass up an opportunity to brag about my work, I chimed in, "From me...I created it."

"Did you really do that?" she asked in a coy tone. Was I detecting a bit of flirtation in it?

"Sure did. That's what I do for a living," I told her. "My name's Jarred."

The pretty lady smiled at me. "I'm impressed. Nice work Jarred. It's great to meet such a talented person." And with that, she grabbed her sandwich and said good- bye as she walked away.

I turned to Rocky and everyone else in the deli with a big grin. "Well, guys, that's a great way to start the day." Honestly, it felt wonderful to have a total stranger appreciate my work, and such an attractive one at that.

A few minutes later I said my farewells, was out the door and en route to my studio. My mind drifted back to my conversation with Sherry about lunch. I did a quick mental run-through of the things we needed to discuss for our upcoming art show, what the artists would be showing, and so on. I would be displaying images from my *Old Toys* project, but there would be all sorts of works represented there.

A stop at Rocky's was a predictable part of my daily routine. After working out at the local gym, I usually stopped there, grabbed a cup of flavored coffee and some sort of healthy nosh then headed over to my photography studio. I guess I'm a pretty typical middle-aged guy in some respects. But pretty unusual in others.

A married, father of two, I feel better now at age 51 than I ever did. I recently lost more than 30 pounds thanks to the guidance of my friend and workout buddy, Mary Ellen, who's one of the personal trainers at the gym. My daily workout helped me feel up to the challenge of whatever life threw at me and helped me sleep better too. I'd be the first to admit that I could be a bit of a bear without it.

My life was one of contrasts and variety. My father, a World War II veteran, navigated a B-17 bomber in England with the 34th Group. (Nicknamed The Flying Fortress, it was one serious aircraft.) Dad died when I was only 16 years old, leaving me pretty much on my own. It toughened me up at an early age. In order to survive, I psychologically constructed internal walls to keep myself safe. Looking back, I see that it was a protection mechanism—it was just something I did to get by. But today, I realize that it was something more.

At eight in the morning of my father's death I woke up with a start, an uneasy feeling in my chest, aware that something had happened. When the phone rang moments later, my worst fears came true. My father was dead. Making funeral arrangements with my Uncle Roger, whom I barely knew at that point of my life, was like a bad dream for me, my worst nightmare. It was an arduous task for a boy of 16, especially just two days before Christmas.

I would always be thankful to my uncle for stepping in the way he did—I didn't know if I could have done it without him. But even with his help, my father's death transformed me into a serious, careful man who was always in control of his thoughts, never allowing himself to drop his guard, nor letting anyone get beyond those walls he built around himself. Just the fact that I talk about myself in the third person gives you an idea of how tall and thick those walls are.

As I continued on in high school after my father's death, teachers often told me that my life would never amount to more than working the business end of a shovel. Right then and there, I made a vow to myself to prove them wrong. Today, I realized that they did me a favor by showing me I was tougher then I realized.

In a way, art saved me. Art has always been a big part of my life in one way or another, whether it be writing, drawing with pen and ink or photography. In my teens, after my father's death, when I wasn't working to survive (which was most of the time), I would sit, quietly writing down my observations on life as I saw it. I could do this for hours on end, alone in my bedroom, headphones on, listening to The Doors, or one of the popular rock groups of the 60s. I couldn't tell you whether I wrote for fun or therapy, or both. I guess I just wrote to survive.

My life experience, even at a young age, had always been wide-ranging. My interests were so vast and eclectic that I never knew what to do first. Even the music I liked to listen to was diverse—it went from *The Beatles* one minute then back to Montovani the next and onto *The Rolling Stones*.

While some people might say I was psychic or had "the shining," as far back as I can remember, I experienced the unexplainable—knowing something was going to happen before it did. I didn't understand much of it. Truthfully, it even scared me a little bit. I never trusted these events or told anyone about them, at least in the beginning. I wanted solid proof, a validation that I never seem to get. So I ignored these episodes...until I couldn't ignore them anymore.

Here's *The Reader's Digest* version of my life: After high school, a failed attempt at college and floundering around in various careers, I finally realized my lifelong dream of becoming a police officer. I spent 10 years in this career, enjoying my work in law enforcement immensely. The nature of the job—and working on shifts— gave me lots of time to spend on writing or drawing. I even dabbled in photography with a cheap 110 millimeter pocket camera. I wasn't able to afford a good 35 millimeter camera until years later.

Then one day at work, my whole world shifted. I was talking about photography with Frank, a fellow officer, who told me about a pretty decent camera—a Mamyia Secor—that was on sale in a Manhattan shop for only $78. It was a steal for such a great piece of machinery. First chance I got, I bought it. Then I needed to figure out how to take pictures, so, Frank and I signed up to attend a Nikon seminar with some of the other guys. "And the rest," as the saying goes, "is history."

From that moment on, nothing ever felt so right to me as being behind the camera. I started my photography business while I was still a police officer. In the tenth year of being on the job, I became so disenchanted with the politics that I decided to retire. Photography was growing into a successful commercial business for me with some art thrown in to keep things interesting. Besides keeping me "right," taking pictures helped me stay in touch with my inner self, and gave me the opportunity to leave the force. Fast- forward to many years later, I have now have built quite a following of photographic art collectors. Not bad for a kid they said would never amount to anything.

One Sunday afternoon, at a time when my creative juices were slowing down, I found myself gazing out my living room window, just watching birds come to my feeder. I laughed to myself thinking, 'Look at all of these freeloaders, coming to me for a handout.' But I kept watching, captivated by their comings and goings. I must have been there for 40 minutes or so when I realized that I was the one getting a great show, and all for the few dollars the birdseed cost—the best deal in town.

A wide variety of birds landed on the feeder. Some shared; some were selfish. (It was pretty much like life, like people, I realized.) The chipmunks, along with the squirrels and juncos (small but brave birds) showed up on the ground below, searching for scraps the pushy blue jays had dropped. They would dance, chase each other and even wrestle. A few squirrels even searched for ways to get to that supply in the sky. Occasionally one would figure it out, hanging upside-down on a tree limb or balancing delicately on the feeder.

All of the different types of birds attracted to the feeder brought an artist's palette of colors—the electric blue of the jays, the vibrant red of the cardinals, the oriole's bright yellow breast. The priceless entertainment they provided gave me an idea for my business. *The Art of Birds*. Hmmm, this was something I could develop into a creative endeavor. I could offer the simple pleasure I enjoyed in my yard to others as art. My creative self was beginning to reawaken and for the first time in a long time, I felt promise. I felt the promise of what could be.

Hell, why not? I figured. As a kid, wildlife was everything in my life. I fished, hunted and trapped to help put food on the table during those hard times after my father died. Now, it was time to return to my roots, to my childhood interest in nature. But could I learn to enjoy the simple things again?

I grabbed my camera and began to take photographs, capturing the birds on film. With each push of the shutter, I felt myself coming alive.

Chapter Two
Sunset Cove

Shortly after I arrived at my photography studio on that fateful, glorious morning, I checked my appointment book. Sipping my flavored coffee (dark no sugar), I smiled. It was a light day, schedule-wise. I had a few things on my "To Do" list, plus lunch with Sherry, and that was it. I finished up some paperwork and before I knew it, noon rolled around, and I was soon on my way to pick her up.

As I approached her building, I noticed Sherry pacing in front of it, impatiently waiting for me to arrive—and I wasn't even late. When I pulled up, she quickly climbed in, smiled at me broadly and greeted me in a warm, inviting tone. "Good afternoon, Jarred," she said. "I've really been looking forward to this."

I couldn't help but agree. "I like Sunset Cove. It has a creative atmosphere— perfect for our meeting." Looking back, I apparently missed what Sherry was hinting at, as well as what her tone implied.

My mind was focused on the variety of subjects I thought we'd be addressing at lunch, not anything else. Although Sherry and I had become friends over the years, she'd always been somewhat distant. She never said much about her private life, always keeping it strictly business—either art or assignments for the agency. Even when Sherry, Bill (her significant other), Carol (my wife) and I occasionally got together for dinner, the conversation was always cordial and pleasant, but never too deep or personal. Bill, a contractor who I also liked, eventually became a client.

Even though it was a bit chilly, Sherry and I decided to take a table outside at Sunset Cove, overlooking the Hudson River. The sky was a deep blue with a few puffy clouds chased across it by the wind. We sat facing each other, with the Hudson over our shoulders. Looking down at my menu, I glanced up for a second to see Sherry smiling at me over her menu. There was definitely something different about her today but I didn't pay much attention to it at first. I smiled back at her nervously and returned to reading the menu but I still felt her eyes upon me.

After another moment, I looked up again. The chill in the air suddenly shifted to a warm, steady breeze that came gently out of nowhere off the river. It was almost as if the breeze reached deep inside me, bringing comfort to my soul. The fresh scent from the Hudson took me back to my younger days when I fished and canoed there. However, I was also aware that this experience ran much deeper than a simple memory. At the time, I didn't realize what was happening, but in retrospect, it's as clear as glass.

Sherry and I arrived at lunch as friends, never guessing that there was so much more in store for us. Perhaps if we had known, we would have avoided each other altogether. Then again, maybe not. I wonder if it was simple destiny or some force beyond our control. But one thing was clear—something was stirring in me and I was pretty sure it was stirring in her as well, just by the way she looked at me. But I tried to shrug it off, thinking maybe it was nothing, just a pleasant breeze lulling me into unknown territory, nothing more.

Or was it some unspoken need coming from within me, a need to know if Sherry felt the same way, a need to understand what both of us felt, for that matter. Friends, yes, but Sherry and I were also strangers, with no real knowledge of each other. Yet, how could I also have this unspoken feeling that she and I had intimate knowledge of each other beyond our friendship? I pushed the thought from my mind or at least made the attempt to do so.

Sherry at I sat there trying to decide what to eat. The conversation was light and somewhat self-indulgent. When our eyes once again met over our menus, I felt strangely drawn to her. Was it the manifestation of that new, warm, eternal breeze coming off the Hudson, completely embracing me, or was it something more? Was Sherry feeling the same thing? No. This had to be my overactive imagination, I convinced myself.

But still, something about the day was different. I found myself oddly attracted to Sherry, unexplainably, magnetically pulled towards her. Momentarily, a vision gripped me—of Sherry and I locked in a passionate embrace. It was like a walk-around dream of a romance in the making.

I quickly shook off the vision and convinced myself that it was nothing more than pure middle-aged foolishness. The truth was I was a little embarrassed about having these unthinkable thoughts about my friend, my poor, innocent unsuspecting friend! *Sherry doesn't deserve this*, I told myself. *She's here as a friend, a business associate. She already has a lover.* I was also concerned about betraying Sherry's trust with thoughts like this. Once again, I stopped myself, chasing these embarrassing musings from my mind. But I couldn't help but wonder if they showed on my face.

Sherry and I sat, quietly enjoying our meal, as well as each other, our time together passing quickly. For once, our conversation became more private, more exploratory. Then we stumbled onto the safer ground of Brush, Chisel & Lens. She was beginning to open up to me, letting me in. Our pleasant lunch ended all too soon.

Outside Sunset Cove, Sherry and I walked slowly back to my car. As I opened the door for her, she told me that she decided to walk back to work. "Is everything okay? I hope I didn't say something to offend you," I asked with concern.

"No, everything's fine," Sherry assured me. "I just want to walk off my delicious lunch. It's such a nice day and the exercise will do me good." I tried to convince her to accept a lift but she politely refused. After quick good-byes, Sherry disappeared down the street alone and I headed back to my studio to work on a few new ideas.

During my solitary drive, I thought about my time with Sherry and realized that much more than a meal had happened. A warm feeling overcame me—that awkward yet wonderful sensation that had engulfed me earlier. Suddenly my current project, which had been so important to me, no longer mattered. I became confused, embarrassed and upset. I felt that I'd committed the worst of all violations—I had betrayed a trust, a friendship. I tried to convince myself that it didn't matter because it was all going on secretly in my head. Sherry would never know. Once again, I shook it off.

Back at the studio, I sat contemplating what to do with my new project. What level should I take it to? Should it make a statement? No, I decided that I'd just have some fun with it. I hated making statements anyway. That always made me think of Frank Capra's old credo, "If you want to send a message, call Western Union." I'd let the collectors figure out what statement, if any, had been made. I always got a kick out of that anyway—collectors come up with much grander, loftier causes and expressions of my art than I possibly could. Nobody ever accused me of being a deep thinker! And, besides, artist statements all seemed to be the same—anti-this, anti-that, angry with...whatever. I just wasn't an angry person. I tried to take my viewers somewhere pleasurable, to a place where they could smile and not be angry.

As I stared at my project notes, I felt lost, something I haven't felt for a long time. I wondered where I might go with this project. I asked myself what purpose it served, or for that matter, what purpose I served. I felt confused as I paced back and forth in the studio, distressed. All kinds of crazy questions went bouncing through my head, like...*What's going on? Why am I so lost? What's in my head?*

I felt the intense need to escape, to get away from my thoughts, so I jumped back into my car, this time heading out to the ocean. I found its constant movements soothing, calming. The second I arrived at the shore, I instantly felt a release, even before I got out of the car. After a brief walk to the sand, I found myself sitting on a bunch of rocks by the water's edge. The waves began beating their mystifying magic into my soul, kissing the shore with a thundering, threatening roar. The rushing of the waves always simultaneously excited me and helped clear my mind. I purposely concentrated on the ocean, not allowing my thoughts to drift back to my studio or the lunch.

When the sun started to set, I was consumed by the colors as well as the salty breeze and the movement of the waves. A feeling of warmth surrounded me. I realized that this was a place I didn't come to enough, one that eluded me far too often.

I sat there silently, listening to the wonderful music emanating from the shore: the percussions of the waves, the strings of the shore birds and the horn of the occasional ship passing by. I observed the palette of colors created as the sun went down, looking on with such envy at its beauty. I watched the clouds blended with the sun to make a momentary painting that changed, second by second, never replicated, nor possessed by anyone, no matter how wealthy.

I chuckled to myself as these thoughts passed through my mind. If only I had the capability to create so seamlessly, as flawlessly. I laid back against the sharp rocks and took in this momentary, magnificent light show. Sadly, it faded all too rapidly into darkness. I watched the full moon slowly rise, its beams reflecting upon the water. The waves raced toward me, pounding, as they beat the hard sand at my feet. The night blanketed me, leaving only my thoughts and the symphony of nature.

I relaxed completely, not thinking of anything in particular, emptying my mind. Or so it seemed. Something strange began to happen to me, something I did not yet realize at the time. A warm, kindling light began to flicker within me, a light which I was not yet aware of then but am so familiar with now.

While watching the stars come out as moonlight danced upon the waters, I remembered the times during my boyhood when my father and I would go out and study a similar night sky. Dad would show me the stars and the constellations, having me repeat them after him so I'd remember them better. We would sit there for hours, studying the Big Dipper, Orion's Belt, the North Star and the like. Those happy times, although long past, were fresh in my memory that night.

As I laid there, searching for familiar constellations, I felt myself slipping into a trance, a semiconscious state. A vision flashed through my head. It was a momentary, quick and confusing, but it seemed to transport me back to a place I'd been to before, a place I couldn't quite remember. A far off place, perhaps a place from long ago.

Then, in an instant, I was back on my throne of rocks, rehashing the lunch conversation I had with Sherry hours earlier. It became clear to me that something similar had happened then too. I was momentarily transported to another time. My thoughts were of Sherry. My smile was for her. Sherry had begun to show me a side of herself that she always withheld from me, perhaps from everyone. I realized then that this secret side of Sherry has always been there, yet, I seemed to have missed it. I began to get a strange feeling—as though I'd known Sherry long before our first meeting at my client's office when I was introduced to her as Valerie's new assistant.

I became aware of the fact that I liked Sherry more than I cared to admit, much more in fact. My thoughts turned to hopes of intimacy. I decided to go along with what I perceived to be a moment of weakness. I allowed my mind to indulge itself. And it felt good. *Why not let yourself go?* I told myself. In the past, I never permitted myself the foolishness of such thoughts. I built a wall around myself that, until now, had kept me protected, detached, and a safe distance from all who could potentially hurt me.

The more I thought about the meal, the more I wondered if my thoughts were foolishness or something more substantial. Perhaps Sherry even had mutual feelings for me. After all, how could you explain all of those weighty glances, those special smiles, her finally opening up to me? No, it couldn't be. These things only happen in movies or in books, never in real life, and certainly not to guys like me with girls like Sherry.

But perhaps, just perhaps? No. I had to find out. But, how? I thought that maybe there'd be a sign, a clear message. In spite of myself, a smile came to my lips. I shook it off and climbed back into the cushion of the night sky, as the sound of breaking waves lifted me farther and farther away. I drifted off to who knows where, who cares where. I just let it take me.

 # Chapter Three
An Honest, Well-Intentioned Man

I remained at rest with my eyes closed, unknowingly in waiting, the waves pulling at me. I allowed myself the freedom of drifting back into the near-hypnotic state I'd experienced only moments before. I fell deeper and deeper into my meditating self. Although it felt as if I were asleep, I was still acutely aware of events as they unfolded before me, almost as if a movie were playing. I drifted further into of the folds of memory into a life I lived before. Was it some form of time travel? I wasn't sure. Although I was confused, I managed to free myself, let go of my consciousness and move into a strange realm of semiconscious travel...

Suddenly a light appears, as if emerging from a fog. I walk toward it, wondering where this could possibly lead. Out of nowhere, a bridge of stone appears. Apprehensively, I move slowly across it, through the fog and toward the light. Upon reaching the other side of the bridge, I find myself in another time, another place that existed years before...

Events from a long-past period in history begin to present themselves to me. It is as if I am in a film. Simultaneously watching a movie and yet starring in it. Although still baffled, I feel no fear of what is unfolding, quite the opposite. I look forward to seeing each new thing that is being revealed to me. It's like turning the pages of a captivating book. Except I am the book.

I see...I see a young man who strongly resembles me. Could this actually be me that I'm watching? What period of time is this? Where am I? I try to push these questions into the back of my mind and simply observe.

I watch this young man working hard on the dock of a shipping town somewhere in New England. The time period looks to be in the early 1800s. The man is loading a ship, which is named "The Four Merry Maids," making repairs and doing whatever his Captain asks with efficiency and skill. Soon thereafter, the ship sets sail. I overhear the crew speak of heading for England.

As darkness begins to overtake the sun, I notice that a beautiful, exotic young woman has come up on the deck. I am startled to see that she bears a striking resemblance to Sherry. It isn't difficult to see that this young sailor has taken a fancy to her. She effortlessly holds his attention as she wanders somewhat aimlessly along the ship's damp boards. Their eyes meet from time to time and she passes him a knowing smile, then approaches him cautiously.

"Good evening, Jeremiah. Beautiful night isn't it?" she says, still smiling. "My father picked a lovely day to set sail."

"It is, isn't it, Jessica?" Jeremiah responds to the Captain's beautiful daughter. He seems a bit bashful but continues speaking. "A good Captain knows these things," he tells her, looking down at the deck with a grin so wide and deep, it lights up the ship.

Jeremiah stands at the rail, gazing out upon the water. Jessica moves close to him, close enough to let him know she is there without arousing suspicion or appearing seductive. They chat amicably as they both lean upon the railing, looking out over the rolling waves. There is an aura, electricity between them. It's clear that they both feel it and this gives them the quiet confidence that only two kindred spirits can feel.

"I've been watching you work, Jeremiah," Jessica tells him quietly. "You work diligently to make sure that everything is just so to ensure a safe passage." Jeremiah says nothing and is plainly embarrassed by the compliment. "Father is abundantly pleased with you and how hard you work," Jessica tells him, embarrassing him further. But this time, he manages to speak.

"Thank you, Jessica. That pleases me," he admits. Jeremiah turns and looks at her, gazing deeply into her eyes and stammers softly, "Your hair looks so wonderful blowing gently in the wind...and it always smells so clean, like lavender."

Jeremiah smiles but reddens as he tells her this. Jessica takes his hand in hers and gives him a gentle peck on the cheek. His blush deepens as he glows with delight, feeling a rush of wonder shudder through him. God, how good Jessica makes me feel! he thinks. At that moment, Jeremiah is certain he could dance across the top of the water all the way to England. He looks at her with a love that penetrates her very soul, so intense that Jessica feels a warm rush flow through her. Life is good, they both think. Life is very good.

The ship gently rolls upon the ocean's surface, slowly heading toward its destination. Jeremiah and Jessica talk tirelessly for hours—laughing, debating, heartily exchanging their thoughts as they slowly and cautiously move closer and closer together. The warm breeze softly embraces them, as the moonlight glitters upon the surface of the sea, turning up the flames ignited within them.

Suddenly, a dark, burly figure appears on deck. The moment Jessica sees it, she moves away from Jeremiah with nervous quickness. "Jessica, how many times must you be told not to fraternize with the sailors?" the man's voice roughly barks.

"But, Father, Jeremiah and I have been friends forever," she pleads. "He isn't just some sailor! We were simply talking about the night, the trip, about our plans upon arriving in England." But her attempt at an explanation are lost on the gruff man.

The brawny Captain is clearly upset with her and will hear none of her excuses. He orders her back to her cabin for the remainder of the evening. Jessica bursts into angry tears and storms off. The Captain now approaches Jeremiah, menacingly. "You are not to associate with my daughter. Do you understand, Jeremiah? Under no circumstances are you to interact with my daughter again," the Captain orders.

"Yes, Sir," Jeremiah says in a small voice, sadly knowing that he must obey his Captain. After the man saunters off, Jeremiah turns back to the ocean and drifts away into to his lonely world.

Jeremiah's heart is heavy with pain. He knows now more than ever that he'll never be allowed to court the woman of his dreams, his friend of many years. Jeremiah is utterly aware that, as a lowly sailor, he will never be of the stature to ask the Captain for his daughter's hand in marriage. He swears to himself that he will never again allow a woman to capture his heart—the ache of forbidden love is too much to bear.

Back in her cabin, Jessica is furious with her father and his nonsensical rules of social standing. When she becomes angry, she is a force to be reckoned with. Jessica knows how she feels about Jeremiah and she is not about to let some old salt tell her what she can and can't do with her life, even if the old salt happens to be her father. She is also irate at Jeremiah for not standing up to her father. Jessica knows the consequences of disobeying a Captain's orders while at sea...but isn't she worth hanging for? Moments later, Jessica laughs at her own foolishness, certain she would not want Jeremiah hanged for disobeying orders, for loving her. After all, what would she do without him?

But how could her father do this to her? She and Jeremiah have grown up together. Jeremiah protected her from the other children who, long ago, taunted her for being a first mate's daughter. That same first mate who became a Captain, as would Jeremiah. He has always been her protector, and now he is her lover, always and forever. A warm smile washes over her lips and the light of love warms her heart.

Yes, Jessica has known Jeremiah all of her life. She knows, as does her father, that Jeremiah is an honorable, well-intentioned man. Couldn't her father see what a fine son-in-law this handsome sailor would make? Does her father not care? Jessica has decided she will see to it that her father's eyes are opened or she will die trying.

With this, Jessica slowly removes a chain which she wears concealed beneath her dress, safely stashed between her breasts. It is a keepsake that she hides from her father. At the end of the chain is a locket in the shape of a heart. Jeremiah gave it to her just before they sailed. Within the locket is a likeness of the two of them. Upon opening the locket, Jeremiah is on one side, and she is on the other. When he slipped her this beautiful gift, Jeremiah told Jessica that the locket would always keep him close to her heart, even when they could not be together. Jessica holds the locket tightly against her chest. She feels warmth emanating from it to her heart. This gives her some comfort, a sense that he is close to her, that he is a part of her.

During the remainder of the journey, Jessica enjoys few stolen moments with Jeremiah. She knows he will not forsake his Captain, but she is determined to keep the fire of their love fanned just the same, always making her sweetheart aware that she is but a breath away. Determined as she is, Jessica lets Jeremiah know that it is their destiny to be together always, no matter what her father thinks.

As Jeremiah works, Jessica slowly walks by, intentionally catching the breeze just so, in such a way to carry her soft, light, floral fragrance to his senses, quickly letting his heart know she is there. But unbeknownst to her, this only causes Jeremiah sorrow and pain, knowing that the object of his deepest desires can never be his. Although he also knows how determined Jessica can be, he never realizes just how determined she is to change the way things stand. *I will find a way to open my father's eyes,* she giggles to herself. *Just wait and see. This will be my life's work.*

After months at sea, "The Four Merry Maids" finally dock in Southampton, England. The sailors are permitted two weeks leave and during this time, it is Jessica's duty to shop with her mother, searching the markets for fine fabrics, teas and fragrances to fill the ship's hold on the return trip. They plan to spend the entire fortnight shopping for all of the wonderful things the new world cannot offer.

One evening, the Captain entertains his distinguished clients and dignitaries at a fabulous dinner in their Southampton home. Their house is lavishly furnished and a warm fire awaits all who enter each room. Rich cloth lines the walls and thick drapery covers the windows. Even those of more means envy their furnishings, which hail from all corners of the world, thoughtfully gathered on the Captain's many journeys. The home resonates with the wonderful fragrance of lavender and sandalwood. To the credit of the Captain's wife, Portia, entering their home is an impressive experience, for it is clear that she takes great care to make it an inviting place which offers comfort to all.

Not only does Jessica's mother proudly display her fine treasures but she also has a generous heart and is quick to share her good fortune. She readily gives the wives of these respectable men, clients of her husband, lovely gifts to show her appreciation for their patronage. The Captain himself, a courageous and tough man, offers superb cigars and brandy to his guests. As a sea captain, he commands a heavy price in exchange for the safe transport of the prized imports and exports shipped by his guests' companies.

Jessica is sought after by these men's wives, who desire such a pretty prize for their sons. A bright, headstrong young lady, Jessica will have none of this silly matchmaking. Her attempts to be pleasant are always pale and forced at best, for her heart and soul are just blocks away at the sailors' pub, with Jeremiah. The more these foolish marriage offers come, the more sickened her heart becomes. This dismay easily turns to rage, a rage toward her father.

Jessica's mother studies her with worry at one point in the evening. She easily reads the pain on her daughter's face, seeing through the mask her daughter dons for polite society. Yes, she knows her daughter well. Portia thinks that perhaps, just this once, in the name of love and matters of the heart, she will defy her husband's demands. Can he not see how Jessica and her sailor feel toward one another? Can he not put this foolish class consciousness behind him? Why is he so unyielding? Portia wonders.

A hard man, the Captain is incapable of seeing or feeling the pain he causes in his beautiful daughter. Oh, such sorrow! After all, women are the experts in such matters, she thinks. Although her Captain is capable of guiding his ship through treacherous seas, he knows little of life's most treacherous tidal wave —love.

Portia takes a deep breath and decides to take the helm and guide her daughter's love ship through the stormy waves kicked up by her husband's blindness to matters of the heart. She deduces that the more these two lovers are kept apart, the more they will desire each other. Perhaps this is nothing more than a longing for the forbidden fruit. Perhaps, if Portia brings them together with her blessings, this romance will fade away and no longer cause such disruption within her family. This is how she will justify to her husband what she is about to do, should he find out.

Once off ship, Jeremiah quickly heads toward The Smuggler's Cove, the public house where the sailors stay while docked in Southampton. As he enters this slightly- seedy establishment, he can smell the stale ale, the smoke of cheap cigars and pipe tobacco. The sawdust on the floor is changed once a week, more often than in the cheaper inns which are swept only once a month. The tavern is empty, but that will change in a few hours.

First, Jeremiah settles into the decent sleeping quarters offered here—decent in comparison to those on the ship and more spacious. The Cove, as it is commonly known, always has a plentiful supply of good quality libations to wash down the simple fare. And there is also female companionship for those with such desires. These men have been months at sea, on a ship devoid of women, save for Jessica, who is clearly off limits. The sailors always set aside some of their wages for a bit of slap and tickle.

What good is it to risk our lives during the treacherous Atlantic passage and not have any enjoyment before the always-hazardous trip back across the pond? they reason. What good would all that hard earned cash do us in the Davy Jones' locker if the trip takes a bad turn? They are hearty, healthy men who work hard and play hard—and shore leave is their time to play.

As Jeremiah sits conversing with his shipmates, he finds little interest in the Cove's women and even less in the food. His heart is heavy and his thoughts are only of his fair maiden Jessica. Who is he to love such a privileged princess? One who travels to such exotic lands, purchasing the finest of goods, silks from China and spices from India? He tries to convince himself that it is for these reasons that Jessica cannot possibly be interested in him.

Jeremiah is a hard working man, it is true, but he is not fine or exotic or exciting. It is true also that he has ambitions of some day becoming the captain of his own ship, but this accomplishment is very far off. Had his life not taken a dramatic turn when he was a lad, everything would have been different. But things are not different, he tells himself harshly, and now it is time for you to understand this and accept it. But like his beloved Jessica, Jeremiah isn't one to accept things as they are. Instead, he is one to take charge of his life and change things. One day, he is certain that he will show the Captain that he is worthy of his lovely daughter.

Jeremiah continues falling deeper into despair, wallowing in his ale as the laughter of the men washes over him. The more he thinks about his unattainable love, the more pitiful he appears. As the effects of the ale begin to become obvious, one of the Cove's working girls senses an easy mark. Katrina is a truly wicked girl. Her soul is so black that she is reputed to have once cut out her lover's heart for betraying her. All the men know better than to take up with her and go out of their way to avoid her.

Katrina strolls confidently and seductively to Jeremiah's side. As she sidles up beside him, uninvited, her intentions far from honorable. Her grimy blouse is just a bit too low, her skirts, just a bit too tight around the belly and even shows a glimpse of ankle, something unheard of in that time. It is also said that Katrina hates men, especially sailors. What barbaric fools they are, she has been known to sneer.

Another of Kat's favorite credos is that drunken sailors can easily be parted from their money. She takes great pleasure in doing just that. In fact, Katrina is something of an artist in this arena. At the right time of night, she accompanies her unknowing victim to his room and lays him on his bed to wait as she "gets ready." These poor drunken louts soon fall into an inebriated slumber, during which Katrina helps herself to whatever happens to be in their pockets. They don't realize that they've been parted from their money until the next morning, if that. Still foggy from the night's whiskey, some don't even remember Katrina's empty promises. Her wallet has grown fat by simply escorting men to their rooms. Such fools these men are, she thinks to herself as she stacks gold and silver coin into neat piles.

Not to be deterred, Katrina fends off Jeremiah's repeated rejection and continues the flirtatious banter. So determined is Katrina is to remove Jeremiah's money from his pockets that she moves closer to him, allowing her blouse to slip off her shoulder, permitting her knee to brush his. Jeremiah moves away slightly, continuing to dodge her advances. He tells Katrina in no uncertain terms that he has no interest in her, that his loyalty is to his lifelong love, the one he grew up with, the one he cannot stop thinking of.

Katrina flies into a rage. "You have wasted my night, you cretin!" she screams and demands that Jeremiah compensate her for her time.

"I have not asked you to keep me company, so any time spent here was time on your own clock," he tells her. "And now it is time for me to bid you a good-night."

When Jeremiah rises to retire, Katrina blocks his way, confronting him once more. He ignores her demands and heads toward the stairs. Enraged at the rejection, Katrina reaches under her skimpy dress and pulls a knife from her garter. With one swift movement, Katrina thrusts the rusty blade deep into Jeremiah's chest. Before she can stab him again, Jeremiah's shipmates grab her and wrestle her to the floor. Jeremiah stumbles to the stairs where he falls bleeding, deeply and mortally wounded.

As the others valiantly try to staunch the bleeding, one of Jeremiah's shipmates runs to the house of the Captain to inform him of this horrible incident, hoping that the Captain's influences *will get swift and sure help for Jeremiah in the form of a trusted physician.*

Just prior to the urgent knock upon their door, Jessica mysteriously falls ill. There is a sick feeling deep in her heart, impossible to describe, but present nonetheless. She grabs onto a mahogany chest to steady herself. Jessica does not know what is wrong—how could she? Nevertheless, somehow—instinctively— she knows. Something has happened to Jeremiah.

As she listens to the sailor telling her father of the incident at the Cove, Jessica dashes hysterically from the house before anyone can restrain her. She runs through the damp, dark cobblestone streets. Her body pierces through the fog that has just rolled in. Her soft, white skin becomes coated with a mist of rain. But Jessica does not care, nor does she notice.

As Jessica enters the door of the Smuggler's Cove, the first thing she sees is Jeremiah lying on the floor, bloody and dying. She falls to the ground and grabs him, pulling him to her bosom. Sobbing, Jessica begs Jeremiah to hold on, not to die. She looks longingly into Jeremiah's eyes. She sees that he is crying—not for fear, not for himself, but for her, for them. For their loss. Their lips meet for one last kiss, and then he is gone.

Later that evening, Portia sits in Jessica's room. Her attempts to console her daughter are useless. Jessica ignores her, sitting in front of a mirror in a corner of her room. Transfixed, she stares at her reflection, yet sees nothing. Jessica's thoughts are of him, and only of him. She tries to be strong but finds only weakness. Jessica places her hand on the locket that hangs around her neck, Jeremiah's locket. She presses it close to her heart, watching the woman in the mirror, then lets out an unearthly wail that could wake the dead. She glances in the mirror at her solemn image and cries.

I woke with a start on the beach, breathless, a pain deep within my own chest and utterly confused. What had I just witnessed? I felt cold and sad and empty. I sat for a few moments, feeling the remnants of what seemed very much like a past life experience. It was so vivid, so real. I didn't know what else to call it.

I had heard about such occurrences but never believed them... until now. In my vision, I could actually feel the passing of Jeremiah's soul. I don't know how this was possible, I just did. I was now certain that the sailor I watched die was myself. I was stunned, confused, shaken and did not completely grasp what had just happened.

Yet if I thought about it, throughout my life, I've always had this underlying sense of a life prior to the one I was currently living. I always seemed to be searching, to be almost driven, throughout my life to find something mystical. But I was never sure of exactly what I was looking for. Somehow, there was always the knowledge, the confidence that the past would somehow find me. And now, it looked like it did.

I walked slowly back to my car for the ride home which seemed endless. The roads were packed with people who had probably just completed long, monotonous days at a job they kept for no other reason than a paycheck. I felt lucky not to be one of them.

As my mind swirled, I tried to put these events together. Bewildered, I racked my brain to try and figure out the meaning of the powerful trip I'd just taken. Was this a sign or some sort of dream? Was I losing my mind? I had a strange feeling that this vision was something I'd lived before. I made a mental note to look into it, then chuckled to myself. Notes of any kind wouldn't be necessary for an event I would never forget.

After I pulled into my driveway, I sat quietly for a few more moments. I took a deep breath and tried to relax. Then another. Breathing deeply, I felt myself beginning to calm down. I knew I had to keep this vision to myself, at least for the time being. I couldn't even share it with my wife. At least, not yet, if ever.

When I felt ready, I got out of the car and walked to the house. Inside, I was confronted with the usual craziness: my wife simultaneously fixing dinner and fighting with my son over not cleaning his room, while my daughter yelled at the two of them to stop fighting. Welcome to my world!

Ah, yes, back to reality. Nothing had changed—at least nothing which I was fully aware of, yet.

Chapter Four
Sherry's Story

While I was wrestling with the strangeness of what seemed to be an out of body experience, I was completely unaware that Sherry was battling with something similar. She later told me that walking back to the office in the warm afternoon sun, she felt good about our lunch at Sunset Cove, although she didn't get exactly what she'd hoped for from me. She was mildly concerned that I hadn't picked up on her not-so-subtle hints and was worried that I didn't appear to be feeling the same emotions that embraced her.

Is this some sort of intuition I've had from the first time Jarred and I met or is it simply just an attraction to him? she wondered. *Are the dreams I've been having some sort of message or are they just dreams? They seem so different than dreams, though.*

Until Sherry confessed this to me later on, I was completely unaware that over the last few years we'd known each other she'd been feeling something eerie, an odd sense of déjà vu that revolved around me. Always a little slow on the uptake, my past life experiences were just awakening in me. I admit, I was a little freaked out by it at first and didn't know how she kept hers a secret for so many months.

A bit of background about Sherry. She worked at a small ad agency owned by my client Valerie. When I walked into Valerie's office for a meeting one day, I had no idea I was about to meet someone who would change my life. I greeted Valerie's attractive new assistant with a warm smile and a very friendly hello. I had no idea that Sherry felt an attraction toward me from the very moment we met. She admitted later that when I shook her hand, she literally felt a spark, like electricity flowing from my touch through her body. "It lifted my heart," she told me shyly.

Sherry didn't think much about this bizarre feeling until she began to have strange, unexplainable dreams soon after. Although she tried to ignore them for some time, it was to no avail. Then, instead of denying that something unusual was occurring, she became determined to find out what was going on. But her feelings were still conflicted. She asked herself, *Should I pursue this interest in Jarred or let it be? After all, he's a married friend of my new boss...and then there's Bill.*

Ah, Bill, Sherry's live-in boyfriend. A contractor by trade, Bill was a hard- drinking man's man. Her life with him was unfulfilling, to say the least, if not predictable. Not only did Bill stop at the bar for a few drinks with the guys after work every day, but afterwards, he'd stumble in for dinner, lie on the couch, turn on the game and eventually pass out in front of the TV. I got the feeling that although Sherry wasn't content with their relationship, he helped pay the bills, kept a roof over their heads and food in the fridge. It was convenient, if nothing else. But I didn't think she was happy.

Like me, Sherry replayed our lunch at Sunset Cove in her head, recalling every little detail:

"I just want to walk off my delicious lunch. It's such a nice day and the exercise will do me good," she had said.

Surprised by her sudden decision, I had asked, *'Are you sure? I'm going right by the office...'*

"Thanks anyway," she had replied. "I need the walk after eating all that food," she'd smiled, patting her tiny belly for emphasis. When she retold the story to me months later, Sherry admitted that she hadn't been totally truthful about why she wanted to walk back to the office.

The truth behind Sherry choosing to stroll back to work? She needed more time to think. About me. She wondered what these odd feelings were about and needed to get to the bottom of them. Sherry recounted kissing me good-bye on the cheek, turning, walking away and not looking back.

When we discussed this crucial meeting months later, Sherry told me what happened when she left my side. It went something like this:

Once I got in the car and drove away, Sherry began her slow walk up the hill, taking advantage of the solitude to muse further. *Oh, how I longed to take him into my arms, hold him close, and feel the warmth of his body against mine!* Then she debated with herself, *Should I be a little more obvious? Jarred always seems so indifferent when he sees me, whether it's at the agency or our artist group. Will my feelings for him create problems between Bill and me? Jarred, will never leave his wife and kids for me...'*

Sherry entered her office building and opted for the stairs. With each step she climbed, thoughts of me fell from her mind. In the office, she saw her co-worker Valerie at the computer. "I see your lunch was a pleasant one," Valerie said with a wink.

Darn, Sherry thought, *Is it really that obvious?* She sat down, concerned that perhaps I had, in fact, picked up on her feelings. Actually, she confessed that she was more hopeful than concerned. Glancing at the phone, she wondered whether she should call me, just to see if I felt something too. But what reason would she give for the call? To thank me for the meal? No, too obvious. She touched the phone hopefully, thinking maybe this action would spark it to ring, then shook her head at her own foolishness.

Little did Sherry know that I had been struck by something more powerful than the simple emotion of love. I was embroiled in so much more. It was as though my heart had been touched by something unspoken but incredibly strong. Touched? No, more like punched...

This might be a good time to tell you a little more about Sherry. In addition to being a sculptor, she was also an accomplished oil painter. Our artist group, Brush, Chisel & Lens, was lucky to have her. I think she's the most successful—and talented— of all of us. She's had her work displayed at a number of prominent art galleries and has had solo exhibitions as well.

Like most artists, Sherry needed to do something else to supplement what she made from her art. For her, it was a matter of personal pride, as well as the wish to take some of the financial pressure off of Bill's shoulders. A true talent, Sherry's dedication to her calling was overpowering, yet she found the so-called romantic notion of being a starving artist unappealing. An intelligent woman with good common sense, Sherry was always the practical one in Brush, Chisel & Lens. She was the voice of reason who kept us grounded.

Maybe this had something to do with her background. She was of tough, sensible, New England stock. Sherry grew up in Cape Cod—Provincetown, to be exact. Her parents owned a small arts and crafts shop in which Sherry spent many a day with her father painting small pictures or creating figures out of Play Doh. She delighted in showing these masterpieces to her mother and father, who acted like each and every one should be in the Louvre.

Sherry took particular delight in telling about the time her father put some of her work on display in their store. That same day, a couple walked in, admiring it. They were especially impressed with one of her paintings and asked if Sherry was the artist.

"Yes, she is," her father responded, proudly. "That piece is called 'Looking Out the Store Window.' It was recently completed and one of a series," he added for good measure.

Sherry beamed as they complimented her work and then asked if they could buy it. "We have just the place for it," they told Sherry's father as he winked at them.

"Well, let's see...I'm not sure you'd be able to afford such a masterpiece," her father-turned-agent began. "I couldn't let it go for a penny less than two dollars."

"Hmmm...," responded the husband, hesitating. But his wife insisted that she needed it for her collection of "refrigerator art," and the deal was complete. The couple finished the transaction by handing Sherry's father two crisp dollar bills. They took the painting and off they went.

Dipping into the cash register, Sherry's father made change and chuckled as he handed her one dollar and eighty cents, keeping his standard 10 percent commission. Upon receiving the money from her first art sale, Sherry happily scurried upstairs to show her mother. She never remembered feeling more proud.

Sherry's mother, a painter who worked in both oil and in watercolor, had a little studio at home. For them, "home" was the apartment above the store. Here, she raised Sherry and her two brothers while her husband ran the shop. Her mother's paintings, mostly seascapes of the area, were very popular with tourists. They also sold crafts made by other local artists on consignment. Most of the time, the shop made enough to get by, but just barely.

Being the oldest child in the family, Sherry would help her mother take care of her brothers, but she also helped her father down in the shop. (They couldn't afford to hire anyone else.) Although Sherry's childhood was a happy one, she was always aware that her family struggled financially. This made a mark on her early on and influenced Sherry's distaste for being a struggling artist. In fact, she did everything in her power to make sure she would never be. She worked hard, saved her money, and even got a scholarship to a prominent art school in Rhode Island.

Immediately after college, Sherry moved to New York City because she felt it was the best place to seek her fortune as an artist. This is where she met Bill. He was one of the carpenters working on a gallery she visited to show the owner her portfolio. Sherry and Bill spoke briefly, then he asked if she wanted to join him for lunch. Knowing no one in New York, she said yes, and the wheels were set in motion. Their relationship quickly moved forward until it stopped moving at all.

Sherry had no desire to work for a large corporation, where office politics and back-biting could suck the creativity out of a person. She learned that much from a summer internship at a Boston advertising agency. Yet, Sherry also knew that she needed a steady income to survive until her art began to sell.

One day during her tireless search for work and a gallery to represent her, Sherry stumbled upon a job at the small ad agency where she still worked. Serendipity, you might say, intervened when she was buying a cup of coffee at a local diner. Sherry happened to overhear my client Valerie telling the waitress that they were looking for more help. Never a shrinking violet, Sherry struck up a conversation with Valerie and realized within minutes that she would enjoy the creative atmosphere at this woman's agency. Val was equally impressed and offered Sherry the job on the spot. And so, Sherry's path to destiny—and meeting me—began.

Always decisive, Sherry knew what she wanted and then went after it. On the outside, Sherry looked to be the picture of confidence, as though she was living a charmed life, but this wasn't the case. Instead, she kept everything to herself. She doesn't bellyache about her problems but she didn't let anyone inside either. Well, not until very recently.

The real Sherry was confused, maybe intrigued, by feelings that began back in those days growing up on Cape Cod. It started when she was just thirteen...she felt that something in her life was missing. Like there was a lost puzzle piece she could never find. Sherry could never put her finger on it, but was painfully aware of an emptiness, a void, a sense of incompleteness.

Whenever Sherry moved to a new place, she expected something to happen that would fill this void. She thought she might find it in college, then when she first moved to New York City. But that "something" never happened, not until that auspicious day when she and I first met at the agency. In that moment we shook hands, Sherry knew that I was the "something" she sought. The void within her began to dissipate when she took my hand in hers in that simple handshake to say hello. At that very instant, the emptiness in her melted away like the wax of a candle. Cautiously, Sherry held that knowledge inside of her, waiting for a sign. Then it came. It came when the dreams began. She knew these dreams were the sign she had waited for. It was now time to explore them further and to find the meaning of it all.

You see, Sherry was a woman on a mission, and as I would soon learn, unstoppable.

 ## Chapter Five
Shooting Nature

The morning sky was beginning to awaken as the sun peeked out over the horizon, flowing into my bedroom and into my eyes. I actually felt my soul warming to this promising day. As I lay there quietly, my brain began to swirl as the events from the day before peeled back the sleep from my mind. Lying in bed, I became embroiled in mysterious feelings, brought on by my lunch with Sherry and by my odd dream-state. Immediately, I realized that I shouldn't let either consume me. Just then, the alarm went off, waking my wife. Carol reached over and gave me her usual hug before getting up to get ready for work.

I lay in bed for a few extra minutes before getting up and getting dressed. After my first cup of coffee, I packed for the gym and then walked the dog in the small, wooded area on our property. The plentiful wildlife in my little patch of woods distracted me for the moment. Watching the chickadees, titmice and cardinals fly about, I thought to myself, *This is going to be a great day.*

After I put the dog back inside, I was off to the gym. Driving there, my mind suddenly wandered back to the day before, confusing me. *A good workout will get me back to where I need to be*, I tried to convince myself. But on the treadmill, I found myself thinking about Sherry and our wonderfully-relaxing meal the previous day. I remembered her unassuming, comforting smile, her bright brown eyes as clear as daylight, her soft, shining hair and her trim, pleasing body.

But I was also puzzled by that "something different" about Sherry, something I was never aware of before. I just couldn't put my finger on it. When I got into the studio after yesterday's lunch, I had a strong urge to call her but held myself back, not wanting to bother her at the office. As I worked out at the gym, I found myself thinking more about Sherry than about the day ahead. Did the bizarre time travel, out of body experience I had on the beach last night have me so confused? Did it have anything to do with Sherry?

Luckily, I was able to snap out of these musings because it was getting late and I had plenty to do at the studio. I finished my workout without any further disruptions and jumped into the shower. Next was my customary stop at the deli for coffee and a quick hello to Rocky before heading to work.

At the studio, I found my mind drifting from the contact sheets spread out before me as it kept trying to get a handle on what had happened yesterday. I was as confused as I'd been earlier. I realized that something significant had happened the day before but I couldn't afford to dwell on it. It was time to get back to my art, wildlife in particular. I forced myself to put all of those crazy thoughts on the back burner, at least for the rest of the day, while I selected photographs to include in my upcoming gallery show.

In my work, just as in my life, I was always seeking a challenge. You might say that challenge was my inspiration. I'd never done things the easy way. Knowing that everyone and his uncle shoots wildlife, I was driven to do it differently. This drove me to look beyond the obvious, to get photos that are not easily captured. I strove to get something interesting as well as something beautiful, not an easy combination.

After some contemplation over my coffee, I decided to try and nab photos of the wood duck and the kingfisher. Both of these birds were shy, small and elusive, and lived in areas that were not easily accessible and where light is often low. Because of this, both birds have a mysterious quality to me.

The male wood duck (or "woody") is incredibly beautiful, painted with exceptional shades of red, blue and yellow in its iridescent feathers, which are accented by one big orange "eye." For some reason, I'd always had a special attraction to this duck. The kingfisher, on the other hand, was another type of bird altogether. Kingfishers were rare, small birds with long bills. Because they were small and moved quickly, to get a good shot of them you had to get close—a near impossible feat. On many occasions, I'd attempted to capture both of these feathered gifts on film and had yet to be successful. *A great challenge!* I thought to myself with a smile. *With some luck, maybe both will be roosting in the same area.*

Actually, the inspiration to obtain a kingfisher's portrait came during my recent photographic field trip to shoot goldeneye ducks. Sitting by the water in a wooded area, I heard a noise to my left which sounded like rocks being thrown into the water. Slowly, I looked over to see what it was. To my surprise, I spotted a kingfisher diving for food. Before I moved closer (for fear I might startle that skittish bird), I attempted to get at least one shot of the elusive creature, so I could have *something*, even if it wasn't the perfect shot, on film.

But just as I turned my camera toward the bird, it sensed my presence and off it flew. This incident stuck with me for years and since then, I've been determined to get a breathtaking photograph of it ever since. I considered this bird a worthy opponent, a true trophy to be proud of, and a great addition to my prized wildlife photo collection.

I decided to take a trip to a small, isolated stream that ran into a pond off the beaten path in Fauhnstalk State Park. I hoped this trip would take my mind off Sherry and force me to get lost in my work. The stream was very difficult to reach because the path that led you to it was steep, hilly, overgrown and hard to follow. Few people knew about it and hearty hikers were the only ones who explored its path. Because of this, it was rare to run into another human being. Which is fine by me because with the crowds of people who run into the woods to get away, combined with over-development, nature photographers like me had to walk miles before seeing elusive wildlife of any value.

When going out into the field, traveling light and being properly equipped was the only way to go. I took out my checklist—a necessity because my mind was always one step ahead of itself and I often forget something. With my list in hand, I approached the black steel cabinet that contained my equipment and began to pack my knapsack with two cameras and several lenses, which would cover just about any photographic situation that might occur.

One last look at my list...cameras, lenses, film. *Oh, shit! I forgot the film.* That would have just made my day...to get deep into the woods only to realize that I forgot one of the essentials. (I confess—I was still a purist when it came to my craft, and preferred the quality of old-fashioned film to digital.) I went to the refrigerator, grabbed five rolls of color and two of black and white. Then I was ready to start a journey, clear my head and maybe even get lucky enough to find a kingfisher. This trip was totally unplanned, spur of the moment, so I had little time, but a strong desire to get out and photograph something—anything— even if not my intended prey.

My thoughts turned to the woody, one of the most beautiful ducks nature had to offer. I could go on forever about my love for these birds, but then again, I could do that about most wildlife. I know I could always count on the wood duck to take my mind off events that seemed to turn my life upside down. Like Sherry.

It took about forty minutes to get to my destination. I pulled into the parking area, hoping I'd be alone. It appeared as though I was—at least there were no other cars in the parking lot. But this never ruled out campers or hikers, who might be connecting to one of my favorite trails from another route. The main trail was short, well-traveled and easy to walk at first, but at the point when it turned for the stream, that all changes. Then the trail became rough and challenging, keeping casual hikers away.

Difficult terrain and a little-traveled path were usually excellent conditions to find shy wildlife. In addition to the trail's toughness, it also wasn't easy to find and this kept foot traffic to a minimum.

I closed the car door, after unloading my knapsack and removing the cameras. I liked to be ready when photographing wildlife. The sun was bright causing the humidity and the temperature to begin to rise. All the ingredients for an uncomfortable situation was also the reason the place was usually so empty.

In the woods, I could hear the sound of the stream just off the path. The sweat poured off me instantly but I didn't let it hinder me. I moved slowly, deliberately, just in case a deer or even a rabbit was around. I didn't want my footsteps to startle any creature, which might in turn, scare away potential subjects. Once, while hiking this same trail, I saw a red fox—a rare sighting but an exciting one. Measured, purposeful movements were important whether hiking or shooting. I was now only a few yards from my destination. The extreme humidity was making the hike slow and uncomfortable, but I hoped it would be worthwhile.

As I turned right onto the path, moving toward the stream, I noticed ferns on both sides of the path, an indication that the marsh was just ahead. I stopped and took a moment to listen. I heard something...I wasn't sure what at first...but something was definitely moving in the water. As the path began to open, I got a clear view of the stream and crouched down. *Damn*, I thought. *It would be so much easier to get my ass out of bed early one day, plan a field trip, set up some camouflage netting to hide under and then just wait for the ducks to fly in.* With camo, birds were so unaware of your presence, they have no fear and often swim within feet of you. *But hey*, I tried to convince myself, *what the hell?* I'm here now. *Let's see what I can get.*

Excitement welled up in me. I felt like a kid at Christmas again, with that same feeling of anticipating gifts under the tree. For me, photographing nature held the same anticipation as I wondered what would be there for me to photograph. Still crouching, I moved very slowly to my right, toward the sound of whatever was splashing the water. I headed toward some bushes by the stream for better cover.

Stopping momentarily, apprehensively, I heard the motion ahead of me stop as well. *Oh no, if this was a woody, had it heard, smelled or seen me? Would it take off even before I had a chance at a shot?* Moments seemed like hours, but I was still hopeful that the sound I heard was a woody allowing me to get that perfect shot. Again, the movement started and again, I moved toward the water's edge. Looking toward the sound, over in the reeds, there it was. Damn! It wasn't a woody or even a duck, for that matter. It was a muskrat, and a very large muskrat at that, gorging himself on the succulent reeds. Slowly, I lifted my camera and clicked off a few shots, consoling myself with the thought that muskrats were hard to come by as well. I could always use one or two shots for my stock collection, though.

Focusing intensely on stalking my new prey, I failed to see the ducks right at my feet. As I moved just one-step closer, to grab one more muskrat shot, the world exploded around me. Mallards flew right out from under my feet. It was their nature to always let the world around them know they were making an exit with extremely loud quacking. Startled myself, I fell back onto the mucky ground, right onto my ass, which was now wet and soggy. Alerted by the ducks—and by me falling—the muskrat slapped its tail and was gone in an instant. A blue jay chimed in, laughing at my predicament.

Now sopping wet from the humidity and from my graceless fall in the mud, I was totally pissed off. I must have violated every rule of nature photography—falling, cursing, etc. I realized how this must look to all the hidden woodland creatures I hoped to capture on film, and began laughing at myself. Well, I was good for a laugh, if anything.

The blue jay sat above me, squawking away. *Hey!* I thought. *Knock it off.* Then, instinctively, I raised the camera and took a shot of the jay. *There! Laugh at me, will you? Well, I'll make a few bucks off of your laughing ass.* With that, I clicked a few more nice shots and thought of what a great image transfer it would make, adding this little hated villain of the woods to my collection. (Blue jays, in case you didn't know, were big bullies.

Larger than many birds, they were good at chasing their smaller neighbors away with their brawn—and their loud, annoying call.)

This pretty much put an end to my hopes for the day. Once again, it ended without my nabbing a much-desired shot of the woody. Although the day was disappointing, it wasn't a total loss. After all, I got some pretty decent photos of the jay before his cry—or was it a laugh?—warned the other woodland tenants of my presence, just in case they didn't notice the mallards' quacking. Trying to look on the bright side, I figured it was better to consider the jay's commotion as his way of saying, *Welcome to the neighborhood,* instead of, *Take a look at that wet fool down there!* Whenever possible, I tried to find something positive in the hand life had dealt me.

And at least my aborted foray into the woods helped get my mind off Sherry...for a few hours, at least.

Chapter Six
Gentle Thunder

Several weeks passed without incident. I kept busy shooting commercial assignments for products like housewares and food. Believe it or not, food shoots were my favorite type of commercial assignments. Why? Because food was romantic. Essential, yes, but romantic just the same. To me, food was like making love. The setting evoked the mood: low, warm lighting created a relaxing mindset, and besides, everything looked good in that kind of light. The aroma completed the experience, bringing about the awareness that something special was about to happen. Add these two ingredients to soft, appealing music which eased the mind and called to the heart, and you've got a winning recipe. For me, soft music not only embraced your mind and heart, but also your entire body.

In addition to being incredibly busy with work, my mind was also consumed with bewilderment. What was that mysterious trip I took at the beach several weeks ago? I just couldn't get it out of my head. I needed to explore that damned dream—or whatever that phenomenon was—a little further. Something astounding occurred on those rocks by the shore and I needed to revisit it. Somehow, I had to reunite with those ghostly figures I'd visualized. Could it be the product of my fertile imagination or something that took place in a prior life. I'd heard a little about the theory of past life experience but needed to learn much more. Was the vision something that captured my soul in a prior life that refused to let go of me?

Whatever it was, during that unexplainable experience, a warm, wonderful feeling enveloped my entire being. It made me realize that there must be more to my life than what I was living now. Past lives? Maybe, but definitely something more. My mind was already made up. I was free for the rest of the day, so I figured, why not? Go for it! Into the car I went, pointed it due south, and headed directly to the beach—to that magical rock outcropping by the shore.

The morning was warm with high, sweeping clouds and the sky was a brilliant sapphire. It was the type of day that made everyone feel good. But as I drove, my mind wandered and apprehension seemed to overtake my thoughts. Would I have the ability— no, the *privilege*—to once again meet the mystical figure of my imagination, past life or whatever Jeremiah happened to be? I was forever searching for answers about this, constantly inquiring and looking deep within myself for answers. Me, a consummate skeptic, was shaken to the root like never before. My mind constantly mulled over the events that took place again and again, not letting me rest.

I found it amazing how quickly time rolled by undetected. The early morning ride to my special place on the beach was over before I realized it. As I reached my physical destination, I wondered if I would ever be able to reach my spiritual destination, which was the goal of this trip. Would I be able to journey back across the sea—to Southampton—hundreds of years in the past. It was a place that felt so familiar, yet I had never physically visited. But spiritually...well, that was a different story.

Arriving at the shore, I noticed that the beach was empty. A slight, balmy breeze was coming off the ocean, sweeping up onto shore, hitting me right in the face, like a subtle slap, then continuing up through my hair. The smell of salty air drew me toward the ocean, pulling me to the moderately turbulent sea. I removed my shoes at the end of the parking lot and stepped onto the beach, enjoying the sensation of the cool sand between my toes.

Slowly, I made my way to my ultimate destination. The breeze grew stronger as I move closer to the water's edge. The gulls were jumping off the sand in nervous flight as I approached, crying out in annoyance as I interrupted their leisure time. They seemed to sit still in the air, to float, wings spread as an invisible force kept them aloft. They made it all look so easy, so effortless. The terns flew low and close to the water's surface in search of the food the sea provided them. Flocks of sandlings nervously tap-danced at the water's edge like a group of children challenging the breaking waves to get them wet. Back and forth they danced.

Walking in the sand offered me a great workout, a welcome alternative to the gym's machines. Nature replaced plastic televisions drilled into walls, tuned to the standard channels offering the same news, the same soaps, adding their own ideology. On the beach, I got a better workout, better scenery. Absolutely nothing the gym offered was as interesting as this.

Only a few die-hard sunbathers and a surf fisherman studded the beach that day. The angler was completely engrossed in the mysteries the depths held for him as he pursued his quarry. A woman and her dog ran along the shore, way off in the distance to my south. Besides them, the beach was mine.

I finally arrived at the outcropping—my magical place. Climbing rocks, always made me feel like a kid or a mountain goat, climbing to its perch. Taking a few minutes to look out over the sea, I was awestruck by the massive sky above and by the might of the sea itself. The salt air continued to cool me, while at the same time, stirring my emotions. As I listened to the symphony of waves crashes upon the shore, I wondered where those waves had come from and what kind of journey they'd had. Were they relieved to have their journey over? But was it really over, though? Was the undertow, which drew the foam back out to sea, the end, or just the beginning of a new journey back to the other side—wherever that might be?

It was all so relaxing...so completely relaxing. There were no words to describe how I felt at my little stone sanctuary on the beach. Sitting there just looking out onto the sea, keeping company with the best nature had to offer... At that moment I released my being to mindless thoughts. At some point, I realized I was stalling and I was nervous that I wouldn't be able to achieve the purpose of my trip. But the apprehension gradually melted away as the sounds and fragrances of the shore embraced me.

I wondered, *Should I try this? Should I let myself go and get lost in my thoughts.* Whatever happened to me weeks earlier, my apprehension was still quite obvious. *Should I lay back and once again allow myself to take that compelling journey to who knows where?* Perhaps it was as simple as a dream, a wonderful, compelling dream that ended in a nightmare. Never one to run from fear, I forced myself to relax so I could continue to do what I'd come there to do.

I watched the wispy clouds moving ever so silently across the bright blue background of the sky. As they drifted past forming new shapes, I felt my body, my entire being, begin to relax. The gentle thunder of the waves against the shore absorbed me into their crashing sounds. The sea pulled my soul out toward the horizon with a strong, spiritual undertow. The longer I listened, the more haunting, the more hypnotic it became.

Soon, I felt my legs grow heavier and the heaviness climbed up the length of my entire body, invading it. I felt the lids of my eyes being pulled shut, almost involuntarily, and they began to close. I surrendered to it. And slowly, before too long...

I am again at that stone bridge engulfed in fog. I cross the bridge without fear or trepidation, but with anticipation this time. As the fog clears...what is this? I see a boy I sense is me, and he is sitting by a window, gazing out to sea. The beautiful moon is full, bright and wonderfully orange. This place is strangely familiar to me.

The boy's small hands rest under his chin, his elbows propped on the windowsill, as he takes in all the gifts his world by the sea gives him. The more I watch this boy, the more I see myself in him...the more I realize that now I am seeing myself. Where is this? I wonder, as I continue to observe this dreamlike experience, like a movie, playing in my mind's eye. As I am swept up in the scene, I know that I have successfully begun another journey back to this past life. My past life?

Seated and peering out his window into the night, the boy is dressed in a long white nightshirt. I can actually feel the breeze come up off the ocean through the window and I now understand why the breeze I had felt on drive to the sea caused me to feel the way I did—it is my transporter of sorts. I notice that the small house the boy is located on the main street of what appears to be the same New England shipping town as before. I am suddenly startled as a shrill voice rings out from downstairs.

"Jeremiah, stop that wasteful wondering and get to bed!"

The boy quickly turns and steps over a small wooden toy, a replica of a merchant's ship. I know instinctively that this is his favorite toy. Jeremiah is in bed with just two quick leaps. He pulls the covers up over his wiry body, lays back and quietly, contentedly stares up at the ceiling.

Lying there, he thinks about how one day, he will be at the helm of a merchant ship, a noble captain steering his vessel to a far-off, exotic land. Jeremiah imagines his ship with tall white sails, the pristine wooden decks crashing through the waves as he guides it safely onward. He maintains a firm grip on the massive, finely finished mahogany wheel that directs the rudder to stay the ship's course. Calling out orders to his crew about the proper positioning of the sails, Jeremiah smiles as the bracing sea air slaps him in the face. He often dreams of this life and it excites every fiber of his being.

The morning sun cuts through Jeremiah's little window and into his sleepy eyes. He slowly awakens to the sound of shore birds crying out to one another as the sea below explodes into a boiling foam and silver eruption. The birds seem to be coordinating their pursuit of the schools of baitfish at the water's surface. These fish are driven upward by larger predatory fish below that are seeking breakfast above. Those who make their living by the sea understand this circle of life. These predators could be bluefish, maybe striped bass, and both are a quarry of the boy's at every given chance.

His mother calls him to breakfast. Elizabeth is a plain, solidly-built woman who stands five foot, four inches tall, with rich, thick, long black hair. Her deep brown eyes are inquisitive and piercing. Elizabeth wears a white cotton top, laced up the front, with a simple, crude brown skirt. As Jeremiah enters the hearth room, she is standing at a stove fueled by coal. Elizabeth insists that Jeremiah, who is ravenously hungry, be seated at the table to eat his customary breakfast of oatmeal. Not a tasty meal, especially the no-nonsense way Elizabeth prepares it (not a touch of sugar or maple syrup), but a filling one just the same. As Jeremiah eats hungrily, his mother barks at him to hurry. She reminds him that he is to get dressed as soon as he consumes his morning's nourishment. It is Saturday, market day, and there is much to do.

Jeremiah tells his mother that sea captains get ready at their will and that he will get dressed when he is ready. Elizabeth shoots him a stern, steely look, one he has seen on a number of occasions. He learned some time ago not to push his mother once that look has been unleashed, so he dutifully bounds up stairs and dresses in his white captain's shirt with brown knickers and brown socks. Jeremiah runs a comb through his black hair that favors the color of both his parents' locks. But his eyes are the deep blue of his father's. Jeremiah sets the comb down on the old oak dresser. He must look his best for Saturday.

Ah, Saturday...Jeremiah's favorite day of the week. No school. His mother and he will go off to the market, she to shop, he to play. At the market there are all sorts of food and staples to sustain him, but nothing so life-sustaining as candy. While Elizabeth shops, Jeremiah visits some of his favorite vendors— vendors who always seem to have an idle piece of something sweet lying around that he could relieve them of.

Once Jeremiah has secured his bounty, he is off to the field where the children gather to play. His two favorites are endless, marathon games of Tag and Hide-and- Seek. The children also run, spinning wooden hoops, striking them with sticks to keep them going. On windy days, they fly kites with long tails made

*from old, worn-out fabric "borrowed" from their mothers. The
more colorful the tails, the more fun they are to watch as they
drift about in the sky, tugging at the children below holding the
string as the kites attempt to free themselves of their bonds to
land and fly off on their own.*

*Jeremiah is the gentle age of eight years old, the same age as
his neighbor Jessica. Although Jessica's home is much more
grand than his, and her family a good deal richer, there is no
indication of this by their joyful play. Jeremiah always sees her
at the fields on Saturday and it is the day's highlight. He actually
seeks Jessica out and tries to look his best. Jeremiah takes great
delight in running up behind her, startling her. He takes much joy
in teasing her, running playful circles around her, pulling her
silky, well-brushed auburn braids. When Jeremiah runs away,
Jessica chases him across the field with a stick. Sometimes, he
lets her catch him, sometimes not. He loves her sky- blue eyes
and rich, reddish-brown locks, the color of his favorite pony.
They carry on for hours until one of their mothers comes
to collect them. Although Jeremiah sees Jessica in school,
somehow, Saturday is always more special. It's a joyful,
unbridled day.*

*On this day, Jessica's father, Adam, is the one who comes to
fetch her. Adam is First Mate on one of the local merchant ships
and some say that he is on the fast track to becoming a Captain
one day soon. Adam lightheartedly scolds the children and then
engages Jeremiah in conversation. "I understand your father is
off to France. When do you expect him home?"*

"Soon, I think," Jeremiah replies.

*"Well, when he arrives, let me know. I insist that he join us
at the pub to tell us about his journey," Adam tells Jeremiah.*

*"Yes, Sir," Jeremiah responds. Then off goes Jessica,
holding her father's hand. Jeremiah watches as they disappear
across the field. He always feels a little sad at the end of their
Saturday outings.*

*Determined to enjoy the rest of his Saturday, Jeremiah runs
off to his other friend—the sea. He never tires of looking at its
face. He misses his father when he is journeying and gazing out
upon the endless sea makes the boy feel closer to him, yet long*

for him all the more. Jeremiah feels the moisture of the sea upon his face and sorrow in his little heart. The pain of missing his father seems to make his little body hurt all over. Is that moisture on his cheeks from the sea or from his heart? He convinces himself that it's merely sea mist because men never cry.

At that moment, I awakened with a start at the thunder of what seemed to be a large wave crushing the shore. I found myself lying on my rocky perch for a few moments longer, gathering my thoughts. So, it worked! I managed to bring myself back to my previous journey. I was flooded with the same warm feeling, the same unexplained glow which embraced me during my last experience. That sense of calm and restfulness, at the same time, left me confused and wondering. What was this soulful journey into the past? And where did it take me exactly? Why was I taking such trips? While I was filled with a fear of the unknown, I also had a strange solace in knowing that this was a very meaningful voyage that was essential to my very being. And I was hungry for more of it.

When I was fully conscious, I hopped up and quickly walked back across the sand to my car. The heavy surf was calling and begged to be captured. Camera in hand, I fired off several photographs—meaningful photos. If to no one else, they would be important to me because they would always remind me of the journey I just took.

Back in my car and on my way home, I contemplated these events on my drive. Should I keep these visions to myself or should I tell someone about these soulful trips I'd been taking? Would people think I'd completely lost it or would they be fascinated? With a slight laugh, I thought, *Hell, no. They'll know I've completely lost it, as many of my friends already suspect by now.* Only one person in my life might be able to understand, but I wasn't ready to tell her yet.

All I could be sure of, at that point, was that these visions, these out of body experiences were doing something to me I didn't quite grasp. But before I started opening up to anyone, I decided to let this thing ride out and see where it took me. I resigned myself to give it time, to see if it went anywhere. And if this turned out to be as pivotal in my life as I suspected it might be, I would take it from there.

 ## Chapter Seven
My Own Private Psychic Hotline

In the weeks that passed since that last out of body experience, two things haunted me. The first, which was really burning up my brain, almost paralyzing me, was the many crazy thoughts I had about Sherry. Not a minute passed without me wondering what she'd been up to...why she hadn't called or even emailed me to just say hello. The second haunting thought concerned my unexplainable the trips into the past. I wondered about their purpose and where they wanted to take me.

At that point, I realized that I was able to take these trips at will. The only thing I didn't seem to have was control over was *where* they took me. I just had to resign myself to relax and travel back to wherever they decided to propel me. And, yes, they always took me somewhere. But why? Did other people experience this or was I the only freak? And what affect were they having on my life? I certainly felt more scattered, more vulnerable and more confused that I usually did. And lastly, I wondered if there was a message I was missing from these experiences.

I was beginning to have more questions than answers. And just what the heck was up with Sherry? Did I say something to upset or hurt her? I sure could have—it didn't take much for guys like me to annoy a woman. (Sometimes I thought that just breathing the "wrong" way annoys them.) But somehow, Sherry didn't seem annoyed with me during our lunch, just the opposite. I really hoped this wasn't the case and that it was just another example of me being paranoid. I didn't think I could deal with Sherry being pissed off at me on top of everything else I was going through.

First and foremost, I needed to figure out what these trips were about. Could I research it online? But I was at a loss at what to do, type in a Google search for "dreams" and see what popped up? That sounded like it could end up being a wild goose chase, unearthing three million or more hits. Reading through even the first thousand would take up too much of my life.

I decided to call two of my friends who are knowledgeable about this sort of thing. It was like having my own private psychic hotline. First, I reached out to Laura, who would give me a quick answer. She owned her own company and was always running. I was never quite sure where she was running to but she was constantly running just the same. Sometimes I got the feeling Laura was running from something, but if so, she kept it to herself. She knew I was there to listen if she needed me but she never took advantage of my offer. I was surprised when she picked up on the first ring. "Hello, Laura. It's Jarred. How have you been?"

"Good, Jarred. And yourself?"

"Fine. Listen," I began. "I'm sure you're busy, so I won't keep you, but I have a quick question. I've been having these out of body experiences recently...I've been taking these trips while in a semiconscious state and..."

Laura cut me off. "Whoa! Nothing like cutting to the chase, Jarred."

"Sorry," I responded. "But you know me, Mr. Cut and Dry. Anyway, it's happened twice now. I go into a sort of hypnotic state and to get there, I travel over this bridge. It's amazing, like watching a movie in my head."

"What else is it like?" she wondered. I could tell that Laura was hooked now.

"Different every time," I began. "Set sometime in the1800s, I think. I've seen a sailor die in one episode. He was in love with this woman, a beautiful, exotic woman. He died in her arms at an old pub. In another trip, I watch this little boy in his home with his mother. They go to the market where he plays with his friends and a little girl..."

" Who is this woman or girl?" Laura asked, intrigued. "Do you think she's the same person?"

"Now that you mention it, I believe she is. But I hadn't given it much thought until now," I said, feeling enlightened already.

"I have to tell you, Jarred, it sounds to me like something is trying to come through to you," Laura told me. "Have you undergone any changes recently in your life?" When I told her that I couldn't think of any, she continued, "How is your relationship with Carol?"

I shrugged. "Pretty much the same. Nothing seems to change. We get along fairly well and there's the usual fighting over money and the kids...nothing new. Why?" I wondered if this was in some way significant or if Laura was just being nosy. Turned out to be the former.

"Well, some of what you're telling me actually sounds like you might be experiencing past life regressions," Laura conceded. "But it's unusual for someone to be able to complete this without assistance." She stopped to think for a moment, then continued, "I'm not sure where you're being taken or what you are being shown, but something has, or is, happening in your life. It seems to me, a message is being sent to you," she informed me. "Give this some thought and give me a call. We'll meet for coffee or something and see if we can't figure this out. But, in the meantime, don't worry about this. I have to run. Talk to you later." We made a tentative date for coffee the following week.

I hung up the phone feeling better. Although I didn't know much more than when I'd picked up the telephone, I knew that I could count on Laura. A client who had become a friend, Laura and I didn't talk as often as we should but I liked her a lot—she shot straight from the hip. Even though she had a very busy life (and so do I), we'd always got each other's backs, no matter what.

Pleased with that hopeful start, I decided to put a call into Peggy. Now, Peggy is a mystic and a good friend whom I met years earlier, working on a committee. She was always upbeat and in a good frame of mind. Nothing ever seemed to bother her, and if it did, she never let on. When Peggy answered the phone, she genuinely sounded happy to hear from me—and knew it was me calling. "Hello, Jarred. It's been a while," is the way she picked up.

"Wow, Peggy! How did you know it was me?" I asked.

"I'm a mystic—remember?" There was silence on the end side of the line. With that, Peggy chuckled, "I have Caller ID, kiddo. Had you there for a minute, though, didn't I?" she laughed.

"Yeah, I was totally floored, sitting here thinking, 'Man, she's even better than I thought," I admitted.

"What's been happening in your life these days, Jarred? I've been thinking about you quite a bit lately. I've been sensing that you're going through some changes," she told me.

Again, I was amazed. "Boy, I've got to admit, you are that good. Something strange has definitely been occurring in my life but I'm not sure what to make of it, if anything," I confessed.

"What is it?" she asked.

"A few weeks ago, I went to my favorite spot at the beach," I began. "I was just lying there watching the clouds, listening to the waves coming in, when all of a sudden, I felt myself drift off into a state of what I can only describe as 'limbo.' Next thing I know, I'm crossing over this stone bridge, through a fog, and I see this other world. It looks like the 1800s, maybe earlier. But it's like I'm watching this movie—or maybe a play—which is playing out right in front of me. All of a sudden, I'm watching—or maybe even becoming—this young sailor, Jeremiah. I watched or *lived*, his life as this scenario plays out. I'm not sure which. It was captivating. The first journey lasted until a prostitute by the name of Katrina killed him. When it happened, I woke up with a start. And that was just the first vision."

I could tell Peggy was extremely interested. "What are you doing right now?" she asked. "I have to know more but I don't want to do this over the phone. But I will tell you that I'm getting a strong sense from you that something is transitioning in your life!" she said with excitement.

"Honestly, all I am doing right now is sitting here and wondering what the hell is going on with all of this," I admitted in a confused voice.

"Okay then, Jarred, come on up. Let's dig into this together and see what it's all about." I promised Peggy I'd be there within a half-hour, and got there even sooner.

I arrived at Peggy's place with mixed emotions. I was happy to see my good friend, who always put a smile on my face, but this visit was more of a serious nature. Would I come away with answers or with more questions? And would the answers be too profound for me to deal with at this point?

Nervously, I knocked on her door. "Hi, Peggy," I greeted her as she opened it.

"Nice to see you, Jarred. Come in." It's a happy mess, as usual, but comforting all the same. "I've made a pot of coffee," she continued. "Would you like a cup?" she asked with a smile—knowing that I would. "Dark no sugar," she remembered.

Entering Peggy's house is always a welcoming experience because it's filled with all sorts of New Age knick-knacks: crystals, feathered items, shells and plaques. I could smell incense burning and wasn't not quite sure what it was—lavender...lilac?—but I found it soothing and relaxing. The gentle flute music that played in the background was also soothing. Peggy handed me a fresh mug of coffee. "Come, sit at the table. Tell me what's up. This sounds really interesting."

I proceed to fill her in on everything, leaving out no detail about the two trips, including the fact that they seemed to be going backward in time, not forward.

When I was done, Peggy spoke with certainty. "Jarred, these are definitely past life experiences. Let me ask, you've observed the same woman in both of these journeys, right?" Once again, she was dead on.

I nodded. "She was older in one journey but she's always the same age as the young man," I admitted, more confused now, trying my best to gather my thoughts.

Peggy spoke quickly, excitedly. "What I'm getting is that there are other forces at work here. I believe that this woman and this young man in your past life left each other too early. I also believe that these people may be you and your soul mate, and that you're reconnecting to complete unfinished business." I think Peggy could tell by the expression on my face that I was floored, so she tried to slow down a tad. "Let's see what the cards say. Sit down and relax," she chuckled.

I didn't realize I was still standing.

Sitting across from Peggy at her pleasantly worn wooden table, I took a deep breath as she doled out the Tarot cards. "Okay...I can see that your life is in transition. New events are occurring. Someone new may be entering your life. This card represents new energy. The connection will benefit both of you," she added. "Jarred, is there someone new in your life, someone you're close to?"

"No, well, no one knew exactly...except...," I began.

"Except what?" she interrupted.

"A friend whom I've known a while now," I admitted. "She and I were having lunch one day, and after leaving, I began to get strange thoughts and feelings about her. I felt really guilty about them and I wasn't quite sure why they happened all of a sudden since I've known her for a few years. But suddenly, it was like I saw her in a different light." I left out the part about the strange, warm breeze and the feelings that overcame me at that point.

"How did you meet?" Peggy wondered.

"We met at her job. I told her boss, who's a client, that we needed some artists for our creative group. That's when Valerie told me about Sherry, her new employee. I immediately went over and introduced myself to her, looked at her work, and the rest, as they say, is history," I recounted.

Peggy nodded knowingly. "The cards are telling me that you're on your way to a new and unexpected journey. Just watch yourself, Jarred. Keep an open mind and see where this journey takes you. I don't know if this person, Sherry, is what I'm seeing, but I would be more aware of your feelings toward her, if I were you."

Then, with her usual enthusiasm, Peggy assured me that this would be an exciting awakening that would somehow enrich my life. I tried hard to believe her as we finished our coffee and moved on to more harmless subjects. After a while, I glanced at my watch. "It's getting late, Peggy. I've got to run. What do I owe you?"

Peggy smiled and pointed to several of my photographs on her walls. "You owe me nothing, Jarred. Every day, I look at the photos you've given me and they bring joy to my life. That's payment enough," she reassured me.

I smiled and shook my head. I think I loved giving Peggy my prints almost as much as she enjoyed getting them. Her genuine sense of appreciation for my work made me feel incredible.

I turned and left with a new sense of exhilaration. Instead of trepidation, I was determined to approach this with Peggy's sense of wonder. Having so many questions answered, I was now sure that I was indeed embarking upon a journey and had a tiny inkling of what it might mean. Moving forward, I promised myself to be more aware of what was going on in my life and those around me—especially Sherry.

Chapter Eight
Little White Lies

Ah, Friday! I thought to myself on my way to the gym. *Fridays are usually pretty slow at work, so I can hopefully get a lot of personal things done today.* Working out also gave me a chance to sort things out and plan my week ahead, or in this case, my weekend. I considered taking it easy that particular weekend but then decided to spend my Saturday trying to make up for that failed impromptu trip out into the field and actually plan my next trip into the wild. On the treadmill, I vowed to get my butt out of bed early the next day—at maybe 5:00 or 5:30--to get a jump on the legions of weekend warriors and tourists.

After leaving the gym, I made my usual stop at the deli to chat with Rocky. He was such a pleasant guy, it was always a great way to start my day. I actually looked forward to it and always secretly hoped that some of his positive vibes would rub off on me. As I entered the deli, the aroma of good Italian food quickly awakened my senses. Growing up in an Italian family, I found that the various pungent cheeses—like provolone—or the perfume of salami and other Italian delicacies, roused my appetite. There was something very inviting about the scents that greeted me as I entered the deli. Add to that, Rocky's wicked sense of humor and thousand watt smile and you couldn't ask for a better way to begin the day.

As I walked in, Rocky shouted out, "Look out ladies, he's here. Hold on to your hearts! This guy will steal them before you know it." I began to laugh. Some of the women making purchases at the counter looked over at me warily while others treated me to a smile.

"You know me, Rock. I never steal anything," I reassured him.—and everyone else within earshot. "If it isn't given to me, I won't take it. Don't worry ladies. I'm married, so you're safe."

"Look out, he's a sharp one," Rocky warned with a laugh. "He's trying to catch you off guard." Then, he pat me on the shoulder. "So, what's new, Jarred?" he asked.

"Not much, Rocky," I told him. "SOS, I'm sorry to say. Nothing exciting ever happens to me."

Okay, so that was a little white lie. However, trying to explain the unexplainable with all of these people around would have been an arduous task. Besides, you never could be sure who was in the deli. For all I knew, there might be a shrink within earshot. Instead of leaving with just my coffee, I might end up leaving in a straight jacket after being shot with a tranquilizer dart. "Egg on a roll?" Rocky asked.

"I'll pass today," I told him. I just stopped by for coffee and to say hello." We chatted for a few pleasant minutes before I realized it was time to get to the studio. "Gotta run," I called out as I moved up to the register to pay for my coffee. "Catch you at lunch. Have a great morning,"

"You too, Jarred."

With that, I was out the door and off to the work. Entering my studio, coffee in hand, I noticed the light blinking on my answering machine. I settled in, turned on my computer, wrestled the top off the coffee container and took a sip. I grabbed a pencil and a sheet of paper and pushed the "message" button. I was happily startled by the sweet, soft voice of Sherry. My spirits lifted and my heartbeat increased as I felt a slight knowing smile come to my lips. "Hi, Jarred, this is Sherry..." There was a long a pause which caused me to wonder momentarily what the call was really about. That pause got me thinking as I put down my pencil. I didn't need a pencil or paper when it came to calling Sherry back after such a short but weighty message.

What I didn't know was, earlier that morning, just after Sherry had just gotten into her office, her boss Valerie approached her with a simple request. They had a rush job for a photo shoot on Monday and Val asked Sherry to contact me to see if I was available to do it. "Or I can call him myself," Valerie added.

Sherry told me later that she couldn't believe the perfect opportunity that had presented itself first thing in the morning. What Valerie didn't know—nor did anyone else for that matter—is that Sherry had spent much of the time thinking about me and her unexplainable attraction to me. (Yep, it came as a pleasant shock to me too!) She wondered how could she explore the possibility of having a relationship with me, which she knew would complicate things for the both of us. But for some unexplainable reason, she didn't care. For once in her life, Sherry was throwing caution to the wind.

Trying to conceal her enthusiasm from Valerie, Sherry quickly shot back, "No, It's my job. I'll do it." Sherry picked up the phone, slowly punched in my number, which, she confessed to me later, she knew by heart. All the while, Sherry was wondering, *What will I say? And, how can I give this guy a hint that I'm interested in him? I swear, he's clueless. If I don't hit him in the head with a brick or something, I don't think he'll ever catch on, and I'll never be able to explore these emotions grabbing at my insides.*

As the phone rang, Sherry anticipated my answering it and how she would accomplish her goal. Damn, the answering machine. Without hesitation or much thought, Sherry's instincts took over. In a seductive voice (but nothing too obvious), she began, "Hi, Jarred, it's Sherry..." Then came her weighty pause for several seconds, "...give me a call at work when you get a moment." *Perfect*, she thought, *If that doesn't make him realize something's up, I might have to consider hitting him with a truck.*

After listening to Sherry's full message, I rushed to the phone, fumbled the receiver and dialed the wrong number. I hung up and started again. When the phone began ringing, I worried, *What do I do if Valerie answers? Does she know that Sherry called me? No, not the way Sherry's message sounded!*

Two rings, three rings, and then four...damn. I considered hanging up, then someone picked up the phone. "Hi, this is Sherry."

My smile broadened at the sound of her voice. "Hi, it's me—Jarred. How are you, Sherry?"

"Oh, hi, 'Me'," she joked. "We have a job for you. Can you hold for a second?"

Crap. A job! How disappointing is that? I bet she's transferring me over to Valerie. I'm on hold, thinking, What a let-down. I could have sworn there was something more to Sherry's call than a job. After a few seconds that felt more like 20 minutes, Sherry came back on. "Sorry, Jarred, I was just finishing up a call. I need to see you..." she began, then paused for several seconds, raising my hopes, only to be let down again. Sherry was unknowingly taking me on an emotional roller coaster ride of a lifetime. Up the slope of hope and back down again. I conceded that maybe I was a little sensitive when it came to Sherry. Maybe I was reading into things that weren't there. "Do you have any time early next week, like say, Monday?" she asked.

"Well, Monday really is early next week," I joked. "Sure, I can see you Monday." All the time I was thinking, *I don't care what I have on the calendar for Monday. I'll change it. I'll move fricking mountains to see her Monday, or any day, for that matter.*

"Great, what time is good for you? Valerie usually gets in at about 10, 10:30."

"Okay...I can be there at eight," I laughed.

"But she won't be in until 10 the earliest," Sherry answered slyly.

"But that will give us some time to talk before she gets in," I laughed some more.

Sherry responded with a telling, "Oh, sounds good to me. But

I'm just getting up at eight."

"Let me get this straight," I began. "You're telling me that I'm not important enough to wake up a little earlier for?"

"No, that isn't what I'm saying, Jarred," she said with concern in her voice.

"Then, just what are you saying?' I asked nervously.

"I'm saying that I don't want to change my routine and arouse suspicion with anyone," she replied coyly.

"Okay then...I can be there at 10:30. I'll wait if I have to," I retorted.

I could almost feel her smile. "Okay, you're in the book for 10:30. Be a little early if you like...so we can talk."

"I will," I told her. "I look forward to seeing you again."

Sherry wasn't about to let me off the phone that easily. "So, what are your plans for the weekend? Doing anything interesting?"

"I'm hoping to head up to the park. There's an area just off Route 301 where I'd love to get some photos of wood ducks. That area is prime for woodies—quiet, secluded. A wonderful place to sit and wait."

"I know," Sherry reminded me. "Remember who told you about it?"

"Oh, yeah...sorry, I forgot. Well, that's where I plan on spending my day tomorrow. Just me and hopefully a few wood ducks...and, well, anything else that might comes my way," I told her.

"I hope you're lucky and everything you're looking for shows up — and maybe something unexpected as well...And, Jarred, seeing as how I'm coming in a little early for you Monday, I take my coffee light no sugar. And make it a large," she instructed me lightheartedly.

"That's a small price to pay for your company on a Monday morning, Sherry. Have a great weekend," I said.

"Okay, 'till Monday..." Sherry hung up. I wondered if she was smiling at the phone with a small devilish grin just as I was. When she and I discussed this telephone conversation a short time later, she admitted that indeed she was. Plus, she muttered to herself, *Yeah, Jarred, till Monday...* just as Valerie walked in.

"What's that, Sherry?" Valerie asked.

"Nothing. Just thinking out loud," Sherry told her. "That was Jarred. He'll be here between 10:30 and 11 on Monday." A cunning move on Sherry's part, giving us more time together before Valerie arrived.

"Good," Val conceded. " I may be a little late on Monday. Maybe you should call him back and tell him to make it closer to 11."

"He was on his way out," Sherry lied. "I'll call him later." Which she didn't. I could just picture Sherry smiling, going back to work and thinking to herself, *He won't mind your being late one bit.*

# Chapter Nine
Retake

The clock radio blared suddenly, startling me awake. I gradually gained consciousness. *Damn! 5:30. I must be nuts getting up this early on a Saturday.* Slowly, I pulled myself out of bed, trying not to awaken Carol. I grabbed some underwear, a shirt and slipped on my jeans. Silently, I padded off to the kitchen to put up a pot of coffee before jumping into the shower. The aroma of fresh coffee first thing in the morning always heightens my senses, pulling me further from the grip of slumber. Did I say "grip?" At that hour, it was more like a strangle hold. At least one eye was completely open, but the other hadn't quite gotten there and my brain was working at half power...okay, more like quarter power. Who was I kidding?

Stumbling into the bathroom, I took a look at myself in the mirror. Man, it was not pretty. My wild hair was standing on end, looking as though it were trying to escape from my head. I hit the shower, washing away what remained of my slumber. I really hoped something showed up today. *I mean, If I was getting my ass out of bed at the crack of dawn...but it's too early even to listen to myself. Okay, stop your complaining, Jarred. No one's forcing you to do this. It's your idea of fun, remember?* There's nothing like engaging in a stern conversation with yourself before six a.m. I've heard that it's acceptable to have talks with yourself like this as long as you don't answer yourself, so I'm not too worried.

I gave my upcoming field day some more thought, planning it right down to the part where the ducks will practically land at my feet. I would leave nothing to chance. No surprises. At that point, I knew I was delusional because when you were dealing with nature, there's precious little you can control. Well, at least I could control my being there alone for a while, thanks to the ungodly hour. But I was losing time and the sun was rising quickly.

I hurried, dried myself off, got dressed and pulled a comb through my unruly hair. After filling my thermos with coffee and a drop of half and half, I headed out to my already-packed car. I arrived at my destination in only 15 minutes. Pulling off the road, I parked my car and took another sip of coffee. I grabbed my knapsack which contained my equipment, threw it on my back, locked the car and headed straight into the woods.

The wilderness welcomed me with the scent of pine. I felt like I was being carried off on a soft, warm, fragrant breeze. I couldn't have ordered a more perfect day. It was maybe 70 degrees and a few clouds decorated the still-dark sky which was lit only by a full moon. This, plus the welcoming chorus of songbirds and the occasional chirp of chipmunks as they ran to hide from this unwelcome intruder, helped complete the scene. One little guy scampered right across my path, tail straight up, pointing to the beautiful indigo sky as it gradually started to brighten. The sun started its ascent above the mountains to my right. The chipmunk bounded into a rock pile and disappeared into a crevice within seconds of my noticing him, to wait out my passing. I could already hear the river below me. It was a welcome, relaxing symphony of nature that brightened my very early day, reminding me why it paid to get up and out at such an ungodly hour.

I traveled slowly along the ravine, just above the river, until I reached a place where the current slowed down. I scanned the scene for hardwood trees like oak, knowing that woodies seek their seed, the mighty acorn. I eased myself into the perfect location from where I could overlook the river and the woods to begin my wait. And as I waited, my thoughts strayed to Sherry. I wondered what she was doing at that moment. Probably sleeping, if she had any sense!

I knew that Sherry's boyfriend Bill often worked on Saturdays and that she relished having the day to herself. I pictured Sherry pouring herself a cup of coffee and taking a few minutes to relax as she enjoyed something sweet, a muffin, maybe...knowing Sherry, probably blueberry. In my mind's eye, she sat peacefully contemplating the hours ahead. She's dressed comfortably in jeans, an old shirt and hiking boots. In my mind's eye, I watched Sherry finishing off her coffee and the last of the muffin, then grab her keys. Did I detect a slight apprehension as she climbed into the car, started it and pulled out of the driveway? I felt a strange excitement watching this simple scenario playing out in my imagination, as if it were something more than a daydream...a fantasy, maybe.

I indulged myself further as I imagined Sherry pulling out of the driveway and going off on her way. But to where? The scenery whizzing past her car windows is oddly familiar. She pulled into a deserted road after only about ten minutes. It was the logging road she told me about years earlier, the very same road I traveled this morning. (Hey, I can dream, can't I?) Sherry turned right and slowly made her way down the road. As she rounded the bend, a smile came to her lips. There it was—my car in the parking lot. She parked beside me, sat for a moment to gather her thoughts and asked herself if she really wanted to begin this journey. When she got out of the car, I had my answer.

Sherry's mind was made up as she slipped out of her car without hesitation and moved deliberately down the path of her destiny. The only thing she knew for sure was that I was there, somewhere in there—exactly where, she had no idea, but she moved instinctively, with purpose.

Nestled in the woods, I heard two birds crying out softly. Breaking out of my reverie, I easily spotted a pair of cardinals who circled me as I watched them. A bright red male and a dusty gray female. They flitted from tree to tree, berry bush to tree, giving me a show. They stopped for a few moments then continued chasing each other through the woods. Disappearing down the path, they resurfaced, as though someone was following them, as though they were leading someone here.

Sitting as quiet and still as possible, I stayed at the ready with my camera and kept a sharp eye out for any wildlife that might wander into the range of my lens. The sound of the slow moving stream was relaxing as it made its way over and around the rocks that cut through the water. My mind drifted from the wildlife and onto Monday's appointment at Valerie's office. I realized that I wasn't thinking about the assignment, but of coffee with Sherry. Was she sending me some kind of message or was I really off target? And what about those pregnant pauses in her speech and the fact that she volunteered to come in a little early to chat before Valerie arrived.

All of a sudden, something crashed into my head. BAM! Like a direct hit between the eyes with a brick. But it actually felt good, not painful as one might expect. I began to think that maybe it wasn't me and there really was something behind Sherry's recent behavior. But I almost missed it. And what about her comment about arousing suspicion? About what? With whom? Maybe I was over thinking things, as I often did, or was there something to this?

The sun was beginning to feel good as it rose above the tree line. By now, the woodies should be moving from their night roosts to the feeding areas which were in the swamp below. Just then, I heard something above the sound of the stream. More crunching leaves and the cardinals have returned, pausing in flight, as if leading something to me.

At that very moment, Sherry bounded into the clearing. At first, I thought it was just my daydream gone wild. But it was Sherry, right there in the flesh, dressed just as I had imagined her. "You looked so intense?" she said in greeting. "I didn't want you to miss your quarry. You know, the shot of a lifetime." But I had a feeling that this might be the shot of a lifetime and I was determined to take it.

Sherry played it cool at first, acting as though she has no idea I might be here. My mind spun through the playback of yesterday's conversation with her. No, she never said anything about coming up here today. Didn't I tell her I'd be coming here? I knew this was no chance meeting.

She moved with such grace and ease, I could watch her forever. Sherry took a step toward me, her bright brown eyes sparkling as sunlight sneaked through the tree branches, gently settling on her face, complimenting her sensual beauty. This was the first time I really noticed how warm and soft her skin seemed, how inviting her friendly smile was. But there was something more to her, so much more than I realized.

My heart raced. "Fancy meeting you here."

She blushed, embarrassed. "Hey, it's a big forest. I doubted I'd run into you. I hope I'm not disturbing you."

"You? Disturb me? Never."

I walked slowly and deliberately toward her, my eyes fixed on hers. I felt weak. My legs wanted to run, but my body held back. There was a pain deep in the pit of my stomach and my knees seemed to want to give out as I got closer.

Sherry watched me coming toward her but it looked like she half wanted to run herself—to me or from me, I wasn't sure which. But she didn't do either, she just stayed put. Sherry maintained her composure, beaming with a smile that lit my heart. She waited anxiously for me to reach her and I seemed to be moving ever so slowly, as if through water. But she waited just the same, not showing too much emotion, holding on to her coolness like a protective shield.

As I moved toward the path where Sherry waited, something inside me was saying, *Run you fool, run! Take her into your arms*. But reason prevailed. Finally we were standing together. I reached out to take her hand and moved to kiss her gently on the cheek—our usual greeting. As our hands touched, I felt a sudden flow of energy rush up my arm and into my heart, which seemed to explode with emotion. When I looked into Sherry's face, I saw that she too felt this unexplainable energy. A tear came to her eyes. When I leaned in to kiss her face, she pulled me into her--or did I pull her into me?

Sherry and I fell into an embrace, hugging one another close. I felt the heat of her body, yet she shook as though she were cold. Our energy seemed to flow from my heart to hers and back again. I wanted to pull her into my body. I wanted Sherry to be a part of me. We stood there stock-still, swaying from side to side gently. I didn't want to let go and it didn't feel like she did either. "I've wanted this for so long," Sherry gasped.

I responded by holding her tighter. "I never want to let you go. You're so beautiful, Sherry, so beautiful."

Maybe it was the warmth of our bodies or the sudden release of so much energy that we'd held back for so long, but I felt so empowered and I thought Sherry did too. But when I heard her sniffle, I pulled my head up from her shoulder to find that she was crying. My heart dropped. "I'm sorry," I apologized. "Did I do something wrong? Maybe I shouldn't have been so forward."

Sherry gave me a bright smile through her tears and said softly, "You haven't done anything wrong. You've done something right. This is what I've dreamed of for so long. I didn't think you cared."

"I felt you pulling me toward you forever. I just never thought..." Sherry touched her fingers to my lips. "Quiet, Jarred."

I began to wipe the tears from her cheeks and when she leaned in, our lips met. The feel of Sherry's soft, warm, longing lips on mine was a dream come true. We kissed long and hard— I hadn't shared such a passionate kiss with anyone in a long time. I felt like a teenager. My head was spinning and my hands were sweating. I felt a strength, an electricity vibrating from within me and from Sherry. We embraced again, her head nestled beside mine, and once more, Sherry broke down and cried. I felt confused and nervous, yet so exhilarated.

"What is it, then?" I needed an answer to clear up my confusion.

"No, it's nothing," she insisted. "Please don't pay attention to my silly crying. Just hold me. Hold me tight and don't let go."

Sherry's response threw me off slightly, but these days, it didn't take much to throw me. I had so many questions yet at the same time, so many answers.

"I will never let you go," I promised.

Sherry and I held each other for what seemed like hours, but in reality, I guess it was only minutes. When I looked into her eyes, there was a new depth and understanding. They seemed to pierce deep into my very soul. "This isn't your normal friendship, is it?" I asked.

She smiled in response. "To say the least," she answered shyly.

Sherry leaned in and kissed me softly, briefly, then hugged me close again. I took her by the hand and led her back to my perch overlooking the stream. We sat quietly for a few moments, her arms twined through mine, her head leaning against my shoulder. We silently watched as the water made its way downstream, billowing over rocks, foaming around the protrusion from the banks. I watched the many shapes and forms the water took on without saying a word. It was so alive, and so much was going on within it, around it. I realized then that the stream was like me—I had returned to life with so much going on in me and around me.

My mind raced, as I imagined Sherry's did too. "What the hell just happened here?" I gathered the courage to whisper. "Where did this come from? Do you have any idea, any idea at all what is going on?"

"I'm not sure, and honestly, I don't care," Sherry told me. "All I know is this is right. I know it. I feel it. So please stop that beautiful brain of yours from thinking and over-thinking. Let's just be silent and enjoy the moment, this journey, each other."

"Point taken."

We sat quietly, savoring the moment. Sherry was so close, I could feel her heart beating and this brought me comfort. As I slipped my arm around her shoulder, Sherry looked up as I leaned in to taste her. A moan escaped from my lips, releasing some of my pent up, long-forgotten feelings.

"I can't tell you how worried I was about coming here, Jarred," she admitted. "I wasn't sure if you would be happy or pissed or if I'd ruin a shot of the wood ducks. But I thought about coming here all night and I couldn't get you out of my head. Morning just didn't come soon enough."

"This was a surprise to say the least. Seeing you here was better than anything Mother Nature can offer me," I assured her softly.

With that, we were disturbed by a noise above us. As we looked up, there sitting on the limb of an oak were the pair of cardinals. I reached over, grabbed my camera and pointed it at them. I could swear they posed for a moment, then began to sing as they flew off. "They are friendly birds, those cardinals," Sherry commented.

"Unusual, is more like it. Cardinals are nervous birds. You rarely see two together like that. I'm not quite sure what that was all about," I said.

"They flew straight down the path. I could swear they wanted me to follow them," she told me.

"Straight? Cardinals never fly straight down a path. At least I've never seen it. They're pretty shy and usually disappear into the woods when someone's around." I stopped for a moment and looked at Sherry who answered me with a knowing smile.

"What can I say? All I know is it that seems like they led me right to you," she responded, cautiously.

Silence surrounded us as we both sat in quiet reflection for a few moments. Then it was almost as though a switch had been thrown. We began talking nervously, hesitantly at first, then nothing could stop us. We both had so much to cover. As if making up for lost time, we talked about anything and everything, important things and seemingly insignificant things. The air around us crackled with pent-up energy. "Come on," I said, pulling Sherry to her feet.

"Where are we going?" she wondered, following me.

"I have no idea but I have to move." The two of us began strolling alongside the stream. We watched the brook trout darting along the shallow bottom, occasionally rising for food. Starting up the path toward the woods, we revealed our feelings for each other, confirming what the other had always surmised.

It was a liberating day, one that lifted me to new heights, as I know it did her. Sherry and I were embarking on a journey...or was it that we were just continuing one?

The hours melted away. Before we knew it, the sun was at the opposite end of the sky. We both knew that it was time for us to leave, something neither of us wanted to do, yet we both knew had to happen. We headed reluctantly to our cars, quietly holding hands, Sherry occasionally took my arm in hers, pulling me into her. Her contagious smile filled me with comfort, easing my worries about how she felt. It was all there in her smile.

Sherry and I talked and talked the whole way back to our cars, until we reached the road. There, we instinctively we moved apart. Maybe it was seeing the road that crossed our paths and getting a glimpse of our cars parked across the lot. At that moment, I realized that we had covered every subject except one—what to do next. And that question would end up haunting us until we had no choice but to confront it.

As we crossed the tiny dirt road, I reached into my pocket for my car keys. The coldness of the metal seemed to force me right back into the real world I was so happy to escape from today. I walked Sherry to her car and watched her slip her key into the door, unlocking it with a swift motion, opening the door to her reality. She turned quickly, giving me a kiss, which numbed me down to my toes. We looked into each other's eyes, brimming with emotion, longing to embrace, yet knowing better. We didn't say another word...we didn't need to.

I stepped back and watched Sherry get into her car and drive away. She was gone in a flash. I slowly walked back to my car, feeling empty inside. How could such a wonderful day, where every minute was filled with joy and warmth, turn so frigid so fast, pinching me back to the cold, hard facts of my life? But I answered my own question: it was easy...Sherry was gone, that's how.

Chapter Ten
Status Quo

As I pulled my car out of the parking space and onto the road, I was preoccupied with the events that played themselves out that day. The joy I'd felt all day ended in emptiness. My excitement melted into hurt. I wanted to be with Sherry, needed to be with her, but I knew better. Reality slammed me like a wrecking ball flying out of control, shaking me to my very soul. The way Sherry came upon me in the woods seemed like a sort of destiny, a force outside my realm of control. I was already missing her and we'd only left each other a few minutes earlier. I craved talking to her, to make sure once again that she really felt what I did.

Maybe I was lost in a crazy, confusing aberration. Or maybe it was my allergies taking over my mind, fogging my thoughts with pollen. Or else magic dust sprinkled from a love fairy hiding in the trees. I shook my head in disbelief at my uncanny ability to divert my thoughts from a reality that I knew I'd have to confront eventually. But I had no interest in reality at that moment. I thought that for once, I'd allow myself the luxury of indulging in happiness. I deserved it.

I veered onto the parkway's southbound entrance just ten miles from home. I hadn't been able to take my mind off Sherry for more than a moment. I wondered if she'd reached home by now and if she was thinking about me like I was thinking about her. I glanced down at my cell phone, asking myself if it would be okay to call her. But what if Bill was there? Would he start asking questions? At that moment, my cell phone rang. I answered it, fully expecting it to be a client or my wife. But it isn't either.

"Hello, Jarred here," I said.

"Hello, 'Jarred here,'" mimicked the soft voice on the other end of the phone.

A smile broke out on my lips and the pain of longing I'd been feeling disappeared. "Hey, how are you, Sherry? I figured you'd be home by now. As a matter of fact, I was thinking of calling you," I said with a smile in my voice.

"I was almost home when I pulled over," she admitted. "I just needed to hear your voice one more time tonight. I am so not looking forward to walking in the front door." Her voice trail off, making me sad.

"I miss you," I said.

"I miss you, too. I'll be thinking about you all weekend. I look forward to seeing you Monday. I'll be there by 9:30," she added with some excitement.

"I'll be there with a large coffee, light and *sweet*." I chuckled, knowing that she doesn't take sugar. I seemed to remember so many little things about her.

"How quickly you forget," she quipped. "I don't take sugar, Jarred. And here I thought you knew me so well."

"What? You don't take sugar?" I joked. "Then how come you're so sweet? Your lips were like honey touching mine," I said laughing.

"Okay, that's it. Time for me to hang up after that one," Sherry laughed.

"Wait...I meant that! You have brought me back to life." I paused. "Thank you for breathing life back into me, into my soul. Thank you for everything, Sherry." I was dead serious and hoped she realized it.

"You're not the only one who feels that way," she admitted. "Now go home and have a great weekend."

"I'll try, but it won't be easy with you rattling around in my head all night," I said, only half kidding. "Good night..." I finished our call sadly.

Pulling into my driveway, I sat looking at my house, unable to go in. I knew I had to eventually but I wanted a few seconds more away from reality. I thought, *For one day after so many years, I felt free, happy, rejuvenated.* I wondered how, or if, I could ever bring back that part of my life—joy seemed to have left me so many years ago. I found that "life" often got in the way of happiness.

Kids, the bills, the house, the parents and the infamous work place often took center stage and a backseat to happiness. With all the stress and ever-increasing costs, the pressure was on everyone. Was anyone really, truly happy? Even the boss, who came to work pissed off, then had to face the very same problems—bills, personality conflicts—at home. He kicked around someone else, who, in turn, kicked around someone else, who drove home at the end of the day angry and did stupid things on the road that pissed off more people, who arrived home pissed.

I began to laugh at my crazy cycle of thought but it did make a twisted sense. Hell, I was lucky not to have a boss, to be the head of a one-man operation. However, my wife had a real prize of a boss at her job—and I'm not referring to myself. After all the pressures of the job, Carol came home to a house made messy by the kids, who got home from school and didn't do anything to pitch in. Add to that the fact that she had to cook dinner most nights and it was insane. I tried to help out where I could but my hours were even longer than hers were. We all worked like dogs. And for what? All in the name of progress, of buying more stuff, of being "successful." But somehow, in the process, I think we lose who we are.

My wife Carol is a good person— there's none better. She was stunningly beautiful with jet black hair and bright blue eyes.

If the truth be told, Carol was a bit self- conscious that she'd put on a few pounds over the years. (But who hasn't?) While I fought to keep the pounds off, she just couldn't seem to be bothered—and then complained how unhappy she was with the way she looked. It's a lose-lose situation.

Over the years, I've made many attempts to keep her happy: trying to include her in my world, and myself in hers. But she continued to reject me and ignored my pleas to join me at the gym, go for a hike or get into the outdoors a little more. Carol's life was the kids and the damn dog. And how could I forget shopping? While I've tried to accompany her on these marathon events, I just didn't get the whole shopping thing. Guys like me know what we're looking for, run into the store, grab it, buy it and go.

The only thing that kept me from killing myself on these sojourns into materialism hell was people-watching. I *loved* to watch people: study their mannerisms, try to guess what they did for a living, wonder if they were content, having an affair...things like that. At least it kept me entertained for a little while. But soon, I got bored and the pain started to set in. Standing on your feet while your spouse poured through racks and racks of clothing. Stuff they had no need for but wanted just the same.

Leaning on the clothing racks in hopes of relieving the pain in your back and legs brought on endless hours of standing (and intense boredom) was excruciating. But mostly for me, it was the chronic pain of knowing it was such a gorgeous day outside and I was trapped in an airless, God-forsaken mall with all this stuff no one really needs but buys anyway.

"The Over-Thinker"...that's how many of my friends described me. And I admit, it was a perfect description. I thought about things (everything!) way too much and in way too much depth. My psychiatrist friend John told me that it was called "avoidance" or something like that. John might be right, because there I was, thinking about a mountain of insignificant stuff just to avoid going into the house.

Unable to put it off any longer, I left the car and slowly made my way toward my house, a sizeable, standard suburban model. I opened the door and called out, "Daddy's home."

In response was Carol's idea of a welcome: "So, what's the big deal? Sorry, I didn't expect you so early or I would have put on my dress, heels, string of pearls with my little apron as I slave over this damn stove."

I guess I was asking for it because by now, I should have known better than to be sarcastic upon entering the sanctuary of the house. I got what I deserved but Carol's retort did crack me up. "What did you do today?" I asked, again not thinking.

"What else? Grocery shopping and cleaning a house that's always left a mess. Welcome to my world," she snapped. So predictable, so tiresome, I thought as I contemplated getting out my hard hat for protection. I could just tell this was going to be a bumpy night.

When Carol and I dated, we always had such a great time. We were into the same things. We would go out, do things spur of the moment. I married her because I knew she was a loving person who would be a good mother, in retrospect maybe not the best reason to marry someone. She and I got along so well and we had so much in common. She was bright, had a good education and a great job as a teacher at a prestigious private school. Carol also had summers off and we would travel to wild, wonderful places like Alaska, fishing and taking photos. I was just an amateur photographer then but it was still so much fun. Carol was always in good humor.

Even after we were married, Carol and I still traveled whenever we could. By then, I had taken the job in the police department but I still had plenty of vacation time. When we had kids, everything changed, as it did for most people. Our lives became all about the kids, Carol's more so than mine. Then I began to truly hate working for the small-minded police chief who was essentially in charge of my life. Einstein said it best in his inspiring words, "Great spirits have always encountered violent opposition from mediocre minds." And that described my relationship with my old boss to a T.

In short, my chief was a moron, a high school dropout and who then ended up in college after getting his GED. Because of this, he became thoroughly impressed with himself. He made his way up in his job through politics, not accomplishments.

Although he thought he was so much more intelligent than everyone else, he was really lacking in so many important areas—like common sense and people skills.

Because he thought he was so much smarter than the average bear (especially me), he constantly attempted to catch me doing something wrong—like minor infractions of the rules—but all of his attempts to undermine me were unsuccessful. I used to laugh at his feeble attempts to quash me and because of this, he tried to make my life a living hell. Recalling the Albert Einstein quote helped me get through it all and I would actually try to find humor in the situation and would go right back at him. A big mistake of my foolish youth because this defiance pissed him off even more. The anger I held inside made me pretty tough to live with but Carol did her best.

My hate for the job and some of the people at it, drove me to start my photography business. After two years of my old chief and playing his cat and mouse games, I left and never looked back. Right off the bat, I was happier. Plus it gave me more time with the kids and Carol. Over the years, she gradually became more obsessed with our children, causing our relationship to suffer. While they are everything to me, it's only up to a certain point. The difference was that I realized a time would soon come when they'd leave us and go off on their own. Carol didn't. She and I needed a reason to keep our relationship together when they weren't in it anymore.

One of the problems was that we always did things as a family, which is fine, but Carol and I never took "us time." For some reason, she always avoided it, no matter how hard I tried. And I desperately attempted everything I could to keep us together. Eventually, I gave up with the understanding that Carol had chosen our kids above she and I, above even herself. I simply surrendered. I gave up. The more she made their struggles hers, the angrier she became and the more our relationship faltered. The more I retreated. Maybe I saw it happening but I chose to ignore it: it was much safer that way. All I know is that I simply gave up.

Over the years, I've done my best to make things good for everyone. I thoroughly enjoyed taking part in the kids' lives as they were growing up. I got involved as much as I could and I have absolutely no regrets doing that. However, now what I'd always feared has come true. With the kids older and more independent, Carol and I grown apart. I hated to think that we were only brought together to have and raise children. I was afraid that once that part was over, so our lives as a couple would be over as well. Now that the kids are older, occasionally Carol and I got out together, but more often than not, she just wants to stay home to watch TV or rent a movie. I felt like I was slowly dying inside.

Carol was never an outwardly affectionate type, nor was I. We never walked around holding hands in public or hung all over each other like others we know did, but still, we had our moments just the same. We were privately loving and had a healthy sex life. I was doing my best to make the most of our relationship, trying to keep it alive. I committed to it, so I resigned to live with it. Carol and I still cared for each other but I suppose we were who we were. Most of the time, I didn't complain, figuring I'd just make the best of it and continue to focus on the positive things about my life. But recently, that became harder and harder for me to do. Especially with what been happened with Sherry. Sherry showed me that there was indeed something else, and it was wonderful.

But Carol...she seemed to be content with status quo. She didn't like change. I guess Carol wasn't much different than lots of other people. I called it the human condition, which plagues so many of us. You know, the type of person who figured, 'I have what I have and I'm happy with it.' They don't aspire for anything else; they're stuck. Well, I'm tired of being stuck.

One thing about Carol that drove me crazy: she always looked at what she didn't have instead of what she had. With her, it was always, "We will never have a bigger house" or "I'm tired of not having anything." My view, which I've told her all the time, was to look at what we *did* have—our health, the kids' health, plus they aren't getting arrested. As for material things, everything we had we earned ourselves—we owe no one. I happened to be very proud of what I'd accomplished. Part of this success was due to Carol—she was a hard worker and a fine mother. But I accepted her the way she was—like I have a choice?—while she couldn't seem to accept anything. I've repeated this so much, I was beginning to feel like a broken record but the situation with my wife truly gnawed away at me.

Part of her attitude had a lot to do with her upbringing. Carol's father was a hard- working, strict man who watched over his daughters like a hawk. He never let them do anything the other girls in their Brooklyn neighborhood did. They had to dress conservatively and most of all, stay away from boys. On top of everything else, Carol's father never gave anyone—including her mother—any money or freedom. These were some of Carol's most vivid childhood memories and I think it explained a lot about why she was the way she was.

Although I did my best to understand this, I just didn't get how Carol couldn't get past her daddy issues and move on. How could she ever be happy living with as much anger as she did? When her father died, she was only 17, Carol's mother—a bitter, angry woman—she took her frustration out on her three daughters. It fell upon Carol to take care of her youngest sister Roberta from the time she was a baby.

To make things even worse when their mother died, Roberta stole everything she could from her sisters. I tried to warn Carol this would happen, but she never paid attention to my warnings. Roberta ended up taking thousands of dollars worth of stocks and antiques that should have been divided evenly among the three sisters. To add insult to injury, Roberta also stole insurance payments and didn't pay the nursing service that took care of their mother while she was sick. When Roberta received the invoices, she told the nursing service to bill Carol and me. We ended up in court and Roberta lost. Carol's sister Debbie and I wanted to have Roberta charged with the crimes but Carol forced us to back down and just cut her baby sister out of our lives, which I knew was devastating for her.

With all of this anger and resentment in stewing within her, I always understood Carol's anger but I just had trouble accepting it. Her way of dealing with life—fighting change at all costs— caused me to envy her in a way because I was just the opposite. I was forever looking for something new, exciting and different.

I was never content with status quo. I constantly wanted new experiences, to meet new people, to create new art.

I admit, I was no bargain. As a cop, I was never home, had crazy hours and was always out doing something. But that was half a lifetime ago. I moved on, accepting the angst in my early life as part of the process. I think made me a stronger person and allowed me to deal with whatever life threw at me. But in contrast, Carol didn't take anything positive from her experiences. Instead, she felt that she deserved a break. Teaching in such a wealthy private school, she was constantly exposed to people who were extremely materialistic, always flaunting what they had. Maybe she did deserve more because she always did so much for others. But I just wish she could put the anger of her young life behind her, move forward and realize how rich she really was.

If Carol couldn't move forward, the anxiety would continue to eat away at our relationship. And now, with the latest events in my life, it might be too late to reverse what was already in motion. Carol might have finally hit that "off" button within me, shutting down the whole system of who I was or more closely, who I had become. Maybe that was what caused me to go out and find something else to fill my life. But in Sherry's case, I wasn't looking for anything, it just kind of found me.

There were many good times in Carol's and my life, which prevented me from leaving. Tough and often funny, people who meet her immediately like her. And what's not to like? But it was the constant anger Carol harbored which I found difficult to live with. Couple that with her never wanting to do anything with me and it was a real challenge. Believe me, I tried everything, including suggesting counseling, which she vehemently refused. About therapy, Carol said, "Counseling is just someone talking to you, like that will do any good. Besides, there's nothing wrong. It's all in your head." What could you say to that?

Well, perhaps it was all in my head...and what if it was? Just the fact that I was concerned about our relationship should make her want to do something—anything—to save our marriage but that wasn't the case. Carol just wanted to stay on the course and maintain status quo. And sadly, her not wanting to work with me on our relationship was what had me rethinking it. Add Sherry to the mix, and let's just say that I've been soul- searching a lot.

But I will continue to be a prudent man and not move foolishly into something I might regret. There's so much said about men my age who go through a mid-life crisis but I knew this wasn't a mid-life crisis for me. After all, I wasn't out buying a "crisis" car like a Corvette, Mercedes or a Portia. I just wanted to be happy again—and I didn't mean happy every moment of every day. That was impossible and pure fantasy.

When I heard people say, 'I want to be happy all the time... I deserve it,' I realized how many people had unrealistic expectations from life. We set goals that didn't make sense, causing us to be even unhappier, adding to the anger already there and preventing ourselves from attaining that unattainable goal. I'd never understand why so many in this world refused to see things as they were. Me, I simply wanted to be happy more often than unhappy. At this juncture in my life, that didn't seem impossible.

Back at home, Carol and I sat down for dinner, just the two of us. The kids had already eaten—or should I say scarfed down their food—and were off to socialize with their friends. Since I knew better than to ask how Carol's day was, I tried to tell her about mine—minus Sherry, of course. But even this made her upset. "So, while I'm working like a dog at home, you're off gallivanting in the woods."

I shook my head in disbelief. "Oh, so collecting photos of wildlife in adverse conditions and trying to sell to try them to keep a roof over our heads is *gallivanting*?"

"Well, I don't see us living in a mansion on the ocean somewhere. Just this old house that's falling apart," she said with a bitter tone.

"Maybe you should go out and find yourself someone with money and stop complaining all the time," I suggested. "I'm getting sick and tired of hearing about what you don't have. I can't seem to do anything right. If I work late or on the weekends, it's no good. If I'm not making enough money, that's not good either. I just can't win and honestly, I'm fed up with it."

" I'm not saying you don't try," Carol conceded. "It's just that every time we get a little put away, something happens, and it's gone."

"Welcome to the real world," I told her. "That's life. But in your eyes, everyone has everything, except us. I just can't live with this negative attitude any more."

With that, I just stopped talking. I just gave up. It was always the same conversation over and over again. It was like our lives were on some sort of short film loop. I left the table and lay down on the couch, burning up inside. I was tight as a drum with tension, totally fed up. I feel trapped, with nowhere to go, no safe place to call my own. I got grief at the studio with difficult clients. I got grief at home with my difficult wife. My only outlet was my time in the woods. I'd begun to realize that it was now up to me to change my life—no one else but me.

I finally fell asleep on the sofa.

Chapter Eleven
Mirror

In the interest of telling a complete, well-rounded story, I thought it was important to give a picture of what Sherry was experiencing as well. She and I compared notes afterwards and were amazed to discover that we'd gone through similar emotional roller coasters with our respective partners. I've retold Sherry's reflections, which mirrored my own, here:

Sherry walked into her house after she and I had met near the stream, satisfied with what she'd accomplished. Like me, she had no idea what would come next, but at least she'd gotten the ball rolling and that was all she could do at that point. She was confident that everything meant to be would be, that was, if she had anything to say about it. She chuckled to herself, thinking how deceitful she was being—but how good it felt. More than anything, though, Sherry wanted to understand what had attracted her to me.

"What's so funny?" Bill asked as Sherry walked into the house, laughing softly to herself.

"Nothing...just something I heard on the radio," she told him, thinking quickly. Not that Bill would notice anything was wrong. As usual, Bill was sitting in front of the television, beer in hand, watching the game. What game? With Bill it didn't matter— basketball, baseball, football or hockey. For him, it is always sports and beer. Sports were always a good excuse for beer. Sometimes Sherry was part of the picture, but most often not. This time, she figured she might as well annoy him, just for the fun of it.

"So, how was your day? What time did you get finished with work?" she asked, knowing he had no interest in having a conversation.

"Same shit as usual," was his short reply, hoping it would be enough to satisfy her. It wasn't.

"Whose house were you working on?" she pried.

"Christ, do you really give a shit whose house I was working on? Are you coming to the job with me Monday to supervise?" he asked sarcastically.

"I was thinking that maybe I should. You know, check out the lady of the house to see who you're flirting with these days."

Sherry knew that Bill always used his boyish charm on female clients to make his life easier. "They don't break my chops that way," he explained once. That's what he always told her when she questioned female customers' late night phone calls to the house and his leaving the room to talk with them. Sherry would have hired a detective to follow him if she really cared. But they'd come to an awkward point in the relationship and were little more than roommates, sharing expenses (he taking on a little more than she did) and little else.

Bill was so withdrawn that Sherry had gotten used to making a life without him. To compensate for what she didn't get from him, she found herself going out with her girlfriends more often, leaving Bill to comb the bars with the boys after work, watch the game, get loaded, stumble in for dinner and fall asleep in his chair. That's what he did most nights, or for a little variety, he'd drink at home in front of that damn TV. Sherry looked forward to his falling asleep because it gave her time to herself without his drunken pawing after the game. She was always relieved when he fell asleep without pressuring her into a slobbering embrace.

"I'm making tacos for dinner," Sherry informed Bill. "Is that okay with you?" She didn't wait for his reply as she proceeded to the kitchen.

"Sounds great," Bill replied. "Just hurry. I'm hungry and half time is coming." "Sure," she said sarcastically. "I wouldn't want you to miss the game."

Actually, Sherry was relieved to see Bill so engrossed in a game. When he wasn't, it would be a grabfest as she tried to cook dinner. He'd come up behind her, wrap his hand around her stomach for all of three seconds before moving his hands down, or up, depending on his mood. If he was in the mood for foreplay, he'd go up and if he wanted a quickie, he'd move his hands down, all the time grinding into her from the rear.

When they were first dating, Sherry thought it was fun. She felt that Bill really desired her and so she found it exciting. But as time went on, Sherry began to feel like she were some sort of relief machine for his never-ending sex drive, just an easy way to get his rocks off. Sherry would fend him off as best she could and he'd give up, momentarily then be back at it again. Bill seemed to have no consideration for her, whether she was sick, upset or menstruating. He always expected some sort of release from Sherry, and it was no secret that he considered it her duty to service him sexually for being a good provider. There was no love or tenderness on his part.

Sure enough, as Sherry cooked that night, during half time, Bill attacked from the rear. Reaching around her body, he moved down the front of her pants quicker than usual. Sherry slapped his hand away. "I'm still sweaty from the hike," she explained.

"Who cares? The dirtier the better," he told her. "Turn off the food, come over to my chair and climb on for a quick ride."

Sherry shook her head. "Sure, climb on while you're watching the game, you mean. Do you have any idea how insulting that is? Then after you get off, I get to come back, finish cooking dinner and serve you in front of the damn TV set."

Still, Bill didn't get the point. Sherry was so angry, she shouted, "No, I don't think so. Take care of yourself if you're so damn horny. I'll finish making dinner, then I'm going up to take a bath."

"By that time, the game should be over and I'll join you in the tub," Bill said, still not understanding.

Exasperated, Sherry thought, *I might as well, if it gets him off my back*. But that made her feel so lonely, so desperate. The thing that upset her so much was how used she felt, without a shred of affection or caring for the man. Sure, they went out to dinner once in a while and had fun with friends, but that was the extent of her pleasure. These distractions helped her hide what she'd really been feeling deep down all along. Perhaps she'd been suppressing it because it was easier not to face things, than to confront things that could bring such a dramatic change to her life.

After giving her situation some thought, it all became clear to Sherry. She needed more for herself. She needed someone who was caring and affectionate—a sensitive man—like Jarred. *He's safe*, she thought, *because he's married. And if we're careful, I can keep Bill as my roommate, while having Jarred as my lover for the caring, physical relationship I know he's capable of. Yes, Jarred can be my dream lover, like in the movies*. At that point, Sherry made up her mind to go forward with a relationship with me. Bill's lack of sensitivity that night — and just about every night — confirmed that her desire to pursue a relationship with me was right.

As Sherry headed up to the bath, Bill instructed her not to fall asleep afterwards. "I'll be up as soon as the game is over."

"Is that a promise or a threat?" she wondered, then added, "Do what you have to do, just don't wake me."

"Don't worry, I'll make it quick so you can get right back to sleep," he shot back.

"Whatever!" she yelled, continuing up the stairs.

"Ouch! Aren't we testy tonight," Bill laughed. "Hey, try to get over your attitude problem before Monday. I don't want you coming to check out my work in a bad mood."

"Monday, I actually have better things to do," she told him.

"What could possibly be more important than me?" he asked.

Sherry smiled to herself. "Jarred is more important than you," She added under her breath.

"What was that?" he asked.

"I said that Valerie and I have a big meeting at nine on Monday with Jarred and a new client. It's a huge project and a rush job. I have to be there early."

"Oh, so meeting with a photographer is more important than me," he whined, only half kidding.

Sherry simply didn't answer. *You have no idea just how important this is*, she thought to herself with a smile. Later, she confessed to me that her heart raced and her soul seemed to jump for joy when she thought of me. Her only disappointment was that Monday was a whole two days away and she didn't know how she could survive until then. Sherry couldn't remember when time has moved so slowly, thoughts which mirrored my own exactly.

Chapter Twelve
A Month of Sundays

Sunday was usually a day of rest for me. I didn't look at a camera. I didn't think about cameras. Well, maybe I thought about my art because I was always thinking about my art but I made it a point not to do anything about it but think.

I was an early riser, as was Carol. Our usual Sunday morning routine was to watch the Sunday morning news magazine shows, and then for me, a fishing show or two on ESPN or on the Outdoor Life channel. When the kids were small, we'd take trips to the farms in South Salem so they could see the animals. We'd get some doughnuts, go up to Sugar Loaf to walk around, grab lunch and come home after a nice day out together. But since the kids have grown, Carol and I rarely headed out on excursions like that, mainly because she had no desire. This was how things had deteriorated between us.

The Sunday after Sherry met me in the woods was a very beautiful, sunny day. I insisted that Carol and I not sit around and do nothing. Since I had an art show coming up for Brush, Chisel and Lens, I wanted to comb through a great little toyshop in a quaint, little town filled with antique shops and restaurants in Putnam County.

Over our second cup of coffee, I suggested to my wife, "Let's head up to Cold Spring. I want to see if I can find an old Jack-in-the-Box to shoot." I could tell by the expression on Carol's face that she might take some convincing, so I persisted, "Come on, we'll stop at 'Serious Toyz,' get some brunch at the Cold Spring Café... I'm in the mood for their Eggs Benedict."

To my surprise, Carol not only agreed, but suggested we call Sherry and Bill.

"They live right there. Maybe they'd like to meet us. Have you heard from Sherry lately?" Carol wondered.

"As a matter of fact, she called Friday," I told her. "We have a meeting at Valerie's on Monday morning about some sort of a rush job for them. I'll give them a call, but you know Bill...it's only 11. He may still be hung over."

"What the heck, try them anyway. They can only say no," Carol insisted.

I agreed. At least it would give me a reason to talk to Sherry. Both Carol and I enjoyed Sherry's company, but we thought Bill could be a bit of a rock head. He was the type that would always lend a hand when needed, which was probably his one redeeming quality. But he was also a drinker and a bit of a womanizer. I avoided unnecessary contact with him at all costs. Now more than ever.

Dialing the phone, my mind was going 100 miles an hour as I wondered if this wasn't a big mistake. Even if Sherry and I managed to keep our emotions at bay, would our partners be able to pick up on the spark between us? Sherry picked up on the first ring." Hello," She cooed, as if expecting me.

"Hi, Sherry, it's Jarred. How are you doing today?" I said.

There was a slight pause on the other end. "Oh, just peachy...," she replied tentatively. I sensed something in her voice.

"Carol and I are headed up your way and she suggested I give you a call to see if you and Bill would like to join us for brunch... Is everything okay?" I inquired.

"Hold on. I'll run downstairs and ask Bill. He's building a cabinet for a client."

"Do you want to call me back?"

"No, I'll just yell downstairs. Hold on a sec."

I didn't like the tone I heard in Sherry's voice—it made me very apprehensive. Perhaps I shouldn't be calling. Maybe she didn't like the idea of my phoning to get together with her and Bill after what transpired between me and Sherry the day before.

Sherry was back on the phone in a flash. "Hi. He said he'd love to meet you guys. In fact, he wants to talk to you about shooting some of his work for his portfolio," she informed me.

"Great. What time is good for you? We can be there in about an hour," I said.

"That's perfect," she told me.

"Great...I have to know... is everything okay? You didn't answer me before," I prodded.

"Everything is fine. I was just worried, for a minute. I thought you might be calling to tell me you were having second thoughts," she replied in a very low voice.

"Me? Yeah, as a matter of fact, I have. Before I walked into my house last night, I asked myself what I was doing. But, within fifteen minutes of being home I had no doubts whatsoever," I reassured her.

"I like what I'm hearing," she told me, sounding relieved. "So, was this really Carol's idea? I always got the impression she wasn't too keen on us getting together."

"I swear it was her idea. I get the feeling she doesn't want to be alone with me," I laughed. "See you at the café in an hour... and I'm sorry if I scared you," I said with a smile in my voice.

Once in the car, I couldn't wait to see Sherry again. I did everything I could not to give away my excitement. But about half way there, my excitement melted into apprehension. What if I said something that gave away our feelings toward one another? What if she did? What if Carol suggested this get-together because she suspected something? I had to make sure to be on guard at all times. I was certain that Sherry would be extra cool because it was in her nature.

Carol and I made small talk during the ride which permeated our long silences. We didn't seem to have much to say to each other these days. The closer I got to Cold Spring, the more my mind raced at the thought of seeing Sherry. My heart quickened as it became light with delight. I thought about the simple, honest beauty that radiated right through her and shone onto me. I pictured the smile that made my palms sweat like a smitten teenager. I pressed down on the accelerator as the excitement of seeing Sherry again pounded at my brain but I felt like she was a million miles away.

Finally arriving in Cold Spring, my next chore was finding a parking space. The weather was still glorious—warm, breezy and sunny. There must have been a million people there that day because there was no parking anywhere. I drove around the block several times before I finally came upon someone pulling out of a spot. Great! "I was just about to say 'screw this' and leave," I told Carol.

"You've got to get some patience! We were bound to find something. We always do," she scolded.

Walking into the Cold Spring Café, the first thing that hit you was the smorgasbord of culinary delights as the fragrance of pancakes, warm maple syrup, eggs, coffee and the like meshed into an intoxicating perfume. People at every table were engaged in animated conversation. Some were seated at the windows, gazing out at the town, contemplating their next stop—antique store or linen shop. The hostess asked "How many?" when we noticed Sherry and Bill waving to us from a table.

"Been here long?" Carol asked when we joined them.

"We just got here a few minutes ago," Sherry said. "We just ordered coffee. Would you like some?" As she looked at me, her face seemed to light up.

"Sure, I'll let the waitress know," Carol responded, signaling the waitress.

Sherry and Bill stood up to greet us. I shook Bill's hand as Carol gave Sherry a quick peck on the cheek. Turning to Sherry, I took her hand in mine, shaking inside. She squeezed it, looking deep into my eyes. An electric current seemed to pass between us, whirring through my brain then stabbing me in the heart with her warm touch. I felt like a kid again. To me, this kind of thing was for adolescents and here I was, past 50. I never thought about older people becoming emotionally involved like this. Maybe I'd become as jaded as Carol.

When we took our seats at the table, I made sure I sat directly across from Sherry. I knew I could justify it to Carol if she complained about being stuck across from Bill later by reminding her how annoying I found him. Besides, it was true.

"What are you guys having?" Sherry asked as the waitress approached.

"I thought about their Eggs Benedict all the way up here," I smiled. Sherry seemed a little disappointed when I said this—maybe she'd hoped I'd thought of nothing but her during the ride.

"That's *all* you could think about?" she asked with a devilish smile. "You never gave us a thought? We're disappointed," she added as she gave me a quiet kick under the table, letting me know her disappointment was real.

"Are you kidding? Jarred was so excited about seeing you guys again, he practically flew up the road," Carol responded.

"Well, that's more like it," Sherry said with a laugh.

"Hey, don't flatter yourself. I was just very hungry." I winked back at them so as not to arouse any suspicion in Bill.

Bill chimed in as though he'd just come to the table and had heard none of what was said. "So, Jarred, I'm finishing up a great kitchen in Bedford. I'll need it photographed when you're free."

"For you, Bill, I'll make time," I assured him. "Just give me a date. Set it up with the home owner and we'll get it done." I didn't have much to say to this guy, nor he to me. "Uh, sounds like you're doing well, Bill."

I feigned interested in Bill and his projects while the ladies talked shopping. This guy was so into himself, he seemed clueless that the rest of us had lives. I felt ignored as Carol regaled Sherry with some of the bargains she'd found over the past few months. Sherry glanced over at me, perhaps feeling as bored with my spouse as I was.

When the food arrived, Bill was on a roll with his endless wisecracking, putting down the women's love for shopping. At least we had a brief reprieve and turned our attention to passing around the salt, pepper and ketchup. Looking down at my plate, my heart jumpstarted as Sherry's foot slowly rubbed my leg. I must have been smiling ear to ear as a feeling of elation embraced me. I no longer felt ignored. Glancing up cautiously, I couldn't believe how cool Sherry was being. She was looking down at her eggs and cutting them as she slowly moved her foot up my leg, then back down. I could feel her emotions as they telegraphed through her into me. My spirit was lifted as it hadn't been in so many years.

Was this just some childish infatuation? Whatever it was, I was hopping on for the ride because it made me feel good about myself again. The bottom line was, I liked the way it felt. Perhaps it was the ultimate in selfishness but I thought I deserved to do something for "me" after sacrificing so much for my family. I'd endured years of Carol's cynicism to the point that I was fast becoming jaded and had lost all hope of ever being happy again.

Bill broke through my pleasant reverie. "So, Sherry tells me you guys have a big meeting Monday," he said with a little sarcasm. *Holy shit!* My heart froze. *What the hell did she tell him?*

Sherry tried to play it cool. "I told Bill about our new client at the agency and how we have a rush job in the works," she explained.

"They sound like an important client," I added, as I shoveled some eggs into my mouth, not looking up.

"They're the biggest we've ever had," Sherry said. "They'll be demanding a lot of our time. Looks like we'll need to have a late meeting at least once a week. And Jarred, you may have to attend them once in a while. But let Valerie fill you in. I don't want it coming from me. You know how she can get," Sherry tagged on, rolling her eyes.

I sat there thinking, V*alerie could care less if Sherry tells me. And late meetings for Sherry...who leaves at four?* I looked up as Sherry began kicking me lightly under the table again. Suddenly, it dawned on me that Sherry wasn't talking about the new client but the new relationship...with me. Sometimes I was a little slow on the uptake.

"Christ, are we getting into those late night meetings and working all the time again?" Carol asked. "I sure hope not."

"You know what, Sherry? Maybe you guys should look for another photographer so I can get home early," I said, half joking, half not.

"Stop making such a big deal out of everything," Carol said, just as I'd hoped she would. "I'm just kidding around. Besides, I don't need you around all the time. I'm a big girl. You guys can keep him all night for all I care, Sherry!" Carol shot back.

Sherry laughed, "No problem, Carol. Just say the word and I'll make sure he works all night long. I'm sure I can come up with something for him to do."

They both laughed while I breathed a sigh of relief.

"Gee, thanks. Anything else you guys want to do with my life?" I inquired.

"We'll give it some thought and get back to you," Carol said.

"But don't be surprised at what we have you running around doing," Carol winked at Sherry and Bill.

"I'll try to find an assignment that will tie you up all night, just to keep you out of Carol's hair," Sherry laughed as she slowly ran her foot up my leg.

The message from Sherry was loud and clear. It was evident to me that she was setting things up to avoid suspicion. *Smart woman*, I thought to myself.

The whole time during this exchange, Bill wasn't paying much attention. He was too busy looking around the room, checking out the various women. Whether they were with or without a male companion, he didn't care. Just the fact that they had breasts and a vagina was all that mattered to him.

I briskly changed the subject to the art show. "Sherry, the show's only in a few months. We need to find the right venue. Would you have some time to join Johnny and me in the afternoon to look at some possible places to show?"

"Sure, I'd love to," Sherry smiled. "When are you meeting?"

"At three this Thursday in Tarrytown, down by the river. I can meet you at Valerie's and we can go there together." I quickly realized that I needed to bring Johnny into this to avoid suspicion. "Better yet, I'll let Johnny know so he can meet me at the studio and we'll come pick you up," I added quickly.

"That sounds great. What other places are you looking at?" she inquired, understanding my true intention.

"We have another in Croton and the third is in Ossining. Nothing like waiting till the last minute, is there?" I laughed.

Sherry knew, as well as I did that we had already secured the space in Tarrytown but I figured this would give us another excuse to meet without raising suspicion.

I turned my attention to Bill, as Carol and Sherry once again talked shopping and jewelry, adding shoes to the mix this time. "Bill, tell me a little more about this kitchen you want me to shoot," I said.

"A huge project. It has a great room and a granite island the size of my kitchen at home with a special setup for the stove. You'll see. It's unreal," he explained.

"Maybe I can take a ride up after my meeting at Valerie's on Monday," I told him. "Give me the address. I'll take a quick look, then we can set up a date."

I looked over and saw that Sherry was listening to our conversation with one ear as she listened to Carol with the other. My wife hadn't picked up on anything. As usual, when Carol talked shopping, nothing else mattered.

As we finished our brunch and said our good-byes, I asked Sherry again what time Valerie would be in the next day. She reminded me that Valerie would be in at about nine. "Don't be late and don't forget breakfast," she added. Sherry took my hand and squeezed it again. It hurt, not from the squeeze but from the pain of knowing I'd have to survive about 24 before I'd see her again.

Outside, Bill had one quick question. "By the way, how much will it cost for you to shoot that kitchen?"

"I get 20 percent of the cost of the job you did," I smiled at him.

"Hell, that sounds fair to me," he said, confused. "Look, thanks anyways but I'll take my own damn pictures," he shot back.

"Hey!" I yelled. "I don't take pictures, Bill. I create images. That's why I get the big bucks. Someday maybe you can build a kitchen like that for me," I joked.

"With your prices, we can start next week!" he chided.

"Don't worry about it, just pick up my costs," I told him.

"Great! Thanks," he said as he and Sherry turned away. As they were walking to their car, I heard Bill comment to Sherry, "Good price. I love that guy."

"Yeah, I love him to," Sherry said quietly. "What did you say?" Bill asked. "I said 'Me too'," she told him jokingly. "I mean, what's not to love?"

After Bill and Sherry left us, Carol and I continued on to the various old toy shops. I ended up finding the Jack-in-the-Box I sought at Serious Toyz, just as I thought. It's a shop dedicated solely to old collectable toys. For me, walking into this little store is like stepping back in time. The owner, Tom, knew I was in the process of creating a book called *My Old Toy Box: Imagination Not Included*. He was a cheerful man with an extensive knowledge of his wares and he offered all the help I needed.

Carol and I headed home for dinner and to finish out the day in the quiet, solitary way we'd fallen into in recent years. Anticipating the next day with Sherry made that Sunday evening the longest night of my life.

Chapter Thirteen
Tears of My Heart

Monday finally rolled around. I woke up at five a.m., an hour before my alarm went off. I felt like a little kid on his birthday. The anticipation of knowing something good was about to happen overwhelmed me. My excitement level was off the charts. I got out of bed in a shot. Looking at the clock, I saw that I had four more long hours to wait before the meeting with Sherry. The energy in me built to the point that I felt like I was going to pop. I grabbed my gym bag and leaned over to kiss Carol. "Why are you up so early?" she asked.

"Couldn't sleep thinking about everything I had to do today," I told her. "I figured I'd hit the gym and get an early start."

"Don't forget the Jack-in-the-Box," she added.

"I left it in the car so I'd remember," I said. "I shouldn't be too late tonight. It all depends on the work I get from Valerie." I purposely didn't bring up Sherry's name. I felt like a bit of a rat lying to Carol but what else could I do?

"Okay...say hello to everyone for me," she yawned.

At the gym, I must have done an hour of cardio without even noticing. Afterwards, I jumped in the shower, was out the door and on my way to Valerie's by 8:30. I stopped by the Moonbean Cafe to grab our coffees but the line seemed 30 miles long. I was only five minutes from Valerie's but I was afraid the wait would be an eternity. In actuality, it only took a few minutes to get the coffee but I guess I was a bit more impatient than usual. I grabbed a few muffins, blueberry, which the both of us liked and was out there like a shot.

I ran across the street to Valerie's building and sprinted past the elevator. Too antsy to wait for it, I decided it would be faster to take the stairs. I bounded up them two at a time like I was a young man of 20 again. Once on their floor, it seemed that no matter how fast I walked toward their office, the further away the door seemed, like one of those bad dreams where your legs move but your body doesn't.

Okay, that's it, I said to myself, *Time to get a grip!* This wasn't me. I'd never been like this in my life. This whole Sherry thing was still a mystery to me but after deciding to surrender to it, I also vowed not to question it too much. I promised myself to take a "wait and see" attitude as to where—and why—I was so captivated by this.

When I reached the office door, it was locked. I knocked, thinking perhaps Sherry had locked herself in. I waited a few minutes...no answer. Damn! Something must have happened, I thought to myself. *Maybe Bill held Sherry up with questions. Why isn't she here? I guess this just isn't as important to her as it is to me.*

I began to feel extremely foolish until I heard the elevator door open. Still totally absorbed in my self-pity, I never even turned to look. I knocked again, this time a little more impatiently. Behind me, an angelic voice cooed, "No one's home." I turned to see Sherry. "Wow, you're early!" she added. "I'm impressed."

I looked at my watch and realized that I was 10 minutes early. Sherry walked past me, gently nudging me aside as she slipped her key into the slot. I was embarrassed at how I'd allowed my mind to spiral out of control My thoughts continued to race as

Sherry opened the door. I followed her inside, waiting patiently as she turned on the lights, the computers and checked the answering machine. There was a message from Valerie saying she would be late. Sherry smiled at me and then headed to her office. I followed her like an embarrassed puppy and stood in the doorway, waiting to be invited inside. I held out the breakfast bag and began, "As promised, I brought the coff..."

Sherry took one step toward me and grabbed the bag without saying a word. She placed it on her desk, held me by the collar and pulled me into her. Sherry kissed me like I'd never been kissed before. It was filled with so much passion and longing that I melted, surrendering to her warmth. I took Sherry in my arms and held her tightly. *I would give anything to become one with her right now, I thought. If only I could pull her into me, into my heart that seems to beat for her.* We stood silently, holding each other. Sherry moved back slightly and looked into my eyes. "I've thought about that all weekend," she whispered. "You have no idea how much I missed you or how hollow I felt without you. I wanted so much to take you in my arms yesterday."

I stood there, holding Sherry, speechless. It was at that point when I realized that we truly were one. Sherry was actually a part of me. She had entered my heart, my soul, my brain, taking complete control of my being. *Well, so much for getting the wrong idea!* I really had to stop thinking and just roll with it. I was certain this wasn't some cheap affair. It was so much more, more than either of us understood, at that point. This was bigger than our very existence. Now everything Peggy and Laura had told me was starting to make sense. The smoke was beginning to clear and my vision was becoming endless, focusing through the tears of my heart.

"Now, what were you saying?" Sherry asked me.

I stood there like some sort of village idiot, trying to remember when all of a sudden, my brain reengaged. "Oh, yeah, I brought the coffee like I promised, light and sweet," I said with a devilish smile. "I even brought breakfast—a blueberry muffin. Baked it myself, just the way you like it."

"Wow, you remembered that I like blueberries and you baked it yourself. I'm impressed! But, you forgot how I take my coffee," she teased.

"How could I forget anything about you? I'm just trying to get a rise out of you."

"I'm guessing I succeeded getting a rise out of you this morning," she chuckled.

"That you have," I shot back, a little embarrassed, admitting that our kissing had excited me. I was hoping she hadn't noticed. "So," I continued, trying to change the subject, "tell me a little about this assignment Valerie has for me."

As she sipped her coffee, Sherry shot me a look that sent a chill to my heart. "You're kidding, right? Like I had you come in early to talk about some stupid project you can do with your eyes closed? No, Jarred, we're here to talk about us."

"About us?" I questioned, as if I had no clue what she was referring to. "What about us? What could we possibly have to discuss?" I asked, teasing her.

Sherry smirked. "We were complete strangers until about six months ago. Something has brought the two of us together, something unexplainable. A few days ago, I realized that from the moment I met you, I couldn't get you out of my mind. I did everything I could to avoid thinking about you. It seemed so bizarre to me. I was in denial about you—and it's something I do well. But at lunch that day, when that warm breeze blew from out of nowhere on such a calm day, it stirred something inside me. It shook me like an earthquake. It was...an awakening of my soul, which seemed to have been asleep my whole life. I did everything I could to keep myself from leaping across the table and taking you in my arms. I was a little embarrassed by the thought."

I didn't know what to say, so I said nothing.

"I hope this isn't frightening you," Sherry said in a small voice, looking down.

I was stunned because she has just described the same thing I'd been going through. This feeling was like nothing I'd ever experienced. It was something I just couldn't explain or understand. I tried to pass it off as purely a physical attraction

but I knew it wasn't. It ran much deeper than that. I
thought about Sherry in a profound, spiritual, ethereal way,
rarely physically.

"I have to be honest, Sherry," I began. "What you just
described was something I also felt. It was like someone
grabbed me by the hand and squeezed it when I first walked
into that office. I think it was a very fateful day for the two
of us," I confessed to her as I reached out and took her hand
in mine.

I felt my eyes beginning to water and when I looked into
Sherry's eyes, I saw that she was crying. I had done everything
I could do to keep myself from getting overly emotional and I'd
done a pretty good job. But when I held Sherry's hand, I felt
weak, almost like my legs were going to give out from under me.
It was like I had finally found something that had been lost to me
so many years ago. I clutched Sherry's other hand and held both
tightly, feeling her energy transfer into me.

It was incredibly intense, as if our very souls crashed together.
A summer thunderstorm is the best way I could describe it. The
power of our inner thunder shook me to my core. It was almost
as if the wind pushed us together and lightening opened our eyes
to each other, awakening us to what had always been but we
refused to acknowledge. The current that traveled from Sherry
into me was all-consuming, taking over both my heart and
my soul.

I couldn't resist another moment. I pulled Sherry close and
embraced her, slowly rubbing her back. With our heads on each
other's shoulders, softly touching each other, I could hear
Sherry begin to sob deeply. This wasn't like her at all—
Sherry was one of the happiest people I knew. I was lost,
not knowing what to do next. And, for probably the first time
in my talkative life, I was speechless.

Then the strangest thing happened and it scared the crap out
of me. I felt my defense mechanisms kick in involuntarily. Those
walls I built to keep others out were going up faster than I could
believe. I was taken by surprise by this wild range of emotions I
was experiencing. Suddenly, I felt as though I'd been ripped
from a thunderstorm and thrown into a tornado. Like Dorothy in

The Wizard of Oz, I was no longer in Kansas. And those defensive walls were flying up around me in a last-ditch attempt to brick up my heart behind them. Suddenly, Sherry pulled me close with a powerful, gripping hug and whispered, "Stop, please stop."

I don't know how she knew that my mind was on a crazy rampage, but she did. And as she uttered those simple words in my ear, the walls began to crumble and I knew from that very moment that I had no choice but to surrender. This was bigger me, bigger than the both of us. It was cosmic in size, with the unbridled power of a hurricane. I was surrendering. But now, looking back, I knew that the choice wasn't mine to make.

"Stop? Stop what?" I inquired.

"I feel it. I feel you trying to pull away from this. No, run away from this. You're building walls again, brick by brick. I can almost feel it as one drops on top of the other. Please don't do that with us. I'm begging you. Give this a chance. This is meant to be and even you've acknowledged it," she pleaded.

"But this is scaring the shit out of me!" I told her. "You know me. I need to be in control of everything I do. This... whatever this is...has taken control of me. I'm sorry. I'm just not comfortable with all of this. I don't want to hurt you. I don't want to hurt the others in our lives. It's selfish and it's not fair to them. They didn't ask for this. They don't deserve this...and you don't either."

But Sherry wasn't having any of it. "I don't want to hear excuses because that's what you're doing, making excuses. You're coming up with reasons to deny yourself the possibility of happiness. The truth is that we don't know what's happening here. It could be nothing, but we both feel it. How do you explain that? This is bigger than you and me put together." I'd never heard her speak so strongly.

Sherry continued, "This is a journey that sought us out and grabbed both of us by the heart. No, by the throat, and dragged us toward each other. As I look back, I realize that my life was always empty. I was constantly seeking something, something more, until I met you. Jarred, the day you walked into this office, into this room, I knew something became complete in my life. At the very moment our eyes met and we shook hands, something enveloped my body and soul. I have no intention of hurting anyone but I'll be damned if I'm going to run away from this. And there is no way I'll let you run away from it either."

"What do we do, then?" I wondered.

She thought for a moment. "We will proceed with caution and move slowly. And if we both have misread this thing, then we will part as friends who have taken a journey that has enriched us."

Sherry lectured me like so many authority figures in my life had done like the few teachers who cared enough to make a difference had done. But there was one difference—I listened to her. Not only did I listen but I heard her loud and clear. I knew she was right.

"Well, this was one of the most productive breakfast meetings I've ever had," I smiled as Sherry and I kissed again. This time it was a soft, yet deep and meaningful kiss, a kiss welding our lives together as one and sealing our fate. "Okay, so where do we go from here?" I inquired.

"We walk together through this darkness, moving into the light of awareness," Sherry said emphatically. I looked at her, puzzled. "Let's not over-think this, okay?" Sherry told me, punching me in the shoulder, smiling, knowing full well my tendency to analyze even most simple things.

I nodded in agreement. "I guess it's time I let go and roll with this. I'm here for the journey. I will walk by your side, your hand in mine, strolling down this unknown path that has presented itself to us. And I will make a promise to you—I won't hide behind any walls. I realize it's time for me to change. It's time for me and for you."

Sherry looked at her watch. "Valerie will be here in about a half an hour. I better head to the ladies room and fix myself up. I don't want her thinking something's up. Have your coffee before it gets any colder. I'll be right back."

Taking a sip of my coffee, I peered out the window overlooking the Hudson River on this gorgeous day. There was a deep blue sky with a few puffy clouds and temperature was in the low 80s, no humidity. *It just doesn't get any better than this,* I smiled to myself.

When Sherry came back, I handed her the coffee and muffin. She sat at her desk across from me and we both were silent for several minutes. I was the one who broke through the quiet. "Okay, so now that you still have my undivided attention, let me ask you: what's the next step?" I asked her.

"What do you want, a road map?" Sherry shot back with a smile.

"Well, yeah. You know us guys. We never stop to ask for directions when we get lost. So before I wander around aimlessly, I want to know where we're going," I joked.

"Tell you what, why don't we meet for lunch later and just start enjoying each other?" she suggested.

"You're kidding, right? I have this rush job for you guys plus I promised Bill I'd stop by his worksite and take a look."

"Oh sure, blow me off for Bill! That's a great start to this journey," she kidded. It was the perfect time to break Sherry's chops. "Besides, I need some time to *think* this thing through."

Sherry broke off a piece of muffin. "Don't even think of starting that nonsense. As a matter of fact, don't even think. Why the hell can't you be like most men and not think at all?" she laughed, tossing the bit of muffin at my head.

I caught the muffin and quickly popped it into my mouth. Smiling, I said, "I knew I could get you to give up some of that. And I've got to admit, that little mouthful was sweeter than my entire muffin. It must have gotten sweeter from your touch."

Sherry rolled her eyes. "Oh please, you're going to make me lose my breakfast, shoveling the shit at me this early."

"Hey, it's true! You know me, I always call it the way I see it. Or is that feel it?" Sherry leaned over her desk and kissed me. "So," I continued, "I guess the next time we get together will be with Johnny, when we look at space we already have."

Sherry gave me a knowing smile. "You're going to make me wait that long before I see you again?" she asked.

"If you stopped to *think* just a little, you'd realize that you'll see me later today or tomorrow when I return with the photos," I said.

"Don't get all smart with me. You know what I mean," she giggled.

I just couldn't tease Sherry anymore although I loved the way she took what I dished out and served it right back at me.

"Thursday, at three, just me and you. No Johnny. It's only three days aw..."

She interrupted me. "*Three days*? That's an eternity to me right now."

"I thought we were taking it slow," I reminded her. "Besides, a fire that burns bright and furious burns out more quickly. I want this to have a chance of becoming something beautiful, something we can have forever. The wait will make our meeting that much more enjoyable," I insisted.

"Yeah, yeah, you win. I guess I'll have to wait until Thursday but be prepared for making me wait. I can't promise I'll be in complete control when I finally see you," Sherry warned.

"I'll take my chances. You know me, Mr. Control," I said.

"Right, a guy who can control himself when he's around a woman! That only exists in movies," she jousted.

"Hey, I'm offended. Are you saying that because I'm a man, I have no self control? Well, I'll have to show you just how much control I can have," I replied, thinking to myself, *Like my controlling my legs, which turn to jelly when you touch me*.

Sherry and I had just finished our coffee and muffins when Valerie walked in.

Chapter Fourteen
Jobsite

Valerie seemed surprised to see me. "Oh, you're here already? Didn't Sherry tell you I wouldn't be here until 10:30?" she commented.

I turned, looking at Sherry. "Actually, she failed to mention it," I admitted. *And I'm glad she did!* "But that's okay, I just got here. We had a lot to talk about with the art show coming. It gave us a few minutes to get that out of the way."

"Give me a few seconds to grab my notes and the products. I'll be right with you," Valerie said, hurriedly.

"Sure, take your time. I'm in no rush," I told her as she left the room.

"Nine o'clock? We forgot Val wasn't coming in until 10:30, did we?" I chided.

"No, actually, I didn't forget. It was accidentally on purpose. Did I tell you nine? I'm sooo sorry," Sherry said with a sly smile. We both broke out laughing. Then it was back to reality for the two of us.

Valerie was there in a flash and began plowing through the details of the project. A job like this was a piece of cake for me but I didn't want her to know because then she would push me to lower the price. I now felt as though I'd spent more than half my life working my lighting and camera angles. I could put a shot together in half the time most others could so I shouldn't be punished for my capability and expertise, right? This was a valuable lesson taught to me by my old public relations client Norm Liss. His words of wisdom have stuck with me, and guided me, for many years. Norm told me he could write a story in half the time others could so he didn't think he should be punished for being so capable.

"Set-up should take me a good part of the day," I told Valerie. "I can have film back here tomorrow morning. Does that work for you?"

"What time in the morning?" Valerie asked. I knew she never got in before ten, so I was going to take full advantage of this.

"Nine, 9:30. Will you be here?" I asked, already knowing her answer.

"No, I won't get in until about 10," she reminded me.

I coolly turned to Sherry. "What time do you get in, Sherry? I have a full day booked for tomorrow, so the earlier I can drop off the film, the better," I said, giving myself a reason to see her.

Sherry looked me right in the eye, smiled and replied, "We'll be here by nine. Oops! I mean I'll be here by nine." We all laughed, but Valerie wasn't on the same page as we were.

"Okay, see you at nine. You're sure you'll be here, right?" I asked Sherry.

"Trust me, I'll be here," she answered, trying not to smirk.

"Then let me run. I want to get started on this as soon as possible. See you tomorrow morning. Oh, and I take my coffee, dark no sugar," I informed Sherry

I moved toward the door with the products in hand. "I hope you don't mind me not being here tomorrow," Valerie said.

"Not at all. I know the pictures will be in capable hands with Sherry. If I have time, I'll try to wait for you," I told her, just to look good, but knowing that wouldn't happen. Valerie consistently tried to run some power games on me—and everyone else she dealt with. I called it "Finding Willy." Invariably, Valerie looked for something wrong to make me reshoot a project. And when I said "looked," I mean she searched, scrutinized and examined my work with such a fine-toothed comb that she would always find something— anything—if for no other reason than to show that she was in the driver's seat.

With the bag of products and the layouts in hand, I was on my way to see Bill. "I have to head further up in the county, to take a quick look at a job," I said to Sherry. "Do you have any messages for my client?"

"Ask him if he's stopping at the bar with the boys later. Actually, if is the wrong word. Just ask what bar, in case I need him." I detected a tone of disgust in her voice.

"Ahhh.... No, I think I'll let you ask him that," I laughed as I walked out.

Without a doubt, that had been one of the most powerful mornings in my life. I knew that Sherry and I would talk about what had been going on, but in a million years I never would have expected that our embrace, our closeness, our unexplained bond, would ever have taken place. I had to say if I'd had any questions about how Sherry actually felt about me before, there was absolutely no doubt about that now. I could stop wondering about my misreading her signals and simply look forward to seeing her. I convinced myself to start enjoying the ride, however bumpy it may be. I was there for the duration or until it ended.

I jumped into the car and secured the products so they wouldn't fly all over the place in the back seat. Then took out the address of Bill's job and checked my road map to figure out the fastest route. Although I promised Sherry I wouldn't over-think our relationship, I found myself consumed by it in spite of what I'd said. But it wasn't in the traditional manner I usually over-think things. I just couldn't stop thinking about her! Yes, I was pleased to have some answers and delighted I was allowing myself to enjoy the journey. Giving myself permission to think about Jarred for a change was a great feeling. For the first time in a long time, I was happy with me. I was determined to see this thing through, to disengage my terminal thought process and simply just enjoy.

I glanced at the dashboard clock as I approached the construction site. Only two cars were there: Bill's and somebody else's. It was clear his crew wasn't there, so I figured maybe it was lunchtime event though it was only 11:15. The door was wide open, so I walked in, knowing he was expecting me. And there was Bill with his arm around some woman. Actually, he had his hand on her behind. Man, I always knew this guy was a player—everybody knew except Sherry—but this was so blatant it disgusted me.

"Hey, Bill!" I announced loudly, as I entered the room. He and the woman turned, with a bit of a start. Bill removed his hand from her ass.

"Hey, Jarred. This is Diane, the homeowner. Diane, Jarred is my photographer," Bill introduced.

"Nice to meet you, Diane," I said coolly.

"Likewise," she smiled. "So you're here to take snapshots of this wonderful kitchen Bill is finally completing for us?"

Snapshots!? Could she be any more clueless? "I'm here to photograph it, yes," I told her. "It certainly is beautiful. I bet you'll be making some wonderful meals here," I added, while thinking to myself, *Like people in this neighborhood cook.*

"Oh, I don't cook. We have someone who comes in and prepares meals for us. We did this for her." *Bingo! What a surprise*, I thought, proud of my intuition.

"That's very nice of you to spend all this money to make someone else's life easier," I said, still holding back what I really wanted to say. Like she really gave a rat's ass about making life easier for the hired help. This kitchen was a status symbol pure and simple, nothing more. Diane couldn't wait to show it off to her Richie Rich friends. I wished I could get this into the conversation but I didn't have time for small talk. I had to get back to the studio and start working on Valerie's assignment. "I have a killer project I have to get to, Bill, but this is some impressive place."

And it was. Black granite countertops with a center island that had two sinks, plus a garbage disposal and all of the latest must-have appliances. There was a tumbled marble backsplash, an expensive marble floor that would kill poor Herve's legs while he stands on it and cooks all day. The lighting was also very high end with strip lights, under the cabinets and recessed lighting in the ceiling, with a unique (and expensive!) Venetian glass fixture hanging over the island.

"When do you want to shoot this?" Diane asked me. "I'd like my husband to be here if possible. He's a photography buff."

Yeah, just what I want. Some asshole who thinks he can use a Point-and-Shoot hanging over my shoulder, questioning my every move. There's nothing like it. "I'm not sure but I never work on weekends," I told her, figuring this loaded bastard was probably out until all hours, making a ton of money to keep his beautiful Arm Charm of a wife flush with materialism to keep her happy.

"Right now, he's away in England, working on an assignment," she told me. "But he'll be home next week. He can stay home when he needs to."

"Really? What does he do?" I asked.

"He's the head creative director for DDBY in New York."

Wow, this guy is someone I need to know. DDBY is one of the biggest advertising agencies in Manhattan.

"Just tell me when he'll be here and I'll see what I can do," I said, trying to accommodate this big wig.

Throughout the conversation, I watched Diane hang all over Bill like an expensive set of curtains, as though I wasn't even there. Bill chimed in, "Hey, can I have a say in this? After all, I'm only the master craftsman."

"I'll leave you two alone so you can figure things out," Diane said as she turned to Bill, running her fingers slowly down his chest to his belt buckle.

I cringed, thinking, *Christ, please don't go any further south with those fingers, not while I'm here at least.* The last thing I needed to know was Bill's business. If Sherry found out I knew something and didn't tell her, she'd feel as though I betrayed a trust and cut me off at the knees. And knowing Sherry, I'd be lucky if it would only be the knees!

As Diane was leaving the room, Bill gave me this "cat that just caught the mouse" look, as though he was proud of his elegant conquest. He really didn't know me at all if he thought I'd be impressed by his screwing around with some rich, bimbo trophy wife.

"I have Wednesday and Thursday open next week," I informed Bill, all business. "Which is good for you?"

"Let's set it up for Thursday," he said. "Don't you want to check with Diane to see if her hubby can be home?" I asked. "Naw, she'll do what I say. She's at my beck and call," he said with a wink.

Since I was about to get more information than I needed to know, I attempted to change the subject. "Sherry asked me to ask you what time you'd be home for dinner." I edited the question a little because I knew if I threw in the stuff about the bar, it would piss him off.

"Home for dinner? Did you get a good look at that dizzy bitch? Not only is she clueless but she's lonely and horny. I have to service my client, so I'll be eating Di...."

I cut Bill off, "Hey, man, WTMI!" *Please leave me out of this one*, I thought.

"WTMI? What the hell is that? Some sort of code?" he quipped.

"Way Too Much Information," I told him. "I'm friends with both you and Sherry. I really don't want to be put in the middle. Okay?"

"What are you, some kinda girl? Be a man, be happy for me that I'm hitting that," he said.

"Okay, I'm thrilled," I lied. "I've got to run. I'll catch you next Thursday, here at 10 a.m. If there are any problems, give me a call. Otherwise I'll see you then."

"Talk to you later," he laughed. Maybe I was being overly sensitive because of my feelings toward Sherry but I thought Bill was a real dog. I could care less what that fool did.

On my way back to the studio, my brain went back into overdrive. I started to wonder if Sherry was aware of Bill's philandering and just wanted to get even by starting something with me. Maybe she was just tired of his nonsense and I happened to be at the right place, at the right time. Was I misreading Sherry's intentions and making more out of our bond than there was?

I tried to flush those negative thoughts from my head. How could I explain the electricity between us and Sherry knowing what I was thinking? She seemed to be experiencing the same feelings I was. What about my dreams or past life experiences? Somehow, I felt she was involved in an odd way. No...I was sure I wasn't misreading this. Sherry was an honest person. I told myself to back down and relax. This felt so damn good, so right. At the very least, it was something I needed right now, so I might as well go with it and let myself have some fun for a change.

Back at the studio, I rushed the set up of my lighting to shoot Valerie's project but once everything was ready, I took my time during the actual shoot. It's a point of professional pride with me plus I didn't want to have to reshoot. (Although reshooting would give me an excuse to see Sherry one more time.) I had to have the film into the lab by four, if I wanted to get it back for next-day delivery. I also wanted to make sure I had every reason to see Sherry alone in the morning without raising suspicion.

Picking up my film later that afternoon, I went back to the studio and checked over every shot, inch by inch, making sure everything was fine. I went through great pains to ensure there were no lights blowing out the product logos, pertinent wording or blotting out part of the products. A real exciting project—foot care products in clear plastic packaging—it was important to see every detail of the insoles as well as the newly-developed logo. It was the pride of not just this new client but of Valerie and her art director, who designed it. So, the pressure was on as far as my lighting was concerned.

As I looked everything over one last time, I felt a swell of pride. *Mission accomplished!* Everything was perfect, in my work and in my life. At least for now.

 # Chapter Fifteen
Solid as a Rock

Tuesday morning rolled around, very much the same as Monday. I woke early, went to the gym and worked out until I knew Sherry would be at work. I didn't want to get there too early. Mostly, I didn't want to scare her by being overly anxious to see her again. I knew I had to be cool or at least make an appearance of being cool. Even so, I was in the car by 8:50. It was a 15 minute ride, so I figured I'd get there around 9:15, mosey in with the film, as calm and businesslike as I could muster.

Within minutes of my getting in the car, my cell phone rang. I picked it up with my customary, "Jarred here."

The voice on the other end said sternly, "Here? No, you're not here, and this is where you're supposed to be. You're late. Where are you?"

It was a gray outside and chilly, the type of day that makes it tough to get out of bed. The moment I heard Sherry's voice, I felt as though the sun had just risen, brightening my day with warm beams of light. As a kid, I always tried to gather those beams in a sock so I could hang onto them to brighten the gray days. Well now, Sherry was those beams and my heart was the sock.

"Who is this?" I asked with a smile breathless from the joy I felt.

"Who is this? You have to ask 'Who is this?' on top of making me wait forever for you to get here? How quickly you forget. Damn you!" she said, laughing.

I felt that this outburst gave me permission to tease her in return. "Hey, it's only 8:55. I thought you didn't get in until nine."

"I've been here for two whole minutes now. I was so looking forward to you being here. I need a hug, Jarred— I need a Jarred hug."

"Okay, okay...I'll be there in a few minutes. Do you have my coffee?" I asked.

"No. I got tired of waiting, so I threw it out. You'll have to get your own coffee."

"I don't need coffee—you just woke me up. Your voice has injected my body with enough endorphins to keep me running on high for the next few days."

"Oh, Christ, that's it...I'm hanging up now. Get here as soon as you can. I'm waiting!" Sherry said.

I pushed down on the accelerator, as I pressed the "off" button on my phone. It only took me about five minutes to arrive, grab the film and bound up the stairs. When I got into the office, Sherry was standing there with her arms folded across her chest, staring at the clock. "What took you so long?" she joked.

"I'm sorry. There was a tractor-trailer overturned, blocking the road. So, I left my car there, climbed over the truck and ran here. I didn't want you to have to wait any longer than you had to," I kidded.

"That's real smart. Throw sarcasm at a woman who's already pissed. Haven't you learned anything in all these years?" Sherry wondered.

"Hey, I'm a guy. What can I tell you? We never learn. So, seeing as how you're pissed off, I'll just give you the film and leave."

I handed Sherry the envelope, which she took, threw down on the desk and refolded her arms, taking me in with half a smile. "You'd better leave before I give you more what-for," she shot back at me.

Undaunted, I walked up to her, took her in my arms and gave her a big hug. Then I planted a kiss on her forehead. "Have it your way," I said. "I'm out of here. Bye."

As I turned to head out, Sherry grabbed me and spun me around, insisting, "Don't you dare walk out of here. Of course, I have coffee for you. You'd better at least finish it before you leave."

"You told me you threw my coffee out!" I told her.

"Just shut up and give me a hug." Again, Sherry pulled me close. I couldn't wait for the inevitable, so I held her tighter than even yesterday. We kissed deeply, soulfully. Her lips were incredibly soft and tasted like strawberries. The natural scent of her body captured my mind like a magic potion. As we pulled apart, her breath was sweet and hot on my neck. I couldn't have asked for a better way to start a dreary, gray day.

"I thought about you so much last night," Sherry confessed. "I couldn't wait until today. You're like a drug. I'm finding that I need my daily dose of Jarred just so I can function," she whispered.

This revelation sent a chill down my spine. How could we both be on the same page, the very same line, the absolute same word? It wasn't normal. We were experiencing something I needed to know more about. Parallel lives? I wasn't sure what to call it but I knew I had to understand it—because it scared the tuna salad out of me.

How could Sherry and I both think and feel the same, never having communicated this to each other before? It was like a mystical magnet that pulled us toward one another. I'd heard many times about two people meeting and immediately having the feeling that they'd known each other before. But this was my first personal experience with the phenomenon and it was freaking me out. It was drawing powerful emotions out of me which both fascinated and frightened me.

I tried to put it into words. "Sherry, I can't believe the depths of my feelings for you. You simply consume my every thought, every fiber of my body. You are my breath. You have become the life blood that pumps through my heart and you give me light that brightens even the grayest days," I managed to blurt out softly.

"Good," she smiled, "because it would be awful if only I felt this way."

I couldn't hold back. "I want you to know my thoughts. As time goes by, I might have trouble communicating them. I don't know why this happens, but sometimes it's right on the tip of my tongue and I just can't get it out. I hate that about me but it's part of who I am. I just want you to know this so when it happens, you'll understand. I don't want you to misinterpret it and leave."

"I don't think I'll be leaving you again all that soon," Sherry told me. "You'll see, this relationship is so much more solid than you think."

I was a little confused. I stood there, still holding Sherry close, listening to her every word...when it hit me. "Again?" I asked her. "What do you mean 'again?'"

Sherry shook her head, as confused as I was. "I have no idea why I said that. I just have this strange feeling that you and I have been together before. It's almost like you were torn away from me unexpectedly in the past."

She paused, as if trying to collect her thoughts. "When I saw you for the first time, walking into this office, something came over me. It's hard to explain and a little confusing, so please bear with me, and hear me out....But when I looked into your eyes for the first time, I felt a sense of completeness. I knew that you were someone I'd been looking for my whole life. At first, I thought maybe it was just that I was unhappy with Bill and I needed someone new in my life. But deep down, I knew it was more than that.

"Even though our first encounter was brief and casual, I couldn't get you out of my mind, Jarred. Meeting you had such a heavy impact on my being. I soon realized that I wasn't looking for you to replace Bill. The more I thought about you, the more at ease I became with myself. It was like I was at rest all of a sudden. I felt calm inside. But the longer I held back my feelings for you, the more I felt a polarizing detachment. I began to experience an internal unrest...Does this make any sense to you?"

I nodded and Sherry continued, "Finally, after a few weeks of living with this, I woke up very early one morning from this strange dream. In it, I saw a couple from another time. All of a sudden another woman killed this young man and took him from his true love. It was strange. I can't remember the details but I woke up with a start, breathless, with a pain in my heart and an emptiness inside. I instinctively knew that this young man in my dream was you. I'm also sure that the young woman was me.

"At first, I thought I was going crazy so I didn't say anything to you. I know you're married and I didn't want to scare you off or have you think I was crazy. But the more I denied my feelings for you, the more I was sure I had to find out what it was that draws you to me."

Sherry took a deep breath. "But even after you and I were together for all those meetings, I never got the feeling you were interested in me. I looked quietly for signs but saw nothing. After several months passed, I had another dream. An old, sad woman came to me and told me to have lunch with you. So I figured why not see what would happen, if anything."

I guess my face showed my disbelief because Sherry paused again. "Please understand that at this point I thought I was losing my mind. But I figured, 'What do I have to lose? Lunch is innocent enough.' I just had to see what would happen. I had to follow the advice from my dream. But I was apprehensive. What if this was all in my head? Would I begin to feel lost and start wondering again? As the time went by and you showed no sign of interest in me other than the art club, I was becoming concerned.

"Then, during the lunch, just as I was getting ready to surrender to the fact that I was crazy, that warm breeze blew from out of nowhere. I don't know if you noticed but it only seemed to affect our table while," Sherry said with deep conviction.

"Yes, I did notice that breeze but..."

Sherry interrupted me. "Wait, please let me finish, Jarred. I felt it pushing me toward you. I looked into your eyes and saw something come over your face. That's when I knew something had happened. After that breeze enveloped us, I knew we had been together before. It was just a feeling. I wish I could prove it, though, but I can't.

I'm just comfortable in the knowledge that it once was and I've stopped questioning it." Sherry took a deep breath, finishing. "Now what did you want to say?"

I was completely blown away by what Sherry had just laid out for me. "I'm speechless, Sherry," I began. "I don't know what to say. I did notice the breeze that day and I felt it pushing me toward you as well. I just didn't trust it. On top of that, I was preoccupied with other things. Please forgive me for what I'm about to say but you've always been a little aloof when it came to me. One day you're friendly, the next, I can barely get you to say anything. I got the impression you were just tolerating me because of the group. But now I know it was because you were wrestling with your feelings."

Sherry looked a little upset but let me continue. "After I left lunch at Sunset Cover, as I was driving around the lakes, I realized that something had happened. I didn't know what but I knew it was more powerful than I was," I told her, trying to sort out the confusion in my brain.

I glanced at my watch. "Look at the time. Valerie will be here any minute and I have an appointment. As much as I hate to, I think we'll have to continue this later."

"You're kidding, right? I'll tell Valerie I have to run out. We can meet later and talk," she pleaded.

"No, Sherry," I told her. "This is more potent than you realize. I want us to take our time and figure this out. We'll talk Thursday night."

Sherry's her upper lip began to quiver. This wasn't like her and it was making me feel very uncomfortable. I took her by the hand and hugged her close, rubbing her back. "Please trust me, Sherry. We're on the same page. This is happening. I want it to happen and so do you. Somehow I don't think either one of us has any say in this. Please be patient and know that I'm here for you now and always," I promised.

Sherry smiled at me through eyes heavy with tears. "I was scared you were going to tell me that you didn't have time for this, that you needed to move on. You know, that those walls were flying up again," she admitted sadly.

"So now who's over-thinking things?" I teased her. "There are no walls this time. I have accepted this as something wonderful. No deterrent, no walls, I promise."

Sherry looked up at me with her warm, knowing smile on her full, inviting lips. I leaned into her to give her a long, passionate kiss, holding her so close that I could feel our hearts beating together. "Trust me," I whispered. "I will not leave again."

I pulled away from her, looking deep into her eyes. When I smiled, her eyes lit up. I could see that she was delighted with what I'd said. "Now, let me get out of here before Valerie gets in and ruins this beautiful day."

"Beautiful day? Have you looked outside lately? It's pouring!" Sherry laughed.

"You couldn't be more wrong," I told her. "It's a wonderful day and almost nothing could ruin it. Notice I said 'almost.' Now let me go before the one thing that can ruin it does. Tell her if she finds anything wrong with the shots—and I know there isn't—I can't reshoot until Friday."

"Will I talk to you later?" she asked.

"Honestly, I'm going to be in meetings all day. If I can, I'll give you a call later or tomorrow but we will be together on Thursday," I sighed.

"You're not going to make me wait that long, are you?" she moaned.

"I'm so sorry, but we have no choice," I told her. "It will be just as painful for me. Besides, it will give us something to look forward to. Now let me run." With that, we kissed again quickly and I was out the door.

On my way down the hall, I saw the elevator door open and Valerie start to exit. To avoid her, I quickly jumped into an office. The receptionist asked if she could help me. I looked around and asked if this was the A & B Insurance Agency, managing my best dumb look and acting as confused as possible.

"They're not in this building. They're down the street," she said, somewhat befuddled.

"Really?" I stammered. "Sorry to bother you."

I listened for Valerie's footsteps to move past and for the door of her office to open and shut. "Not a problem," the receptionist responded cautiously. "Good luck finding them."

I politely thanked her and left the office, on my way to my next appointment.

I could just imagine the exchange between Valerie and Sherry. The minute Valerie got in, she would stalk into Sherry's office. "Hear from Jarred?" she would ask hurriedly.

"He just dropped off the film. I'm surprised you didn't run into him in the hall," Sherry would say.

"Why didn't he wait for me?" Valerie would inquire, a bit short.

"He was in a hurry," Sherry would sigh. "He said that he had another big assignment which would tie him up until Friday."

Sherry might look down and notice my coffee cup sitting there untouched. "Here, I bought you a coffee," she'd quip, ever the quick thinker. "The film is on the light box. It looks great, by the way."

Always one wanted to be in control and call all the shots, Valerie might say, "I can't believe I missed him....He must have taken the stairs..."

Knowing Sherry, she'd be thinking, *He must have seen you coming and jumped out the window*, and then she'd have to choke back her laughter.

"Are you feeling okay, Sherry?" Valerie might prod. "You look a little pale." "Never better," Sherry would smile. "Never better."

Chapter Sixteen
The Salty Mistress

I woke up very early that Wednesday morning, unable to sleep. My head was swimming as I tried to figure out just what the hell was happening. I needed a place to clear my head. I did some of my best thinking hiking at Rockefeller State Park or at my favorite spot by the ocean. After giving it some thought, I figured it was best to take a ride out to the ocean. There's nothing like the salt air to clear your head. Perhaps it would also lead me to another journey into the past.

As I drove, I recalled the conversation that Sherry and I had the day before. I rewound it over and over again in my head until the tape was ready to snap. I couldn't get my head around the fact that Sherry had the same dream I had and a very similar out of body experience to mine. Something odd and other worldly was definitely in play here and I was on a mission to figure out what it was. I resigned myself to accept the journey that had presented itself to me, and was open and eager to take it.

But I was still filled with questions and actively sought answers. I couldn't help but wonder what would happen if

Carol and Bill found out about me and Sherry? Would I be willing to leave Carol? Would Sherry leave Bill to take this path life has offered up to us? So many questions but only time could answer.

As I pulled into the parking lot near my thinking rock, I noticed that the beach was empty. I was the only soul there. Completely unaware of the time, I checked my watch, wondering why it was so empty. Only 5:30 a.m...that explained it. The sun was just beginning to peek over the horizon as I approached my station. The sunrise was filled with color, bright pinks and oranges. With very few clouds in the sky, it was turning from a warm kaleidoscope of color to pale blue.

I climbed up on my perch and observed the shore birds as they dove for breakfast just offshore. There was no wind to speak of, just a light breeze blowing from the west. As I laid back and fixed my focus on the sky, I felt my legs grow heavy and slowly the weightiness moved up to my arms and my eyes became heavy as well. Counting backwards, I felt myself sinking deeper and deeper into a trance.

But that was as far as I went. I felt some sort of blockage holding me back and I couldn't get any deeper. My mind just refused to shut down as it continued to race through bits of my conversation with Sherry the day earlier. *This isn't going to happen*. I became upset, nervous and jittery. The harder I tried, the worse it became. I sat up, frustrated, and gave up, knowing it wouldn't happen today.

Never one to totally throw in the towel, I decided to make the best of my trip to the water's edge. I climbed down off the rock, took off my shoes and began to walk in the sand. Out over the ocean, I saw that the waves were relatively calm. My head still spun with thoughts of Sherry and our puzzling relationship. I worried again that this wasn't real, just some sort of midlife crisis, but I knew in my heart that wasn't the case. I stopped dead in my tracks after walking several yards down the beach when I remembered my promise to Sherry—and myself—about not over-thinking the situation. I peered out over the ocean and noticed that the breeze has shifted. It was coming off the ocean now, not from the west as it had been.

This new wind had a calming effect on me. I smiled, took a deep breath and let it out slowly as I began to relax. I made my way back to my rocky perch as I allowed myself to be taken in by the effects of the shore. I noticed for the first time that morning, the sensation of the warm sand between my toes, the salt air rushing into my nose, massaging my mind into a relaxed state. I seemed to be lifted by the actions of Mother Nature herself, as she cradled me in her arms, moving both my body and soul into a space of calm. Totally relaxed, I drifted into this landscape painting of life at the shore.

When I reached the rock for the second time that morning, I climbed back up, slightly tired from my walk in the sand. I succumbed to the breeze, along with the soothing sound of the waves breaking upon the shore. I laid back on my rocky pillow, trying to push the anxiousness from my being---the fear that I would never again return to the places in the past I had visited twice before.

Taking a deep breath in through my nose, I held it for a few seconds then let it out through my mouth, a yogic breathing technique that works often for me when I need to release tension. Again, I stared up at the sky and concentrated on my legs as they grew heavier and heavier. The weight invaded my arms, as they felt weighed down, too heavy to even lift. The sensation sifted up to my eyelids as they closed. I began to count backwards again: Ten, nine, eight...

The door opens, putting me at the foot of a stone bridge. A thick fog engulfs me. I cross through it and upon reaching the other side, I see Jeremiah sitting in some sort of classroom, behind Jessica. He seems to be distracted as he looks out the window. The teacher is at the blackboard. He, too, seems preoccupied. In the classroom several seats are empty. I sense a sadness in the room. Jessica gazes over at Jeremiah and rubs his arm softly. Tears glisten in her eyes.

The other children in the room range from the ages of twelve to sixteen. Each desk is small, fashioned from honey-colored wood and has a seat attached to it. A potbelly stove burns wood for warmth. The room itself smells of burning pine, a tree indigenous to the area, which is used to heat the schoolhouse.

Each student has their own black slate for writing. There is wide planking on the floors and thin boards cover the walls. Three large windows and a handful of oil lanterns light the room.

After a few minutes, the teacher turns to the class, noticeably upset. He takes a deep breath and speaks slowly, with feeling. "Children, the loss we learned of today is devastating. Your classmates who have lost their fathers when the Emma James sunk need your support. This weighs very heavy on their souls and the souls of their families. It is almost too much to bear. Let us take a moment and pray silently for the souls of the brave men who were taken from us by the cruel way of life at sea," he tells them.

The students bow their heads and pray for their friends to gain spiritual strength, and for the souls of those ripped from their families. After a moment or two, the teacher raises his head and tells the class that they will be dismissed early so that the children can head home to help their parents prepare for the burial at sea ceremony, a common occurrence in New England towns whenever a ship is lost.

I notice now that there is a United States naval vessel in port. Several scruffy- looking sailors are being taken off the ship, their hands bound behind them. Their clothing is in tatters, mostly black in color. Their skin and hair are caked with dirt. Jeremiah and Jessica, now dismissed from school and on the cobblestoned streets, watch this closely, as do the other children. "There they are!" Jeremiah says to the others. "Those are the pirates that attacked the Emma James."

With that, a young boy, of perhaps twelve years old, runs from out of nowhere and begins punching and kicking one of the pirates, screaming at him, "You killed my father! You killed my father! Now I must kill you!"

The sailor escorting the pirate doesn't make a great effort to stop the boy because he's so little and so angry. He lets the boy get in a number of kicks and punches before getting between them and pulling the boy off the pirate. As the filthy brigand is dragged away, the boy shouts, "I hope they send you to Davy Jones' Locker!"

It seems that pirates have become a menace off the country's eastern shore in the early 1800s. It's so devastating, in fact, that the President has sent the Navy to protect the merchant ships and capture or kill the pirates. This effort is just too late for the Emma James and her crew, but the navy was able to sink the pirates' ship. They also managed to pull the surviving pirates from the water and bring them back for trial and hanging in this town which has suffered the loss of many fathers, sons and brothers. As the children watch the spectacle, Jessica takes Jeremiah's arm and pulls him close to her.

"I worry about our fathers," she whispers to him. "Jeremiah, you're fifteen. You will be going to sea yourself in just a few years. I don't want you to leave me. I don't want to lose you like these wives lost their husbands."

"Husband?" Jeremiah smiles at her. "Are we getting married?" he asks with joy.

"You know how I feel about you. We will always and forever be together for eternity. Both our fathers will one day be captains of their own vessels. We will be equals in society and we will be allowed to marry."

"And if we're not?" he wonders, a bit breathless.

"I will marry you, no matter what happens," Jessica tells him.

With those words, Jeremiah kisses Jessica. "I will be yours always," he tells her. "I promise, when I am a captain I will have you by my side at all times. We will never be apart for I will not be able to live without your love. I am so happy when I'm with you."

Jeremiah and Jessica walk together through town, holding hands as lovers do, talking about their hopes and dreams for the future. At their young age, in those times, they are ready to set out into the world, much younger, I realize, than in this day and age.

I get a strong sense that I am watching myself as a boy, in years past. Jeremiah talks like me and acts like my twin. These two are the same young couple I had seen before on the ship and in England, and playing in the field on my previous journey.

The town prepares for a trial that is to take place the next day in the tavern, The Salty Mistress. This is the center of society, the gathering place, if you will, where the town's men often congregate after work, to meet and exchange tales of their days— whether they are seamen or merchants. The air always smells of stale ale and old pipe smoke. A large fireplace provides heat in the winter, which also serves as the place food is prepared all year round for those who have no wives at home to cook a hearty dinner. The bar is small and made of oak. There are no stools. Anyone who bellies up to the bar will have to stand—if he can't then he has no business drinking. Several oak tables with chairs nestled around each, are placed around the open room. The sawdust on the floor serves to absorb the spilled ale, lost by those too drunk to hold their cups steady.

Behind the bar are several barrels of ale and other types of beer. The finer liquor is stored beneath. Hung from the low ceiling are several oil lanterns that provide a dim light. A staircase to the right of the bar leads up to a balcony, which, in turn, leads to six small bedrooms. These provide sleeping quarters for visitors or for those too drunk to make their way home—mostly single men fit into this category for the wives of the married sods come to collect their drunken spouses and chide them all the way home.

It is the tavern's owner that tends bar. He is an unsavory type, short, stout and unshaven. Balding, with stringy, long, unkempt hair, the man will do anything to part his patrons from their money. His wife, if she is, in fact, his wife, from time to time will lie with some of the patrons for the price of several dollars. The men must be extremely drunk to lie with a wench so brash, overweight and unwashed. Her hair long and greasy, she favors blouses that are low-cut and expose her ample bosom.

There is no better place to hold a trial than The Salty Mistress. Common practice back then, local taverns offered large spaces and were customary places to hold trials and other meetings of importance. The bar owner charged, or perhaps a better word is, gouged, the government for the use of his establishment while the trial went on.

Collected in the tavern that night is the prosecutor from the Maritime Authorities, as well as a lawyer, to defend these despicable men. Presiding over the trial is Judge Rear Admiral John Buchanan, a Scotsman, sent from the naval department, expressly for this purpose. The Judge is a tall, impressive man, who stands almost six foot tall. His uniform is impeccable and he carries himself with confidence, showing pride in his position. The Judge sits tall at the table in the front of the room as the men discuss how they will proceed. The Judge announces to all the people present that henceforth, the pub will be closed, and no one is to serve whiskey or ale. All who attend must behave in an upstanding manner, or they will be charged with disruption and jailed.

The three officials select a jury to sit at the trial which will begin at sunup. Only seven pirates have survived the battle with the Navy and they will all be tried together to save time and expense, the Judge commands. The other men agree.

Just before sunrise the next day, the town becomes an active beehive of activity. The shops are closed for the trial, and twelve men have been picked to sit in judgment of the seven. Promptly at seven-thirty, the pirates are brought to the impromptu courtroom in shackles and seated before the table, where Judge John Buchanan will preside.

The courtroom is filled to the bursting with townspeople, mostly family and friends of the fallen seamen. Jacob Wilson, the attorney for the pirates sits talking quietly to them. They mostly ignore him, offering him no help to defend themselves. The prosecutor, Captain Smith, from the United States Navy, will try the case. He is a short, thin man, with a long ruddy face. Clean-shaven, as all military men are, he cuts an impressive figure in his well-kept uniform. Captain Smith speaks with a deep, determined voice that is clear and always to the point. He pays close attention to every detail.

The townspeople have already grown impatient in their seats. All are angry but they restrain themselves and as difficult as it is they do their best not to become unruly. When Judge Buchanan enters, everyone rises. "Please be seated," he commands with a stern, authoritative tone.

Everyone sits, with the exception of the defendants, who defy the authority of the court and anything else that has to do with the law. "It is this very insolent attitude that brings these individuals into this court room," the Judge admonishes their attorney. "Please advise the defendants to respect this proceeding or the sailors will see to it that they do."

Pirates on the high seas believe that they are above the law and should anyone dare attempt to bring them to answer for their transgressions, they will unleash a violent, lawless retaliation feared by many. Their wrath includes horrors such as murder, robbery, torture and rape, for they know no limits and answer to no God.

The first witness called is Captain William Joseph, commander of the naval ship that arrested the seven. After the good captain takes his oath of honesty, the prosecutor begins his questioning. "Captain Joseph, would you please tell us, in your own words, how you came upon the defendants?" Captain Smith inquires.

Captain Joseph nods in assent and begins in a clear, strong voice, "We were on patrol about two miles off the coast when we noticed a steady stream of black smoke. Upon investigation, we saw the small pirate ship, the Black Rock, tied to the merchant's ship, the Emma James. The defendants were in the process of setting it afire. As we approached, they cut loose and attempted to run. We fired upon the vessel, striking it twice. There was a secondary explosion—we knew it was their gunpowder blowing. As we drew closer, we noticed eight men in the water. We pulled all eight safely from the sea. And when we did so, we observed that the men had items upon their person from the Emma James," Captain Joseph states with assuredness.

"Was there anything else, Captain?" Captain Smith asks.

"We also retrieved several bodies, sailors from the Emma James. Most had their throats slashed and stab wounds, as well as gunshot wounds. They were brutally murdered," Captain Joseph's voice trails off, a hint of sadness painting the memory.

After taking a moment to compose himself, Captain Joseph continues, "The seven pirates attempted to fight with my men, *but we were able to overpower them. We shackled them and put them in restraints below."*

Captain Smith turns, walks slowly toward the pirates, looking them straight in the eyes, his back to Captain Joseph. "You are convinced, Captain, that these seven are, in fact, part of the crew from the pirate ship that attacked the Emma James, are you not?"

"Yes, these are, without a doubt, the men that attacked the ship," Captain Joseph states with conviction.

"Thank you. No more questions," Captain Smith concludes.

Next, Defense Attorney Wilson steps up to cross-examine Captain Joseph. He is a small, squat man with a poorly trimmed beard and mustache. His gray hair is long and unwashed and his clothing is also unkempt. Wilson swaggers toward the stand much like the fat cat that just caught the mouse. " Captain Joseph," Wilson begins in a sneering tone, "were you on the Emma James before the attack?"

"No, I was not, sir" states Captain Joseph.

"So, Caaaptain Joseph," Wilson drawls, drawing out the name like taffy, "How can you be so sure these fine, seafaring men were attacking the ship and not attempting to pull survivors from the unfortunate accident that befell the Emma James?" Wilson stares at the jury with a smug, self-satisfied look as he concludes his question.

Unruffled, Captain Joseph responds, "They all had personal belongings and artifacts from the Emma James on their persons."

Wilson shoots back, "Perhaps they picked up these items from the sea, to return them to the families of the unfortunate men who died."

Captain Joseph shakes his head. "No. Most of the items we found on them were the items kept in the holds of ships, not personal belongings. This proves they were on board prior to the fires," Captain Joseph replies.

"But you don't know this for sure, do you, Captain Joseph?" Wilson prods in a snide voice.

"Yes, we do know this for sure," the Captain answers.

"Oh? And just how is that?"

Before Captain Joseph can respond, Wilson continues sharply, "And, let me also ask you, what you did with the eighth sailor you pulled from the water? Could it be that you tortured him? Tell me this, why am I not defending him?"

"No, we tortured no one," Captain Joseph answered loudly. "The eighth sailor was not a pirate at all. He was the First Mate on the Emma James!"

The Defense Attorney steps back, takes a deep breath and looks sternly at his defendants. It is clear they did not advise him of this important tidbit. There is an outburst from the crowd. Everyone seems to be bewildered but Wilson plows forward with his questions, "Who was it that they pulled from the sea? Is he alive or was he so badly injured that he died?"

Captain Joseph steeled his jaw and answered. "He is Ezra James, the son of the Captain your men so brutally murdered. Ezra has survived his wounds and is recovering in a safe place to protect him from retaliation by your clients' friends. Ezra is the one who told us who these rats were and everything he saw them do to his father and the others," Captain Smith rudely informs Wilson.

This doesn't deter Wilson's full-on attack. "Why hasn't this Ezra shown his face here in this courtroom? I have the right to cross-examine him!" Wilson cries out angrily.

"Mr. James has been on the mend for the last several days," Captain Joseph responds, unmoved. "He will be ready to testify tomorrow. Ezra will then tell this court just what happened."

"You hid this man from us. No one here knew he survived. I call for a mistrial!" Wilson shouts at the judge.

"No!" exclaims Captain Joseph. "Your clients all saw us pull him from the water, as well as saw us attend to his wounds. As a matter of fact, one of your clients, Mr. Wilson, attempted to escape our brig and harm Mr. James several times without success. They knew he was alive; they should have told you."

Upon hearing this revelation, the crowd is on their feet, calling for these seven to be turned over to them. They exclaim their right to impose justice on these scoundrels— immediately! Several of the Navy sailors move forward and stand between the people and the seven. Judge Buchanan slams down his gavel. "Order! There will be order in this court or you will all be removed."

As the sailors close in, the crowd settles down, their anger simmering. In light of the disturbance, Judge Buchanan wisely calls a recess. He orders the prisoners to be taken upstairs and kept under guard, and for all spectators to leave the premises until one that afternoon, after lunch.

"You may step down," Judge Buchanan says to Captain Joseph, "When you return this afternoon, you will still be under oath."

Chapter Seventeen
The Water's Edge

Jeremiah and Jessica run from the courtroom to the docks by the ocean. They breathe deeply and freely—as though the tense, stuffy air of the tavern has been smothering them. There they sit, as the shore birds fly overhead, diving into the sea, foraging for small fish that have been driven to the surface by the predator fish underneath. The wind blows a steady current of salt air into their faces. They sit silently, both feeling the hurt and anger from the loss the town has experienced. Jessica takes Jeremiah's hand as if perhaps her touch will somehow soothe him. "I hope the other pirates don't come here to try to save their friends," Jessica frets.

"I wouldn't worry," Jeremiah tells her reassuringly. "The Navy is here to protect us and we all have rifles. The pirates know this. If they do anything, it will be to try and sneak in and out at night. They will not stop to harm us." For emphasis, he puts his arm around her, pulling her close to him and states, "I will always be here to protect you, Jessica. We will be together forever. I promise."

"That makes me feel so much better," she sighs. "I will never leave you either. We will journey together through all of eternity," she adds, professing her love and faith in him with confidence. The two hold each other tightly, the fear in their hearts more overpowering than the sorrow for the losses experienced by their friends and neighbors.

These past few days have weighed heavily upon them. So young, so fragile. Yet, this is the way of life in that difficult age where life could end more abruptly than it begins. Jessica and Jeremiah look out in silence over the ocean, the powerful body of water that gives them life by providing food and work. This same mistress, from whom so many benefit, also takes life away, seemingly at will. It is a power never harnessed by man or beast and one respected by all who know her. Those who harbor no respect for her might will quickly perish beneath her surface. As their lungs fill with her salty essence, their hearts are squeezed by her cold embrace. Both Jessica and Jeremiah are intimately aware of the kind and cruel sea's capabilities as they have witnessed this drama play out much too often in their short lives.

The couple sits quietly for what seems like days, lost in their own world. Suddenly the streets come alive behind them as the townspeople rush back to The Salty Mistress, for the trial is about to resume. Jessica and Jeremiah rise quickly and hurry back to join the others in the courtroom.

As the crowd settles in, filling the seats and standing, the seven defendants are led back to the seats before judge and jury. A low undertone of conversation continues in the court as they wait for Judge Buchanan to enter. The one unasked question that weighs heaviest in the room is why there is even a trial at all. It had been the way of the past to simply hang these culprits as soon as they were captured and dragged back to town. Something was different now, yet no one could figure it out.

A Naval lieutenant acting as the clerk jumps to his feet. "Please rise," he shouts above the din of the crowd. The Honorable Judge Rear Admiral Buchanan reenters the impromptu courtroom and again takes his seat behind the makeshift bench. The lieutenant commands, "Be seated." And the proceedings continue.

Judge Buchanan orders, "Captain Joseph, please take the stand,"

At that very moment, there is a bustle in the back of the courtroom. A late entry, a stranger to the town. The sailor posted at the door notices the man, then nods to Captain Joseph. The Captain makes a subtle gesture of acknowledgement, bowing his head slightly. As Defense Attorney Wilson rises, he glances toward the back of the room and upon noticing the man, also gives a slight, knowing nod. He approaches Captain Joseph. "You have told us about a witness, Seaman James, who has been wounded," Wilson begins. "He will be here tomorrow so that I can cross-examine him, will he not?"

"That is correct," Captain Joseph states. "He is very anxious to tell his story." "Just where is he now?" Wilson inquires. "He is resting, with a nurse watching over him." "Resting where?" Wilson prods.

Captain Joseph looks at the Judge. "Must I answer?" he wonders. Judge Buchanan nods—indeed, he must. "In the house on the hill, just outside of town on the south end," Captain Joseph responds, somewhat reluctantly.

"So he is under the protection of the Navy as we speak?"

"No, no armed guards protect him," Captain Joseph admits. "There are plenty of people there during the day. Those that would have been a threat to him are here or dead, so we have no worries. He is best left alone at night so he can rest."

"I have no more questions for this witness, your Honor," Wilson says.

As Wilson leaves the bench, the Judge asks the prosecuting attorney. "Captain Smith, do you need to redirect?"

"No, Judge, I have no more questions for this witness," Captain Smith concedes.

"Do you have any more witnesses?" continues the Judge.

Captain Smith responds, "Just First Mate James, tomorrow morning, your Honor ."

Judge Buchanan strikes his gavel. "This court will recess until tomorrow morning, at six a.m. At that time, you will present your next and final witness, gentlemen."

*The courtroom springs to life once more and begins its
transformation into a tavern. Some leave while others stay and
approach the bar. The stranger who had arrived late at court
does not tarry at The Salty Mistress. Instead, he slips out
unseen. It seems as though he came just to hear Captain Joseph's
testimony then the mysterious stranger is gone.*

*Night falls upon the village. As the town sleeps, there is
movement out in the harbor. A large ship, flying the pirate's
colors, slips in, close to shore. Upon dropping anchor, they set
two rowboats into the water. Eight men begin rowing ashore
under the cover of darkness, moving silently and deliberately, so
as not to attract attention. They beach their crafts, check to
make sure their guns are loaded, then make their way up the
embankment, toward the small, isolated house where First Mate
Ezra James lies healing from his wounds. They approach the
house, confident from the information their lead man has
gathered in court. They are certain they will not encounter any
resistance or problems reaching the only remaining witness
against their seven brothers standing trial.*

*Using only the light from the moon to guide them, the men
approach the house on the hill. They stand watching the windows
for any movement. Just as Captain Joseph said under oath, there
is no one outside guarding the First Mate The pirates joke and
make jest of honest men and how they can always be counted on
to give away their position while under oath.*

*Their leader dispatches the men to strategic points, stationing
one at the beginning of the path that approaches the house and
two at the front entrance. He sends two more to the house's back
entrance to ensure that no one approaches from the rear.*

*Finally, the leader and the last two men enter the house. They
immediately notice the stairs as they open the door. They quickly
look around and see that no one else is afoot. One man stays at
the bottom of the stairs as the leader and the last man creep
upstairs. Slowly, stealthily they move, hoping not to wake First
Mate James before they kill him.*

*Once at the top of the stairs, they see a bed with a sleeping
body nestled in the dark. It must be James because he is the only
one there. They quickly approach the bed, confidant that they are*

alone. The lead man takes out his gun and points it at the man in the bed as he rapidly approaches it.

But before the pirate has a chance to cock his pistol, he realizes, a moment too late, that the man lying in wait in the bed is a Navy officer. The officer rises quickly, gun in hand, and fires a shot at the startled pirate, hitting him in the chest and killing him instantly. The other pirate attempts to run, but from behind the door, out steps another Navy officer, killing the second pirate deftly with one shot. The other brigands on watch below are confused by hearing two shots and call out to their men upstairs but get no response. Realizing they have walked into a trap, they panic and tear down the path, toward their ship.

As the pirates flee, they are confronted by several more Navy sharpshooters, who order them to halt. Refusing to be captured, the pirates fire shots at the sailors instead, narrowly missing their targets. Once being fired upon, the sailors open a barrage of fire. The six remaining pirates drop like ducks from the sky, all at the same moment, falling dead upon the ground.

At the same time these eight meet their demise, canons fire out in the harbor. The firefight awakens the townspeople as burning gunpowder lights up the night sky. The USS Sally, hidden by the shadows of the cliffs, lies in wait for the pirates. The Sally approaches the pirate ship known as The Swordfish Kurt lets loose a volley of canon fire at her. But these guns are small and no match for the Sally's artillery. The inexperienced pirates on the Swordfish fire too quickly, not waiting for the Naval ship to get into proper range, a grave mistake. The guns from the Sally explode, firing all eight guns at once, striking the Swordfish with every shot. It is literally blown apart, setting gun powder afire as the rounds destroy their target. What is left of the ship burns as it slowly sinks, dragging all the crew with her to the sea's floor.

Prior to this dramatic exchange, Naval intelligence had revealed that the pirate ship was hiding in the area, uncovering the plot to liberate the captured seven. It was now obvious why there was a trial—for the testimony it generated. The Navy was setting a trap in the guise of a mock trial, to bring down one of the most notorious East Coast pirate crews and their ship. The Captain of the Sally was none other than Captain Smith, who

had set up this cunning trap, along with Captain Joseph and
Admiral Buchanan.

The magnificent battle is over in a matter of minutes, the
townspeople watching in awe the short but explosive fray,
witnessing firsthand how impressively the Navy handled this
matter. In the end, the citizens settle down, a little uneasy at
first, but reassured that the Navy had the situation under control
at every turn. The little town seems to sleep a bit easier that
night, even Jeremiah, whose nerves are jangled but lets
sleep overpower him. He slumbers like a newborn a babe
until morning.

Upon the dawn's arrival, the townspeople rush to the court to
get a better understanding about what transpired the night
before and to see what bearing these events will have on the
trial. By the time Jeremiah arrives, court is already in session.
The defendants, who also witnessed the evening's events through
their cell windows, are alone. Their attorney Wilson, who
mysteriously arrived in town just at the right time to defend the
seven, is nowhere to be found. The captive pirates are asked if
they know where Wilson is and their only response it to look out
the window toward the harbor.

Judge Buchanan pushes them further, "Would you not like to
defend yourselves in this matter?"

One pirate speaks up, "You can take this court and ram it in
your asses, your Honor...sir ."

Upon hearing this, Admiral Buchanan orders the seven to be
hanged by the neck until dead, at sunset. This is the fate that
befalls all scoundrels, even these. When the sun goes down that
evening, the pirates are hanged without much ceremony. Their
bodies decorate the yard irons and are left there for two days for
any pirates who may be crossing the harbor to see.

The following day, the town holds a solemn ceremony at the
Fallen Sailor Memorial in memory of the seamen lost that fateful
night. Standing tall, with his arm in a sling, is First Mate Ezra
James, trying his best to console his mother, who stands bravely
beside him as a Captain's wife should, for she lost her husband
on the Emma James, which had been named in her honor.
Jeremiah, Jessica and their parents are also in attendance, along

with practically all who live in town, for it is an important event. They all know, yet do not say, that it could have been any one of their loved ones among the dead, and indeed, many have lost their fathers, husbands and sons.

At almost sixteen, Jeremiah and Jessica know that the time for them to begin their venture into the often-hazardous life of sailing is just a year away. He, as a sailor and she, to travel with her mother and father, who will soon be the captain of his own vessel. For now, they long to spend as much time together as possible.

After the ceremony, the two sneak off unnoticed to the woods just outside of town. There, they kiss and innocently embrace for hours. It has been a sobering time for the two youths, and it has shaken them to their very roots. They simply want to spend quiet, safe moments in each other's arms. Neither brings up the uncertain future that lies ahead for them. They simply live in the joy of the moment. And their joy, the depth of their love, is almost palatable, like sweet honey on the tongue.

As I watched Jeremiah and Jessica embracing, they slowly faded off into the distance until they were so small, I could barely make them out. I found myself back at the stone bridge, emerging from the fog that carried me into their world. I was observing the scene from a great distance, from above, until it all whited out.

Completely conscious now, I opened my eyes, blinking up at the sky in what seemed like only moments later. I heard children playing on the beach, and realized that now the once-empty beach has filled with sunbathers. I must have been under for quite a few hours. As I sat up, I was still a little groggy and I felt as though I had just awoken from a long sleep. As I looked out upon the sea, I watched the waves rushing in, pounding the shore as children laughed and frolicked. There were shore birds feeding nearby, in this very typical seaside scene, but the experience I just woke from was anything but typical.

Never one to pass up a photo op, even after waking from a trance, I decided to run back to the car, grab my camera and take a few shots. On my way back to the shore, a little girl stopped me. "What are you doing with the camera, mister?" she asked.

I looked down at her and smiled, "I'm going to take a few photos of one of nature's sustaining dramas," I said.

With a confused look, she inquired, "What?" "I'm going to take some pictures of those birds feeding over there," I explained. "Oh. Is this going to be on TV or in the newspaper?" she wondered. "No, I'm just taking them for myself, to look at whenever I want," I told her.

The little girl smiled then ran off, excitedly yelling to her mother about what she just learned. Then she dashed away to play with her pail and shovel in the sand, our conversation no more than a distant and momentary distraction for her. I watched her a few more moments, envious of how simple life was at her age. In a way, I wished I could return to those days, when being content with just a shovel and pail was a distinct possibility. Everything in that little girl's life seemed so uncomplicated and neat—living for the moment, not worrying about the future. Children live life as it should be lived, without concern about what might or might not be.

I sat with my knees at chin-level, camera perched upon them at the ready, watching the birds' feeding frenzy through my lens. When I saw a moment of interest, I committed the image to film with the click of a shutter, a moment in time frozen forever in celluloid. I zoomed the lens from wide angle to telephoto as the mood suited me. The music of life played in the background, joyful voices rising and falling, and waves striking shore. They served as background music to the birds' cries. The gulls communicated with each other while hanging effortlessly in the sky; watchful eyes upon the water, waiting for the opportune moment when food arrives to their watery table.

Completely relaxed, I was momentarily distracted while soaking in the warmth of the sun, enjoying the subtle, cool breeze whispering off the sea. Moments like these made me wish this type of easy existence could be a way of life for me—no deadlines, no worries, no bills. I felt like I belonged here. This was my life as it should be. I never wanted to leave. But soon, reality began to set in as the birds finished their feeding frenzy and returned to shore. I put the lens cap back on my camera and got ready to go.

 # Chapter Eighteen
Reality Check

I forced myself to head back to my studio, to my business and the cold reality of my life. It was difficult to pull myself from that tranquil seaside vista. I didn't want to leave. I allowed myself the luxury of remaining there for a few more minutes before I dragged myself up onto the beach and headed to my car. *There will be other times*, I tried to tell myself. *I know there will be.*

I pulled out of the parking area and headed north, absorbed in my thoughts for quite some time before the real world reached in and dragged me back against my will. As I drove, I felt exposed and vulnerable about the events that had revealed themselves to me in my vision. What did it all mean? I guess it caught me off guard, because then came the worry, doubts and confusion about Sherry and me.

In an attempt to save myself from my own foolishness, I slipped in my favorite Josh Groban CD. His music immediately began to take me over. There was something about his voice and the songs he sings that captivated my total being. I turned up the volume, hoping the music would overtake my mind and stop it from swirling. I became completely absorbed by Groban's voice, which sounds like God himself reached down and touched the man's vocal cords. I was pulled into the music, the sound vibrating into my being. I'd heard this album many times before, but something was different this time. What was it?

Her. Sherry. She was the difference. Like a salmon was mysteriously called upstream to his ultimate destiny, I felt Sherry pull me toward her from afar. The uncertainty of our destinies pained my heart. My emotions were so high it made me dizzy. I considered myself a pretty strong person—in fact, others often described me as being a "tough guy,"—but for the first time in my life, I felt weak, exposed, confused.

Not only that, but I'd become an emotional wreck. Despite the closeness Sherry and I felt toward each other, she and I were just getting to really know each other. I never wanted her to see this vulnerable side of me. I was afraid she might misinterpret or misunderstand it. Neither of us sought out this relationship—we'd just been unexplainably drawn to each other and thrust into it. I didn't understand these feelings...but then again, "feelings" was such an inadequate word to describe what was happening. There was a terrible jumble of emotions. Should I run, leave her alone? Or should I stay and face this maddening uncertainty. Would Sherry ever understand what was happening in my mind and who I really was? At this point, I was so confused and had buried so much, maybe I didn't even know who I was!

There I was again, wrestling with my wild thoughts. I had to take control of my mind once and for all and just live life for the moment like that little girl on the beach. I had to enjoy the journey and not over-intellectualize it, just like I promised Sherry—and myself. I resigned myself to go along for the ride and take everything as it came. Nothing more.

Shaking, I turned up the CD, listening to Josh as loud as the volume would go, hoping to stop my thoughts, my feelings, my mind. But the vibrations seemed to pierce my soul, my heart, and a tear came to my eye. *What the hell is happening? Where will this go?* I would soon see.

The voice on the CD rescued me. It pulled me back in and helped put the brakes on the insane thoughts that rushed through my brain. Josh's voice soothed me. I took solace in knowing that things would be okay. I would be totally convinced when Sherry and I met again—I would know when I looked into her eyes again, when I touched her. I had to wait until our next meeting, suffering through my pain silently, a pain Sherry would never know. But maybe, just maybe, she was feeling the same torment.

Ah, Sherry...I wondered if we were doomed to live this uncertain life that had befallen us, moving from one kiss to another, sharing stolen moments when we could, surviving only on the knowledge that we would soon see each other again. We trusted the knowledge that our lips would meet again, and lived just for that. It embarrassed me to admit that Sherry's embrace was the kindling that warmed my heart. Would we be able to sustain the emptiness of not being together for long durations? We would have to. I tried to remind myself that Sherry and I were blessed with living this dream that was sent from above. Somehow I knew this experience would enrich us more than torture us.

She and I were to meet again the following night—Thursday. I would soon be reassured about what was happening between us. I would make it clear, once and for all. I would do everything in my power to bond with her every chance I got. Thursday couldn't come soon enough.

But once I was home for the evening, I began to feel guilty about my involvement with Sherry. I had always pictured myself as a family man—a good husband, a dedicated father—but now, I wasn't so sure. I was steps away from becoming an adulterer.

It was a typical evening at our house. Carol was banging around the kitchen and the kids were in their rooms, doing whatever they did there. My oldest, Joann, had just graduated from high school and was looking forward to going away to a college upstate in the fall. A good student, Joann enjoyed school and learning, and always excelled academically. She was also a solid athlete but an inept softball coach soured Joann on sports the rest of her high school career. Jo now immersed herself into work and school. She was very bright, great with children and had a good head on her shoulders.

Joann favored me more than Carol. She had my curious nature and determination. I could look at anything I decided to tackle and figure it out, take it apart and put it back together again so that it worked even better than it did before. Joann had the same knack and never stopped impressing me with her abilities and her drive.

Another thing she did very well was writing, maybe because she was such an avid reader. I knew she would love to be a writer but as a side gig. Even at 18, she knew that very few writers made a living from their craft, and Jo was very pragmatic, even at this young age. A hard worker and a caring person, she had been burned by friends and relatives, so she also had both feet firmly planted on the ground.

As her father, I thought Joann was beautiful but most people considered her a very attractive girl as well. Plus, she was very active which kept her in good shape. This winning combination caused some jealousy among her girl friends. I swear, the fighting and backstabbing that went on in high school was unreal. I was glad it was over now.

Another of my daughter's great points—and stumbling blocks—was her persistence. Joann wouldn't back down to anyone. She simply plotted her course and stayed with it, no matter what. All of the above succeeded in molding Joann into an extremely worldly young lady in a very short time. Nothing got past her, and like most adolescents, she was convinced that she was smarter than her parents.

On the other hand, my son Jamie, who was 16, was very different than his sister. He tolerated school because we pushed him. All we wanted him to do was get through high school and hopefully some college. After that, it would be up to him if he wanted to continue with college or go straight into the workforce. Carol and I explained to him (over and over again) that without at least some college, his future would be limited. It didn't seem to faze him, though.

Jamie like his sister, was very bright, but for some reason kept his smarts in reserve, rarely using them in the traditional way. He would much rather be in the woods hunting, fishing or hiking, doing something, anything, that got him outdoors and away from school. Athletic, Jamie played sports in school—baseball, wrestling, etc.—but he stuck with football because he loved it, even though they didn't play him very often. The wrestling coach he loved left the school so Jamie's interest in the sport waned.

The more he became disenchanted with school sports, the more he put into outdoor sports. Jamie knew game animals and their habitats inside and out. He could track just about anything plus tell you if it was male or female. When it came to fishing, he was out on the water whenever he could—sometimes a little too much—neglecting his schoolwork. Jamie recently took up shooting trap and really enjoyed the challenge of a sport where you compete against yourself as well as others. When it came to things he was interested in, Jamie really committed himself to them. He had an unbelievable team spirit and was even supportive to his opponents, something that never failed to impress me. Like his sister, Jamie was headstrong, and when he believed in something, he got behind it 110%. I only wished he put some of that intensity toward school!

Thinking about my kids, which always gave me great pleasure, gave me the opportunity to stop obsessing about Sherry...at least for the moment. I had a good relationship with both Joann and Jamie. I gave them the space they needed to grow and learn life's lessons by themselves. I loved watching the people they were becoming and looked forward to seeing what kind of adults they would mature into. A chill ran through me as I asked myself if I was willing to give them up for Sherry. I hated to admit that I didn't know the answer.

Grabbing a book, I headed downstairs to do some reading in my favorite easy chair. I hoped it would take my mind off my new situation but it didn't work. My latest worry was about the kids. What would happen to them if I decide to leave or worse, if they found out about Sherry and me? It was something I didn't think they could ever accept or forgive. And forget about Carol. She was the other monkey wrench in a complex situation that grew more complicated with every passing day, every vision. I chuckled at my fleeting thought of selling my story to Hollywood—I was sure a sitcom writer could put this convoluted relationship into a neat, little package that would wrap up nicely in 30 minutes. If only real life were that easy.

I reminded myself that what was happening was more powerful than me, Sherry, my family, and even stronger than all of us put together. I was extremely curious about where these visions were leading me and I knew that I needed to follow them to the very end and explore them to the fullest. (To me, Sherry and the visions were one in the same.) If I didn't allow myself to see where the road led, I might end up resenting Carol—and resentment is the death of any relationship. Even if I thought our relationship was half-dead already, I still needed make sure it was really gone.

I also had to make sure that it wasn't just an infatuation with Sherry, though deep in my heart, I knew this wasn't the case. Even when we were at our best, Carol had never shown interest in me the way Sherry did. Sherry's lack of cynicism was also a breath of fresh air. I'd had to live with Carol's bitterness over the years and it was strangling me. When I tried to point this out to her, Carol's response was that I was crazy.

Call me selfish, but I wasn't going to deny myself the chance for even 15 minutes of happiness. I realized that an affair, if that's what this relationship with Sherry would turn out to be, was complex and morally wrong, but I had to explore it to the fullest. I owed it to myself.

Proceed with caution, a little voice inside my head told me. I didn't know if this was possible but at least I would try.

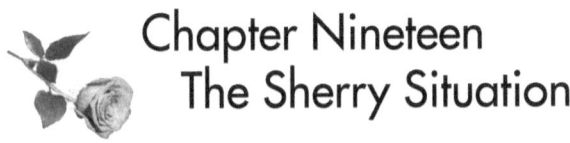# Chapter Nineteen
The Sherry Situation

And so it began. Again. It was Thursday morning. At the gym doing my usual workout, I tried not to be apprehensive about the afternoon, when Sherry and I would be alone again for the first time in many days. We had been alone in the woods the weekend before but that was just the beginning, and so much had transpired since then, namely my vision the day before of the pirates' trial. Somehow, I sensed that Thursday night would be a new beginning for Sherry and me.

Working out with weights, my concentration was off because my head was clearly in the very near future. Or was it the past? Whatever. I had to stop torturing myself—mentally, at least— and start torturing my body with an intense workout so I could forget about Sherry, at least for an hour or so.

Almost on cue, Terry, one of the instructors at the gym, approached me. I knew what she wanted. Terry was on a never-ending quest to get me to take one of her classes. Terry smiled, "Come on, Jarred, you know you want to!"

"It's all women," I bantered. "What if I make a fool out of myself?"

"Just come up. No one will even notice you," she told me. "Everyone will be doing their own thing and just trying to keep up."

"I don't want to be the only man there."

"We have a few other guys today, so just come up. It's in Studio A. We start in five minutes...Please?"

I convinced myself that Terry's class might just be the answer. At the very least, it would take the edge off my anxieties and at worst, it would kill an hour. (Or kill me!) So I went up and joined Terry's kick-boxing class. Before I knew it, I was kicking, punching and jumping around like a hyperactive kid. I completely lost myself in the workout and my mind rarely strayed to Sherry and my visions. But afterwards, I realized that in true Jarred fashion, I over did it. I was so tired, I could hardly move my legs. Legs? What legs? I could barely feel them. I was upset with myself about going overboard. When Sherry got to the studio, I might not be able to move at all.

Hobbling down the gym stairs, every step hurt. Well, I hoped Sherry wouldn't mind wheeling me to my car and pouring me into it later. I laughed to myself. At least this relationship had brought back my sense of humor, something I seemed to have lost over the years.

In my studio, I got piles of paperwork done—any chore I could do sitting down. Before I knew it, the clock said 2:30. I wondered why Sherry wasn't early. Maybe she was having second thoughts like I'd had. My heart sunk when I realized that I hadn't even called her the day before, having lost myself at the shore and then in the bustle at home. Was she pissed off at me? Idiot! I didn't even phone her to say hello. Was she so upset with me that she wouldn't come today?

Three o'clock and Sherry was still a no-show. Where the hell was she? Was she one of those "fashionably late" types? (I sure hoped not because I hated that bull.) Finally, at 3:15, I saw her pulling into a parking space outside. A few minutes later, she was standing in front of me, looking breathless and beautiful. "Sorry

I'm late," she began. "Valerie had me doing this special project and it took forever."

Then Sherry walked straight up to me. My heart racing, my palms sweaty, I leaned forward to kiss her hello—and she slugged me in the shoulder. "Ouch! What was that about?" I inquired, rubbing my arm. Just what I needed, more aches and pains.

Sherry stood silent, looking at me with eyes filled with longing. When I reached out she didn't punch me this time. We were both unable to resist the impulse to embrace. I felt her body shaking, as mine was, trembling with desire and want, begging for a release of pent-up emotions. At that instant, we both knew that we could no longer hide from ourselves.

I was concerned about not saying the wrong thing, careful not to say that I had fallen in love with her. Love, real love, was not something you fell into, like a black hole. No, to me, love was a living, breathing organism, always growing within you, in your heart, your soul. If nurtured properly, it continued to grow stronger with each moment, each day. I told myself not to over-think the Sherry situation, just to let things happen. If it was real, if it was meant to be, then it would be. It was no longer in my control. All of yesterday's concerns fell away—they were no longer concerns to me. This was a first–no worries, casting my fate into the wind. I liked it—it felt more like "me" and who I really was. Or at least the man I wanted to become.

My eyes locked with Sherry's and we melted into a long, hard kiss. Again, I had the odd and overwhelming desire to be one with her. We held each other more tightly. All the physical and emotional pain sifted out from my body. Like magic, I only felt joy. Pure, simple joy.

After a silence, I had to ask, "Okay, what's up with the punching?"

"Why do you think?" she responded.

I hoped this wasn't one of those lose-lose situations, where no matter what you said, it would be wrong. My mind was racing, searching, fast-forwarding for a response. "Your kiss, your embrace, has left me numb with joy. I can't seem to think straight right now. Why don't you just tell me what's up with the abuse?" *Abuse? I didn't just use that word, did I? Man, did I just put my foot in it...*

"Abuse!" Sherry repeated. I steeled myself for a cup of verbal abuse. Sherry began with a slight smile curling her lips, "I'll tell you what real abuse is!" Now I knew I picked the wrong word... "Abuse, my dear," she continued, "is when you don't pick up the phone and call to simply say 'hello.' I waited all day yesterday for that damn phone to ring, to hear your voice. Just a simple 'Hello, Sherry' was all I needed."

I took a deep breath, certain that the best retort would be to tell her the truth. "I'm sorry," I told her. "But I spent the day at the beach and..."

But I couldn't get another word out. "*At the beach?* You're telling me that you were having a good time at the beach and never thought to call?"

"I...I thought of you all the time," I stammered but Sherry was on a roll and she ignored me.

"You let me sit at work all day wondering how you were, where you were, whether you were having second thoughts about us and you were out having fun!" she quipped, a slight smile flickering in her dark brown eyes.

"Hey, wait. Let me finish. Christ, woman..." There I go again, putting my foot in it. *Did I just call her 'woman?' Judging from the look on her face, I did*. But I continued digging my own grave before Sherry could get a word out.

"Yes, I was at the beach...thinking about you. I wasn't having fun..." *Oh, no. I couldn't dig a deeper hole if I had a shovel*. I tried again, "I mean, I needed some time to myself so I could think...about you and how much you mean to me. I lost myself in you and the joy you bring me." Good save, I thought. "I never realized the time. Before I knew it, it was almost four and I knew you had left work." Sherry stared me down. "Hey, I was upset. I missed talking to you, but I didn't want to call while you were with Bill. *This might just work. Or not...*

Sherry shook her head. "Oh, man, you are so full of crap. But I'll just pretend you're telling me the truth," she laughed, letting me know she was pulling my aching leg.

"No, I swear it's true. Trust me."

"Whenever a man says trust me, you shouldn't," Sherry added.

I wasn't ready to tell her the details of my voyage back in time on the beach. She'd think I was crazy for sure if I told her about this one. Besides, I wanted to wait until I met with Peggy before sharing the details of these trips with anyone else, even Sherry. I might even take Sherry to meet Peggy at some point.

I could tell that Sherry was about to continue our playful repartee, but she glanced at the clock and knew we only had an hour left before she had to get home to Bill. I touched her lips gently with my fingers and kissed her more softly this time. As we embraced, I pulled her close to me. My excitement was becoming more obvious.

Embarrassed, I hoped she didn't realize what was happening but how could she not. Sherry responded to my arousal by pushing herself into me. My embarrassment was short lived, it was now clear that we both wanted the same thing—each other.

As we kissed, I moved my hand slowly down Sherry's back, holding my breath, waiting for her to stop me but she didn't. Cupping my hand on her buttocks, I pulled her into me tighter and she responded passionately. Both on fire now, our bodies moved against each other like flames. My boldness was starting to surprise me.

I moved my hand to Sherry's breast when she suddenly stopped me. "I want this as much as you do, Jarred," she began, "but we only have about 30 minutes left before I have to leave. I don't want to rush our first time together. And I don't want it to be on the floor of your studio!" I knew what she was saying was true. She continued gently, "It needs to be special like all other aspects of this relationship. A quickie wouldn't do."

But that's not what I heard. In typical, self-depreciating Jarred fashion, all I got from this was, 'I really don't want you...'

I just wilted, a jumble of mixed emotions. "I'm sorry, Sherry. I didn't mean to be so pushy. I hope you didn't get the wrong idea. We don't have to make love. I'll behave myself from now on."

"Didn't you hear anything I said?" Sherry told me. "All I'm saying is that our first time has to be special because this relationship is special. If we do this now...here...like this..." She paused to gather her thoughts. "I desire you as much as you do me, Jarred, just not like this."

"You're right," I admitted. "I'll wait until you say it's okay. But promise you'll let me know when the time is right."

Sherry was getting exasperated by now. "You're still not listening! Look at me." She took my face in her hands so that our eyes locked. "I said it needs to be special. Got that? I want this as much as you do. Got that?" she said sternly. Then Sherry kissed me hard on the mouth for emphasis.

"Got it. Loud and clear," I slurred, still dizzy from her kiss.

"Good! Finally!" she sighed. "It took some doing, but I think I finally reached you," she chuckled.

"Yes, you did. So, when are we getting together again?" I asked.

When Sherry laughed, it was like music. "You're just like all the others," she smirked. "Just can't wait to get into a woman's pants. You're all dogs."

My turn to torture her, I thought. "I'm like all the rest? Did you just accuse me of being a dog? I'm hurt. Truly, deeply hurt. I thought you knew me better than that." I couldn't resist giving Sherry a taste of her own medicine. I even pouted a little, raising my lower lip over my upper lip like a petulant three-year-old.

"Oh, so now you're sensitive all of a sudden?" she fired back.

"Hey, I'm a sensitive guy," I said, still pouting.

"I know you think you're kidding, but you're honestly more sensitive than you let on," Sherry told me.

Her remark took me by surprise. Carol, whom I've been with for several decades, never picked up on that. Maybe it was because I was pretty good at hiding it. I was raised to think that sensitivity wasn't a good quality in a man, so I didn't know how to respond to Sherry's revelation. I simply took her in my arms and held her tight for the few remaining moments we had left. We embraced in total silence, knowing, but not wanting, to acknowledge that our time together was almost over. I didn't want Sherry to leave, nor did she want to go but, this was the way it had to be, for now, at least. We had to be careful not to be stupid or lose sight of our other lives. I knew we would do everything we could not to hurt anyone else and be careful not raise suspicions.

"I have to leave now," Sherry said in a soft, sad tone.

"Just a few more minutes...please?" I asked. Her response was to stand there holding me for a little while longer.

"Okay...I really have to go," she told me. "I can't be late or else Bill will..."

"I know, I know. But letting you go is hard to do," I admitted. We kissed once more, then released each other.

Sherry slung her purse onto her shoulder. "I'll call you tomorrow when I get in, seeing as how I can't rely on you to call me. That is, if you're not off having fun at the beach or off in the woods, not giving me a second thought," she jabbed, grinning.

"Are you ever going to let that go?" I chided with a smile. "Talking about not listening, did you even hear a word I said?"

"Okay, we're even," she laughed as she headed for the door. I followed her there. Sherry stopped for a moment, turned and gave me another kiss, followed by a powerful bear hug. "I'll miss you tonight," she added, for good measure. "Think about me."

I shook my head, "Once you're out that door, I won't give you a second thought."

With statement, Sherry punched me again, laughed and left. As I watched her walk to her car, I began to hurt again, not from the punch, not from the exercise but from her absence and my longing. I sat back down at my computer, trying to get my head into my work but it was futile. I smiled, picked up the phone and dialed. "Hello," answered a voice that was both soft and sweet.

"I just wanted to say I missed you, Sherry," I said with a smile. "And I miss you too, you big, old, romantic lug," she chuckled. "I look forward to tomorrow when we can talk again," I told her. "'Till tomorrow," she echoed. "Have a good evening."

"That's impossible," I shot back.

"Here too," she admitted. We both laughed wistfully and ended the call.

I stayed at the studio later than usual that night because I simply wasn't in the mood to head home to the fighting and the general negativity that filled the house. My legs began to hurt again, bringing me back to reality, a new reality, almost. I realized now that the Sherry situation was exactly what I thought it was. It wasn't in my head—it was real. I vowed never to doubt what has blossomed between us. Seeing her again gave me a reason to live. Right then and there, I gave myself permission to be happy and to move forward on this journey without my usual resistance.

I also realized that by granting myself this permission to live a life of happiness, the resentment I'd been feeling toward Carol was slowly dissipating. I understood now that Carol wasn't the problem—it was me. In the past, I'd denied myself so much because I felt it was the right thing to do for my family, never realizing how much I was hurting myself. I had an obligation to my family, true, but doing things that were right for me was also important. It would have eliminated so much of this resentment and in turn, made things better for those around me. I was sure that I was now on the course to becoming a better person and Sherry was responsible for that.

Finishing my work, I stood up and tried to move my legs, which didn't seem to like the idea. I pulled myself up to stand slowly, bracing myself on my desk for a moment. Then I put one foot in front of the other and limped to my car. A sudden leg cramp forced me to stop worrying about where things would ultimately go with Sherry and simply enjoy where they had taken us now. I took this as a sign to stop my bullshit. Pain wasn't always bad, I remembered, because sometimes it lets you know that change was coming. This might be just what I needed in my life.

Pointing my car toward home, for once, I looked forward to being there. I now had so much to look forward to. Maybe Saturday, I'd take another field trip back to the stream where the woodies often go. *A good day afield, something else to look forward to.*

At ease with myself for the first time in a long time, I became content in my skin and with who I was. True, there were more questions than answers but at least I knew the answers were coming. Perhaps they were a little slow for someone as impatient as me, but I knew they were coming just the same. I would surrender my constant need for control and open myself up to receive what would be my destiny. Just like a flower opens itself to the sun or Sherry opens herself up to me. Something seemed to be steering us together. Whatever it was and whoever was in the driver's seat, I resigned to let them take me and drive me to where I needed to be. No questions asked.

I merged onto the parkway north, slipping into a comfortable place—a completely new feeling for me. I pushed the button on my CD player to hear Josh Groban's voice flow from the speakers, through my ears and into my heart. If only I could express myself as eloquently he did and with such ease. Overpowering me with both his song and his voice, as "Oceano" began, I was no longer there.

Chapter Twenty
Steam

Friday morning, I found myself staying at the gym a little longer than usual. The pain in my legs was still there, so I made sure to stretch and take a steam. Sitting in the sauna, I jumped up with a start when I realized that Sherry was going to call. I leapt out of the steam, hopped into the shower and rushed off to my locker and dressed as quickly as humanly possible so I could get to the studio in time for Sherry's call. The clock on the gym wall read 9:15 already. Damn!

Throwing on my shirt, I was pulling my pants out of the locker when I noticed I had a message on my cell. I fumbled with the phone, hit the "message call" button and Sherry's lovely voice filled the locker room. Everyone looks over, expecting to see a beautiful lady to match that captivating voice. I'd totally forgotten that the speaker was on. So much for keeping this thing under wraps.

I pressed the speaker off and Sherry continued, cooing in my ear, "I call the studio, no answer. I call the cell, no answer. I know you have caller ID and I think you're avoiding my call.

I hope you're not upset about yesterday. Anyway, you know who this is. Call me back as soon as you get this, if you know what's good for you...and me!"

For a brief moment my heart fell, thinking Sherry had the wrong idea. I hit the "redial" button lightning fast. Sherry's phone rang and rang. I knew that the office also had caller ID and that Valerie wouldn't be there at the time. *Was Sherry avoiding me now? Was this our first fight? Will we survive it if it is?* In the middle of my insecure reverie, Sherry picked up. "Had you going there, didn't I?" she laughed.

"Damn you. I owe you one," I said with a laugh and a sigh of relief.

"Don't tell me you're at the beach again, enjoying yourself without me, not even thinking about me. How quickly you men forget," she joked.

"Yeah, that's it exactly. I'm sitting on my beach blanket with two Playboy models, forgetting all about you and everyone else," I said in a serious voice.

There was a brief hesitation on the other end of the line, dead silence for what seemed like an hour but was only just a few seconds. "You are?" Sherry finally said with a slight tinge of insecurity. The vulnerability in her voice honestly took me back a step.

"You're kidding, right?" I began. "You don't really believe me, do you? Like centerfold girls would ever think of hooking up with an ugly guy like me. By 'ugly,' I mean ugly to them, which means no money."

With that, Sherry started to chuckle. "Wrong answer! The right answer would be that you only have eyes for me." She continued, "For a second, I figured: you're a photographer and maybe you had some special assignment I was unaware of."

"No assignment from *Playboy*," I reassured her. "Actually, I was in the steam room with a bunch of guys, who to be honest, aren't my type. When we did talk in there, it was eye contact only or we looked up at the ceiling."

But Sherry kept up the jealous act. "If I find out you were out there with another woman, you'd better watch your ass. No, scratch that. Not your ass, your balls," she laughed. "I have a hard enough time sharing you with Carol..."

I interrupted her. "You really don't get me, do you? I'm honestly not one of those guys who are out dogging after every skirt they see. I never cheated on Carol in 21 years of marriage. You're the exception... no, the surprise. I never expected this to happen. There seem to be other forces at work."

"Other forces? What do you mean by that?" Sherry inquired.

"You know, something else seems to be pulling us together," I attempted to explain. It would be difficult enough trying to fill Sherry in about my most recent visions, much less in front of a bunch of guys in a locker room who barely knew me. "We'll talk about this another time, okay?" I suggested.

"No, tell me now. I need to know. I won't let you off the phone," she warned me.

My heart dropped. "Trust me on this. Not now, not here," I told her.

"Yes, here and now!" she pushed. "I insist! Start talking, fella. If I mean that much to you, then you shouldn't care who hears it." Then she burst out laughing.

Busting my shoes again, Sherry was well aware there were too many people around for me to discuss this topic. "Okay, you got me....again. Now let it go," I said.

"I will. Just give me a hint what it's about," she asked sheepishly.

"Okay, here it is. You said you had a dream about a couple who lived years in the past. Right? Well, it's about that...about them," I conceded. Again, there was silence.

"Got it. I'd like to talk some more about that," she agreed. "It was the strangest thing. I rarely dream but this was vivid... different than a typical dream. I was thinking of talking about it with someone who analyzes dreams."

"We'll discuss it when the time is right," I assured her. "I have someone I'd like you to meet. Have I ever told you about my friend Peggy?" I asked.

"No, who is she?" she said, a touch of mistrust in her voice.

"A friend. A good friend. Peggy has a special understanding of these things. She won't judge us. She'll just educate us about your dream—and mine. Trust me."

"I do," she said, "trust you, I mean."

I struggled to button my shirt with one hand. "Can I call you back later when I get to the studio?"

"I have to head out with Valerie. We have a client meeting and we'll be gone all day. As a matter of fact, I'm expecting her any minute."

"Okay then...I'll talk to you on Monday, I guess. Do you guys have plans for the weekend?"

Sherry sighed. "Bill will be working all day Saturday and I have to work on my sculptures if I'm going to be ready for our show. How about you? What are you doing?"

"Carol has a baby shower tomorrow out in New Jersey so I figured I'd head up to the stream to try and get some of those wood ducks on film, seeing as how I was rudely interrupted last week," I joked.

"Well, I'll make sure not to interrupt you this week," she pouted.

"You can interrupt me anytime," I insisted.

"I'll take you at your word, so watch out," she laughed. "I have to run. Valerie's here. Later!"

"Bye for now. I miss you," I told her. "Me too," she said just before she hung up.

After I closed my phone, Lou, one of the guys I've gotten to know from the steam room, came over to me.

"Do you miss me too?" Lou wondered. "After all, you ran out of the steam room so fast, I thought it was something I said."

"Oh, Lou, I didn't think you cared," I laughed. "Don't flatter yourself," he poked back.

"Sorry, Lou. Bald isn't my type. You just don't do it for me on so many levels. Have a great weekend. See you Monday," I said, walking out the door.

"Same to you, Big Fella," Lou grumbled.

I looked back and smiled at him.

"Big Fella? Lou, you devil...you peeked! Shame on you. I'm not going into the sauna with you anymore."

With that, I eased slowly out of the locker room and hobbled downstairs.

Chapter Twenty-One
Almost Normal

I knew it was going to be a really long day because I had all kinds of stuff coming at me from every which way. It would be one of those crazy work days, not your standard lazy Friday. I hated days filled with lots of dry, boring computer stuff but at least Claudia, my part-time bookkeeper would be at the studio so I wouldn't be alone in my agony. I enjoyed talking to Claudia and she was a great person. She was also very levelheaded and always made a lot of sense, a real numbers person, I guess. Calm and easygoing, Claudia was the type who thought things out before she put her two cents in— and her two cents was always welcome. Sometimes I was afraid I might talk to her too much and keep her from getting her work done but Claudia didn't seem to mind.

Once Claudia and I had the computer work out of the way, I planned to head up to shoot the kitchen for Bill. We were supposed to do it the day before but he called at the last minute and changed the date, explaining, in no uncertain terms that his client wanted a "private meeting" with him before her husband came home on Friday. I didn't mind because I had no desire to see Sherry's wolfish boyfriend.

The work I had with Claudia took a little longer than we'd anticipated since we'd gabbed a little more than usual. Well, maybe it was me who did most of the talking because I was in no hurry to get to Bill's shoot. It was already 12:30 when Claudia said to me, "Don't you have to be somewhere at one?"

"Damn, I almost forgot," I blurted out. "I have to do an interior shoot for Bill, a contractor client."

Claudia made a face. "That jerk who lives with your friend Sherry, the sculptor?"

"Yeah, that jerk," I told her. "The shoot was originally scheduled for yesterday, but Bill claimed the client's husband got delayed on his trip, so he pushed it back a day."

"Is that really the reason? From what I saw of Bill—and granted I only met him once—I'll bet there was more to it than that," Claudia said with a knowing look.

"Is he that obvious?" I asked her.

"Well, yeah," she admitted snidely. "Anyone can tell what that guy's about. He's a real ladies' man. You know, the type who will take advantage of anything in a skirt."

"Sherry obviously doesn't think so," I replied.

"If she doesn't know, she's the only one. I couldn't stand being in the same room with that guy. He gave me the creeps," Claudia said, shuddering.

"Speaking of creeps, I better call him to let him know I'll be delayed."

Bill didn't seem upset that I had to push back the meeting from one to two. "Sure man, no problem," he said. "I'll let Diane and John know. I have to head off to another job but you don't need me to be here. You know what I like."

"Don't worry, you'll get great shots," I said, "but if there is anything special you need, just let Diane and John know. They can fill me in. I'll have the photos for you next week. Either I'll give you a call or if I have them in time for our Brush, Chisel & Lens meeting, I'll just give them to Sherry to bring home. That is, if she comes to the meeting next Thursday," I added coyly.

"Nah, nothing special, just your usual crap," Bill shot back. "That's a good idea, just give the shots to Sherry. It'll make things easier. I have so much other shit to do next week. And send me the bill when you're done."

"Don't worry about it," I informed him. "I have some contracting stuff I'll need done. We'll work it out."

After hanging up, I went from my pint-sized office into the studio adjoining it, packed up my equipment and was ready. "Claudia, I've got to run," I told her. "Do me a favor and leave any messages on my chair. Have a great weekend. Talk to you soon."

"You too," she said. "And have fun with that guy."

"Luckily, he's not going to be there," I replied. "But Diane's husband John will, and he's a would-be photographer. I don't know what's worse: Bill, the jerk, or some wanna-be who'll be on my back all afternoon."

"Look at the bright side. At least Bill isn't going to be there," she pointed out.

Heading up to the jobsite, I thought about the lighting and possible angles. I like to do interior shots with as much natural light as possible, enhancing it slightly with my own lights. I also like to use a wide-angle lens to give the setting some distortion and make it a little more interesting. When a prospective client calls in an interior designer, architect or contractor client of mine to look at their work, I want their books to pop and sparkle. After all, a kitchen is pretty much a kitchen so a portfolio has to stand out. You want potential clients to remember them—and you want your client to get the job. That's why they hire me—to make them look good.

I pulled into the driveway and parked by the side door that led directly to the kitchen. Diane greeted me soon after I rang the bell. Trailing Diane was her husband John, who looked to be an intense Type A guy. Expensive clothes, sharp haircut, mint running shoes. Even when he was just relaxing at home, you could tell that he was on the fast track. "Sorry about yesterday," Diane apologized. "I hope you didn't mind rescheduling but John wanted to be here for the shoot. Glad you could make it today."

"Actually today works better for me," I assured her. "Jarred, this is my husband John," Diane introduced.

"Hey, John, nice to meet you." I put down my equipment and shook his hand.

John had a good, firm grip. "I've heard so much about you from Bill. When he showed us his portfolio, I noticed it was different from all the others, which impressed me. That's when he told me about you," John explained. "You have a keen eye."

"Thank you very much," I said sincerely. "I take my art very seriously. Whenever I approach a project, I try to get the message across as vividly as possible without compromising the product." I explained to John my approach, my thought process and how I continue to examine the project at hand even as I shoot.

"I can see you have a unique way of capturing the selling point with your image without getting caught up with the 'artist' bullshit," John conceded. "So many other photographers try to play off on the clients or potential clients. Most photographers think they know better, which is so often a source of frustration for us at the agency."

I knew exactly what he was talking about. "John, I've been doing this for a bunch of years. When I approach a project, I consider several things. One is what my client went through to sell the concept and I'm not here to change it after all the time and money they spent developing it. But if I see something that may work better and I can enhance the image to make it unique, I'll show the art director. We discuss it and do what's necessary to ultimately make the client very happy. That's what this business is all about: creating images for a client as a team effort."

"A refreshing attitude," John admitted.

"And to keep myself sane, I have my art which is all me," I laughed.

"Well, I'm impressed with what I've seen of your work. If I can be of any help while you're shooting, just let me know. I'll be happy to assist you. Otherwise, I'll stay out of your way and watch, if that's okay with you," John said politely.

"Thanks, John, I appreciate that. Actually, I might need a hand." Why not? I figured. I liked him right off the bat. John turned out to be a very nice guy. I breathed a sigh of relief because it didn't seem like he'd turn out to be a real pain in the ass. I knew the type all too well— always asking questions, wanting you to give them blow-by-blow descriptions on every lens you touch, every shot you take. But from the moment I met him, I knew John was the sort who could just hang back and learn quietly.

I set up my equipment in the kitchen, first positioning my camera, then looking through the lens to find the correct angles. I moved out some items like the toaster, vases and small kitchen appliances. From a nearby shelf, I took a few books to fill in empty countertops. When I shoot, I like my kitchens to look homey and lived in, not a pristine, empty room where no one cooks or eats. Once everything was in place, I asked John to move things around while I surveyed everything through my lens. I usually did this myself but I wanted to let John feel he was a part of the process. Plus, it would save me a few steps and save time as well.

Once I had everything positioned the way I liked, I started to set up the lights. This involved taking meter readings and explaining to John what I was doing and why as I went along. I even let him take a look through the camera, which he really seemed to enjoy. Normally, this could be a real pain, but he was so easy going, I didn't mind. I let him know I was happy with the set-up and proceeded to expose my film.

Moving around the room, I shot three different angles, showing an important aspect in each. After about two hours of working, I told John I was finished and began to pack up. He and I chatted while I did. "I appreciate your letting me participate in the shoot," John said in a tone reminiscent of a kid who'd just gotten a treat.

"I couldn't have done it without you," I assured him. "You have a good eye too. And it's always better to have two pairs of eyes on projects as big as this."

John smiled. "I enjoyed working with you, Jarred. You're easygoing, you know what you're doing and you're open to suggestion. I like that. Would you be interested in working with me on some print ads? I think you'd be a pleasure to work with."

I was pleasantly shocked and fumbled in my pocket for a business card. "I'd love to. Feel free to call me any time."

John took a card from a burnished silver case and handed it to me. He called in Diane and we exchanged pleasant good-byes. It was almost four when I put my equipment back in the car. This took a lot longer than I'd thought, probably because of my chatting with John. But it proved to be well worth the extra time and effort because there was a strong chance he'd use me for DDBY work in the future.

I figured that since I was up at the northern end of Westchester, I'd head home instead of going all the way back to my studio. On the drive, I thought about the shoot. I had to admit, I was pleasantly surprised with Bill's client. He wasn't full of himself or obnoxious about his wealth. He worked hard for it and appreciated what the hard work got him, the luxuries it bought, what he was able to give Diane because of it.

I wondered if John would ever call me for work, though. This happened often— people told you they would hire you or wanted to buy your art and you never heard from them again. It happened so often that I'd become cynical about it. I usually didn't give it a second thought. If they contacted me, I was happy. If not, I wasn't disappointed. I'd give them a call occasionally to see if I could shake some branches and some low lying fruit might fall down but I never got my hopes up too high.

But if John did call, I wonder how I'd feel working with him, knowing his wife had fallen victim to that slug Bill. I stopped myself. I wasn't not going to put Bill down. He was what he was and who was I to judge? Besides, he could be totally bullshitting me about Diane. I never saw him do anything, so how did I know if he was for real or not? It could just be male bravado rearing its ugly head instead of a real conquest.

As I pulled into my driveway, I noticed that my lawn had somehow grown out of control. Even though I hated yard work, I thought maybe I should pay a little more attention to my house. After pulling the car into the garage, I dusted off the lawn mower and set out to cut my mess of a front lawn. Just what I needed—a mindless chore to help me relax. I realized that I'd been so busy during the day, I barely thought of Sherry, something that both worried me and pleased me. Maybe I was on the road to finally stop obsessing about our relationship and enjoy it.

The sun was setting, pleasantly cooling down the day. A nice change from the heat. My mind settled down as I guided the mower across the grass, slowly, methodically working my way back and forth in even lines. Before I knew it, the job was done. I'd be able to head out tomorrow without hearing Carol complain about the lawn this week. The worst part about her griping about the grass was that I knew she was right.

When I entered the house, Carol was laughing," I guess you're finally learning, after all these years, that doing the things that need to be done saves you grief."

"Hey, it only took me a couple of decades. Not too bad," I said.

"How many years, exactly?" she wondered.

"Hey, give me a break. I just finished cutting that stupid lawn. I'm tired and you know I can't think when I'm tired," I admitted, laughing. "Stop breaking my balls and get dinner ready," I joked as I dashed downstairs to avoid getting my head taken off.

Carol yelled down the stairs, "I hope you remembered that I have the shower out in Jersey tomorrow. You'll have to fend for yourself. Please don't starve to death by the time I get home."

"I'll do my best," I promised. "I plan on heading back out to the stream for the day, to try to get those wood duck shots. I'll be there from sun up till sundown because I have to get something—anything—on these damn elusive ducks."

"You and those stinking woods! Why don't you just move there?" she jibed.

"I just might! You know it's been my dream to shoot wildlife, live and work some remote place. Besides wolves and grizzlies would be a lot easier to deal with than you," I said, laughing.

"I hope one gets your ass tomorrow," Carol said sweetly. "That will teach you."

"Dear, what would you do without me?" I asked.

"I'll survive. Just make sure the life insurance is paid up," she shot back.

"I canceled it. I wanted it to be a sad day when I depart this life and I figured that would be the only way I'd get you to be sad. No big payoff for you," I kidded her.

But Carol wouldn't be duped. "I'll check the bills and make sure your policy's up to date. And it wouldn't be that sad a day. I'd just bury you in your precious woods. Or leave you there for your furry friends to eat you. That way I'd save on a funeral."

"Thanks. Now at least I know where I stand."

Carol and I shared a good laugh together. The kids were both out, so it was just us. We sat and enjoyed dinner, chatting about the day's events. I filled her in on John, leaving Bill and Diane out of the discussion. She wasn't a fan of Bill's to begin with and it was just easier not to go there. Carol talked about her day, her work and the kids. It was a pleasant night for a change. No fighting, no yelling. Almost normal.

# Chapter Twenty-Two
Into the Woods

The alarm went off at five a.m. I looked up with one eye half open, not believing I was getting up this early on a weekend. But if I were to stand any chance of getting my equipment set up before the woodies flew to the stream to feed, this was the price I had to pay. I hit the "off" button on the clock-radio quickly so Carol would sleep through it. She had a long drive ahead of her and I didn't want her doing the hundred-mile round trip all the way out to New Jersey and back being tired.

I dragged myself out of bed and headed for a quick shower, taking with me the clothing I'd laid out the night before. After shaving and brushing my teeth, I grabbed the lunch I'd packed the night before and was out the door. On the way to the stream, I stopped at a bagel place, grabbed a nosh a large coffee for my ride north. It was a short drive—about a half a cup of coffee and a bagel's worth, I figured sleepily.

I was the only car in the dirt parking area I noticed as I pulled in. Out of the back seat, I grabbed the knapsack I'd packed for the trip, stuffed with the essential camera equipment, lunch and a blanket to soften the hard ground I'd be sitting on all day. The sunlight was just beginning to peek over the horizon and filter through the trees as I entered the woods. I hoped I wasn't too late. I should have been in place by now so that when the ducks arrived (usually about 15 to 30 minutes after the sun rises), I'd be in position, camera ready, and I wouldn't startle them. It was only a short walk—maybe 200 yards or so. I'd be set up in five or ten minutes.

I hurried, walking double time with the backpack heavy on my shoulders. The songbirds were all beginning to awaken as I arrived at my spot on the stream. I unpacked the blanket and food, then set up my tripod in the mouth of a cave I had found on previous trips. The cave gave me a great vantage point to shoot from plus the wood ducks would most likely not notice me there. A slight breeze blew toward me, away from the stream where I hoped the woodies would land. The breeze coming from that direction would prevent them from picking up my scent, which might alarm them.

I was no sooner unpacked than I noticed silhouettes in the sky above. I recognized them immediately—they were woodies coming through the trees. I held my breath in anticipation as they flew past me overhead. At first, I was upset, but they suddenly changed their course, turned and headed right for the water just below me. I settled down and waited as a display of natural wonder unfolded before me.

The wood ducks landed gracefully and began to calm down, calling to one another in their soft, squeaky voices. I was just about to grab a few shots, when I noticed a few more come in. So much better than I could have ever imagined, I waited for the new arrivals to land and settle down. Slowly, I pointed my lens at one brightly-colored male sitting in the stillness of a pool, out of the rapids. The sun, which was behind me, hit his brilliant feathers, lighting him in all his glory. He was a beautiful creature with iridescent feathers and a bright orange "eye" glowing in the morning light. His reflection stared back at him from the clear, dark water. I hit the shutter again and again until I was satisfied that I had a shot. Finally, I had a shot!

I did my best to keep my composure as I pulled my zoom lens to a wider angle. Now the shot included a female swimming not too far from this gorgeous male. After I clicked off several more shots and began to bring my camera down, I noticed two more males sitting on a fallen tree trunk partially submerged in the water. Was it my imagination or did these two seem to be getting a little nervous? I quickly adjusted the meter for the light and clicked two more shots. Just in time, because in the next breath, both males jumped off the log and swam to shore. I watched silently as they waddled into the woods, scratching at the leaves for acorns.

The woodies still had no idea I was there. I sat back and observed them in complete anonymity. The joy I garnered from just watching them amazed me. Since I was always running from one thing to the other in my day-to-day life, just to be sitting there quiet and still, watching these little birds play out their own survival game, was incredible to me. Actually, the fact that I was *able* to sit so still surprised me. I'm a firm believe that it's the little things in life that matter and this was one of those moments. If I didn't see another woody that entire day, it would still be a perfect outing. I grabbed a few more shots, varying them as much as possible to keep it interesting.

Taking another sip of coffee, I noticed there was less than a half cup left. It was still good even though it had gotten cold—the sign of a really good cup of Joe. Sitting in the woods for over an hour, watching and snapping photographs, I noticed that the ducks were beginning to get even more jittery. Those that were in the woods quickly returned to the water, their chatter picking up. I sat up straight as I noticed them all swimming off in the same direction. I wonder what could have spooked them but don't give it a second thought, readying my camera, waiting expectantly to see what was driving them.

Suddenly a red fox flies out of the woods, chasing after the ducks. The birds explode into flight. I began snapping furiously, capturing the drama as it played out at the water's edge. Within seconds, it was over and my models were gone, while the fox just stood there looking perplexed, his front paws still in the water. I ripped off a few shots as he looked over in my direction and surveyed the woods around him. He scratched the ground, sniffed, looked up again then was off as quickly as he'd appeared.

What a day so far. This just couldn't get any better. If I didn't see another thing that day, it still would have been wonderful, memorable. I studied the shadows of the woods as they grew shorter, as the sun moved higher up into the sky. I laid back watching the clouds pass, listening to the birds and chipmunks chatter to one another as though I wasn't even there. Although this wasn't the shore, it was just as relaxing. Both had special qualities I enjoyed equally.

A blue jay screamed out, jolting me awake. I must have dozed off for some time without realizing it. One minute I was lying back looking at the clouds and the next thing I knew, a jay was jabbering at me from a tree limb. I checked the time—11:30. Lunchtime. I grabbed the ham sandwich from my pack, got up and walked around to stretch my legs, watching the birds and the chipmunks scurry about.

I scrambled up to the top of my cave, watching the stream flow down to meet the Hudson River. It spilled over rocks, around the fallen tree and bubbled as the water struck along the shore. The muted sound and the movement mesmerized me. I began to daydream, picturing the water's journey to the Hudson, a river that now had a new meaning to me. It was much more than just an impressive waterway that flowed more than 300 miles from Lake Tear of the Clouds in the Adirondacks and emptied into the Atlantic Ocean at New York Bay, forming New York Harbor. It was a river that breathed new life into my soul.

Other birds nearby began flying off, calling out to the others. I froze, thinking that maybe a deer was approaching. Another potentially great shot, this time of a deer drinking from the pristine stream, practically made me salivate. But as I listened to the sound, I soon realized that it wasn't a deer. No, it must be hikers. I felt a small sense of loss when I realized that I would no longer be alone. I stood up to see who had violated my peace, my space, and saw a slight figure coming toward me through the brush, slowly working its way closer and closer. Whoever it was, he was alone. As he hit the clearing, I could see that he was a she. And it wasn't just any woman—it was Sherry.

I stood up on top of the rocks so she would see me. "Hi!" I yelled and waved.

Sherry's face lit up with a sheepish smile as she responded with a slight wave. I climbed down from my perch and as I reached the ground, Sherry approached. "Just when I thought this day couldn't get any better," I beamed. "To what do I owe the honor of your company?" I questioned her in a stodgy way.

Then I ceremoniously reached out to shake her hand. Sherry looked at it as though it were a live eel. "You're kidding right?" she said. Then she proceeded to slap away my hand. I looked down at my hand, then up at her, with mock sadness and shock. I took a determined step toward her, gazing into her soulful, dark eyes. She smiled as I grabbed her around the waist, pulled her close and kissed her hard on the mouth. Sherry sighed deeply and seemed to melt in my embrace. I lost myself in her arms, her velvet lips on mine, her warm breath breathing new life into me. We broke apart, stared into each other's eyes in complete silence and smiled. I held Sherry tightly and whispered, "You have made my day. Hell, you've made my weekend....What I mean to say is, you've made my life."

After a beat, I added, "So, I thought you were staying home this weekend to get some work done."

"I was," Sherry admitted, "but I couldn't get past you. Every time I tried to concentrate on my project, I looked into the clay and saw your face. Knowing you were here alone distracted me to a fault. The harder I tried to get into the sculpture, the less coordinated I became. It was like something had tied my hands. And whenever I was able to push you to the back of my mind, all of a sudden, without warning, I visualized you rushing toward me. I saw us so vividly, remembering the two of us together on Thursday night, and that was it. I had to see if I could find you," she confessed.

"Thursday. What happened on Thursday?" I inquired with a wicked smile.

"What happened Thursday?!" she shouted, pretending to be hurt.

"Help me out here," I said. "I forget,"

"I'll just leave you to your duckies," Sherry told me, trying to break away and leave. I pulled her into me.

"Wait, wait!" I laughed.

"Wait for what? If you can't even remember..." she struggled slightly.

"Oh, you mean...last Thursday. I'm so high just being here with you, I'm not thinking right. Can you forgive me?" I begged.

"No, you forgot me. I guess I don't mean as much to you as I thought." "You do! Please give me a chance to make it up to you," I pleaded, grinning.

"What do you have in mind? Before you answer, I have to warn you, it better be good," Sherry smiled.

"Why don't you just come up to my room so we can talk about it?" I said as I took her by the hand and pulled her gently up to my new found home in the woods.

"Where do you think you're taking me?" she pressed, still breaking my chops. "Just shut up and come with me," I told her. Trust me, you will not be disappointed." *I hope*, I said under my breath.

Once we reached the mouth of the cave, I held Sherry close and kissed her hard and long. I felt this tough woman coming apart in my arms. My excitement mounted and my desire to make love to her, to be one with her, was overtaking me. But this time, I didn't feel embarrassed or try to hide my arousal. Instead, I pressed my hips into her and relished her response as she pushed her hips forward to meet mine. Sherry wrapped one leg around me as I moved my mouth from her lips to her neck, just behind her ear. She writhed her head from side to side as I kissed her gently, trailing down her neck to her exposed chest. Sherry threw her head back, losing herself, moving more firmly against me. I kissed a path back up her neck to her full lips and we kissed like a couple of kids experiencing this crazy, stupid thing called love for the first time.

I stopped, gazing into her eyes and softly said, "Come with me." And she did.

Chapter Twenty-Three
The Man of Her Choosing

I took Sherry's hand and led her back to my little camp. The blanket, the knapsack, my equipment, were just as I'd left them. She looked me and smiled, her eyes sparkling with love and desire. Sherry's beauty was a subtle beauty, a quiet radiance that emanated from deep within her. I was truly in awe of this and of her. How could anyone so lovely in so many ways be attracted to someone like me? I was confused, happy and elated to be the man of her choosing. She smiled at me so warmly and with so much emotion that it almost took my breath away.

Sherry seemed to look *through* my eyes and into my heart, my soul. Her feelings for me were so intense, I could almost taste it. I held her hands tightly in mine as we stood in silence, gazing at each other. I leaned in, kissing her gently, sweetly. She squeezed my hands so hard in return that I thought my fingers might break.

I kissed her long, elegant neck. "You make my knees weak," she whispered, pulling me down to the blanket with her. On the cushion of the earth, our lips met again tenderly. Sherry lay back, pulling me half on top of her. My leg slid between hers and she opened her thighs to meet it. Sherry pressed herself into my knee, breathless.

I don't think I'd ever been so aroused. I knew that this time, sex would be different. It felt as though I were about to make love for the first time. I was nervous and my body ached. But I was lost in Sherry, lost in her soul when we kissed.

Slowly, I slid my hand down to Sherry's breasts. Full, warm, firm, they filled my hands as I cupped them, teased them, pleasured them. She moaned softly as I explored the curves of her body. I took one perfect, pink nipple in my mouth—it was already erect with anticipation, waiting for me—then the other. Sherry arched her body toward me. "More," she breathed. "More."

I moved my hand down to Sherry's taut belly and tried to unbutton her jeans but fumbled like a teenager. "Wait," she said, her hand covering mine. *Shit. That's it. I did something wrong. I'm moving too fast, I...* But instead of stopping me, Sherry smiled and unfastened her jeans herself, sliding them off her body in one swift motion. She wasn't wearing any panties.

I trailed my hand down her tummy, past her mound to her thighs. Sherry gasped as my fingers briefly grazed her mounds then darted away. I softly massaged her inner thighs, which were as creamy as satin. I could feel the heat of her sex pressing against my arm. I moved my hand up her thigh as I kissed her more deeply. Sherry raised her hips to meet my hand in expectation, but again, I bypassed her tender parts and slowly traced my fingers down her other thigh. Apparently this was too much for her because she pulled me on top of her and pressed her pelvis into me. I pulled back slightly.

Aroused and excited, I also became apprehensive. *Could I satisfy her? Would this be all she anticipated?* My insecurities were pushed aside as Sherry began to unbutton my pants and ease down my zipper. When I stopped her, she looked up at me pleadingly, biting her lower lip. She watched patiently as I removed my pants. I hoped she wouldn't touch me because that might put me over the edge. I needed to calm myself down because I wanted to give her as much joy as I possibly could.

We'd both waited so long for this and I didn't want to disappoint her.

Lying side by side, skin to skin, with each heartbeat, I throbbed against Sherry's thigh. I almost lost it when I slipped my fingers to discover her soft wetness, slowly massaging her. Sherry let out a small cry and buried her face in my neck, rising up to meet my hand. "Slow down," I whispered. "I want you to enjoy this...please."

Sherry gazed into my eyes, smiling, her lips slightly parted. As I slid one finger gently into her body, she gasped, gripping me. Palm pressed against her mound, I immediately was engulfed in warmth. We kissed with such deep passion, with so much elation, that I could barely breathe. I moved my mouth to her breast, all the while pleasuring her with my hand.

Sliding her fingers down my stomach, Sherry gently grasped my hot, hard shaft and squeezed. This was such a delight, I was afraid my heart might jump out of my chest. Slowly, I moved down, kissing her belly, caressing her breasts. Again, Sherry raised her hips in anticipation of my mouth replacing my fingers. But I slipped past Sherry's moistness to her creamy thighs, kissing the entire length to her knee. Slowly I moved back up, until my head was just above my hand, then I trailed my tongue down her other thigh. Sherry trembled beneath me in this sweet torture. She tried to move her body to meet my mouth, but I didn't let her, and she whimpered in response.

I ignored Sherry's silent complaints, kissing her thighs. Just the thought of giving her pleasure brought me such joy and delight. I moved up between her thighs, replacing my hand with kisses as she cried out, climaxing against my face, trembling, spasming and sobbing in an orgasm that was both intense and sweet. I held her tightly as she cried in my arms, trying to recover. All the while, we looked into each other's eyes, kissing passionately, deeply. I tasted the salt of her tears then went back to her mouth.

When Sherry was ready, she rolled on top of me and took me inside her body. I was engulfed in a sea of warm wetness, lost in her, joined to her. Sherry moved like a soft wind above me. As she kissed me, hard and deep and serious, it was as though our hearts became one, beating in unison. Our worlds spun wildly together as Sherry rocked her hips, slowly at first, then building to a crescendo. I exploded into her as I felt her tight, damp furrow, throbbing around my shaft. She fell onto my chest, heaving.

For a few moments, we said nothing, did nothing, just lay in each other's embrace, reveling in the sensations as our bodies settled down and our breathing returned to normal. My world was spinning, as I imagined hers was, but we didn't speak. There was no need to. We lay there, holding each other silently, just simply *being*.

My emotions flowed like waves to the shore, endless, relentless, one falling onto the next, then disappearing. My heart was light, almost as though it were floating freely within my body. I felt my soul joining Sherry's with the power of lightning striking an oak. The electricity that flowed between us shook me to the core. I was lost, so lost.

Suddenly I was overwhelmed with the knowledge that I had been with Sherry before, that we had made love before, just like this. I'd had unspoken inklings of this previously but now I was certain. When Sherry and I made love, I felt I had been rejoined with someone from a past life, someone I had lain with before, loved before. It was long ago, the memories little more than a ghost to me now, yet it was crystal clear. She was Jessica and I was Jeremiah, I was certain of that now.

Sherry lay lightly on top of me, her head on my shoulder. She kissed my neck gently, then spoke, breaking through my reverie. "Wow," she said, with a subtle, telling groan. I let out a nervous chuckle. "Laughing at me, are you? What's that about?"

"Nothing. Trust me, it's nothing," I assured her.

"Oh no, you don't! You're not getting off that easy," Sherry grinned. "Tell me what you're thinking." But still, I was silent. "I can stay here all day. I won't let you up unless you start talking," she added for emphasis. "I'm serious."

"I don't know...It's just that I never expected this today, or ever, for that matter. I'm filled with happiness but I'm also conflicted at the same time," I responded shyly.

Sherry said nothing. She just smiled at me knowingly as I pulled her into me to comfort and reassure her. "What do we do now?" Sherry asked. She shifted her body and slid onto the blanket beside me, legs still intertwined with mine. We both knew it wasn't going to be easy — we were committed to our other lives, yet committed to each other on a much different level, and a level that neither of us completely understood.

I pulled Sherry a little closer, my arm around her waist. "I think we have to be true to each other, as well as to the others we're committed to."

She looked at me, confused. "How can we manage that?"

I shrugged. "I know it sounds complicated but nobody involved here has asked for this to happen. Not even you or me. It just happened. For some crazy reason, the two of us have been on a collision course from the first day we met."

Sherry started to laugh but when she saw how serious I was, she stopped. "No...I honestly think this started *before* you and I first met," I continued. "I know it sounds insane but I really believe that unexplainable outside events in our lives pushed us toward this day. Think about it...you leave the Cape and end up here with Bill. Then you take a job in a small agency that I happened to work with. Strange coincidence. And had you ended up with one of those mega-agencies in Manhattan, we would have never met," I explained. "Everybody wants to work in a place like that."

"Everybody but me," she conceded.

"And me," I added. "Did you ever think what brought you here?"

Sherry thought for a moment. "It was...it was just a feeling. I could have easily commuted to the City. But something made me want to stay here."

"See what I mean?" I told her. I pulled the blanket around our shoulders and held her closer. "And the dreams. How do you explain the dreams?"

It was the oddest thing— my revelation about Sherry's and my connection simply came to me as I spoke to her. In fact, it practically spilled uncontrollably out of my mouth. I had never given our unusual bond much thought before then. But I spoke almost as if someone were whispering into my ear. The words I uttered seemed not to be of my doing; I was just a messenger. Now, I usually didn't believe in this sort of thing but how else could I explain how these words just seemed to be pouring from my mouth?

"I'm confused," Sherry admitted.

"I am too," I told her.

We both were silent for a few moments. "What will we do?" she worried. How will we cope or continue to be with each other. Or worse, how will we not be with each other?" There were no answers, just looming questions. "Hold me tight," Sherry sighed. "I need you to hold me, to reassure me that this is okay and that it's not a mistake."

I pulled Sherry against me, skin to skin. I didn't answer her. What could I possibly say? I was as confused as she was. I had never cheated on Carol before and this relationship with Sherry violated everything I'd ever believed in about marriage and fidelity, yet it didn't feel wrong. In a sense, it was beyond right and wrong.

And the sex...the sex was so much more powerful than anything I'd ever experienced before. It was as though it transcended the physical and existed in a whole new spiritual realm. It was so meaningful, so deep, like praying, but without words. And now that we'd crossed over the line where the physical meets the divine, everything changed. Where this spiritual journey would lead was anyone's guess.

Sherry looked at me with unspoken questions on her lips. "How about we just take a step back from all of this to clear our heads?" I suggested. "Let's enjoy the rest of this day. It belongs to us. Right now, there's no one else is in our world except us. Why don't we take a walk? It may help us look at this from another angle."

Sherry nodded as we both stood and dressed wordlessly. She took my hand and stood there, looking like a little lost girl for a moment. "Things will work out," I reassured her. "Trust me." I held her close and kissed the top of her head. Her hair smelled like lavender.

"We're both intelligent people," I continued. "As we grow to understand this, we'll work everything out. Just take comfort in the fact that everything happens for a reason and that things always have a purpose."

Sherry nodded against my chest. "I know but I don't want to let you go."

I agreed. "Me neither but eventually, we'll have to. Eventually, we both have to go home." Sherry zipped up her jeans and laced up her hiking boots. "Come on, let's see if we can find something else to photograph. A herd of bongo, maybe?" I teased.

"Are bongo dangerous?" she inquired.

"No, especially not here in Fahnestock State Park," I said.

"Not even in Kenya," she smiled. "I know you're trying to make me feel better, Jarred. Thanks." Sherry grabbed my hand, looking sad and serious. "Where are we headed?" she asked.

"We'll go up that hill first and then we'll take it from there."

"You know what I mean," she nudged me.

"I'm serious," I told her. "Let's go." Maybe that was the answer—to step back and survey the big picture from somewhere on high.

I climbed off our rock and helped Sherry down. She stumbled slightly, falling into my arms. When I caught her, our eyes met for the first time since getting up to dress. She smiled nervously. Maybe she was sensing my confusion. I was sure she knew what was going on in my head because she was incredibly intuitive about our relationship. But rather than talk about it then, I knew we both needed time to process what had happened.

Sherry and I slowly made our way up the path which led to the peak of a small mountain. About halfway up, we heard a ruckus above us. We looked up to see a male and female cardinal chasing each other before landing on a branch together. Again, this was a behavior I'd never seen in cardinals past mating season. They looked down from their perch and began to sing, almost like they were giving us a private performance.

"I wonder if those are the same two birds that led me to you the first time we met here," Sherry asked, breaking the silence.

"They could be," I admitted. "I've never seen a male and female interact like these two have."

Sherry smiled thoughtfully. "I know the feeling."

"Me, too." I told her. "Are you okay?"

Sherry nodded and reassured me that everything was fine. I couldn't help but wonder if she were being truthful or just humoring me. Sherry took my hand. "Are you sure you're okay?" Sherry inquired nervously.

"Yeah," I said. "Yeah, I am."

"I hope so," Sherry told me, "because you're being a little strange. Maybe we shouldn't have made love—if it bothers you. I hope you're not upset I came here today. I can feel something's up by the way you're acting. You're scaring me a little."

I stopped walking, took her hand and turned her to face me.

"Don't pay me any mind. I'm fine," I said. "I really hope...I hope it was okay for you. If I wasn't up to your standards, please tell me, I..."

Sherry looked at me, shocked. "You really have to stop being so ridiculous. We have so many other things to discuss and this simply isn't one of them."

My mind began racing about how many other things I could have done wrong but once again, Sherry rescued me from myself and brought me back down to earth. "What happened between us...I never experienced anything like it. In a way, it frightened me...Please, just hold me tight and don't let go. Please, don't leave me."

I did as she asked. It was all I could do. "I'll never leave you," I promised. "Ever. I'll always be with you in spirit, even when I'm not by your side."

I felt Sherry smiling into my chest as I held her even closer.

 # Chapter Twenty-Four
Top Ten Day

Sherry and I walked for what seemed like hours in complete silence. I was deep in thought, as usual, and Sherry seemed to be as well. But it was odd, even though no words passed between us, I felt as though she and I were continuing to connect, and that our spirits grew closer with each step. We were in tune with each other, even in our silent thoughts.

The day was perfect weather-wise, a "Top Ten Day." Cool, with a soft, steady breeze, the sun was bright and high with some billowing white clouds set in the deep blue canvas of the sky. Just being there was so relaxing. It was the type of day you wished would last forever, the type of day that felt like nothing could go wrong, ever.

As we walked, Sherry gently brushed up against me, very subtly. When I reached out and took her hand, she smiled softly and gave me a squeeze. I held her hand tighter, so comfortable there with her, comfortable in my own skin beside her. I knew Sherry felt it too, felt right, felt like she belonged, felt like we belonged together. She slid her arm through mine as we continued our hike.

After a few more steps, I stopped, turned to her and took her into my arms. Quietly, we stood in a warm embrace, slowly swaying, dancing without music. I felt like this was something right out of a Hollywood romance, like it was scripted. You know, cue the breeze, the perfect blue sky. Cue the star-crossed lovers who might, just might, have a happy ending. I knew it sounded like some sort of childhood infatuation or midlife crisis yet I didn't care. I would enjoy this for as long as I possibly could. I'd denied myself for too long and now gave myself permission to do something for me. I was accepting this, embracing this, and it felt incredible.

As Sherry and I held each other, I looked at the woods around us. We were completely alone. This was our place, our world, and no one else's. I smiled and pulled Sherry even closer as she brought her arms up to my shoulders. I rubbed her back gently and she gazed at me and smiled back. Her head on my chest felt so right. I took her chin between my fingers and lifted it. Warmly, softly I kissed her. And felt nothing but joy. "It looks like I'm in this for the long run," I told Sherry softly.

Not saying a word, she just looked up, smiled again, then lay her head back down on my chest, snuggling into me. We continued to stand like this for several moments, just enjoying our strong embrace. Sherry looked up at me again, "Are you sure?"

"Believe me, I'm sure," I told her. "I'm more sure of this than anything in my whole life."

We continued to hike the trail, enjoying each other's presence, stopping briefly every so often to embrace and kiss, building upon our new-found love. We walked aimlessly about from trail to trail, without a care in the world. For one brief day, I was suspending all thought and worry—concern about the struggles of the photography business, my family, my loveless marriage, the bills, the house. My brain finally had taken a sabbatical from thought as it simply drank in all this short, relaxing day with Sherry had to offer. We are in no hurry to go anywhere—like old times as a kid, when everyone would take things as they came, not running from one point to the next—just enjoying what destiny had bestowed upon us.

At one point, Sherry and I stopped, sat upon a rock and watched a couple of blue jays chasing each other around the pines. "So, what do you have planned for the rest of the weekend?" Sherry asked.

I looked at her, smiled, and put my fingers upon her lips to quiet her thoughts. "Let's just take this day for what it is and not even think about tomorrow...or even tonight. I'm here with you. You're here with me. This is our life now, this moment, and I would like to enjoy this time...enjoy you."

She smiled in return, then kissed my fingers and the palm of my hand. "I'm shocked," she admitted. "Mr. Deep Thinker isn't spinning his brain about the future or past. How did this happen?"

"You happened. We happened. God has given us a perfect day to enjoy and fate has given us each other."

Sherry blushed. "Your words are...amazing. Comforting and reassuring. You make me feel so good about myself, Jarred. You lift my spirits and me. When I'm with you, I feel as though I've been removed from this world and placed gently into another dimension. I enjoy you so much. I can't find the words to do justice to the way I feel."

"Don't look for words," I told her. "Words can't come close to your actions or the energy, the vibrations, I get from you. When you're around, there is this electricity in the air. It seems to flow from you into me. I've never experienced anything like it."

"So, you feel it too," Sherry admitted. But then, quick as a flash, her face changed, clouding with worry. "But what if this isn't real? What if this is just an infatuation? A middle age crisis? Our hormones running wild?"

I looked into Sherry's eyes, so deep and brown and serious. "Now who's over- thinking this? Why don't we take it one step at a time? Let's make a pact. We take this for what it's worth. Let things happen as they may and enjoy every minute of it."

Sherry nodded. I was on a roll. There was no stopping me, so I just went with it, "Look, there are too many other things out there for us to worry about. If this isn't what it seems to be, then what have we lost? Nothing. What have we gained? Everything. We have gained something that we will remember for the rest of our lives. Thinking back about this when we're old and gray, well, it will bring us peace until the day we leave this beautiful earth. Can you ask for anything more? We have been given a gift, Sherry. Let's accept it and commit to it. You're burned into my memory and our relationship is burned into my memory for all eternity."

Sherry chuckled and gave me a tiny round of applause. "I like that. You're so right. I just worry that this will end and I don't want it to ever end, Jarred."

"Okay, the answer is simple, then," I told her. "Let's not let it end. Let's always remember this day when we run into troubled times."

Sherry looked worried. "Troubled times? You mean with our relationship?

I gave a reluctant nod. "Like it or not, it's bound to happen. You've got to admit, this thing is pretty complicated. But when we do run into trouble, we have to promise to work with each other, to get past it and back to us."

Sherry looked at me with eyes weighed down with sadness. "I hate to admit it but I know what you mean. Even though you do sound pretty negative."

"I'm not being negative, just realistic," I told her. "I just want us to be prepared and promise each other we will work through things, no matter what. The way we feel about each other, with so much emotion, so much love...it's bound to happen."

Sherry looked at me with shock and surprise. I knew instantly that I'd screwed up, and she caught it. I stood there holding my breath, waiting for the explosion. *"Love?"* she said with a gasp.

I shook my head. "I'm sorry. I don't know where that came from. It just slipped out. Please, I know it's too early to know whether or not this is love."

I was almost in a panic but then Sherry smiled, as though she found the look of panic upon my face humorous. "Sorry?"

Another one-word sentence...That couldn't be good.

"And just what the hell are you so sorry about?" she began.

Relief momentarily washed over me. "I didn't mean to scare you. It just slipped out. I misspoke."

"Oh, so now you 'misspoke,' how nice," Sherry snapped, then burst into laughter. "You got me again," I conceded.

"Relax, will you? Stop acting so scared."

I let out a nervous laugh. "Well, I am kind of scared, aren't you?"

"Scared? Me? Not in the slightest," Sherry said surely. "Your words surrounded me like a warm, settling breeze. Words I had only dared to think but was afraid to say out loud. I'm glad you feel the same way I do."

We kissed then Sherry continued, "But please, take your own advice for once, will you? Just let this happen and stop worrying."

"I'm letting it happen...it's happening," I told her. "And how could I ever forget how I feel about you? I have you in my heart no matter what happens."

I pushed a stray hair out of Sherry's face. "One last thing on the subject," she began. "Have a little more faith in me. My heart is yours."

"Okay, you've made your point," I told her. "I will no longer question this relationship as long as you make me one more promise, as I will promise you...."

Sherry cut me off. "Oh, my God! What is it now?" she cried out in mock exasperation.

I continued, undaunted, "Promise me that if, at any time, your feelings for me change or you feel like you can no longer stay with whatever this relationship brings, that you will be honest and tell me. I promise you the same. It's only fair."

Sherry nodded seriously. "I promise. Now, shut up, and come with me," she demanded as she took my hand, pulling me back down the path we'd just come from.

"Where are you taking me?" I asked. "And what's the hurry?"

"We're going back to our perch, to our cave," Sherry insisted.

"Do you know how to get back?" I asked, breaking her chops a bit.

"I can always ask the cardinals for directions," she quipped. "Now, I know if you got us lost, being a man you'd never ask directions, even from birds, and we would be doomed to wander endlessly in the woods," Sherry shot back as she pulled me along.

"Why are we in such a hurry?" I asked. What are we going to do there?"

"Let me put it this way," Sherry told me, licking her lips. "We will not be photographing your duckies," she laughed.

 # Chapter Twenty-Five
Joy Eternal

After a long, quick walk, Sherry and I reached our destination. She turned to me and took my hands. Leaning into me, our lips met and we shared a long, passionate kiss. When Sherry suddenly pulled back and laid down upon the blanket, I just stood there watching her, still in disbelief at the recent turn of events. "Are you joining me or are you just going to stand there with that stupid look on your face?" she wondered.

I didn't need to be told twice. On the blanket beside her, I took Sherry into my arms as our mouths found each other. I didn't know how much more of this heat, this excitement, I could take. We stripped off our clothes, laughing, panting. Naked, I felt the heat from her body rise up and envelope me. I struggled to control my excitement as our bodies touched, her silky flesh against mine. Like two kids discovering the wonders of a new toy, we enjoyed each other's bodies in every way possible. This time, it was more relaxed, but every bit as loving. We savored each other hungrily, lustily, and soon became one again, our bodies melting together on that hot afternoon.

Afterwards, Sherry and I laid there, quietly embracing, our bodies limp with joy and exhaustion. We watched the color of the sky deepen and the clouds pass overhead, not saying a word, simply enjoying the warmth of each other's bodies. I wasn't sure how much time has passed, but the joy I felt was eternal.

After a time, Sherry rolled over, chin on my chest. "You don't play poker, do you?" she asked out of the blue.

"I don't like to gamble," I told her. If I'm laying down money, I want something in return. I think..."

Sherry cut me off, grinning. "Spare me the lecture. I only ask because you can't hide anything. Your face is so easy to read. It's a good thing you don't gamble."

I stroked her hair as I talked. "Yeah, I found that out today, didn't I? I just can't get anything past you," I admitted. "We waited a long time for this. I hope you're not disappointed."

Sherry looked at me, puzzled. "Disappointed? How could I possibly be disappointed?" I shrugged in response. "No, today couldn't have been any better. I hope you feel the same way I do. I hope I wasn't too forward coming here or that you didn't feel pressured in any way."

"This seems to be turning into a 'let's be polite session'," I joked.

Sherry laughed at herself. "Let's not go there. But let's also not take each other for granted. Ever. We'll just accept each other's shortcomings..."

"Shortcomings?!" I blurted out.

"I wasn't referring to the size of your...no, that's just fine, more than fine," Sherry blushed. "But we're both pretty insecure. Let's just enjoy this...please?" We embraced, lying still and quiet, listening to each other's hearts beating, blurring together.

The shadows began to grow longer and the sky began to morph into a bluish pink, then yellow and eventually orange. "The day is ending," I said sadly.

"I can see that. Why are days like this so short?"

We both sat up and slowly began getting dressed. "I don't know," I admitted. "But the longest days are the days before I know I'm going to see you. That day is at least a week long."

Sherry smiled at that, pulling her shirt over her head. Then I noticed shadows moving above the treetops— wood ducks coming back to feed. "Don't move," I whispered to Sherry. "Lie still."

"That sounds exciting," she whispered back in a sexy voice.

I fumbled for my camera and began shooting the flock's return. I managed to get a few just as they were about to hit the water. "What a way to end the day," I grinned.

Sherry sat up and pulled on her hiking boots. "You can say that again."

We quietly packed up our things and slowly descended from our perch, careful not to disturb our new visitors. At the trail's edge, I slipped on my knapsack and took Sherry by the hand as we slowly headed to our cars. I couldn't help but feel a little melancholy that such a wonderful day was ending. "I'm so glad I came here," Sherry admitted softly. "This has been one of the best days of my life."

"One? Not the?" I shot back. "You know what I mean," she said quickly. "Yeah, I do," I told her.

At the parking area, I dropped my pack into my truck, then turned to face Sherry. We looked at each other in silence, not knowing what to say after all we'd experienced. We hugged briefly for what I knew would be the last time that day. Then I slipped my hand around her shoulders and walked her to her car, then watched her as she got in. I leaned into the window and kissed her. "What are you going to tell Bill when he sees that you didn't get anything done on your sculpture today?"

"You're kidding, right?" Sherry said. "I don't think he's ever asked me about my art, my day or my life. He just comes home, bagged up, drops into his recliner and says 'Feed me!'"

"Unreal," I told her. "Well, I just wanted to make sure you covered yourself, so you don't get caught off guard."

"I'll tell you what...if he asks, I won't lie to him." My stomach dropped into my hiking boots. "I'm serious," Sherry continued. "I'll tell him I went for a hike in the woods—that's not a lie. But, trust me, he never asks, so why would he start today? Now, give me a kiss and let me get going."

We both laughed as we kissed, our teeth softly clanking as our mouths met. I closed Sherry's car door and watched her pull onto the road and drive off. *This is going to be tough on the old heartstrings,* I thought, leaning against my car to watch the sun begin its descent beyond the mountain crests. Somehow, I knew that for me, this was more than just the end of the day. It was the end of my safe, little life as I knew it. Nothing would ever be the same.

Behind the wheel, I had a tough time, turning the key to start my journey home. Not just home but the journey that destiny had served up for me in the form of Sherry. I turned the key and the truck jumped to life.

I arrived to an empty house. *It's better that way,* I told myself. I realized that I was famished, so I grilled myself a burger and threw together a quick salad. I ate my solitary dinner on my deck overlooking the woods, listening to the night. Chewing thoughtfully, I reflected on the events of the day as though they were scenes from a movie I'd just watched. Then I poured myself a scotch, sitting a little longer. My muscles ached pleasantly from the hikes, the rock-climbing and from Sherry. After a hot shower I headed to the den, turned on the TV and laid down on the couch.

The next thing I knew, Carol was waking me. "How did you do today?" she asked. "Did you get any good shots of the ducks?"

"Yeah, I got some great stuff today," I admitted. "I accomplished a lot more than thought I would. How was the shower?"

She made a face. "It was okay—typical baby stuff. Nothing new or exciting. What's on?"

"I don't know. The woods always knock me out. I fell asleep."

"Let's head up to bed then," Carol suggested. "I'm beat too."

As we lay in bed, Carol reached over to cuddle for the first time in a very long time. This time, I didn't resent it like I usually did. I suppose bickering constantly about minor nonsense took its toll romantically. I couldn't remember exactly when it happened, but our marriage had become platonic. We were a living, breathing example of that old joke: "One night you realize you're sleeping with a relative."

But I had some comfort in the thought that Carol and I weren't alone. So many couples succumbed to this sad, boring existence of just plodding along. But being with Sherry earlier that day, changed everything for me. The realization that my unconscious resentment of Carol had subsided and that I was finally accepting what our relationship had become, was more than I could have hoped for. I curled my body around my wife and drifted off to sleep.

Later, Sherry told me about the very similar scene she came home to after our foray into the woods. When she pulled into her driveway, Sherry noticed that Bill's car—and Bill—were among the missing. The house was dark except for the light she left on in her studio. Feeling relaxed and happy, she noticed the message light on the telephone answering machine blinking "1." She instinctively knew what the message would be because she heard the same one almost every night.

Without much of a choice, Sherry pushed the button to hear: "Hey, Babe, it's me. I'm at O'Donahue's with the guys, playing pool. Be home about ten." Sherry shook her head and thought, *You mean more like twelve or one.* But she smiled this time. This time, she didn't resent the message but was happy to hear it. At least Bill didn't leave her hanging and she knew he was safe. Drunk, but safe.

Content within herself, Sherry padded into the kitchen, fixed herself a salad and went into her studio. There she studied her sketches while munching on her salad. Putting down the bowl, she picked up her tools and began to work the clay, molding it slowly into her vision. As she worked, she began to smile, realizing that for the first time in a long time, she was able to focus on her work and not be distracted by the underlying anger she felt toward Bill.

Sherry worked for hours undisturbed, without stopping, the smile never leaving her face. Not once did she look up at the clock to see the time. (She usually made sure she was in bed and asleep before Bill stumbled in drunk, high or both, depending which friends he hung out with.) *My God,* she thought, *This guy is 50. Is he ever going to grow up? Or will he always be looking*

to get high? Maybe it's time for me to do some soul searching.
Why do I need to be captive to this man?

When Sherry tired after working for hours, her thoughts
turned to me and our day. Her heart was lifted by the knowledge
that she'd finally found what she'd been searching for all these
years. She confessed to me that she felt so happy she almost
cried for joy.

Sherry covered her clay so it wouldn't dry out, washed off her
tools and scrubbed her hands. She glanced over at the clock and
noticed that it was already one a.m. Slowly, she climbed the
stairs, jumped into the shower and cleaned the clay from her
arms and fingers. Toweling off, her thoughts again turned to
me—my caring touch, my soft, yet powerful kiss that moved her
right down to her toes...

No sooner did Sherry hit the sheets than she fell asleep—into
a deep sleep she hadn't experienced in years. So deep she never
heard Bill come stumbling in at two or so, nor would she have
cared. Her life had taken on a new, exciting turn, a turn brought
on by destiny. The very same destiny that grabbed me by the
shirt collar and dragged the two of us together with a cosmic
crash that would impress even the most jaded astrologer.

Chapter Twenty-Six
Typical

I spent the next day doing a bunch of things around the house, trying to get some of the chores I'd neglected under control. It was a long day and a hot one too. As I worked, my mind was on Sherry. As I went through junk in the garage or replaced a washer in the kitchen faucet, I was replaying in my mind everything that happened the day before. That's part of who I was—my mind never stopped, even when I slept or worked. I was my own worst enemy and it was a constant source of frustration for me. I'd rehash things in my head, things that weren't resolved, as well as things that went well. You could say that I was on a quest—a crusade to always improve myself and perfect whatever I could. It was a real pain in the ass sometimes! Sometimes I wished I could just relax and enjoy.

For example, as I fumbled with the garden hose, I asked myself if I should have held back the day before and not made love with Sherry. Should we have waited several more weeks or even months? Up until this point, my sexual encounters had been purely physical, but this was different, with spirituality thrown into the mix. It was so difficult to put into words. The whole time I was with Sherry, I didn't once think about myself or my pleasure but only of her. It was as though another being had entered my body and took control. Like I went into automatic pilot and someone else was doing the driving. Yet, I was there. I was present. I couldn't explain it. Words didn't seem adequate.

I was harshly yanked from my reverie by the sound of Carol yelling inside the house. She was screaming at one of the kids for doing—or more likely, for not doing— something. That woman just couldn't seem to let anything go. Everything was a tragedy to her. She'd scream about a wet towel being left on the bathroom floor with as much fervor as she would if they'd cracked up the car. All three of them yelled at each other on a regular basis. It set my teeth on edge. I couldn't wait until Monday to get back to work where I could relax and at least have some peace and quiet.

I didn't mind work. I loved what I did. This week promised to be a particularly busy one for me. Monday, I had an assignment for one of my major clients, shooting electronic products for their sales sheets. Barry usually gave me about four assignments a year, and this was one of them. Then on Tuesday, I'd be off to New York City to show my work around. Wednesday, I would head down to southern New Jersey, to a high-end gun shop that sells to a very distinctive group of people. (Shooting was one of my hobbies. Believe it or not, I found it very relaxing.) Thursday...Thursday would be a slow day and I hoped to spend most of it by the shore, photographing for my portfolio. What, I wasn't sure yet, but I usually poked around until I saw something interesting. If I didn't see anything that struck my fancy, then at least I'd enjoy the day. And Friday would be a day to play catch up with paperwork.

The week went by slowly. Monday was a rainy, miserable day but that was of little consequence to me because I was shooting in the studio all day with Barry. He was great to work with because he knew exactly what he wanted and was good at communicating it. And when he wasn't sure, he always trusted my judgment and was willing to let me stretch my creative muscles. Although Barry was a good client with a wicked sense of humor, his products were tough to shoot. The plastic bubbles enclosing his wares were a bitch to light correctly. Light and shadow were especially important to these shoots and always offered me a challenge, which kept me interested. I liked to be challenged. It kept me fresh, kept me on my toes.

I was done with Barry's shoot by about four, so before heading home, I decided to tackle some laborious paperwork. Of course, when it was occupied by mundane tasks, my mind always went to Sherry. I was actually surprised that I was able to keep from being distracted by thoughts of her throughout most of the day. There were times, though, when I was setting up a light and I got a flash of her beautiful breasts in my mind's eye or the way she trembled in my hands like a tiny bird when she climaxed.

I glanced over at the phone, wondering if I should give her a call. About now, Sherry would be on her way home from the office. All of a sudden, the phone rang. I picked it up on the first ring. "Hello, Jarred here."

"Hello, 'Jarred here,'" said the melodic voice on the other end. "When did you change your last name to 'here'?" My heart lifted.

"Yeah, I changed my name yesterday, so I could hide out," I quickly responded.

"Are you trying to hide from me too?" Sherry wondered.

"From you and everyone else. I'm ready to run away from home," I laughed.

"Yeah, me too. Let's run together. Where do you want to go?" Sherry asked.

"I'm up for suggestions. Maybe I'll follow my dream to live and work in the wild," I told her.

"Maybe I'll follow you," Sherry contemplated. "Where?"

"I don't know...we can start in Alaska, then head to Tuscany. I saw an Andrea Bocelli TV special that was set there," I said. "I never wanted to go to Europe until then, but Tuscany looked so peaceful. Maybe it was his songs that drew me in. I was just listening to him when you called. I find Bocelli so incredibly relaxing. His music has a very powerful affect on me," I confided.

"Really? I never heard him," Sherry told me. "You'll have to play his album for me one day. Is he as good as that Groban guy you love so much?"

"I love them both. Three years ago, had anyone told me that I'd be listening to either one of them, I would have laughed, 'Not in this lifetime.' I must be getting old or something," I chuckled.

"No, you're just becoming more in touch with yourself. Maybe they're helping you to bring about this change," Sherry enlightened me.

"You may have a point there," I told her. "The way I see it, there are two kinds of thinkers—those that use the creative brain and those that use the logical brain. The logical people are the ones who help us function by making computers work or by building bridges. And then there's us, the artists. We don't create anything that's of use, but it's still important...to the soul, at least. And a lucky few can transcend both the creative and the logical."

"Sounds like you've thought a lot about this subject," she said.

"Maybe too much," I admitted. "It helps me tolerate others who don't understand me or understand what I do or who I am. Well, lesson over for today. I'll fill you in on it another day when you have nothing better to do than be bored."

"I never find you boring," Sherry said. "In fact, I can't think of anyone who finds you boring. You're a lot of things, Jarred, but you're certainly not boring!"

"Aw shucks, I'm embarrassed now," I teased her. (I did feel a little embarrassed actually.)

"So, when am I going to see you again?" she asked. "How about five minutes from now?" I shot back without missing a beat. "You men are dogs. Give a guy a little and you don't leave us alone," she kidded.

"I'm hurt that you'd lump me together with other guys," I jabbed.

"Why? Aren't you all the same? That's been my experience so far," Sherry jousted. I loved our mental sparring—it was something I'd never had with another woman. But once again, my insecurities began to gnaw at me. A little voice inside wondered if Sherry might not be kidding anymore. After living with Bill all these years (and his friends were just like him), I worried Sherry might actually feel that way. I figured it would be a good time to test her out.

"Yeah, we're all the same," I pushed. "Give me the remote, a beer, the game, a toilet and, oh yeah, feed me and I'm happy," I said with sarcasm.

"Have I offended you, Jarred?" she asked in a soft voice.

"Kidding or not, I don't like to be compared with other guys," I admitted. "Because, let's face it, Sherry—I'm nothing like other guys. Never have been and never will be. True, I have my faults..."

Sherry cut me off. "Hey, I was only kidding! Really, I was just busting your shoes," she said. "I swear."

I regained my composure quickly when I realized that it was Sherry who was allowing her insecurity to show. She'd been burned before and I couldn't fault her for trying to make sure I wasn't another Bill, consciously or subconsciously. Who would want to have two jerks in their life?

I pulled back a little bit. "Sorry for jumping down your throat, Sherry," I told her. "But I'm a little tired, and maybe a little sensitive in that area. You see, all my life, whether playing football, or as a cop, I've been unpopular because I wasn't one of the boys. I just think differently than most guys."

"And that's one of the things I love about you," she broke in.

I smiled into the telephone. "Another reason it's a sore spot is that when I was a kid, all the girls fell for the guy's guy, while I was always the one they only liked as a friend or, worse, a brother. You know, the nice guy you want to take home to the parents but not to the prom. If a woman ever tells me I'm a nice guy, I cringe."

"Why?" she asked. "Because nice guys never get laid," I joked. "Well, I think you're a very nice guy...and didn't you just get laid? Twice?" "I didn't consider that getting laid..." I stammered. "So, I wasn't good enough for you?" she said, offended.

"Give me a chance to finish," I began. "What we did was beyond sex. It was beyond making love. It was so much more.

For me, it was more spiritual than physical. I hope that makes sense."

"Wow, nice save," she admitted, trying to lighten things up.

"It wasn't a 'save.' It was the truth. But if you look at this as just getting laid, maybe I took this whole thing the wrong way. Somehow, it was different from anything I'd experienced in the past. You're different. The way I feel about you is different. How am I sure? Well, afterwards, I didn't just want to get up, get dressed, and leave."

"Me neither," Sherry admitted.

I took a deep breath. "So, it's more than just physical for you too?"

There was silence on the other end of the line. A minute maybe but it seemed like an eternity. A loud, deafening silence. I could hear my heart beating in my ears. I thought I'd just blown it. My stomach ached with butterflies. "Hello?" I asked quietly.

"I'm here," Sherry said. "Where else would I be?"

"Are you okay? I hope I didn't say something to piss you off," I told her softly.

"No...just the opposite," she responded, her voice quivering with emotion. "Do you really feel that way?"

"How long have you known me, Sherry? When have I ever said something I didn't mean?" Again, silence, but I pushed through it. "If I have something to say, I say it. Otherwise, I keep my big mouth shut. Don't you know that by now? "

"If I didn't, I sure do now," she said with a smile in her voice.

"Now, back to where we started...when am I going to see you again?" I asked.

"I wish I could turn the car around and come over," she said in a tiny voice. "I want to see you so bad. I need a hug... a Jarred hug."

"So turn around and come over," I told her.

"I can't. I have to meet Bill. Some of his friends coming over for a barbeque." The disappointment in her voice was obvious.

"So, call him and tell him you're going to be late because you have to get some barbeque sauce," I laughed.

"I can't," she said sadly. "I know... I'm just teasing...Okay, I wasn't teasing. I figured I'd give it a shot." She chuckled, "Nice try. What are you doing Thursday night?"

"Nothing. I'm heading out in the morning to shoot at the shore. I need to add to my water birds collection. I'll be back by about four. What time do you want to meet me and where?" I asked.

"I get off at four so I can be at your studio by 4:30. It's comfortable enough and we don't have to waste time going somewhere else," she said slyly.

"Good. What do you want to do?" I asked, somewhat stupidly.

"Hmmm...I figured we could have an in-depth discussion about the situation in the Middle East," Sherry replied, slightly sarcastically. "Something along those lines."

"Okay, I'd better start watching CNN tonight so I can keep up my side of the conversation," I jabbed.

"Yeah, you do that," she laughed. "I have to go. I'm headed into a bad area and I might lose you. We'll talk tomorrow."

"Have fun with the boys," I told her.

"I'm sure it'll be a blast. I can't wait until after their fourth beer. That's when the real fun begins," she said with a touch of anger in her voice.

"So, excuse yourself and meet me," I suggested.

"Don't tempt me," she sighed.

"I'm tempting you," I said. But, I never got an answer because we lost the signal. I knew it wasn't right for her to meet me. We didn't want to piss Bill off and raise suspicions. After all, he needed his waitress and when he got high, he could get nasty.

I finished in the studio, recalling snippets of our conversation, which made me realize that Sherry had some issues with men. With her being so insecure, it wasn't hard to figure out why she ended up with Bill. The older I got, the more I realized that we picked our lifestyle and our partners because of our experiences growing up.

I've always been attracted to women who are strong because my mother wasn't. She relied upon my father for everything and when he died, she fell apart, leaving my younger sister and me to fend for ourselves. I even had to make my dad's funeral arrangements by myself. My mother just shut down, broke down. My sister was raised by an aunt but I was pretty much left to my own devices. Even though I loved my mom, I hated that weak, clinging quality in her. The minute a girl or woman I was dating showed she was dependent on me, I was history.

Likewise, I assume something in Sherry's life must have made her into a woman who's attracted to abusive, selfish, hard-drinking guys. But I'm not her psychiatrist. What was I to her, exactly? I hoped, that by being myself, she could learn how to be herself, and accept me for who I was, understanding I wasn't the typical guy. Far from it!

I wrapped things up for the day, finishing one last invoice for the job I just completed. I checked my appointment book to see what was on the agenda for tomorrow and called to confirm each appointment. I turned off the lights, locked the door, and headed home for the evening. Pretty typical.

The next morning, I went to the gym as usual. I met Mary Ellen, my personal trainer friend, and we worked out together and talked about our lives in general. I would never let on to Mary Ellen about what was happening with Sherry and me. Mary Ellen saw me as a father image, which drove me crazy. We joked about it and I still busted her chops about it on occasion but it still got under my skin. Beyond that, she would never accept the fact I was involved with someone outside of my marriage, even if it was on a metaphysical level.

Mary Ellen and I did some upper body work before she had to run out to train a paying client. Then I headed to aerobics class for an hour-long workout. Terry's class was as intense as she was. I was usually half dead when I finished but I figured it would help me stay in shape for hiking.

I went to class, minded my own business, tried to keep up and not to pass out. There were mostly women in the class and usually one other guy who'd been there before I started coming. In my head, I called him "Apha Male." He was pleasant enough but one of those fellows who always tried to be the center of attention, no matter where he was. Loud, always with the jokes which were rarely funny. But the women in class seemed to like him, so I just shut up and worked out. At that point in my life, I wasn't looking for more friends so I had no intention of socializing. I just did my thing then headed off to the shower when Terry's class was over. After a morning of intense working out, I seemed to be a lot less stressed out and I had more energy.

I made a quick stop at the studio, checked my email and the office phone, grabbed my appointment book and was off to the city. Although it was easier and cheaper to take the train, I preferred to drive so I could get in and get right out again. I guess it was a control thing—not having to wait for trains or busses, but it worked best for me.

It was a hot, humid day, not perfect conditions to be in a concrete metropolis. I ran from one appointment to the next, grabbed some lunch at a café, and before I knew it, was off to my last meeting. I didn't know how I'd done that day or if I'd get any work from the effort. I found it tough to tell if art directors or art buyers would ever use me. They were tough to read. Most had their suppliers and it was difficult to get them to change how they did things.

My biggest problem was follow-up. Once you were out the door, they seemed to forget about you. You really needed to call these people every so often if you hoped to get work from them. I found this tough. Being chief cook and bottle washer, I was always running from point A to point B to produce something. My desire was to concentrate on art—wildlife art in particular. If I had the opportunity to shoot just art and live on what I got from sales, I would in a heartbeat. The concept as photography as an art is up and coming so it was still nearly impossible to make a living at it, so I just supplemented it with the commercial aspect of my craft.

I finished my last appointment about 2:15, got my car from the lot and I was soon headed north to the suburbs and the studio. As I rolled back up to Westchester, I went over the events of the day in my head. I would love to be able to say screw the advertising clients and just shoot for myself. This business has changed so much it wasn't fun anymore. To me, the world of advertising was going the way of the American automobile. They had this "It's good enough" attitude and never tried for anything more than average. Most advertising agencies were happy with stock images that looked like everything else out there. They figured the public wouldn't know the difference and it saved them time and money by not doing anything different. Clients were charged a premium price for mediocre product. This was the direction I saw the ad world taking. Clients were beginning to realize that advertising wasn't working like it used to and they just didn't understand or want to understand exactly why.

I shifted my attention to what lay ahead for me the following day and my presentation to a client in New Jersey. This came on recommendation from one of my clients, Jonas Brothers of New York. Mary and Carl Jonas were great people to work for and they appreciated what I did for them. They also knew my policy—if they were unhappy, I'd do whatever I could to fix it. I wasn't the type to take advantage of my clients. I wasn't out there buying cheap and selling high, like most agencies did now that they were publicly traded and had to answer to their investors. The only one I had to answer to was myself, so I could uphold a strong work ethic. That was the only way I could operate.

As I reached Westchester, I decided to check my voice mail to see if I had any pressing issues. Nothing of consequence except a message from Barry, who wanted me to know he received all the images and was very happy with them. I decide to head home early, get the lawn cut, do some other chores and then sit out by my pool and relax.

The following day would be the same routine: the gym, the studio, check emails and voicemails, confirm with a potential client that I was on my way to him. Monotonous. A little boring, and no Sherry.

On Thursday, I might be able to squeeze in the shore, which was always relaxing. I was thinking of getting some shots of the waves hitting the rocks and maybe some shore birds and some grasses. While I was there, I'd try to get in some relaxing on my rock. I tried to keep my mind off seeing Sherry because that would make Thursday seem like it was light years away instead of just a day away.

Chapter Twenty-Seven
A Man Between Two Worlds

It seemed like forever but Thursday finally came. To get an early jump on my trip to the shore that morning, I skipped the gym and headed off after a quick bite to eat and a hasty slug of coffee.

I arrived just as the sun was coming up. Taking my knapsack and my equipment out of the car, I hustled down to the water's edge. There was "my" rock, waiting patiently for me. It was actually part of a large group of rocks that jutted out of the ocean and expanded onto the beach. That day, I perched myself as far out onto the ocean as possible and was sitting above the water's edge. Looking down at the point where the water ended its journey, abruptly releasing its energy, violently exploding upward, wildly about, made for interesting photos. You could just feel the violent blast. The sound could be frightening, even deafening at times, but it was that very power I craved to capture.

Unfortunately, the water wasn't as rough as I'd hoped and my opportunities for outstanding shots were limited. As I tried to do with most things in life, I did the best with what I had. The air was thick with humidity and it felt like you could cut through it with a butter knife. It was a sticky day, even for the shore, with no breeze to cool me off.

I sat and watched the sea striking the shore, looking for a point of contact that was lively and compelling. Once I located a promising area, I sat, camera to my eye, watching and waiting for something, anything. Soon, the pattern of the waves striking the rocks captivated me. About every fourth wave gave an especially explosive splash. I grabbed about two or three shots before changing my position to see if I could get more action from another vantage point. But still, it didn't look too hopeful.

I decided to take a hike to the dunes to see if I could get any good shots there. After walking around and searching for about a half an hour, I realized that the day would be an uneventful one. This sometimes happened with nature, which was so wonderfully unpredictable. Sometimes you had a good day, even a great day, and sometimes the day just plain sucked. And that day seemed to be the latter.

I ambled slowly back to the rocks with hopes of the wind picking up... something... anything worth photographing, but was even too muggy for the shore birds, who weren't even feeding. I packed up my camera, scrambled further up my rock and laid back. *Maybe the day wouldn't be a total wash, I thought. I'm here so why not see if my friends Jessica and Jeremiah are here too.*

Finding a comfortable spot, I laid down using my knapsack as a pillow. My skin was already sticky, so I unbuttoned my shirt to ease the discomfort from the humidity. Looking up into the cloudy sky, I noticed a small opening where the blue behind the clouds was attempting to break through. I began to draw myself back, further and further into a state of limbo. My eyes closed, almost involuntarily. I felt my body growing heavier as I counted backward from ten, going deeper...*three, two*...I sunk even deeper into myself...*one*...

The door opens to the now-familiar foggy stone bridge. I slowly, cautiously step across it to the other side. This time I feel a strong sense of discomfort as I approach my destination on the far end of this bridge. Perhaps it is because my last trip here was so violent. But I try to put the thought behind me and just enjoy the journey.

It is evening and the town has gathered at some sort of church function. A long, wooden table is covered with food. There are many people dancing and having a good time here. Immediately, I spot Jeremiah, his mother Elizabeth and two other children as they enter the big banquet room and search for a table. Jeremiah is the oldest child of the group. There is another boy who looks to be about thirteen and a young girl who seems fifteen. She is helping her mother carry a basket brimming with food to add to the large, communal table while Jeremiah banters amicably with his brother.

"Stop picking on your younger brother, Jeremiah, and help your sister carry the basket to the table," his mother grins. "Some gentleman you are! It's too heavy for her."

This is the first time I realize that there are more members in Jeremiah's family than just him and his parents. I never thought about this before but back in the early 1800s, families were large, so why not his?

His mother continues, "Jeremiah, when you're done with helping your sister, go fetch Jessica and her family and have them join us."

With that, Jeremiah runs, pulls the basket from his sister's hands and quickly sets it on the big table, then runs back to where his mother and younger brother are setting up napkins, plates and cutlery. It's as though just the sound of his beloved's name makes him hurry. Elizabeth watches him with a slight smile on her lips, remembering how it was to be young, impatient and in love. A small, thoughtful chuckle escapes from her as she continues setting up a simple yet neat table.

Jeremiah runs as fast as he can toward Jessica's house. But before he reaches it, he sees Jessica, her mother and her three sisters approaching. The second child of four, Jessica totes a large basket, but not the largest. They too are carrying heaps of food and beverage to the town's church social. It is Sunday and all the townspeople return home after church, prepare food and bring it to share at the evening's gathering. There is music, polite dancing, games for the children and good conversation for the adults.

"Hello, Jeremiah," Jessica's mother Portia says, greeting him with a smile.

Jeremiah barely manages to stammer a greeting before running up to Jessica, taking her basket and smiling shyly at her. Like his own mother, Portia knows the depth of their affection for one another and excuses his slight social bumble. But if his own mother had witnessed this behavior, she surely would have grabbed him by the ear and brought him back to say a proper hello. Although Jessica's mother fully understands the urgency of young love, her sisters do not. They look at one another and roll their eyes. "I have a basket too, you know," Jessica's sister Molly quips. She walks up to Jessica and shoves her basket into her sister's hands.

"Mary, you stop that this instant," scolds Portia with a slight smile. "Yes, Momma," she whines, then runs toward the social with her younger sister. "Momma!" Jessica cries out in objection.

"Hush, Jessica. You're older," her mother says. "Jeremiah took your basket, now you take your sister's and stop your bellyaching. The sooner you stop complaining, the sooner you will be at the church hall."

Jessica gives a hearty "Humph," flashes a big frown and strides off with Jeremiah. "Young love," her mother sighs, as she makes her way to the festivities, with her oldest girl beside her.

I can see now that the church hall is actually an old barn which has been converted, probably by the town's men, for events such as this. Upon entering the hall, Jessica, her mother and older sister, along with Jeremiah, bring the baskets to the main table, then join Jeremiah's mother and siblings at their nicely-appointed table. Elizabeth has even set out a bunch of wildflowers. "Hello, Portia," Jeremiah's mother says, bowing her head in a polite greeting. "How are you this evening?"

"I am fine, Elizabeth. And yourself?" Jessica's mother replies. "I am well, Portia," Elizabeth responds with a little concern in her voice. *"Are you certain? You sound a little concerned tonight,"* Portia observes.

"Well, to be honest, Phillip's ship was due back three days ago. There has been no word about them for days. Besides that, Jeremiah has not been himself either. I don't know what has gotten into that boy. When I ask if he is all right, he insists that he is, but a mother always knows when something is wrong with her child," she says sadly.

Portia tries to reassure the other woman. *"It's always a worry when a ship doesn't return from its journey on time but I'm certain they are fine. Perhaps they were just delayed at port in Spain. You know how the Spanish can be. They can take forever to load a ship."*

Elizabeth nods in agreement. *"That is very true. Maybe I'm a bit nervous with the events of the past few months...the pirates and all,"* she confesses.

"Then perhaps this is what has been bothering Jeremiah," Portia concludes.

"No, this behavior began only a few days ago. He has been very quiet and to himself," Elizabeth responds.

"Now that you mention it, I have also seen a slight change. But he always seems so happy around Jessica," Portia says.

"Maybe I am imagining things because of my worries over the Native Spirit's lateness," Elizabeth responds softly.

Portia squeezes Elizabeth's hands warmly. *"Well, let us try to enjoy ourselves tonight and not give it a second thought. There is no reason to worry for now,"* Portia tells her friend, all the while hiding her own concerns.

Elizabeth shakes her head sadly. *"But fall is fast approaching and you know as well as I that autumn is the most dangerous season for storms out at sea."*

Portia reluctantly nods in agreement. *"But we are wives of the sea. This is the lives our men have chosen. We just abide by it and stand as strong as we can. And we pray. We pray hard."*

Elizabeth bites her lip to hold back the tears that threaten to come. Portia squeezes her hands tighter and gives them a little shake. *"Let's try not to upset the children. The little ones have enough on their minds with school starting up soon. And*

Jeremiah is beginning his new job as a laborer in the shipping yards, is he not?"

Elizabeth nods. "And how is Jessica adjusting to the life of a homemaker now that she has finished her schooling?" she asks.

Portia smiles. "She has much to learn but is doing fine. She and Molly are both learning to sew and cook. Some day Jessica will make someone a fine wife." They both watch as Jeremiah and Jessica slip off with their plates of food. Portia whispers to Elizabeth, "Now what do those two think they're up to, sneaking off like a couple of foolish love birds?"

Elizabeth smiles and taps Portia on the shoulder. With her chin, she gestures to Jessica's two younger sisters who are skulking off behind the couple, undetected.

Portia nods. "Ah, yes. They are upset that Jeremiah came up and took Jessica's basket without so much as a hello to them. Seems to me they are planning a little revenge of their own. I doubt Jessica and Jeremiah will be alone tonight, no matter how hard they try." With that, the two women laugh and set to fill their plates.

The church hall bears little resemblance to its former self as a barn, except for the hayloft, which is still intact. Jeremiah and Jessica manage to climb the steep ladder, dishes in hand and search for a private place in the back of the loft behind a few bales of hay. Jessica's two younger sisters wait a few moments then slowly sneak up the ladder behind them. Upon almost reaching the top, they peek up over the top step, hoping to be undetected as they watch where Jeremiah and Jessica are headed. Once the girls see them settle in behind a few bales of hay with their food, the sisters climbed the rest of the way up onto the hayloft's floor. There they wait quietly for a few minutes, silently giggling between themselves until they are sure the coast is clear.

The loft is open on one side, exposing this drama to the folks down below. Portia and Elizabeth stand there with a sharp eye on the goings of their two teenagers. "Those two girls of mine can certainly be a handful when they start conjuring up plans to make Jeremiah's and Jessica's lives miserable," Portia admits.

Once the mischievous sisters are certain the two lovebirds are settled into their secret hiding place, the two little ones begin to tiptoe there, quiet as barn mice. Foolishly, Jeremiah and Jessica are confident no one saw them sneak off. As the little girls reach the hay, they leap on top of the bales, screaming and laughing, attempting to scare the two love-struck teens encamped behind the hay. Success is theirs, for Jeremiah and Jessica both jump up with a start, dropping their plates, scared out of their wits. The entire hall looks up at the commotion.

Jessica gives chase to her sisters as they run off, laughing and yelling, "Yuck, they were kissing! They were kissing!"

The two girls leap onto the ladder and scuttle down as Jessica stands threateningly at the top, chiding them. The people below begin to laugh at the spectacle. Mortified, Jessica runs back to Jeremiah who stands there laughing as well. She runs into his arms, burrowing her head into Jeremiah's chest. But soon, anger overtakes embarrassment, and Jessica stalks down to her mother, upset. Portia struggles to keep a straight face as she summons her two youngest daughters to her side.

"Apologize to your sister this instant, you two," Portia insists, trying to mask her laughter .

The two mischievous girls look at her and say in unison, "Sorrryyy..." in very unapologetic voices. Then, adding for good measure, "But you were kissing Jeremiah...ewwwe, that's so disgusting."

"Mommaaaa!" Jessica objects.

Portia has had enough drama and hysterics for one evening. "Jessica, go up and get your food...and your beau. You left Jeremiah standing all alone. Everyone in town knows you like the boy, so stop your nonsense," she says sternly.

At this point, everyone else has lost interest in the brief floorshow and have gone back to what they were doing. The music has resumed and many continue dancing, while others prefer to eat and talk. Jessica climbs back up the ladder to Jeremiah who is holding both of their partly-filled plates. Jeremiah hands Jessica what remains of her dinner. Then the two walk over to the edge of the loft, their feet dangling over the side. They sit and eat what is left on their plates as they watch the

*town folks dance below. "I'll get even with those two brats,"
Jessica exclaims.*

*"Why? They were just having a little fun," Jeremiah says.
"That's why we have these get-togethers, isn't it? For fun."
Jessica continues to scowl, eating slowly, thoughtfully.
"Besides" Jeremiah adds, "How we feel about each other is no
secret. We're both grown up and out of school. We're adults
now. There's no shame in it. When I become a first mate on a
ship, I will ask your father for your hand in marriage. This I
promise you."*

*"Only my hand?" Jessica smiles, a bit naughtily. Quite
satisfied, she continues to eat, as does Jeremiah. Upon finishing
their meals, they set down their plates and sit holding hands,
making certain to keep their joined hands low to the floor, back
from the edge and out of sight of the others below.*

*The music begins to grow louder and more and more people
are drawn to the worn wooden floor to dance. Jessica stands and
takes Jeremiah with her, leading him toward the ladder. "Where
do you think you're taking me?" Jeremiah wonders, knowing full
well her desire.*

"I'll give you just one guess," Jessica says.

*"I'm really not in the mood to dance tonight,"
Jeremiah objects.*

*"Why? What's troubling you this evening?" she
asks impatiently.*

"Nothing," he tells her sadly.

*"Hogwash! Something is bothering you," Jessica insists.
"Come, let's dance. Maybe it will cheer you up."*

But Jeremiah is firm. "No, please, I really don't want to."

*Jessica lets go of his arm, but holds fast to his hand. "If you
will not dance with me, you must trust me enough to tell me what
troubles you. I can tell something worries you. I just need to
know what it is," Jessica insists again.*

*Jeremiah thinks for a moment, then relents. "Only if you
promise me not to say anything to anyone. They will think the
devil himself has gotten hold of me and they will hang me or
worse," he says in a concerned voice.*

"I cross my heart, Jeremiah," Jessica swears dramatically. *"I promise I will not say anything to anyone. Just tell me what the trouble is,"* she pleads.

Jeremiah takes a deep breath, then begins. "On Thursday morning, I had a strange vision. As I awoke, all of a sudden, I saw my father. He came to me and told me that bad news would be coming soon and that he would no longer be with us."

Jessica gasps but allows him to continue. "He said that I was to be the man of the house and that I should take care of my mother, of all of them." *He takes another breath, and says thoughtfully.* "This dream, this vision, was so real and now with the Native Spirit being late to port, I'm wondering if it was a dream or if it was him, speaking to me from beyond."

For perhaps the first time in her young life, Jessica is tongue-tied. "It has been bothering me four days now," *Jeremiah continues.* "My father came to me again in my sleep Friday night to tell me that he was at peace with the rest of his crew and that he would always be with us in spirit." *Jessica begins to cry silently now but still says nothing. Jeremiah bites his lip, coursing forward to conclude his story,* "Father told me to let the men's families know when the time is right."

"To let them know what?" she wonders, though she knows the answer. *"That they are all at peace,"* Jeremiah confesses. *"Now, remember, you promised not to say a word to anyone. Right?"*

"I promise," Jessica whispers. *"It is our secret. But I'm sure it was just a bad dream. Perhaps from something you ate that day. Or else..."* her voice trails off.

"Maybe you're right," Jeremiah concedes but neither of them believes it. *"But I just don't feel up to dancing."*

"I understand," Jessica says.

"Do you think I'm crazy?" Jeremiah wonders in a small voice. *"I get these feelings all the time. These visions. They come and go. Sometimes I think it was just a dream and then it's all too real to deny. This has been very bothersome to me."*

Jessica brings his hand to her lips, kisses it. "We'll just sit up here watching and talk about this until you feel better," she says.

As Jessica promised, she and Jeremiah sit side by side and chat until the evening draws to a close. After the last waltz has been played, the two families walk home together, down the cobblestone streets sheathed in night, to the edge of town, to the little houses where they live. Their homes are only a few yards from each other and the families have always been close. The close proximity is a comfort with the men of the houses gone to sea so much of the time. The younger boys and girls run ahead, playing tag as they go. Their mothers walk slowly behind, talking and watching their offspring who have grown so quickly, becoming young adults before their very eyes. Yet tonight, they behave as children for at least one more night, and this too is a comfort.

They arrive at Jeremiah's house first and say their good-nights and sleep-tights. Jeremiah tells his mother that he is going to walk Jessica and her family home.

"But come back as soon as they are in their house," she instructs. "No shenanigans now."

Portia steps in. "I'll make certain he gets right back home to you, Elizabeth, just as soon as we're safe inside." Portia and Elizabeth share a knowing smile that their children will dawdle just a little bit.

Upon reaching their home, Portia and three of her daughters go inside, while Jessica pauses for a moment, looking down. "In a moment, Momma...please?

Portia nods. "Five minutes Jessica, no more. And Jeremiah, I know you will be respectful of my daughter." But Portia has no fears for she knows Jeremiah has always been a true gentleman.

"Yes, ma'am," Jeremiah says shyly. " Don't worry, I will." Portia and the girls go inside and close the door softly, leaving the two beaus alone.

"Good night, Jeremiah," Jessica says gently. "Thank you for seeing us home."

He nods. "I just wanted to make certain you were safe. You know, with all of those pirates about," he says in a strong, proud voice.

Jeremiah reaches over and gives Jessica a quick peck on the cheek. She giggles and smiles at him, then kisses him hard and fast on the mouth. It takes his breath away. Then she goes inside, shutting the door, then bolting it securely. Jeremiah turns and *runs toward his house, his heart both light from the kiss yet heavy from his troubling vision. A man between two worlds.*

 # Chapter Twenty-Eight
Native Spirit

In retrospect, this was to be my longest out of body experience to date. During it, I had no idea where I ended and where Jeremiah began. We were seamless. I also had no idea how long I'd been sitting there on the beach. I just let the vision take me...

As Jeremiah approaches the door to his house, he hears a commotion inside. There is the sound of crying, of wooden furniture being scraped along the wooden floor. He enters quickly to see what is wrong. Standing over his mother as she sits in her straight-backed chair, sobbing, is Mr. Peabody, the owner of the shipping company. With him are several other men in suits, wearing grave expressions.

Elizabeth looks up at Jeremiah with tears in her eyes. His siblings stand there crying as well, trying to console their mother. The men observe Jeremiah and his family with somber faces. Jeremiah's heart drops and there is a chill in his chest. He chokes back the urge to vomit, as his knees become weak. Although he knew what had happened before anyone could say a word, it still is not easy to bear. His father is dead. His dream was not a dream after all. Instinctively, he knows that now in his bones, in his being.

It takes all of Jeremiah's strength not to cry, not to show his fear. "What happened?" he asks, even though he knows the answer.

It is round, little Mr. Peabody who speaks. "Jeremiah, I am deeply sorry to have to tell you this...but the Native Spirit has sunk." Jeremiah sucks in a sharp breath. His mother and siblings cry harder. Mr. Peabody plods ahead, undaunted. He has done this many times before and will probably have to do this many times after. "It was caught in a terrible storm, just five miles offshore. The poor ship was battered and destroyed. The Navy discovered pieces of it while on patrol."

There is silence except for the sound of muffled sobbing. Mr. Peabody continues, "Your father and all of the others onboard are missing, presumed dead. I am sorry to bring you such terrible news..."

Jeremiah's family and the other men in the room study him, holding their breath, trying to gauge his reaction. It takes all that he has not to falter, not to break apart. "When?" he stammers. "When did this happen?"

One of the other men clears his throat, a sailor, clad in plain blue wool. "By our best estimation, the storm hit early Thursday morning. It was a powerful storm that rose up unexpectedly." The man pauses, then adds, "Your father was a fine seaman. The best. I had the honor of sailing with him on several voyages...sir."

"Thank you," Jeremiah says with a slight waver in his voice.

But it is too much for the children to bear. Jeremiah's sister Franny lets out a low, deep wail, like that of an animal. Without warning, she runs out the door and up the street before anyone can catch her. Franny bangs on the door to Jessica's house wildly. Portia opens it quickly, her daughters piled up behind her. "Why I could swear it was the devil himself..." she begins.

But Franny cuts her off, sobbing. "It's my father! He's dead. Everyone's dead. The Native Spirit went down." Before the girl can give further details, Jessica is pulling on her shawl and is out the door. "I knew you'd come," Franny cries. "He is just standing there like stone. He needs you," Franny pleads, following her.

Portia and the entire family hurry out the door behind them. The women cry softly as they rush toward Jeremiah's house, for the fear of every family has struck Elizabeth and her family with a vengeance. Jessica is particularly stunned, as she is still reeling from the conversation she'd just had with Jeremiah at the social.

Upon entering the grieving home, they come upon the sad scene of Mr. Peabody addressing Jeremiah. "You're the man of the house now, son," the serious, owl-like man says. "Please know that you will always have a job with Peabody & Company. Be strong for your family. Stay by their side through the services. They will be held day after tomorrow, dockside, at the Sailors' Memorial. Come see me about work when you are ready."

Mr. Peabody goes over a few more details as Jessica impatiently waits to embrace her beloved. Standing there, she feels his pain as it emanates from him like the heat from a fire. She sees the shock in his pale face. He glances up into her eyes, biting his lip, attempting not to cry. Jeremiah's eyes fill as his younger brother embraces him, weeping, seeking solace. But it is as though a bolt of lightning has hit this young man. He can't move. He doesn't know what to say or do. He holds his brother tight to his chest as Jessica embraces them both.

Jeremiah thinks silently for a few moments and then, almost from nowhere, the strength comes to him. It fills his veins like blood. Perhaps it is his father, his father's spirit, filling him. Jeremiah stands tall and kisses Jessica on the forehead, then takes his brother's hand as he approaches the men.

The young man's voice is sure and strong, much like his father's was. "I would like to thank all of you for your compassion," Jeremiah begins. "Telling us this unthinkable news must have been so incredibly difficult but it is important for us to know what has happened."

Jeremiah turns to Mr. Peabody. "I will come to your office after first light tomorrow, after gathering the other family members who lost loved ones on that good ship. Speaking of

which, you should be off to inform the others, Mr. Peabody."
Jeremiah and Mr. Peabody shake hands. "If you would be so
kind as to advise them to meet me at the church tomorrow
morning. We will say a prayer for the souls of all these brave
men, including my father, before we come to see you."

Jeremiah's mother comes to him and falls against his chest.
"Mother, everyone, please listen closely to me for I have
something important that I need to say," Jeremiah begins. "I
know that all of these men walk with God now. They are safe and
at peace. We are the ones who now have to learn to go on with
this hardship weighing heavily upon our hearts. Our wounds will
take time to heal but we will heal—we must if we are to survive
in this life. We will always carry the scars from this wound but
we mustn't let it destroy us. If we let it weaken us then we will be
damned to a life of pity and bitterness. If we find strength in it,
we will not only honor their memories but also, ourselves. Let
us all take one moment to silently say our good-byes to my
beloved father."

The women, as well as the steely men, look at Jeremiah with
surprise and admiration. Mr. Peabody is the first to put their
collective feelings to words. "I am impressed by your strength
and wisdom beyond your years," he says. "As I speak with the
remaining families my intent is to reassure them that you will
help them through these trying times. I will ask them to meet you
at the church as you requested. Until tomorrow, then." Mr.
Peabody bows and is gone.

The men give their final condolences to Jeremiah and his
family as they exit the small house, so full with people, yet so
empty. For the remainder of the evening, the two families sit and
talk, trying to ease each other's pain. Jessica does everything she
can to help Jeremiah cope with this sadness. She, as well as
everyone else, is taken with the leadership Jeremiah showed at
this time of crisis.

After many hours, everyone falls asleep, all except for
Jeremiah, who is too frightened to sleep, afraid of what he will
dream next. Will his father visit him again? Or will it be some of
the other men this time? Whenever he dozes, he wakes with a
start. By morning, he is exhausted, and even a strong pot of tea

can't rouse him properly. But still, he does his duty and greets the day as best he can.

Just before sunup, Jeremiah is at the church, anxiously awaiting the others. His father Jacob was first mate on the ill-fated Native Spirit but ten crew members in all perished, including the Captain. All of their families have come to the church, just as Jeremiah asked. Many are angry as well as grieving, and looking for someone to blame. That person, that fall boy, is Jeremiah. He has witnessed this reaction many times before and expected it this time, girding his loins for the worst. One young man by the name of Jonathan, is especially furious, and speaks for the others.

"Your father was a poor example of a first mate," Jonathan shouts through gritted teeth and tears. "Had he been better at his job, all would be alive today."

Although Jonathan's words wound Jeremiah like a knife, he listens patiently, silently, not uttering a word, just allowing the man to say his piece. When Jonathan finishes speaking, shaking with anger, Jeremiah approaches his hand and takes it strongly in his. "Please," he begins softly. "Let us all join hands..."

But Jonathan pulls away and shouts, "I will have nothing to do with you for what your father did to mine, to all of them. Damn him!"

Jeremiah calmly stands his ground. "I know this is very difficult for all of us," he says. "The storm that rained down upon them was no one's fault. I know that your fathers, as well as mine, did everything within their power to overcome the elements but fortune was not with them on this journey."

There is a soft mumbling of agreement amid those who have gathered. Jeremiah continues confidently, "They were not the first, and they will not be the last, to fall in such a way. Please take heart that your fathers are here with us right now, watching over us. They are giving me the strength to work through this as they are here to give all of us strength. The choice is yours whether to accept this strength from them and make them proud or to blame others for what was no one's fault."

Even Jonathan is silent now and bows his head, reflecting. "Before we go to the office to help with the memorial, we need to get our composure and show solidarity," Jeremiah tells them. "We need to be strong for our friends and neighbors who will be hurting for us as well as with us. This is why I have asked all of you to meet me here today...so we can work through whatever it is we need to work through together."

Jeremiah looks at each and every one of them, eyes full and weighty with emotion. He notices that some are still in shock, but that all are still hurting. Jonathan's rage still seethes beneath the surface, perhaps because he is among the youngest of the group. As Jeremiah studies Jonathan, the boy's eyes begin to well up. When Jeremiah puts his arm around Jonathan's shoulder, the boy begins to sob uncontrollably. "What am I going to do" Jonathan cries. "How will we survive? I miss him. I miss him something awful... Daddy, please come back. Please..."

It takes all of Jeremiah's fortitude not break down crying himself but some of the others are not nearly so strong. All he can do is hold Jonathan tightly as he cries. He does not utter a word to the boy, simply comforts him, rocking him slowly back and forth as a father does to a sorrowful child. Although Jeremiah seems like a monument of hope, strength and life, there to help them heal and move through these dark times, he is actually numb and empty inside. He feels a depth of pain that he had never before experienced.

When Jonathan settles down, Jeremiah speaks. "Let us all join hands and pray for our fathers and for those with whom they have joined in the life beyond. Brave souls all, we will miss you. Let us gain our might from you and build upon what you have given us in this life for the short time you were here. We know you walk with God. Please give us the strength to help us through this time of darkness. Amen."

These words filled Jeremiah's heart, then his mouth, as though they are seeds that were planted there. But by whom? He is no pastor or man of God. He simply does what he can to try and comfort these children and wives of lost seamen. Jeremiah then concludes, "Now, we will pray silently within ourselves, say our good-byes as we pick ourselves up and journey forward with strength." After a few moments, Jeremiah looks up, eyes moving *from one to the other. "Are you ready to go make our families proud and do what we need to do?" he asks. All nod.*

Together, the grieving families walk to Mr. Peabody's office. A kind man, he assures them that Peabody & Company will be there to help in any way possible. Then they take their places at several long tables and plan the memorial for their loved ones. Mr. Peabody has done this far too many times for his liking but he always does a fine, respectful job. The following morning, one representative from each family will say a few words and then will lay a wreath upon the water. Within the wreath will be a small portrait or memento from the departed. Wreath and all will then be set out to sea. Afterwards, there will be a supper at the church hall, where plans will be made to support those in need. This will indeed be a long two days for the families. As soon as the wreaths disappear beyond the horizon, the healing must begin. Especially in those days, it was important to get back upon one's feet as quickly as possible in order to survive.

The following morning, all of the town's business stops. The Four Maids, Jessica's father's ship, arrives in time for its crew to pay their respects. The ceremony is somber and heartfelt, led by Mr. Peabody. Also lending a hand is Jeremiah, who makes all who watch him admire him, especially his mother and Jessica. At the luncheon that follows, it is Jeremiah who visits every family for a few moments to console them. When he returns to his own family, Jessica's father approaches him. The stern, bearded man is clearly moved. "Jeremiah, you did your father proud," the Captain says. "You handled this like a true gentleman."

Jeremiah is caught by surprise, for the Captain is a man of very few words, most of them harsh. On a good day, the man is cold and detached and on a bad day, you best steer clear of him altogether.

When the luncheon is almost through, Jeremiah excuses himself to go lie down for a few moments. It has been a difficult few days for the young man. Now with over the memorial nearing its end, he needs some time to reflect, to regroup. Before leaving, he turns to Jessica. "Tomorrow, I would like you to come with me to Clemont's shop," he tells her. "I would like to have our photographs taken. It is important we have them as a

*remembrance, should anything happen to either one of us,"
Although this thought worries Jessica, she doesn't object. She
understands Jeremiah's sense of urgency and immediately agrees
to his request.*

*Alone, Jeremiah walks to his empty house and goes straight
to bed. There he lay and stares up at the ceiling. It is only then
that he begins to cry for the first time. He feels all the pain of
losing his father with whom he was close. It is then that he
acknowledges the sad truth that he will never again be able to
see that fine man, to hug him or hear of his adventures in strange
and exotic lands. Jeremiah feels as though the ceiling had
come down upon him. There is a crushing pain in his chest.
Embarrassed by the depth of his emotion, he turns his face into
the pillow to muffle his sobs.*

*Unable to leave her beloved alone in his grief, Jessica follows
Jeremiah home, unseen, but upon seeing him break down, she
stands there like a statue by the door, unable to move, listening
to her darling's sorrow. She waits until he is asleep before
entering his room. There she sits on the bed at his side, tenderly
stroking his hair and wiping away his tear before they have the
chance to dry.*

*Back at the luncheon, there is a conversation as to Jeremiah's
fate with Peabody & Company. Although Jeremiah must work his
way up the ranks, Mr. Peabody tells Jeremiah's mother that he is
extremely impressed with the way her son carries himself. "Mark
my words," he says," that young man will make a fine captain
one day." But the words are lost on Elizabeth, for she fears that
she will lose her son to the same fate as her husband. "Yes, a fine
captain indeed..."*

With Mr. Peabody's words echoing in my head, the scene
faded as the smoky bridge once again appeared. Reluctantly, I
slowly journeyed back over its expanse, feeling the wet stones
beneath my feet. Five, four, three, two, one...

Almost fully awake now, I was sweating. There was also a
hollow feeling inside my chest, a sensation more dramatic than
in any other of my previous visions. I was numb, unable to
move. It felt as though I had lost my father all over again. The
feeling was so pronounced that it took me several moments to

compose myself. A strong wind whipped across the rocks, pulling me back to full consciousness. It was an odd, cold wind on this humid day, a shocking wind. A wind that didn't belong, that came from somewhere else.

I got up on wobbly legs and made my way to my car. The thought of seeing Sherry that night brought me around quickly as I started my journey northward.

Chapter Twenty-Nine
Sherry, Through the Lens

Driving back to the studio, I fell into my usual deep thought about the odd, dreamlike journeys that I'd been taking back and forth through time. I began to realize that during my entire life, for as far back as I could remember, I'd had passing thoughts of the ocean and an anonymous shipping town. Whenever I went to a museum that had pictures or replicas of old ships from the 1800s, I felt a strange sense of déjà vu. Like I'd been there before. I never gave it much credence, because it was so abstract, just a feeling I couldn't explain. But now, it all made sense.

On top of that, I had an unexplained love/fear of the ocean. I was always pulled to it as though a distant, magnetic force field were drawing me there. Then, once I was at the water's edge, the closer I got to it, my feelings became polar opposites and a slight fear began to grip me. When I went back in time to visit these folks in their charming little shipping town, it was like I'd once lived there. I knew where certain shops were, where specific people lived. Slowly but surely, I was beginning to finally accept that these visions weren't dreams but were more significant events meaningful to my life today. I actually started a journal to chronicle the images that began to consume me.

As I drove, I decided to write down one of my "Observations" as soon as I got to the studio, while it was still fresh in my mind. My "Observations" were usually one page long and I'd been jotting them down from the time I was a teenager. For example, I would see something like the "Close Door" button on the elevator button panel and this would spark an "Observation." I would write a short dissertation about how elevator "Close Door" buttons always seemed to be worn out and explored why this was in a one page exposé. Then I'd do a photograph to go along with the writing, to document it, in a sense. Similarly, I figured that maybe if I wrote about these vivid, colorful time-trips I took, it would help me to further understand them. During my whole ride to the studio, my thoughts wavered back and forth between my dreams and Sherry.

Sherry... Darn, what time was it? I'd been so engrossed by my visions that I never gave the time a thought. When I remembered, it was almost 3:00 and I would make it back just in time to call her, as long as there were no accidents or broken-down vehicles to delay me. I kicked down the accelerator a bit and picked up the pace to make sure I'd make it.

As I drove, I decided to make a journal entry instead of an "Observation." How the hell would I take a picture of what I just dreamed? I figured that when I finished the journal entry, I would contact Peggy again, get together with her and talk about it. I might even bring Sherry to talk about her dreams as well.

The second I unlocked the studio door, I rushed to check my telephone answering machine to see if anyone had called— "anyone" meaning Sherry. I wanted to be sure she could still make our appointment and didn't have to cancel. Then I realized that she would have called my cell, not the studio, and relaxed a bit.

Actually, I was glad to get back a little earlier than I'd planned. This would give me time to set up my lights and prep the studio. I'd decided to take some photos of Sherry that night and hoped she would agree to being my model for the evening. My intention was to make the shots artistic as well as interesting.

But I had to proceed with caution, making sure Sherry knew that I did not in any way intend to get physical again. Not that I didn't want to—it was incredible—but I wanted to transcend beyond the physical. I was inspired to see if I could capture that inner, subtle beauty that emanates from her in such an unassuming way.

I didn't think Sherry really knew how quietly beautiful she was and I wanted to show her. The most stunning things about her weren't visible to the eye. Yes, she wore a little makeup and, true, her hair always looked beautiful, but that wasn't it. I was honestly at a loss for words to describe her allure. The French called it *je ne sais quoi*, which roughly translated to "that certain something." But that still didn't quite nail it. Instead of trying to put Sherry's beauty into words, I would attempt to do her justice through my lens as I burned her image onto film. I mentioned earlier that I loved challenges, and to me, there was none greater than taking the physical three-dimensional image of a vibrant individual and attempt to translate it onto the one-dimensional medium of a photograph.

Sherry arrived early that night, just as I was setting up my lights. Maybe she was just as anxious as I was. As she walked into the studio, my heart thumped so loud, I was afraid she could hear it. My eyes must have lit up with the sheer delight of seeing her. Even though I was a pretty damn good photographer, I didn't know if I could do her justice on film but I would sure as hell try. She looked a bit apprehensive at the barrage of lights that surrounded me. "We're still on for this afternoon, right?" Sherry asked. "Or are you still working?"

"Yes and no," I told her, confusing her even more. I gestured at the lights. "This is for you. There's a little project I've wanted to try and you're the perfect subject for me to try it out on," I tried to explain. I didn't want to lay it on too heavy because making her feel apprehensive or uncomfortable would pretty much guarantee failure. After all, I wanted to pay tribute to her, not scare the crap out of her.

"And what project is that?" she asked, pulling me to her by the belt buckle.

"I'm looking to do black and white portraits of women and I need some samples," I stammered, stretching the truth just a bit. "I can't think of anyone better than you to test my lighting."

"Oh, so now, I'm your Guinea pig," she laughed. "No offense to your 'art,' Jarred, but I can think of better ways to spend these scant few hours we have together."

"So can I," I admitted. "But, this is something I just have to do and it would be a great help to me, if you don't mind." Sherry looked doubtful so I pressed on. "Come on, this can be fun. I promise to make this as painless as possible. Look, I don't bite... at least not when I'm taking photos," I joked.

"Okay but you have to promise me that next time biting is included," she shot back.

"Duly noted," I said coolly, but the truth was that I was getting nervous about capturing Sherry on film. I tried to shrug it off and continued perfecting the lighting.

On occasion, while creating an image, something travels through my mind, my body, down my arm, through my finger, up the shutter button and onto the film. Something unexplainable— it's much more than pointing and shooting. It's an amazing phenomenon, the reason why so many photographers who are truly dedicated to their art resist taking digital images. Something is missing in digital. It simply isn't as visceral or as physically rewarding.

"What do you want me to do?" Sherry asked, looking especially vulnerable.

"Just sit on the stool," I told her. "I'll put on some music." I gestured toward the CD player. "What kind of music will relax you? You know, take you in, put you in a romantic frame of mind. What will move you?"

"You mean, besides you?" she retorted wickedly.

"Yeah," I admitted. "Besides me."

Sherry shrugged. "Well, we like the same type of sound so put on whatever you'd like," she said. "Besides, I'm already in a romantic frame of mind." She smiled seductively.

I picked up the remote for my five-disc CD player, hit play and on came Josh. Next it would be Andrea, then the Righteous Brothers and so on. I turned off the studio's overhead lights so that the only source of light in the room was the warm, soft glow from my strobes— and from Sherry.

I turned up the music slightly, slowly raised my camera and observed Sherry through the lens. She seemed a little tense, so I approached her, camera in hand, and slowly stroked her hair with my other. I lifted her hair from her neck, moving my hand down the side of her face, her cheek, and gently lifted her chin. Sherry looked into my eyes and half-smiled. I lightly caressed her lips with the back of my fingers. She kissed them. The mood of the room was changing and Sherry was beginning to react to the music as well as to my touch. I leaned forward her, kissing her mouth lightly. I thought I detected a blush. Slowly, I moved back into position, the music playing softly in the background. I raised my camera.

"Let the music take you. Let it lift you," I whispered.

Sherry began to allow her creative spirit to combine with her emotions. She looked down, turning her head slightly— click!—I exposed the film. She moved slowly, glancing to the side and again I exposed the film. There was electricity in the room between us now, her eyes meeting mine darkly as I studied her through my lens. I felt Sherry's heart beating from way across the studio—we were connected. I felt our energy rushing toward each other, intertwining, then embracing us both. Melting inside, I exposed a few more frames of film, my fingers weak, almost too weak to push the shutter. But I did. I captured Sherry's magic as best I could.

I stopped and walked up to her again. This time I took her chin in my hand and lifted it as I leaned in toward her. Our lips met in a tender kiss. I felt myself being drawn into her like a tidal pull, like the wind tugs at a leaf. Sherry moved toward me for a hug, her arms outstretched but I stopped her. She gave a tiny pout but I didn't want to break the magic, not yet. "A few more minutes," I promised. "Please let me capture your beauty a while longer."

Sherry's smile was a telling smile. I unbuttoned her blouse, slightly opening it at the neck so that her vulnerable throat and just the top of her lovely breasts were exposed. Again, she melted. I exposed a few more frames then I approached her and moved her hair back as I kissed her neck. Her head tilted back submissively, seductively, as she gave herself to me. It took everything I had not to completely undress her and take her right then and there, right in the middle of the shoot. I resisted the impulse. "Please take off your bra," I whispered to her. "Then put your blouse back on."

Sherry looked up at me curiously and smiled without saying a word. She unbuttoned her blouse, with deft, sure fingers. I think she was beginning to understand what I was trying to do, how I wanted to immortalize her. Sherry turned her back demurely as she wriggled out of her bra and back into her shirt, buttoning it quickly to just above the breastline. I exposed a few more frames of film then moved up and adjusted her blouse until it draped off her shoulders. I positioned Sherry with her back toward me and had her look up to the left, head slightly tilted. Now she moved deliberately, letting her sexual self drive her positioning.

Unable to resist, I approached Sherry and kissed the back of her neck. I laid her upon the floor and unbuttoned her blouse completely. I also unzipped the front of her pants until just the top of her lace panties showed. "Take them off," I told her, "and put your slacks back on." She hesitated, for a millisecond. "You can change in the dressing room. I'll wait."

Sherry stood and looked at me hard, dropped her pants and slowly peeled down her panties. She gave me a quick glimpse of her downy thatch, partially obscured by her shirttails. Coquettishly, Sherry pulled her panties back on one finger, aimed and fired the lacy fabric directly at me. "Missed," I said, laughing.

Sherry smiled and poured herself back into her slacks. After a big, passionate kiss, we were ready to continue the shoot. Like a pro, she moved back to position and lay down on the floor. I straddled her body and positioned her clothing as she moved languidly, lazily, making love to me without touching me. I lit her skin with soft, warm light and again set to work, capturing her beauty on film.

We worked at this for about an hour but it didn't feel like work. My concentration slipped back and forth between my desire for her and my desire to make Sherry part of my art. After three rolls of film, I found myself completely drained emotionally. I'd poured everything I had inside of myself into her to create these sensual images. I wondered if I'd been successful in putting the deep emotions I felt for Sherry onto something as cold and tactile as film.

The photo shoot over, I reached out to take Sherry's hand and lifted her up to me. She embraced me tightly, her bare breasts resting upon my chest. She looked into my eyes with a warm, wanting look and then we fell into a kiss. "Do you think you got what you were looking for?" Sherry asked. "I know I did," she added, more shyly. "That was really hot."

Her hands were warm on my shoulders as she looked deeply into my eyes. Pulling me toward her, our lips again met as we melted into one another. The photo shoot left me emotionally drained—I'd felt so much energy flowing back and forth between us that now I felt spent. I used all my strength not to buckle at the knees when she kissed me. I desired Sherry so badly, but knew she had only a few minutes before she had to leave. "I want you," I said softly.

"Me too," she conceded. "But it's too late now, so hold onto that thought." Sherry began dressing. "You wasted all that time taking your little pictures. Now I have to run, so you will have to suffer until we meet again."

I helped Sherry fasten the last few buttons on her blouse. "I didn't waste my time. I wanted to see if I could capture your essence on film to cherish forever. And I wanted others to see you, who you really are, as I have. I experienced you, as you did me. No, this wasn't a waste. This was one of the most erotic moments of my life," I confided.

Sherry's eyes filled up instantly. "That's one of the most wonderful things anyone has ever said to me. At first, I thought you might be stalling because you didn't want me again. I was worried you were disappointed Saturday. But then...then it became something more, something...holy."

"I could never be disappointed in making love to you," I assured her. "I have never felt anything like that day we were together. The intensity...your body against mine..."

Sherry looked down, shyly. "It was pretty intense, wasn't it?"

"This might sound strange," I began, "but with us, it isn't so much about sex. It's deeper than that. It's...enjoining our bodies, our souls together as one. It's about me being a part of you and you being a part of me. The heat from our bodies melts us together as one. I feel your heart beating with mine. Nothing like this has ever happened to me before."

I finished buttoning her blouse and kissed the top of her head. "I know," she admitted. "It's a little freaky...but sooo nice. I love it but it also scares the crap out of me. Just a little bit." Sherry gave me a hug so intense I thought it might break my back. We embraced for several minutes then she gave me a quick kiss on the mouth. "Man, that was hot!" she said, beaming. "I don't know how I'll be able to hold up until I see you again."

She walked toward the door with a slight hesitation in her step. "Think about me," I called after her.

Sherry laughed, "I'm not sure I'll be able to think about anything else."

I stayed at the studio late that night to develop the film. I simply couldn't wait to see it. Once out of the processing tank, I held the ribbon of film up to the light. It looked great but I wouldn't really know how great until I printed it. Unfortunately, that had to wait until the next day. I shut off the studio lights, taking one last look over to the set where I'd photographed Sherry. Her essence seemed to still be there, hanging invisibly in the air. I could smell her on my fingertips.

Smiling, I left the studio and locked up. I was almost to my car, when my cell phone rang. "So how did it come out?" the sweet voice on the other end of the line wondered. The sound of Sherry's voice always delighted me. "So, were you able to accomplish what you wanted with plain, old me?" she inquired.

"How could I have missed?" I told her. "Plain, old you is exquisite."

There was a silence on the other end of the line. "You've got to stop being so nice to me," Sherry sighed.

"I'll try," I whined.

"I only have a few minutes before I have to go into the house," Sherry said. "I pulled over down the road from the house so Bill didn't ask who I was talking to. I just wanted to ask you how I looked and if you got what you were hoping for."

"What made you think I developed the film?" I asked her.

"Because I know you," she laughed. "And I saw how excited you were. I also know that when it comes to your art, you're too impatient to wait. It's who you are, Jarred. Everyone who knows you knows that."

I couldn't help but smile. "Well, the negatives came out great. Your image is striking. I know I got what I wanted," I said. "But I hope you weren't disappointed that we didn't..."

"That we didn't what?" she asked devilishly. "You're going to make me say it, aren't you?" "Oh, yeah," she giggled. "I'm waiting."

"You know...that we didn't make love," I advised her softly.

"Are you kidding?" Sherry asked. "It was so incredibly erotic. Like foreplay."

"I just don't want you to be disappointed right now," I told her. "I'm sure there will be enough disappointment later as you get to know me better." I was only half joking.

"Trust me, Jarred, I already know you and I don't think you could ever disappoint me. Although, I can read you like a cheap novel," she jabbed.

"Ouch. Cheap novel? And here I thought I was more like War and Peace," I told her. "You know, a classic with lots of substance."

"I think you've spent too much time smelling those chemicals you used to develop my negatives," she laughed.

"It's more like I'm high from your scent, your soft kiss, your warm touch," I said, trying to be serious.

There was a momentary silence on the other end of the phone. "I'll have to put on my hip boots if this conversation continues," she responded with a laugh. "I'll talk to you tomorrow. Let me know how they came out."

"I'll call you when I get the contact prints. If you have some time, maybe we can meet for lunch by the river at Sunset Cove," I said.

"I should have time for lunch tomorrow. Will you have them done by 12:30?"

"I might actually have a print or two done by then. Can I pick you up in front of your building?" I asked.

"Sure. I can't wait."

"Me neither," I said with a smile, ending the conversation. But as usual, tomorrow seemed very far away.

Chapter Thirty
Beautiful Wreck

The next morning, I decided to blow off the gym so I could get to the studio early and print Sherry's film. But on the way, I did stop by the deli to say hello to Rocky and grab a quick breakfast to-go. That guy always made me smile. "Morning, Rock," I greeted him. "How are you today?"

"Not bad. What are you doing here so early?" he wondered. I noticed a new tone in his voice. Rocky hadn't been the same fun, "up" guy since the deli was sold and new owners took over the place.

"I figured I'd get an early jump on the day," I told him. "I have some darkroom work I wanted to get done this morning. My client needs to see them at a lunch appointment."

"So, we won't see you at lunch today?" he asked. "Sorry, Rock. You won't have the pleasure of my company today," I laughed.

"I don't know how I'll get through the day today without your happy face," he joked. "Ditto. But we'll have to manage somehow," I shot back. "Do your best to get through it, Jarred."

"You, too. See you tomorrow for coffee. Have a great day, Rock."

I seemed to be walking on air, maybe left over from the exhilarating photo shoot with Sherry the night before. I couldn't wait to see the prints. At the studio, I was anxious to get into the darkroom and get printing. I turned on the lights and the computer, did a quick check of the voice mail (nothing important), then brought my coffee and egg into the darkroom, eating as I set up.

After the contact sheets of the film were ready, I turned on the lights and looked at each one through an ocular. In them, Sherry was spectacularly beautiful, her inner light shining through. She seemed to glow, luminous as the full moon. Each and every photo seemed to be a winner. The shots with her blouse and pants slightly open immediately caught my eye. Even though you couldn't see much flesh, they were incredibly arousing, inviting. Maybe more tantalizing than if they'd been nudes. I seemed to capture her sensuality, her very essence.

I pulled four negatives from the bunch and printed several eight-by-ten's of each. I figured Sherry would like one or two for herself. I wanted the rest for my samples and for a scrapbook I decided to create of her. The thought came to me as I was climbing into bed the night before and was still hyper-focused on how erotic the session had been. So absorbed in my thoughts of Sherry, I thought that perhaps there should be a book or a journal devoted to her. I thought of the painter Andrew Wyeth and his muse Helga.

Maybe I would even be able to get a publisher interested. It would be a challenge to write the supporting text without any mention of the physical relation between Sherry and me—and I didn't think I was a good enough writer to pull that off. It would have to be a generic journal and just list Sherry as a model for the book. That would hopefully take away any suspicion from what had really happened between us. Although I had a burning desire to tell the world about how this wonderful woman crashed-landed into my life and rocked my world, I had to keep it under wraps. At least for now.

And I also had to focus, to focus and get the shots done. After working on the prints for some time, I was satisfied that I'd achieved what I sought. Looking at the clock, I realized that I had completely lost track of time and had to run if I was going to pick Sherry up by 12:30. I'd gotten so caught up in her image and getting each print perfect, that I ran the risk of standing up my flesh and blood model in favor of her likeness. I took the prints, grabbed my keys and was off.

As I stepped out from the studio, the brightness, heat and humidity of the day hit me like a brick. A perfect day to sit out by the Hudson and enjoy a meal in the company of a beautiful woman. The ride seemed longer than usual and leaving a little late didn't help. It seemed that every slow driver in the world was on the road and had somehow managed to get in front of me.

As I approached Sherry's building, I saw her pacing. I checked the clock—I was right on time, but she still seemed agitated. Pulling to the curb, I reached over and opened the door for her. "Good afternoon," I said with lots of energy, attempting to get her to smile.

It didn't work. Sherry had fire in her eyes—and not the good kind. I couldn't help but think that someone had pissed her off and I was hoping it had been Bill or Valerie and not me. Sherry climbed into the car. I reached over to kiss her hello and she stopped me. "Just drive," she said in a very pointed voice.

After an uncomfortable silence I quipped, "Was it something I said? Or maybe it's my breath," I joked, still trying to get her to grin. But instead, Sherry shot me a look I thought might turn me into a pillar of salt.

"Listen, if you don't mind, could we skip lunch today and go somewhere where we can talk? Somewhere without people around?" she asked sternly.

Anytime someone uttered any form of the statement "we've got to talk," you knew nothing good would come of it. I began to tense up and braced myself for whatever was coming. "Sure," I told her. "We could head over to Croton Point Park if you'd like. It should be easy to stay away from anyone who might be there. Should we pick up something to eat?"

"You can get something if you want. I'm not hungry," Sherry said flatly.

Not hungry. This was really going to be a disaster. No food. We have to talk. All I needed now was for her to open the conversation with: "You know..." or "I have something really important I need to..." and that was it! Those are doomsday words in a relationship.

As I drove toward Croton Point, Sherry sat silently staring out the window. Not a word. Not a look. No sign of things to come. The frost was so thick, I thought of stopping at the hardware store for an ice pick. But I thought better of sharing this observation with Sherry and decided to avoid thinking any negative thoughts. I almost let out a nervous chuckle but that would have meant instant death. I bit the inside of my cheek to prevent one of my usual inappropriate jokes I have the habit of dropping at times like these to lighten the mood.

I pulled into the park and found a spot. Before I even shifted gears into park, Sherry got out, walked to the front of the car and stood there waiting for me. As I approached her, Sherry threw herself into my arms and began to cry. "What's the matter?" I asked.

"It's Bill," Sherry started. I held my breath. The way she said it, I thought maybe the guy was sick, seriously ill, and she was about tell me that she needed to be by his side.

"What's up with Bill?" I queried nervously. Sherry took my hand. "Come on, let's go sit by the river where we can talk."

More suspense. "Why can't we talk and walk? I know I'm a man but I have evolved," I joked. "I can walk and talk at the same time, I swear." I noticed a very slight smile painting her lips. A good sign, I hoped.

"No! I just want to sit and talk," she insisted.

I didn't push anymore. Instead, I gently pulled Sherry along as we strode toward the river. We found a nice flat rock, large enough for the both of us to sit. Once we got settled, Sherry looked at me and she began to tear up again. I was so nervous about the impending doom that I thought I might throw up.

Sherry took a deep breath and started talking. "I went to bed last night about 12 and Bill wasn't home yet. I fell asleep but he woke me up when he came stumbling in at 3:30. I could smell perfume on him. I could smell another woman all over him. When I asked him where he'd been, he told me that he was out playing pool with Jim."

I tried to reassure her. "Well, he has stayed out before with the guy. Maybe Jim's girlfriend there, too. You know Jan, she loves to hang all over other guys. It gives Jim a rush."

"The problem with that theory is Jim and Jane are away fishing this week," Sherry advised me in a short, smart tone. "I ran into her on Sunday and she told me that they were headed up to Eagle Lake in Maine to fish for brook trout."

"Maybe they came back early. You never know what could happen. Maybe they hit bad weather and decided to leave," I said, attempting to cut off what I felt was coming.

"First, that's a 13-hour ride, so they wouldn't just leave there because of a little rain. Aside from that, Jim will fish in anything. And they went with another couple, who they swing with, so they'd find something to do in the rain. Trust me," Sherry informed me.

Her eyes narrowed slightly. "And why are you trying to defend Bill anyway?" Sherry asked, suspiciously.

"I just don't want you to get upset for nothing," I told her. "This whole thing could be innocent enough." I couldn't believe I was defending Bill either. Especially since I knew his game. Plus I'd seen the way he carried on with his client in front of me.

Sherry snapped, "If I find out for sure, I will dump him as fast as look at him. I give that man everything he asks for. I cook for him, do his laundry...you name it, I do it. He has no reason to cheat on me."

My first thought was, *Wow, here she is involved with me and she's accusing Bill of not being loyal.* I wasn't sure I understood it but knew that we'd crossed the line where things became complicated. In the beginning, she and I might have been having a simple affair but now it was so much more than that.

Sherry knew the ache of discovering that someone you cared for was cheating on you. Did this mean Sherry truly loved Bill? The way she was acting, it was quite obvious she did. Although I didn't think you could call it love, I still had feelings for Carol, which explained why I had so much guilt about Sherry and was always second-guessing myself. But before I opened my mouth (and the can of spiders inevitably fell out), I decided to just sit and listen.

But Sherry beat me to the punch. "Look, I know we're sort of doing the same thing but what we have is not a physical, dirty sex thing. And I know that if Bill's fooling around with one woman, he's fooling around with more. You and me...that's coming from who knows where. There's an unexplainable force behind it. We were meant to be together and this thing found us. But with Bill, it's like he goes out and looks for it. I realized this morning that he's a dog, a womanizer, and us...we just happened. Neither of us was looking for this. It just happened and we're being careful not to hurt anyone. We never take time away from them. Besides, we don't know where this will lead...Damn, this is so complex," she confided in me.

I couldn't avoid asking the question even though the answer might kill me. I held my breath then let it out and spoke. "Do you think we should end this...whatever this is? I'm not really sure what to think now." I was caught halfway between anger and sorrow.

Sherry didn't answer immediately and the silence was killing me. She looked up at me with tear-filled eyes as she squeezed my hand and began to cry. "Now that I know the pain it causes, I think maybe we should," she admitted softly.

Shit! There it was. I just knew it was coming. Damn that guy! My initial reaction was anger. How the hell could she do this to me? To us? I then became numb, hard as stone. When I thought about Carol, I figured that maybe it really was the best decision for all involved. But I was speechless. I just didn't know what to say or think. I just sat there in shock, quietly, looking out upon the river. My heart was in so much pain, I could barely take a breath. I was lost, confused, angry and hurt. She and I sat side by side, silent.

"Say something. Don't just sit there! Yell at me. Do something," Sherry pleaded.

"What am I supposed to say?" I snapped. "Should I beg you to rethink this? You've made up your mind and, honestly, I'm so fucking numb with shock that I really don't know what to say. On one hand, I understand completely, but on the other hand, I don't want to lose you. Most women would have done the opposite. I really don't have anything to say except that I think I should take you back to the office."

Sherry shook her head. "We don't have to leave right away. Maybe we should talk about this. I don't want you to be mad at me. Please try to understand."

"I'm not angry. I'm just stunned...numb. And please don't ask us to stay friends. I can't possibly just be friends with you after what we've experienced. So, please let me take you back to work now. I need some time for myself," I told her as calmly as I could.

"Okay," she said. "I'm sorry. Please believe me. I really am sorry."

I got up without saying a word. We began to make our way back to the car in silence. Once inside, Sherry put her hand on my shoulder, which made me even angrier. "We're making a break, right?" I sighed. "Well, let's just do it. Make it clean and simple. No questions asked. Nothing." Sherry slipped her hand from my shoulder and let it fall, limp, into her lap. She hung her head and let me continue my tirade. "Let's just go our own ways," I said. "We'll just deal with each other in business and for Brush, Chisel & Lens, but that's it. I promised you that I would walk away if you ever decided this wasn't right and I'm a man of my word. I appreciate your being honest with me," I told her.

The ride back to Sherry's office was long and very quiet. I pulled up right in front of the building because there was nothing to hide anymore. As Sherry grabbed the door handle, she looked over at me and said, "Please try to understand and please don't hate me."

"I could never hate you," I told her, reaching into the back seat. I grabbed the envelope of photos and handed it to her without saying a word. Sherry took it and gave me a kiss on the cheek. I watched her walk into the office building and disappear into the elevator.

Sitting there, I asked myself how pissed off I should I be. Was I really angry or just hurt? I decided not to push myself into answering any questions. All I knew was that I was upset, not at Sherry, but at myself for dropping those walls. I should have known that nothing good could come out of this. I should have known that this was a train wreck waiting to happen. But what a beautiful wreck it was! This will never happen again, I promised myself. Never .

I quietly drove back to the studio with no radio, no music, nothing, just dead silence. Just the road and me. Before I knew it, I was there with nothing to do. I couldn't bear to look at Sherry's photos again. I walked into the studio, checked my email and voicemail. There was nothing. I sat at my desk, not thinking, not wondering, just hurting. My body felt leaden. I had lost all feelings inside. I sure could use someone to talk to as I sat there in total disbelief, squashed like a fly on the window of life. Damn! I was even starting to hate my stupid puns.

The telephone rang, crackling through the silence. I didn't answer it because I couldn't bear to speak to anyone, especially not her. I let the machine pick up. It was Sherry, saying, "I just wanted to tell you again how sorry I was. Please don't hate me...please."

As soon as she hung up, I deleted the message. I just needed to heal and Sherry's voice on my machine was like salt on this fresh, new wound. I couldn't just sit there. I had to get out. I turned off the lights, got into my car and headed up to Rockefeller Preserve, to a spot I loved there perched on the top of a hill, overlooking the Hudson. At least there I knew I would get some privacy, some solitude.

The parking lot had only a few cars in it. I had a long walk ahead of me and I enjoyed every step of the arduous climb up the path to my special place. It gave me a chance to think things through—what was happening and what should I do, if anything. I took my notebook with me.

Once I arrived at the peak, I sat down and rested as I gazed out over the treetops at the Hudson River. I immediately opened my book and began to write, starting with a question: "How could something so passionate, so powerful one day, turn so cold and lifeless the next?" I couldn't comprehend how or why this was possible.

But at least I learned a valuable lesson. I made a vow to myself never to fall for anyone again. I sat silently looking at my chicken scratch and at the blank pages that followed. I simply stared with no answers, nothing to say. My mind was completely empty. Something inside of me died that day. The little light that seemed to slowly grow brighter with each passing moment was suddenly extinguished more quickly than it had been lit.

I later learned that after we parted, Sherry had sat silently alone very much the same as I did. Thankfully, Valerie was out of the office on appointments, so she could wallow and sob when she needed to. She felt injured and confused. *What have I done?* she wondered. *Why stay with Bill if he's such a jerk? Why give up Jarred...he was such a prince?*

Sherry understood that Bill was her comfort zone when it came to financial security but he was also her ruin. Maybe it was her realization that she and I could never be together as she would have liked, as we deserved, that made her stay with him. But still, she couldn't understand why she was so hurt by Bill's actions. Was it simply a bruised ego or something more? She was afraid that she would never know the answer and that the question would haunt her for eternity.

Chapter Thirty-One
Clock Hands

A week passed since I climbed down the peak at Rockefeller's. My journal remained unattended with only one unanswered question scrawled across the top of the page. It sat idle on my desk. I carried the damn thing around all the time, hoping to add something inspiring but never found anything to write. The only thing that kept my mind occupied was the nagging pain in my knees I experienced working out in Terry's class at the gym or thinking about my debt that always seemed to be climbing. It was amazing how all the negative things in your life take precedence when you're in a sorry state.

I planned to go through the junk I'd accumulated at the studio and toss out as much as I could but somehow, it kept piling up on me. I considered renting a large dumpster, throwing everything out and starting over. It seemed easier than sifting through memories. Twenty-eight years of negatives, props, books and papers. I felt like I was drowning. There were art negatives that needed to be printed, letters that had to be written and sales calls that should be made but I didn't feel like doing any of it. I seemed to be overwhelmed these days.

Plus the photography business seemed to be changing daily. Quality no longer matters like it once did. My love for commercial shooting was all but gone. I wanted to be able to concentrate on my portraits and my art. I was doing mixed media these days— writing down my observations then creating a photo to go along with it. The wildlife shooting was always refreshing and forever a challenge. I put out feelers with a number of agencies that would allow me to concentrate solely on wildlife but I hadn't heard back from any of them. I also had two new irons in the fire, but both included a move from New York to out west. I was also checking into moving to the motion picture side of the photography industry. There were lots of possibilities but I had passion for nothing.

All I could seem to do was to sit unfocused, staring into the emptiness of my studio. My inspiration was gone completely. My mind wandered. I found myself sitting, wondering what the hell had actually happened with Sherry. One day, she was asking me to never again leave her, then, bam!—the next, she walked out of my car and never looked back. All because that bastard Bill might have cheated on her. Damn, did everyone but Sherry know he'd been screwing everything that breathed? I'd known pretty much as long as I've known him.

After a few hours of this nonsense, I couldn't stand sitting in the studio any longer, asking myself questions that had no answers. I grabbed my camera equipment from the cabinet and headed to the car, forcing myself to do something besides feeling sorry for myself. I was determined to push myself back into my life as I knew it before that fated almost-lunch with Sherry on the Hudson. This time, I planned on going a little further east to explore new horizons.

As I drove, it was almost on automatic pilot as my mind drifted in and out of the events with Sherry, trying to make sense of all it. I made my way out to the point where the beaches ended and the houses began. From the road, I spotted a point that had water on both sides of the road, a peninsula, I guess you'd call it. Seemed like a great place to explore. After I parked, I started toward the harbor side, knowing it often had more wildlife than on the ocean side. Off I went, camera in hand, moving slowly with no intention of heading back to the studio or home too soon. I was going to make a good day of this mess if it killed me.

I found it fascinating that while I was at the water's edge, struggling with my emotions, Sherry was also struggling with the horrible turn our lives had taken. She confronted Bill every night for about a week about his suspected philandering. Well, not every evening, just the nights he came home at a reasonable hour, reasonably sober. All he did was deny, deny, and deny. He told her she was being paranoid, that he was drunk when he'd said he'd been out Jimmy and Jane—he'd really meant John who was joined at the hip with some new girl Sherry didn't know. This nameless lush was supposedly wasted and had been falling all over him. Bill made sure to tell Sherry that the woman smelled like she took a shower in perfume, which was why he smelled the way he did. Finally Bill told Sherry to knock off the cross-examination—if she didn't trust him, she could leave. He knew she had no place to go so he'd hoped that would be the end of it.

The night after that exchange, Sherry decided that she needed to see what Bill was up to, firsthand. She found a quiet spot and parked her car by the back wall at the north end of the bar's parking lot. From that point, she could see into the bar through the open door. Luckily, it was a cool August night, so instead of running the air conditioner, the pub always left the door open so their patrons could sit outside on the patio to smoke and drink. A nice perk for drinkers, plus the pub saved on electricity.

Sherry saw Bill leave the bar several times with John and a girl Sherry didn't recognize, but the floozy was hanging onto John like wallpaper every time Sherry saw them. Maybe Bill was telling the truth. Confused and a bit guilty, Sherry didn't hang around much longer. At that point, she wasn't sure whether she didn't want to know the truth or whether she simply didn't care. Sitting there in the obscure darkness, spying on this guy she could barely tolerate, Sherry reflected upon what she had done to me, to us.

A million thoughts swirled through her mind but the most profound was that she couldn't believe she sacrificed something so important to her. Me! What was she thinking!? Sherry knew she had driven a spike into the heart of our relationship and doubted that she had any chance of reclaiming me so we could continue upon the journey we'd begun. Sherry was confused, worried, lost. She knew it was too late to call me and I'd been avoiding speaking to her anyway. The following day, Thursday, she would have a full day at work and no chance to phone me. And would I even talk to her anyway?

Sherry started her car and was about to shift into drive, when everything hit her all at once. She began to sob uncontrollably. Her world began to spin as she surrendered to her feelings. It was several minutes before she was finally able to collect her thoughts and could think more clearly. That's when Sherry remembered that Thursday was "our day"—it had become our usual day to meet. She was sure I'd be in the studio and decided to surprise me with a visit, pleading for forgiveness. Maybe not plead because she also knew that I hated any sign of weakness and dependence in women because of what I'd witnessed with my mother.

Her plan was simple. She would show up, walk over to me and give me a warm passionate kiss that would make my hair stand on end. (Well, maybe not just my hair.) In spite of her wrecked emotions, Sherry began to smile as she amused herself with thoughts of our reconciliation. With that, she put the car in drive and headed home for a good night's sleep, resting up for what she hoped would be a very eventful afternoon.

Sherry admitted to me afterwards that Thursday had been a very long day, perhaps the longest day of her life. She watched the clock constantly, which made it chug along slower than usual. Even being as busy as she was, the hours seemed to drag. As the clock moved closer to four, she became more excited at the thought of seeing me and the hopes that she would win me back.

Finally, the little hand was on four and that ever-so-slow big hand struck twelve. Sherry grabbed her purse and was out of the office like a shot. Within minutes, she was in her car, headed to my studio. The closer she got, the more apprehensive she became. Her palms even started to sweat and she had to struggle to breathe normally. As Sherry turned onto my street, her heart began pounding. *Maybe I should have called,* she thought. *No, I don't want to give him a chance to tell me not to come.* She resigned that even if I tried to push her away, she was going to fight to get me back, promising that this would never happen again.

When Sherry pulled up to the studio, the first thing she noticed was that my car wasn't in its usual spot. Her heart dropped. She thought that maybe I was at the lab or somewhere else nearby doing an errand and might come back soon. So Sherry decided to park her car, pick up the book she'd been reading and wait maybe 30 minutes or so.

As the clock continued to tick along, she began to give up hope. After a half hour passed, she figured another 15 minutes wouldn't hurt. What Sherry didn't know then was that I was off on my weekly shore visit. Only this time, I had no reason to rush back. I wouldn't return to the studio any time soon. As a matter of fact, it turned out that I wouldn't be back that night at all.

By five o'clock, Sherry realized this was fruitless, but she still wasn't giving up that easily. She vowed to come back as many times as it took to surprise me and revive what we'd begun to build. Sherry was convinced that it was stronger than both of us, mystical, even, so she promised herself that she would do whatever it took to win my confidence back. Instinctively, she knew that the flame in my heart was still burning— because the fire in hers glowed stronger than ever, no matter how she tried to ignore it. No matter what I said or how I tried to ignore her telephone calls, I still carried strong feelings for her. She was sure of it.

Back at the water's edge, I sat quietly in the tall grass at the top of a sand dune, photographing the songbirds as they landed upon the grasses and the sand. They were a colorful lot, and watching them in their quest to sustain life provided an interesting and relaxing distraction. For once, thoughts of Sherry hadn't even crossed my mind. The salt air and the lulling sound of the water was so soothing, it drew me in. Despite the wreck my life was in, I was really enjoying the day. But for some reason, at about four o'clock, Sherry crashed back into my brain with a vengeance and I was feeling this unexplainable pull drawing me back to the studio. Little did I know that was the time Sherry had arrived at the studio.

Although I gave serious thought to heading back to work, I resisted because I didn't want to be caught in the middle of rush-hour traffic. But still, I couldn't understand where this mysterious pull came from. I finally convinced myself that it was just because it was Thursday, the day Sherry and I usually shared some stolen moments together. I successfully fought off any desire to head back to the studio, pushing Sherry to the corner of my mind again.

But it didn't last. I tried to remind myself how I'd looked forward to watching the sunset in a few hours and how good the breeze felt. But again, thoughts of Sherry won out. I convinced myself that no matter what happened, I would never let myself get into a situation like that again. It just wasn't worth the pain. I was so much better off by myself, even though my relationship with Carol was unfulfilling at best. I wouldn't allow anything else to distract me from my business or my art.

As I snapped photographs, feeling light in spirit for the first time in a long time, I told myself that if I could realize my dream of living and photographing wildlife in the back country, this never would have happened. If Sherry folded that quickly, that easily, she couldn't have cared for me as much as she said she did. She never even called to see how I was holding up. (Except for that one time I didn't answer.) And she never tried again. How much could Sherry have possibly cared? I must have been filling in for her loneliness when Bill wasn't around. That was it, I decided. I wasn't going to give this another thought.

A red-winged black bird called out to the others, pulling me back to the moment, and away from my pain of Sherry.

Chapter Thirty-Two
Refuge

There were no rocks on the side of the bay where I'd taken refuge so the sounds of the waves splashing upon the shore were more subdued, gentler in this protected cove. After several hours of bird-watching and studying the horseshoe crabs and fiddler crabs scrabbling around, I decided to lie back and watch the sky. It was a clear day, with only a few clouds that lazed by. The sand I laid back upon was warm and comfortable, like a hard, heated mattress. The breeze teased my skin as the sound of the dry grass shuffled in the wind. The smell of the salt air was intoxicating and relaxing.

I found myself drifting, almost falling asleep and wondered if it would be possible for me to take one more journey back to my little village nestled in the 1800s. Would it work from here and from not my magical rock? Could I bear another emotional upheaval with what I was going through with Sherry? I decided to surrender, to give it a try. At the very least, I'd get a relaxing nap. At the most...who knew what I'd find?

Gazing up at the sky, I began to count backwards...ten, nine, eight, seven, six, five, four, three, two...

I find myself again at the familiar, fog-engulfed stone bridge. Dare I go any further? What the hell, I figure, what do I have to lose? I slowly make my way across to the other side. As I reach the end of the bridge, I come out of the haze and I once again see my tiny town. But there are changes—dramatic changes. The ships are different and Main Street also has a new face.

The clothing the townspeople are wearing is also different, so much so that I begin to wonder if I am, in fact, in the same village. But the feeling, the sense that I've been there before, is the same. Looking around, I notice that some things haven't changed. The Peabody's shipping company is still there and so is Jeremiah's house. Jessica's house is there as well, so I realize that I am in the same town, only it is years later, perhaps the late 1800s but I couldn't be exactly sure.

It is early morning as I watch a woman in a bonnet, face slightly obscured, leave Jessica's house. She looks vaguely familiar but I can't quite place who she is yet. Could this be one of Jessica's aunts or perhaps her mother? But this woman looks different in both body and hair. This woman has a rounder shape with gray tresses, much older, yet not elderly. I watch her make her way down toward the new store I noticed on Main Street. The woman takes out a key and fits it into the shop's door. It is then I notice the sign, which reads, "Captain Jeremiah's Import and Export."

Inside, the woman moves back toward a small office in the shop's rear. From a drawer in an old oak roll-top des, she removes a small box then takes it out to the wooden counter, which also looks to be made of oak. Back in those times, I know that oak was considered to be one of the finest woods one could use. The poor used pine but oak was a product for the wealthy, the well-to-do.

It is at this point that I detect the scent of several fine fragrances—spices such as cinnamon and nutmeg, and perfumes like lavender and sandalwood. I also notice large rolls of rich fabrics—silks, satins, linens and cottons. There is a case where several types of buttons are on display—mother-of-pearl, whale-

bone and even ivory. A cabinet of oak drawers stands behind it, one of the drawers partially open. Inside, I see a good supply of threads and ribbons of every color.

This shop is stocked with quality items for making fine food, clothing, curtains or to upholster furniture. Its contents are intended for those who have the means to live a good life. Just the smell of this place, the leathers, spices, herbs, and the rich colors, surrounds me with the sense of being cradled and gives me a warm, happy feeling. Yet this old crone looks anything but happy. She is truly a lady, though, subdued, refined, and obviously a proper woman thanks to years of elegant upbringing. If I were to guess, she was the wife of a captain, and most likely a daughter of a captain as well. Captain Jeremiah, whoever he is, must own the place. There is no sign of him there, however. Perhaps he is out at sea or still at home. Or, from what I had seen from my trips into the past, perhaps he is even dead.

I watch the village as the day begins. I see women and men alike, merchants and private citizens, come into the shop to browse and to purchase items. They always engage in polite conversation about their mornings or a particular project they're working on. They ask this woman for advice and she gives it readily, kindly, but seems to hold back something inside, never smiling widely, never laughing deeply.

I wonder why my travels have taken me to this woman and why I haven't seen Jeremiah or Jessica. But I've come to accept that these trips take me to where they want me to go. Finally, about mid-morning, a young woman in her twenties runs into the store. She is well dressed, as is the woman I have been studying. The young lady seems flustered and agitated as she rushes up to the old woman.

"Aunt Jessica, I am so sorry I am late," she says breathlessly, "but Ericka refused to go off to her first day of school. She was impossible this morning, much more so than usual."

The old woman smiles knowingly. "Catherine, this happens often with small children, so often that I expected you to be late on this fine September morning," she replied in a soft, calming voice. "So, by my estimation, you are actually quite early." Both the young and old woman smile.

Jessica? She called this old woman "Jessica." Is it possible that the woman I have been watching is Jessica? Jeremiah's Jessica grown aged?

My observations continue throughout their day, which moves forward at a gentle pace. Jessica seems to be extremely tired and not at all well. The customers flow in and out of the shop, spending time with the both women. Shopping is so different back then— no one is in a hurry, everyone seems to take time to politely socialize. They share ideas, dress patterns and their thoughts about their friends and neighbors. The women are toughest on each other, teasing each other in a joking way. But it is all in good fun and based in caring.

At one point, Jessica begins coughing. One of her customers turns to her and scolds her. "Jessica, you must take better care of yourself. Who would we have to share our deepest secrets and desires with?" she chuckles, trying to make light of the merchant's poor health.

"Oh, Sally, I am sure you will find someone to complain to about that old man you call a husband," Jessica says with a smile.

All within earshot laugh. "Speaking of that 'old salt,' you wouldn't have any of that nice rat poison here, Catherine, would you?" Sally jokes.

"You best check at Shaunessy's down near the docks," Catherine, the younger woman, suggests.

"Never mind, I would never be able to poison him anyway," Sally admits.

"See? You do love him after all," Jessica points out.

"Love him? It is that what you call it?" Sally shoots back. "Why, he's always hanging around that pub. He's never home long enough to give me a chance to poison him. Besides, he so pickled with ale, I don't think anything could kill him!"

The three women share a hearty laugh until Jessica begins to cough again, this time longer and deeper. She has a difficult time catching her breath afterwards. Catherine brings her a dipperful of water.

"That's it, Jessica. I'm bringing you some of my home remedy for that nasty cough when I come back next week," Sally says

firmly. "It will take care of that cough and anything else that ails you."

"I'd think twice about taking one of your home remedies after what you said about poisoning your dear husband," Jessica kids Sally.

"I would never want to lose you, Jessica," Sally tells her. "I would miss you terribly. And what would happen to this store?"

"Catherine will take over when I'm gone," Jessica remarks. "She knows how to run it better than I."

"Enough of this foolish talk!" Catherine exclaims. "I will not have it, not in front of me. I can't bear the thought of this place without you."

"Neither can I," Sally says softly. She apologizes for upsetting Catherine, pays her bill and leaves with a promise to see them both next week.

When the door closes behind her, Catherine turns to Jessica and pleads, "Aunt Jess, Sally is right. You've had that cough for quite some time and it keeps getting worse. Perhaps you should head up and see Doc Jacob."

"Nonsense. I feel fine, child. It's just a little cold. It will be gone before you know it." She puts her arm around her niece's shoulder. "Now let's head up to the docks to see if our shipment from India has arrived."

Wearing bonnets and shawls, the two walk arm in arm toward the docks and Peabody & Company. Upon entering the establishment, the clerk, an old gentleman by the name of William, greets them. He rises from behind the front desk with a smile.

"Good morning, William," Jessica nods. "And how are you today?"

"Well, Jessica, it has been a wonderful morning. And, just when I thought it couldn't get any better, two of the most beautiful women in the county walk into my little corner of the world," William says with a flourish.

Both women blush and thank him for the kind compliment. After they exchange pleasantries, Jessica inquires, "Has our shipment from India arrived yet?"

*"Oh, yes," he says. "I saw it here early this morning—
two large crates. Too large for you dears to handle. Would you
like me to have them delivered? For you, Jessica, there will be
no charge."*

*"Thank you, William. Please do have it dropped off but I
insist upon paying for it," Jessica states.*

*"Jessica, when are you going to allow me to do something
kind for you," William pleads. "We have done business together
all these years."*

*Jessica thinks for a moment. "All right, William," she
concedes. "I will allow you to deliver it for me for free of charge
this one time. Thank you." Upon giving her gratitude, Jessica
begins to cough uncontrollably once again. Catherine grabs her
around the waist, both to steady her and to comfort her. William
seems concerned as well and offers to fetch the doctor but
Jessica will hear none of it.*

*Poor Catherine is near tears. "Aunt Jessica," she begs.
"Please allow me to take you to Doc Jacob's. You have been
suffering with this cough for more than a year now. Why are you
so pigheaded about this?"*

*But Jessica is unmoved. "My dear, doctors never help. They
only make things worse. Besides, it's only the dampness. Let's get
back to the shop now and make room for the shipment. I will lie
down in the back for a short while to rest. I promise."*

*Catherine shakes her head. "Oh, you are just so impossible.
I give up."*

*The two ladies bid William farewell and walk arm in arm out
of his establishment. "Aunt," begins Catherine. "I was hoping
you would come again for dinner tonight. Ericka is looking
forward to seeing you after her first day of school. She wants to
tell you all about her day. It's the only way I could get her to go...
with the promise of you supping with us this night." When
Jessica hesitates, Catherine proves to be as headstrong as her
aunt, adding, "And I will not take no for an answer."*

*Jessica is clearly moved by her nieces' depth of feeling for
her. "I could never let that lovely little lady down," she smiles.
"But I insist on helping you prepare dinner."*

Catherine consents, "It's a deal, then. The three of us will prepare it together. Ericka will feel so grown up."

And with that, the ladies, one very old and one very young, continue their slow morning stroll back to their fine shop on Main.

Chapter Thirty-Three
Captain of My Heart

It amazed me how I could be a bird on a wire, so to speak, observing what was happening undetected. I followed the two women back to their charming little shop on the main drag of this picturesque seacoast village...

Upon reaching the store, Jessica goes straight into the back room to lie down, just as she promised her concerned niece. I have the sense that this is unusual for a woman as strong as she. As I continue to watch, people come in and out of the shop to chat, to make purchases. Somehow, I become aware of Jessica's personal history. It just comes to me, as though I have known her for years, like she is an old friend. Maybe she is.

Jessica has a reputation in town for being a tough but fair businesswoman. Years before, she opened the shop with her mother, Portia, taking advantage of her father's respected position as a captain. Her mother would sail abroad with Jessica's father, buying the finest fabrics and spices available, then bringing them back to their new shop where they would sell these wonderful items from near and far.

Jessica is the only one of the four sisters who never married, so she is the only with time and independence enough to run a business. Still, in that day, it was unusual for women to have a business endeavor of any sort. But Jessica and her mother built their small but substantial shop into a formidable import/export emporium. Soon, other captains joined into the enterprise and brought back wares to sell in the store.

When it came time for her parents to retire, they gave Jessica their home and the business, and happily moved down the coast a few miles from the center of town. Once a week, they came to help out at the store, that is, until they passed on, both peacefully in their sleep from old age, only six months apart. Until that time, the shop kept them busy and Jessica appreciated the help—and the pleasure of their company. A generous soul, Jessica dutifully sent them money to help them along, but in truth, they were very well off and didn't need it. They saved the money in an earthenware jug, which, after their deaths, was divided equally among the four sisters.

When Jessica sought someone to help with the shop, her niece, Catherine who was always very close to her, offered to lend a hand. Catherine, Jessica and Catherine's daughter Ericka spent many hours working side by side, talking, and making lovely dresses and dolls. Jessica cherished both of them. She spent a number of her days and nights with her nieces and with Jessica's sister, Molly, who is Catherine's mother. Catherine appreciated the opportunity to have something to do while her husband George, a first mate, is away at sea.

But now, Catherine worries that Jessica is more ill than she thought, for to head straight to the back room simply wasn't like her. Aunt Jessica would never lie down in the middle of the day like this, although during the past several months, she has rested more and more frequently, she thinks.

After several hours, the crates are delivered to the shop. Jessica hears the men and greets them at the front of the establishment. She politely asks them to move the large boxes to the rear of the store so they will be out of the way. "Just point out where you'd like them," one of the burly men tells her.

"Thank you, Michael. You're so kind," she smiles. "Near the back wall would be perfect."

"Not at all, Miss Jessica. We're only too happy to do it," he replies. The big man and his helper move the huge boxes as though they are children's toys. Jessica stops them before they exit and hands them each a two-dollar tip. At first they refuse but Jessica insists, and one thing the townspeople know is not to bother arguing with Jessica when she sets her mind to something.

At the end of this bright, sunny day, the two women close down the shop and slowly make their way to the schoolhouse where Ericka waits for them. The child rushes into her favorite aunt's arms and excitedly tells her of her day. Then all three head home for a nice, relaxing dinner together. Their supper is a simple but hearty stew with fresh bread Catherine baked just that morning. The women happily peel and chop side by side, then continue to chat as the delicious meal simmers and bubbles in the big pot.

After supper, Ericka sits on Jessica's lap as she tells her which boys at school are yucky and which are simply all right. It is clear that Jessica and Ericka are thrilled with each other's company. As she clears the table, Catherine watches the two with a smile for it is such a delight to see them together. Ericka inquires, "Auntie Jess, why did you never have children?"

"I never married, dear," Jessica softly smiles.

"Then if you never married, who is Captain Jeremiah, the man whose name is on the store?" Ericka wonders.

"He is someone I knew many years ago, dear," Jessica admits, with a touch of sadness in her voice. "Had he been around today, he surely would have been a captain. I named the store in his memory, for he will always be the captain of my heart."

"But where did he...?" Ericka begins.

"Now, Ericka, that's quite enough!" Catherine says sternly.

Alarmed by the tone of her mother's voice, Ericka knows she has made a big mistake. "I'm sorry, Mommy," she gasps. "I'm sorry Aunt Jess. I'm sorry." Ericka treats her aunt to a big hug. Jessica cherishes these embraces for they make her feel so warm and loved. Tonight, feeling a bit melancholy, Jessica especially welcomes them.

After the dinner dishes are washed and put away, the three ladies sit sipping tea, chatting and laughing until it is Ericka's bedtime, a bit past her bedtime, in fact.

"Would you mind if I tucked in Ericka tonight?" Jessica ventures.

"Yes! Please!" Ericka pipes up before Catherine can assent.

"Be my guest, Aunt Jessica," Catherine says. "I'm sure this little imp will love it." Catherine's eyes sparkle in the candle light as she smiles beneficently at the two. "I will put some more tea in the kettle while you're gone."

Jessica takes Ericka by the hand and leads her up to bed. It's a small, cheerful room at the top of the stairs. Jessica mounts the steps slowly, so as not to tax her breathing and spark a coughing fit. The girl quickly changes from shift to nightgown and jumps beneath the covers, tired but content. As Jessica tucks her in, Ericka reaches up to give her a big hug. Jessica wraps her arms around the girl as they hold each other for several moments. So much emotion passes between them that I can feel the warmth.

"I love you, Aunt Jess," Ericka confesses, somewhat shyly. "It makes me happy when you're here with us."

"It makes me happy too, dear," Jessica says.

"Maybe you could move in so you never have to leave," Ericka adds excitedly.

"But I'm here all the time, sweetheart," Jessica tells her. She gestures to her chest and the heart that beats within it. "I'm in here. Besides, I don't want to wear out my welcome. I will always be there for you. I love you so much," Jessica reassures the child as she kisses her cheek.

Ericka lays back on her pillow and smiles as Jessica smoothes her hair away from her face. "When I wake up tomorrow, I'm going to ask mommy if you can stay here with us forever and ever." She rolls over to her side, fitting a ragdoll (which I have the distinct feeling Jessica made) into the crook of her arm. "I love you too, Aunt Jess."

Jessica plants a kiss on Ericka's forehead and tucks the quilts around the girl's little body. A golden locket slips out from the bodice of Jessica's dress, which she deftly slips back inside. "Good night, sleep tight. Don't let the bed bugs bite," Jessica whispers.

"You always say that," Ericka chuckles.

Jessica smiles at her niece and pulls the covers more tightly around her to make sure she feels safe, secure and well-loved. Only after the girl's eyes flutter closed does Jessica return to the sitting room where Catherine sits quietly waiting in her chair. Jessica takes the seat beside her and takes her by the hand. As they talk amicably and sip their tea, Jessica toys with the locket on the golden chain. "My dear Catherine," she says. "When my time comes, I want you to have the store. Please promise me that you will always keep it in the family." With that, Jessica reaches into her dress pocket and removes a folded piece of paper. She hands it to Catherine.

"What's this?" Catherine wonders.

"Open it," Jessica tells her. As Catherine does as she's told, Jessica continues, "I had these drawn up a few weeks ago. It gives you sole ownership of Captain Jeremiah's Import and Export upon my passing." Catherine's initial reaction is to pull her hand away, but Jessica places her own hand on top of Catherine's to hold the papers in place there.

Catherine bites her lip. "I'm sure it will be many years before this happens. Maybe you should think about giving the shop to Ericka when she becomes a woman," Catherine suggests.

"No, my dear," Jessica says surely. "Take this and take good care of the shop."

"I will not have any more of this kind of talk in my house," Catherine replies, a bit too firmly.

Jessica smiles, "Yes, Cat. It's been such a lovely evening. Let's enjoy our tea."

The two sit chatting or an hour more, discussing everything and anything, reminiscing, laughing until tears almost come. Jessica tells Catherine stories about herself and what a headstrong young girl she was. She delights her with tales of Catherine's mother Molly, of the mischief they got into when they were little girls. "By the way, dear, where is your mother tonight?" Jessica wonders.

"She and father went to grandmother's old house to spend a few days by the shore," Catherine replies. "Father fancied a bit of fishing and mother wanted to make sure everything was in order down there. They will be home next week."

"It is so nice they have each other," Jessica reflects wistfully. Then she pulls herself out of the doldrums that threaten to take her away. "Well, my dear, it's time for me to go home," Jessica says as she stands and prepares to leave.

Catherine rises and takes her hands. "I look forward to seeing you in the morning." Catherine walks her aunt to the door. "We'll stop by your house on the way to school so we can walk Ericka there together. She was so disappointed you couldn't come with us this morning."

"Hopefully I'll feel better tomorrow," Jessica says. "I will see you in the morning, my dear." With her shawl around her shoulders, Jessica sets out and Catherine softly closes the door behind her.

The following morning, as promised, Catherine and Ericka head up to Jessica's house. They knock and knock on the door but there is no answer. Ericka is upset. "Did she leave before we got here?" she asks her mother.

"That isn't like her," Catherine says. "She knew we were coming." Catherine opens the door and calls out her aunt's name several times, her voice getting more urgent with each calling. She is clearly worried. "Wait here," Catherine tells her daughter. "I will check. Maybe she is still asleep."

As Catherine makes her way into Jessica's bedroom, she notices her aunt sitting at her little corner vanity table. Her head rests upon its smooth surface, as though she is sleeping, perfectly still, but Catherine senses that she is not.

Clutched in Jessica's hands is a tiny photograph. Without even looking, Catherine knows who it is. It is the likeness of Jeremiah, the man whom Catherine has heard so much about from her mother. This is the man Jessica had loved so dearly but never had the chance to marry. Her aunt carried his picture with her in her locket and kept another in a frame. The love of her life, Jessica's heart belonged to only him, and though many tried to court this lovely woman in her youth, she showed no interest.

Jeremiah is the reason Jessica never married. Jeremiah is the one whose name the fine shop on Main Street bears—Jessica christened it after him and his memory. Going to the shop each day always gave Jessica the feeling of being close to her beloved Jeremiah.

At first Catherine thinks her dear aunt is merely asleep, but as she approaches the woman's slumped form, she realizes that Jessica has finally gone to meet her darling Jeremiah. Catherine's heart aches in her chest and she begins to cry, when suddenly she hears a little, frightened voice behind her. "Momma, please tell Aunt Jessica to wake up. Tell her to hurry. We'll be late for school."

But as Ericka looks at her mother, then at her aunt, she knows that the kind, old woman is gone. "No, Momma, no. Please... wake her up...please!" the girl shouts.

Catherine falls to her knees, peering into Ericka's eyes as they began to well up. "Ericka, honey, Aunt Jessica is..."

But the child won't let her finish. "No, Momma, no!"

Catherine holds her close. "Aunt Jess has gone to visit her momma and poppa. She is no longer sick. She is at rest."

But Ericka will not be comforted. She tries to shake free from her mother's embrace. "No, Mommy, I don't want her to leave. I love her. She can't...she can't." Ericka begins to sob in Catherine's arms.

Through tears, Catherine whispers to Ericka, "I will miss her too but remember, she will always be with us, in our hearts."

Ericka shakes her head. "No, Mommy, you don't understand. She promised me that she would always be here. Just last night..."

Catherine holds Ericka firmly by the shoulders and looks into her red, swollen face. "You must know that your aunt loved you very much and she will always be here. In here." Catherine gestures to her heart.

"She said that to me last night," Ericka sighs. "But now..."

"Ah, yes," Catherine tells her. "As she told me each and every night she tucked me in as a little girl." Catherine and her daughter speak softly and kindly of Jessica and when the girl is

*ready, her mother tells her, "Come, we must take care of Aunt
Jess now as she did to us."*

*As they turn to walk out of the bedroom, a small locket falls to
the floor. Catherine remembers it as the one Jessica wore around
her neck every day. She bends and picks it up, prying it open
gently with her fingers. Instantly, she recognizes the portrait
of a youthful Jessica. In the locket's second compartment is a
portrait of a young man, the same man in the larger photograph.
Jessica's Jeremiah.*

*Catherine takes Ericka's hand and gently presses the locket
into her palm. "Aunt Jessica would want you to have this,"
Catherine says. "Let's put it around your neck. This way she
will always be with you. She and her dear Jeremiah will watch
over you."*

*Ericka examines the beautiful locket in her hand, smiling
sadly. "Would you help me put it on?" Catherine does, beaming
through her tears. As the two slip from the room, Ericka takes
one last look back at her aunt, lying peacefully at her dressing
table, Jeremiah's portrait clutched in her hand. Then they leave.*

*Against my will, I find myself leaving too. I am once more at
the wall of fog and my journey ends as abruptly as it started. I
walk across the stone bridge and begin to count backwards from
five to awaken.*

It took me a moment or two before I remember where I was.
Slowly, the view of the harbor filled my vision. At first, I felt an
overwhelming sadness for Jessica, whom I had followed on all of
my previous trips. I tried to absorb what I just saw...or dreamed,
wondering if this would be my last trip there.

I laid back and watched the sun begin to set. As I returned to
a more conscious state, my eyes began to focus and I studied the
sky as it changed colors—a phenomenon that never ceases to
amaze me. I finally pulled myself up to a sitting position,
clearing my head to full consciousness. Looking out over the
harbor for a moment, I smiled and headed back to my car. But I
didn't leave right away. Instead, I sat inside, reflecting on Jessica
and Jeremiah. A feeling of emptiness overwhelmed me because I
realized that I had now lived two lives with two separate endings
and had experienced two losses— Jessica and Sherry.

I sat quietly for several more moments as I thought about the latter, how Sherry walked away from me and never looked back. This took me on a journey from sadness to anger. I put the key in the ignition, started my car and headed north, more pissed off than when I began. All I wanted was to relax in front of the TV and watch a mindless comedy. I needed to laugh, not think—just to forget about life for a few hours. Because if I thought about what had happened—to Jessica, with Sherry—I would surely break down and cry.

 # Chapter Thirty-Four
Determined

I spent Saturday doing chores around the house, as usual. Then I rewarded myself with a trip to my favorite stream in the park again and waited for something of interest to happen (it didn't) but it did give me a chance to relax by the water, which wasn't a bad thing. On Sunday, I mowed the lawn, which I'd neglected for some time, as well as completed many boring items on Carol's "Honey Do" list.

At least working on these projects helped keep my mind busy. I felt relieved that Sherry never entered it ...well, maybe once or twice for a moment but at least she didn't dominate my mind. It would be two weeks that Thursday since our split. In general, I felt good. I was getting back to the old "me" quickly and still felt adamant about never allowing myself the foolishness of being hurt like that again.

As I buried myself in my work, I began to acknowledge that Carol and I did have a number of problems which I would love to fix, only I really wasn't sure how. She had become so cynical and I didn't understand why this happened. Maybe it was the way I treated her or talked to her. I know that sometimes I could be a bit short, what with the commercial side of the business—the side that pays the bills—slowing down and all of the pressures of daily life.

Plus, I was beginning to feel that it was time for a career shift because the photography business had changed so much. Art directors were under increasing pressure to get it done "right now," and as cheaply as possible. They didn't really care about quality. The same "good enough" syndrome that killed the US auto industry was now killing the advertising industry. The business simply was no fun anymore. Photographers weren't allowed to take the necessary time to do quality set-ups, and that was just the beginning. Instead of feeling sorry for myself, I tried to concentrate on how to change my fate. I would seek more wildlife assignments that would take me away from civilization for long periods of time. A welcome change and a positive step toward fulfilling my dream.

When I arrived at the studio that Monday, I went right to the computer and posted my contact information on several websites, listing myself as a wildlife photographer in search of assignments. I also included a link to my website so they could see samples of my work. I answered a few ads seeking photographers for similar outdoorsy assignments. Honestly, it felt really good putting my plans to make a career shift into motion. I'd spent the good part of the last several years pursuing of such assignments with no luck. This type of work was few and far between, so I had to be patient.

I also had to prep for a food shoot I had in the city on Wednesday. I'd been doing them so long, I could shoot them with my eyes closed, but at least it kept me from thinking about how things had gone to pieces with Sherry.

Wednesday arrived soon enough and the shoot wasn't until one that day. To keep my mind occupied, I decided to leave early—about 11, which would give me plenty of time to relax—and not feel pressured if I had trouble finding a parking space. But the truth was, if I sat around the studio waiting, I knew my thoughts would drift to Sherry.

I packed everything up I had to bring, double-checked it and changed the message on the answering machine to let anyone who called know that I was on location. A quick glance at the clock told me that I was moving faster than I'd thought. Damn, it was only 10:30. I figured, what the hell, I'd stop at the deli, grab a coffee and shoot the breeze with Rocky for a few minutes. I loaded up the car and I was off to the deli in a flash.

While I was wrestling with the minutia of my Wednesday, Sherry worried that she had blown it with me altogether and was nervous about calling me. She planned to do it as soon as she cleared some work off her desk and got in early to accomplish the task. She hoped to talk me into having lunch with her. *After all, what would he have to lose?* she thought to herself. *I may have lost everything already.* Sherry was feeling very foolish about what she'd done two weeks earlier. She realized that it must have hurt me more than she imagined it would but was surprised that I hadn't called her at least once.

It was already 10:30 when she decided to phone me at the studio, which offered her more of a safety net than calling my cell. On the cell, I could always say I wasn't around if I wanted to avoid her, but if I picked up at the studio, she knew I was local and had a better chance of saying "yes" to lunch... especially since she was treating. But the phone rang and rang until the answering machine picked up. When she realized that lunch wasn't happening, she hung up without leaving a message.

Although disappointed, Sherry's determination to see me again would not be deterred. She later explained that she needed to look deep into my eyes once more to see if there was a chance to win me back, to regain the time we'd lost and hopefully repair the damage done.

Sherry also knew that I was the type who never looked back. She remembered our conversation from when we'd first met when I'd told her that once I moved on from something that failed, I would never go back. It was my philosophy that if something didn't work after you gave it your best shot, it wasn't meant to be. As hard as it was, you had to move forward or you would be taken down by it. I told her that I'd watched too many people in my life get stuck in the past and that most of them never got out.

This memory of this conversation really started to resonate with Sherry as the day went on. As the hours ticked away, she vacillated back and forth between walking away from the relationship and giving it one more shot. Suddenly, something I'd said hit her: "Do what you can to repair any damage." That's exactly what she resigned to do and she hoped I would respect her for giving us one more shot. After all, this wasn't some sordid affair—it was so much more than that. Like me, Sherry still wasn't exactly sure what it was, but she instinctively knew that we had traveled great distances to come together and she wasn't about to lose it.

At that moment, Sherry decided that she would continue to drop by the studio and keep calling me until she actually reached me...and got through to me. She smiled to herself, knowing deep inside that it was the right thing to do. And I, for one, was very glad she did.

Chapter Thirty-Five
The Beat

The food shoot was pretty much like most food shoots—uneventful, unexciting, lots of hurry-up-and-wait. Once I was through, I headed back up to Westchester, stopped at the studio, dropped off my equipment and drove home. Also pretty uneventful.

One thing that was on my mind now more than ever, was how much I enjoyed my little trips to the past. I began to wonder if I wasn't enjoying the past more than I was enjoying the present. Another thought that crossed my mind: were my voyages now complete? After watching Jessica pass away and seeing Jeremiah murdered, what was left? What was the purpose? Was any of this significant to my life today? Was there a message I was missing? I decided to give it one more try as soon as time would allow.

No one was there when I got home. The house was quiet, still. Being alone and a tired from my long day, I figured it was as good a time as any to attempt to take a trip back to the past. I'd never done it without being outdoors but what did I have to lose?

Maybe Jessica and Jeremiah would appear again from some point in their lives that I had yet to witness.

I lay down on the couch and counted backward, fully expecting to be in the 1800s again. But that wasn't what happened..

I cross the stone bridge that is becoming so familiar to me, I can probably navigate it with my eyes closed. The thick fog greets me and I cut through its moist curtain expectantly. But, what is this? Where is my quaint, beautiful village?

I find myself in a city during what seems to be the early 1900s. It doesn't look like New York but more resembles Chicago, with a lake and rivers surrounding it. I stand on a side street made of cobblestone, lined with trees. It is dusk. The streets are pretty deserted, except for a police officer walking slowly up the middle of the block, with his nightstick in hand. The policeman hesitates when he sees a woman come around the corner toward him. I am able to get a closer look at him at this point. He is young and fresh-faced, with the expectant air of a rookie.

Then I notice something else that floors me. This guy looks almost exactly like me when I was younger. The moment he gazes upon the young woman's face, his eyes light up; he seems to know her. The woman gives the policeman a big smile as she approaches. Now that she is out of shadow, I can study her face. My heart leaps as she comes closer and into focus, and I am shocked by what I see. It is Sherry! Confused more than ever, I wonder if this is a dream or if I was transported to another time, another place? Although Jessica and Jeremiah strongly resemble Sherry and me, these two are almost identical. They could be our twins.

"'Evening, Mary. How was your day today?" the policeman inquires.

"I was very busy, Robert. And how about yours?" Mary answers.

"Mine? Let's just say mine has been very interesting." Changing the subject, Robert asks, "May I escort you to your door this evening?"

"I only live a few houses down, Robert. I think I will be safe," she smiles boldly. "But please be my guest if you so desire."

Robert doffs his cap, turns and the two proceed to walk slowly until Mary is at her front stoop. They make small talk and from the sound of it, these two have been running into each other for quite some time. Mary stops at the bottom of the steps and turns to Robert. "This is my stop," she says with a giggle.

"Ah, I have done my duty and made sure another of this city's special citizens arrived safely at her destination," Robert jokes. Mary looks around to see if anyone else is approaching, then leans in and gives him a kiss.

"What time are you coming by to get me tonight?" she asks. "I get off at 11, so I can be here by 11:15. Perhaps we can go down to the Water

Front Café for coffee. It will be a wonderful evening—just the two of us," he tells her. "I hate when you have to work the three to 11 shift. By the time you come to me,

I'm so tired I can hardly think," Mary admits.

"Then we can skip our coffee if you'd like to catch up on your beauty sleep," he quips with a devilish smile. "Not that you need any more beauty. I can just go out with the guys in my squad."

Mary pokes him playfully in the belly. "I will go up and take a nap right now so I will be wide awake for you tonight." She is up the stairs and gone in a shot.

Robert continues on his patrol with a spring in his step. I get the feeling that the streets in those days were a very dangerous place for the police, especially an honest one like Robert. From what I'd read—and what I feel—there were many corrupt cops on the beat, looking out for themselves, ready to take a kickback. Honest cops were their enemies, so that the good ones had no one watching their backs.

Street gangs were also coming up fast and furious in those days, and every ethnic group had one. It was also a time when gangsters were especially dangerous and plentiful. They would just as soon cut a good cop's throat as look at him. And the dirty cops who ran with them would cover up any "mishap" involving an honest cop, making it look like a suicide or an accident. Or *else they would just arrest some street bum for a cop's murder, knowing full well they were innocent. Either way, you lost.*

Something tells me that Robert is an honest cop and that he is in trouble. Something also tells me that he is pretty sharp. Robert knows that he must watch himself. The politicians are all in someone's pocket, so the honest young rookie keeps a keen eye open, always looking over his shoulder, hoping some day to change things, but knowing that day will not be soon.

The evening is not a demanding one for Robert, only some minor public drunkenness which he takes care of without a fuss. The officers always try to get the rummys to go home quietly before taking them in, and this evening, Robert works extra hard not to lock anyone up. He wants to be on time to meet Sherr... Wow! Talk about a slip...Sherry looks so much like Mary it's eerie.

As promised, Robert is sure to be at Mary's apartment on time. Her mother and father always stay up to greet him. They are proud of the fact that their daughter is dating one of the city's fine, upright police officers, and they know Robert will make an excellent husband and father himself some day.

The two leave Mary's apartment after a brief chat with her parents and rush off down the street to the café. Robert seems to be in a hurry to get there. He also seems to be avoiding conversation with her, giving short answers or not speaking at all. He is a man on a mission.

When they arrive at the café, the owner appears to be waiting for them. "Good evening, Robert...Mary," he nods with a flourish. 'It is a lovely evening, no? I have saved a special table for you."

The owner leads them out to the deck, which overlooks the lake. It is a pleasant night, dark and still, with a crescent moon lighting the scene. As they follow the man to the verandah, Mary leans into Robert and asks, "How did he know we were coming? Or does he save a special table reserved for you and a sweetheart every night?" Mary pinches his arm for emphasis and giggles.

"Ouch!" Robert says, rubbing his arm. "You're the only girl for me, Mary. Don't you know that?" Mary beams contentedly.

The moon smiles upon the water with its warm, beneficent glow, comforting those who take the time to let it into their souls. The water slowly laps the shore as a subtle breeze blows in from the lake.

Once seated at their table, a waiter brings them a pot of tea and two cups. Mary stares at Robert as though he is the cat that caught the mouse. He reaches across the table, takes her hands in his, and looks straight into her eyes as the moon teases them with its light. "As you know, I have a good job with a future," Robert begins. Mary nods in agreement. "I have a simple question for you." Robert becomes suddenly serious and drops one of Mary's hands. He takes a deep breath as she holds hers. "I was hoping that you would become my wife," he says.

Mary sits there for a minute, somewhat stunned, as Robert slips a ring from his pocket and drops it into her hand at the very same moment. She looks down at the golden circle in her hand, not quite grasping what Robert is doing. When it finally hits her, everything becomes clear—the clipped conversation he had with her parents (he was always rather chatty with them)...the café owner having a special table for them..."What do you think my parents will say when we ask them?" she says.

Robert laughs, "They gave me their blessing tonight before you came home. I stopped up on my beat and asked their permission. I was nervous, but they were thrilled—I was relieved actually—because I had already bought the ring."

"That was a little presumptuous of you, wasn't it?" she jokes.

"I figured I would take a chance," he shrugs. "Now are you going to answer me or are you stalling?"

"As I recall, you never did ask me a question," she tells him.

Robert clears his throat again. "Mary, will you marry me?" he asks , his expression deep and serious.

"Oh, yes! Yes!" she shouts excitedly. Mary leaps up and gives Robert a powerful hug and a big kiss. The owner brings over a bottle of fine champagne after observing the events, replacing the tea cups with carved crystal goblets.

"This is on the house...for two of my favorite customers," he explains, overcome with emotion.

"Fritzie, you seem as excited as we are," Robert remarks. Fritzie leaves, embarrassed, shaking his head and mopping his eyes with a huge handkerchief.

Once they settle down, Robert and Mary sit and talk for almost two hours, making plans for their future: the wedding (simple, small and elegant), an apartment (ditto) and perhaps even children. They decide. without hesitation, that the wedding will be held right there in that very café. Realizing the late hour, the two leave the café and practically float back to Mary's house.

Despite the time, her parents are anxiously waiting for them, still sitting on the stoop. They take one look at Mary and Robert, trying to read the happy verdict. Without a word, Mary smiles and lifts her left hand to show the beautiful diamond ring on her finger. Her mother leaps to her feet, grabs Mary's hand and gushes over the ring . Mary's father is bursting with pride. "You'll make a fine policeman's wife," he says, then hugs his daughter. "And you, a fine husband for my baby," he admits, patting Robert on the back. Then he puts his arm around Robert's shoulder and grabs him in a bear hug, holding him for several minutes.

After the men break awkwardly from their embrace, all four go into the apartment but I do not follow. The door to the building closes before I can enter and I suddenly find myself back at the stone bridge, walking rapidly back to the other side.

The noisy entrance into my house by my family shook me right out of my vision. I lay there, trying to absorb these new events, reveling in the happy ending to this one. It was now clear that Sherry and I were together in at least two other lifetimes before, perhaps even more. I was now convinced that Jessica and Jeremiah inhabited the same souls as Mary and Robert. I was sure also that Sherry and I were these souls, and that we had found each other in this life as well. It was all making sense now.

Later that evening, I sat quietly eating dinner with my family, contemplating what I had witnessed, my realization and my understanding of these events. Tomorrow, I would call Peggy and have a long conversation with her about my latest vision to resolve this thing, once and for all.

I tried to watch some TV that night, to no avail, because I was completely overtaken by my trip into the past. Thoughts of Sherry also crashed back into my head. I knew we were meant to be together but why didn't she? I fought to keep my feelings of love from turning into anger as I worried that I wasn't important enough for her to try to hold onto while she resolved her issues with Bill. I did everything I could to stop myself from thinking about Sherry, to little avail.

At eleven o'clock, Carol and I made our way to bed, as though neither of us were looking forward to it. I tossed and turned most of the night, hoping I wouldn't dream, both fearing and looking forward to the dawn and the answers the next day might hold.

 # Chapter Thirty-Six
Deja Vu Stew

The following day, I decided to forget about the gym and head back to the shore. I couldn't wait to find out more about this new cop and his soon-to-be wife. But I had some matters to resolve before I could leave for my favorite spot. I made a quick stop at work to get what needed to do out of the way—some correspondence, mostly—then planned to take off for the water's edge. But first, some more important business.

I arrived at the studio at about seven a.m., my head still swimming in the swirl of Sherry, Robert, Mary, Jeremiah and Jessica. I knew my friend Peggy was an early riser, so the indecent hour of 7:30, I was on the phone to her, explaining what I'd just experienced the previous evening.

"This is very interesting, Jarred," Peggy began, calmly, as though it were the most natural thing in the world. "What you're doing is reliving past life experiences. Soul mates can come from a variety of unresolved relationships. You're seeing these two as married, or as lovers, in two separate situations. This tells me that someone in your life, or someone who is about to enter your life, is a former lover from a past life. It's believed that many of us who come together in this life could have been sisters or brothers, even mothers and sons, with unfinished business. So, we come together again in this life, in different ways, to complete what wasn't completed before. A cosmic event, if you will."

I interrupted her. "Slow down there, Peggy. You're giving me way too much information to absorb all at once. All I'm concerned with right now are these couples I've seen. What's your take on it?"

"All I can say, Jarred, is to be very cautious with any woman who enters your life now," Peggy advised me strongly. "This could cause trouble in your marriage. And if something does happen, remember this: you have the power to avoid a disaster."

"Thanks, Peggy," I said. "Your advice is always good and right on target."

As I was finishing my conversation with Peggy, I heard someone come into the studio. I figured it was one of the attorneys who worked next door, stopping by to say hello, so I didn't turn around right away. But after I said good-bye to Peggy, I turned around, and who was standing there but Sherry. I was more than surprised—I was in shock because she appeared almost as if on cue.

Sherry leaned against the door of my office looking as nervous as I was. After the initial shock, a range of emotions shot through me—from delight to anger to angst. "Good morning, Jarred," she said with trepidation.

I opened my mouth to speak but nothing came out. Sherry talked fast, as though she were afraid I might send her away. "I wanted to see you so figured I would come here, sit in my car and wait for you no matter how long it took, even if I had to call in sick," she blurted out breathlessly, with trepidation.

"Well, I'm here," I told her with an edge of anger. "Nice to see you, too."

I didn't want it to come out that way, but it did. I'm not sure if it was because of the walls I'd put up or the conversation I'd just had with Peggy, but whatever it was, I was standoffish, to say the least. But it didn't appear that my demeanor put Sherry off one bit, because she continues to approach me with determination in her dark, fiery eyes. Sherry leaned forward and nailed me to my chair with a long, passionate kiss that might have killed a lesser man. She stepped back and smiled, "I have missed you so much, Jarred. You have no idea."

"Well, you have a hell of a way of showing it," I shot back. "It's been two weeks and not a word from you. If you cared so much, how could you stay away like that?" Again, I wasn't able to hide my anger, hurt and disappointment.

Sherry bowed her head. "I didn't stay away. I tried to call but you weren't in. I even came by last Thursday and you weren't here either. I waited until almost 6:30," she told me in a plaintive voice.

I knew Sherry was telling me the truth because it was true—I wasn't here those times she mentioned. Slowly dropping a few more bricks from the wall that encased me, I stood up and looked in Sherry's eyes, knowing I just had to kiss her. Not simply because of my deep passion for her but because I was convinced that a kiss I initiated would convey her real feelings.

I took Sherry's face in my hands and pressed my lips to hers. Her knees buckled slightly as her body swayed into mine. And me, I felt like I was levitating. I knew at that very moment that this was real. Sherry wrapped me into her arms and held me close with everything she had. My head began to swim with confusion, emotion and even a healthy dose of fear. I thought about what Peggy had just told me about the past-life journey I'd taken last night. This was it. This was the cosmic event she spoke of. I began to laugh.

"You find this funny?" Sherry inquired.

I couldn't possibly have told her what about that "cosmic event" crap. Hell, I didn't even believe in that stuff or—I should say—didn't then. "Not at all," I lied. "It's just nerves."

"We have a lot to talk about, Jarred," she began. "I hope you can forgive me for being so selfish and confused at our infamous lunch two weeks ago," she said softly as her voice trailed off.

"We'll talk," I told her. "But not now. We don't have enough time before you have to go to work. So let's save it until we can be together for a whole day."

I had barely finished when Sherry took out her cell phone and dialed. Changing her voice to sound sick, she groaned, "Hi, it's me...Sorry for the last minute call, but I woke up feeling really ill. I can't make it in, Val. I'll try my best to come in early tomorrow to catch up." She hesitated for a minute, listening to Valerie's response. "Thanks for being so understanding. I'll talk to you later. I just want to get back to bed."

After Sherry hung up, I looked at her and laughed, "Academy Award-winning performance."

She smiled, leaned into me and said, "If you're not worth a little, white lie, tell me now, and I'll head off to work."

"No, stay here. You can do some work for me then, instead of Val," I kidded her.

"Oh, no...no work. We have too much to discuss," Sherry said emphatically. "I have something I need to tell you about."

"Like?" I inquired.

"I had this strange dream last night," she started. "I went to bed early because I knew I was coming here at the crack of dawn." I held my breath as she continued. "In the dream, you were this cop in some city at the turn of the century. Your name was Robert and you were with a woman by the name of Mary. They were in a café where he asked her to marry him. There is more to it, but that was the gist of it," Sherry said. "And I had the strange feeling that this Mary...that she was me."

When she broke off, I finished the sentence for her. "And, when they got back to her parent's apartment, they all embraced."

Sherry looked at me in amazement. "How did you know?"

I took her hand and brought her over to the couch. "Sit down," I told her. "We have so much to talk about," I smiled. "I think I dreamed the same dream."

The two of us sat and talked about the experiences I'd been having and Sherry's as well. Both were startlingly similar, if not exactly the same. The only difference was that Sherry's came to her as dreams, not as visions. Now more than ever, I was convinced that there was more to our relationship than met the eye. She and I also realized that we wouldn't d be able to prove anything scientifically but we decided to accept this and not question it. After all, we always knew somehow that we were being pulled together from some unknown place, for some unknown reason and these dreams were our proof.

Somehow, the hurt and pain I'd experienced over the past weeks without Sherry were beginning to gradually sift away and be replaced with a sense of wholeness, goodness and belonging. But I wasn't going to let her off the hook so easily. I knew we were destined to be together but I wasn't about to be put through the emotional wringer whenever Sherry felt guilty or had doubts. It had to be all or nothing and I had to make sure she knew this. "Okay, with that understood," I started, "We need to address what just took place. Why you ran away from me and didn't trust me enough to tell me you were scared. Why you didn't ask me to stand by your side till you sorted this through."

Sherry didn't respond. Instead, she moved closer, slid her arm around me and looked into my eyes. She smiled softly and gently kissed me. The scent of her skin paralyzed my mind and my heart, almost to the point that I was sorry I was resuming this tempestuous relationship. If I were to totally let down my emotional walls, I couldn't keep putting them back up again only to have them torn down by my captivating soul mate. Sherry and I kissed for a few more minutes before I regained my composure and pulled back. I tried again. "I need to know what you were thinking while we were apart," I told her, more emphatically this time. "I can't go through that again."

Sherry looked at me and shook her head. "I really don't know why I did it. I regretted it the moment I stepped out of the car. There were so many things flying around in my head. I was confused, hurt and scared all at once." She paused, then continued, "But the one thing I understood a little too late is that I needed someone to talk to and you were that person. By the time I realized that I'd pushed away my best friend, I felt that I'd hurt you so much I couldn't bring myself to turn to you for help."

"How do you know I was so hurt? I never said a word."

"You didn't have to," she replied. "I saw it in your face."

Sherry bit her lip. This was clearly hard for her. "But I needed to be with you so bad I broke down and called. Only I was afraid to leave a message because I felt you might think I was avoiding you by leaving messages. Jarred, I promise you I have learned a lesson. I missed you so much and I realized what a mistake I'd made. I vow I will never let that happen again, I swear," she said with conviction.

"I'll take you at your word and give you a second chance but I will always be a little cautious," I advised her.

"I understand and respect that but please don't punish me for being stupid," Sherry pleaded. "Give me a chance to make it up to you." She began to tear up.

I rubbed her shoulder to assure her. "I have no intention of punishing you. It serves no purpose. Let's just accept this as our first fight, move forward and mend."

Sherry looked at me with tears rolling down her cheeks. *"Our first fight?* What do you mean? Are you planning on others?" she asked, smiling through her tears.

"I don't think I can take another fight like this," I told her. "Look, with two people who care about each other so strongly, emotions are bound to run high. But it's the strength of their love for one another that will prevail and move them toward a stronger bond."

"That is powerful," she said. "I never thought about it like that."

Sherry grabbed me, pulling our bodies together. The moment our mouths met, all of my concerns melted away. I kissed a damp trail down her neck. She moaned and pushed me back onto the couch, straddling my body, wedging her leg between mine. Pressing her hips into me, she opened my shirt with clumsy fingers, still kissing me. Slowly, she began moving down my chest to the top of my pants, which she started to unfasten. Although I felt like I was going to explode, I stopped her. I wanted to feel her hot, mouth on mine and feel her embrace more than anything but I also wanted to savor her. Wordlessly, she understood.

I unbuttoned Sherry's blouse and begin kissing her neck, slipping down to her chest. I slid the soft fabric over her head and dropped it to the floor, nuzzling her breasts, getting lost in her warmth and sweetness. Control was no longer ours. Our only desire, our only goal, was to please each other. Within moments, our bodies were bare and we slowly, fervently became one. There was a power flowing through the two of us, from one to the other, and back. The passion was deeper, more potent than anything I had ever known. We held nothing back, becoming lost in each other, so that I wasn't sure where I ended and Sherry began.

Afterwards, we laid there quiet, spent, in awe of the way our bodies transcended the physical and interacted on a purely emotional level. I felt more bonded to Sherry than I ever had to another human being, not wanting to say a word, not needing to say a word. The energy that poured from her body to mine was amazingly electric. I whispered to her, "I never want to let you go. I want to stay like this forever. Please don't let go."

Sherry smiled and sighed, pulling me closer. I never felt so relaxed, so much a part of anyone before. Our relationship was now cemented and the future ahead of us filled with hope. We let the past go, left it behind us on this path, this journey, and the only way to continue was onward and upward.

I began to lose track of time, but I figured that we lay there an hour or so, simply holding each other. We were both getting hungry so we decided to have a nice lunch and spend the rest of the day together. And we wanted to start where it all began.

Sherry and I drove to Sunset Cove and asked for a table overlooking the water. We chatted, laughed and thoroughly enjoyed our lunch together. From there it was just a short ride to Rockefeller State Park. I took her to my perch overlooking the valley and the Hudson, where we spent the rest of our day learning each other's secrets.

Before long, the sun began to set over the river. Sherry and I knew, sadly, that this day had come to an end and that we had to return to our other lives. But we were ever so grateful that we had this day to enjoy. We traveled slowly down the path in the dwindling light, trying to make our remaining moments together last.

I turned to her before getting into my car. Sherry smiled at me, saying nothing. I kissed her and held her tightly before we drove to the studio to get her car. Sherry caressed the back of my head and neck during the short, quiet ride. So closely bonded were we that words were unnecessary things.

Outside the studio, Sherry leaned over, gave me a quick kiss and thanked me for such a wonderful day. Before I knew it, she was off to her car. It jumped to life as she turned the key. I smiled sadly and blew her a kiss. Watching her drive off, I knew that she was disappearing from sight, but not from my life.

My emotions were mixed. I felt wonderful, privileged, to have experienced such a day yet sad that it had to end. I knew instinctively that there will be more such days ahead of us and probably some tough ones, too. But I also knew that the tough times would be short-lived. Once behind us, they would bring us even closer.

I put my car in drive and head off to my previous life.

 # Chapter Thirty-Seven
Cloud Nine

Time has flown. It's difficult to believe that three years have passed already. Yes, it's been that long since I wrote my last journal entry. Over the years, I've showed these chapters to Sherry and she thinks they're wonderful. (Of course she would!) She also thinks I should publish them. I'm not sure about that. They're too personal, too private, too "out there." Besides, who would believe them? "Well, you could always publish it as fiction," she says with a wry smile."

For now, I think I'll just finish up our story, writing it in the past tense, even though the past is very present for me.

It was beginning to snow and I wondered if Sherry would cancel our regular Thursday night meeting. It's been more than three years now since we met for lunch that significant day at Sunset Cove. With every week that passed, Sherry and I continued to grow closer. The idea that we were completing something that once was—our past lives together—seemed to have created a strong bond between us.

Our relationship, being limited to seeing each other once or twice a week, kept strong and fresh. I always looked forward to seeing her, as she looked forward to seeing me. It was mutual and still very exciting. When Sherry and I got together for lunch, we talked about things we enjoyed, things we had in common, not the day-to-day garbage that everyone has to deal with. That could really kill a relationship and ours had already been killed so many times in the past, in the guise of different people. Together, Sherry and I laughed and had simple, honest conversation. I felt blessed to have met such a wonderful soul and to have her in my life.

To this day, when I saw Sherry, my eyes lit up and my heartbeat kicked up a notch. Her touch still made me tingle, filling me with a comforting warmth that was indescribable—it never failed to put me on Cloud Nine. We had something very special. Did I wish we'd met before we were involved with others? There's no doubt about that, but we've been dealt this hand and now we must play it out for all was worth. To us, this special relationship was priceless and we cherished any bits of time we were able to spend together.

I'd be a liar if I said I didn't struggle about having an affair with Sherry. I'd always been one of those guys who looked down on anyone who violated the trust between husband and wife. But the sad, surprising reality was that this thing with Sherry actually helped my relationship with Carol. I lost the anger and resentment I held toward her for always putting the kids before our relationship. I was no longer resentful about what we didn't have in material wealth. My kids were just as important to me as they've always been but then again, I always knew there would come a time when they'd leave the nest, leaving Carol and me to live the life we should have been building all along. Instead we grew apart. But that's all right now. That's all right because I have Sherry.

At about 4:30, I looked outside the studio. It would be dark soon and the snow seemed to be coming down hard. I was sure the phone would ring at any moment to cancel our weekly get-together, but it didn't. I went back to my computer to finish some work and check my emails. I opened a message from a potential client and as I read, my mind spun out of control. It presented new possibilities and I was confused and lost about what I should do.

I jumped out of my reverie when I heard stomping feet behind me. "You'd better make my time worthwhile tonight since I braved the dangerous elements to get here," Sherry laughed as she brushed the snow off her shoulders. I closed the email

Sherry dropped her coat on an empty chair and kissed me hard. Any snow on us at this point would not only have melted but it would have evaporated. My knees became putty. The smell of her hair, her skin, her soft, tender touch worked the magic it had for many years now. The snow, the wind and the treacherous driving conditions were of no concern to me. My world was now sunny skies with big, puffy clouds and rainbows.

"What were you reading that you clicked off so quickly?" she inquired when we broke out of the kiss.

"It was nothing. I really didn't get a chance to read it because you got here," I told her. "And I couldn't wait another second to hold you."

"Oh, crap, you don't really think I'm going to buy that, do you?" she smiled.

"Really! I just started to look at it," I shot back a little nervously. "Hey, we can read it together. How's that?"

Sherry looked outside and said, "As much as I'd love to, with this weather, we have precious little time." She dragged me to the couch. It was a place we would talk and do projects together. Sherry would help me with my photos and I would exchange ideas with her on her work. Our relationship had moved so much deeper than merely the physical, although the physical was an important part of what bonded us. You see, this sofa was also our bed as well as our place to brainstorm.

That afternoon, time was of the essence. We embraced quickly, passionately. Moving down her neck, I unbuttoned Sherry's blouse, kissing a slow, wet path, bypassing her chest and moving lower until she melted beneath me.

Even after dozens of months, the passion that invaded Sherry and my bodies was incredibly intense—always growing, deepening, strengthening our bond with a power that was almost frightening. Each time was as exciting as the first time. Uniting with Sherry was my life's one true pleasure. At the very moment we became one, my body shook with delight, feeling her warmth engulf me. Our eyes met, looking deeply into one another, which heightened the passion. I pulled her soft, moist lips to mine, gently kissing her as I slipped her body around me and I was lost. The pure joy of being one lifted me to heights I never thought possible and grew every time I was with her.

Afterwards, Sherry and I lay there, holding each other, not moving. She placed her head gently upon my chest as I slowly, softly scratched her back. She moaned and smiled, looking up into my face. Sherry kissed my chest softly, her hand flat upon my belly, the other hand on my shoulder. With her body upon mine, I was flying among the clouds under the warmth of the sun and the weather outside was of no consequence to either of us at that moment. I began to chuckle.

"What's so funny?" Sherry inquired.

"I was thinking about us, the passion, all of this kissing at our age," I told her. "I always saw this passion stuff as something for kids. But this...our relationship, our love has proven that passion is ageless when two hearts become one and souls come together."

"A little sappy, yes," Sherry quipped. "But very true. I never thought about it like that. I always believed that passion was possible, no matter what age. But you have an interesting point. It proves another thing, though."

"What?" I asked.

"It proves that you're still thinking way too much about stuff that is so unimportant. I give up on you," she laughed, as she pinched my chest.

"Ouch! What the hell?" I chided her, as I rubbed my chest.

"Oh, did I do that?" she gasped. "It must have been an involuntary reaction to your consistently over-thinking things." Sherry smiled as she got up and began to get dressed. "It's going to take us forever to get home in this weather," she added, looking out the window.

"Just call Bill and tell him you're staying here with me tonight. I'll do the same." "You're going to call Bill, too?" she joked. "You know what I meant," I said.

The two of us bundled up and left the studio after a few more minutes of sitting and caressing, and chatting amicably. I walked Sherry to her car, where we kissed good night, the snow swirling wildly around our bodies. "Do me a favor and call me when you reach your driveway," I told her. "I want to know you made it home safe."

"You're too cute," she smiled and kissed me again. "Me, cute? Well, that's one thing we agree upon," I laughed.

"Oh, Lord, that's it for me. I'm out of here. I'll call you," Sherry said as she got into her car and carefully drove off.

When I got home that evening, I didn't say much to Carol. I was deep in thought about the email I'd received that day. "How was the trip home tonight with all that snow?" Carol wondered.

"A bitch, as always, when there's any kind of weather," I responded. "Hey, what's up with you? You seem distracted tonight," she asked. "Nothing. I just have some business things to think about. SOS," I fibbed.

"Well, dinner is on the counter," she told me. We rarely ate together at the table, especially when the kids weren't there. I grabbed a plate, dished out some food, went downstairs and joined Carol in front of the TV as we had dinner in silence.

My head was still spinning because the email wasn't completely clear. There were a lot of unanswered questions surrounding it. I would give the sender a call first thing in the morning to clarify it before I said anything to anyone.

At about 11, Carol and I went upstairs to bed. Although I was tired, I was also wired. All I could do was lay there and stare at the ceiling, trying to figure things out. I tossed and turned until about three a.m. before I finally feel off to a dreamless sleep.

Chapter Thirty-Eight
Loose Ends

At six a.m., the alarm clock shook me awake. I was up and off to the gym in a flash, trying to avoid any thoughts about the email until I got to the studio. But then I met Mary Ellen there, my buddy and workout partner. A good friend, I confided in her my dilemma. Just as I knew she would, Mary Ellen told me that I shouldn't get ahead of myself and should find out all the facts before I drove myself nuts. I needed to think things through before I made much ado about nothing.

After this sound advice, we lifted weights and did a little cardio. After my vigorous workout with Mary Ellen, I went to Terry's class, joining the 30or so women in attendance. I hoped that with so many people around, I'd be a little distracted but it didn't work. That day, my concentration was off. I didn't seem to know my left leg from my right but I did my best and resigned myself to do the best I could with my head up my behind. As soon as class was over, I hit the locker room. The clock on the wall told me that I had several hours to kill before I could make that call, so I took a steam and tried to relax before hitting the shower.

On my drive to the studio, I stopped at the deli to talk to Rocky but his jokes and good humor were lost on me. I talked with him for a few short minutes because I was driven to get to the studio and start my phone calls.

By the time I got to the studio, the clock said 10:30. I fired up the computer, opened the email, read off the telephone number and dialed. "Hello, this is Jarred Stone.

I'm calling regarding an email a Mr. Peterson sent me yesterday. Is he available?" I inquired. I was placed on hold, which only took a minute but seemed like forever. My heart was racing and I tried to breathe normally.

"Peterson here," a solid voice said.

"Hello, Mr. Peterson," I began. "This is Jarred Stone, the photographer you emailed yesterday. How are you?" I asked.

"I am fine, Jarred," he told me. "Listen, I received your application and I had the opportunity to look at your work. We have a project that will be starting soon and we think you'd be perfect for it. Would you still be interested?" Mr. Peterson asked.

"I may be," I told him. "Could you fill me in on the details?"

We spent about 30 minutes talking and after the first five, I knew I had to do this project. I agree to meet him in two weeks time. Before going to meet him, I needed to get some business in order.

First, I called Carol and filled her in on my conversation with Mr. Peterson. I told her that we'd talk more about it when I got home and we'd take the weekend to work through the details. After I hung up with Carol, I looked around the studio and realized what a life-changing situation this would be for everyone in my life, including me.

Even with all I had to do, I couldn't stay cooped up in the studio any longer. I had too much to think about and wasn't in the mood to field calls or sort through photographs. I wanted to do some hiking at Rockefeller's. The snow had ended early enough the night before, so the highway department was able to get the roads clear for rush hour. I hoped Sherry was able to make it into work and would be free to grab lunch with me. I had a lot to share with her. Sherry picked up the office phone after the second ring. "Hi, it's me. Do you have time for lunch today?" I asked.

"Sure," she told me. "Valerie just called and said she wasn't feeling well. It's slow around here today, so sure, let's meet. Where and when?"

"I'm headed up to Rocky's estate to get some snow shots for my Christmas card. Why don't we meet at this little place in Irvington called River City Grill? It's just past the Main Street traffic light on the right," I told her. "Let's say 12:30."

"Perfect. I'll see you there," she said. "Hey, is anything bothering you?" "Why?" I asked. "I hear something in your voice. You sound sad," she told me. "No, I'm fine. Just a little tired. See you in about two hours."

I was one of only two cars in the Rockefeller parking lot. As I walked the snowy path, I was taken in by the scent of the pines and the crisp, cold air. I always find it invigorating and it woke my sprit. The freshly fallen snow and the moist, chilly breeze worked some sort of magic on me. Days like that brought me back to when I was a boy playing in the fields behind our apartment, exploring the vast tundra that the barren place had become in my young imagination. My friends and I searched those snow-covered fields for animal tracks left by small creatures like rabbits or birds like the ring-necked pheasant, both in abundance back then. We would follow the tracks until we flushed out whatever it was that created them. Life was always an adventure for me back then. To this day, that excitement of being out in the snow soon after it fell, still carried the thrill it did so many years ago.

The cold wind on my face heightened my awareness of my surroundings. The silence was wonderful. Because snow acts as a sound absorber, the woods were quieter than usual, giving me the peace I needed. I wasn't really concerned about getting photos of the snow today. After all, it was the first snowfall of the season and there'd be many other opportunities. This trip was all about me for a change.

Hiking along the trail, I was completely self-absorbed and feeling a little sorry for myself. Camera on my shoulder, I was startled by the sound of a big tussle in front of me. A red-tailed hawk swooped down on a squirrel and missed. So did I, because I never managed to get my camera off my shoulder. It would have been a great shot too but I took solace fact that this amazing sight would be filed away forever in my memory. I smiled, thankful I was able to witness it.

Seeing the hawk helped change my mood and made me realize that if I spent more time in the woods, I would experience wonders like this more often. I stood there watching the disappointed hawk perched back in his tree, scanning around for the squirrel he hoped would be his breakfast. The squirrel scurried to a nearby tree which camouflaged his thick, gray fur that blended in nicely with the tree's bark. Before I knew it, it was time for lunch with Sherry and I left my wooded haven behind.

At The River City Grill, Sherry and I chatted about putting together a show for Brush, Chisel & Lens in the spring. We discussed where the show should be and managed to bring in other things that were in our lives. I was at peace with Sherry now. I watched her soft, warm lips as she spoke, wanting to lean across the table to kiss them, yet I knew better. I wanted desperately to tell her what was happening with Mr. Peterson but there were still some details to be worked out, still questions to be answered, so I held back. I was afraid she wouldn't understand right now and that she'd take it the wrong way. I knew she would fire a barrage of questions which I had no answers to.

"Listen, I'm thinking of putting together a dinner party next Saturday night at my house," I told her. "Do you think you and Bill would be able to make it? I want to have all the people important in my life there."

"I'm pretty sure we can," she said. "Sounds like fun. We always enjoy getting together with you guys. Bill thinks you're interesting."

"Only Bill finds me interesting?" I asked, smiling. "Yeah. Why? Who else would?" she commented, busting my chops. "No one. Actually, Bill is all I need," I told her, and we both burst out laughing.

After lunch, Sherry and I headed to the parking lot, satiated and happy. I stopped Sherry as she was getting into her car. "Listen, I want you to know that I have a business opportunity that may be coming up," I began. "I don't know much about it right now but as things progress I'll keep you informed. This could be an opportunity for both of us."

"Sounds interesting. What else can you tell me about this business opportunity"? Sherry inquired with a sly smile.

"I honestly don't know if anything will come of it. I have so little information about it but I promise to fill you in as soon as I have all the details."

"Give me a call when you have something to tell me," Sherry said. "I really have to get back to work. If we don't have the chance to talk, I'll see you next Saturday at your dinner party," she said quickly. "I'm holding down the fort today."

Over the weekend, Carol and I had some very intense conversations about my future and hers—where we were going and the new events in my life. We talked for hours about the possibilities and examined all sorts of different scenarios. In the end, we agreed to wait things out and give it a day or so of thought. We also spent some time planning our dinner party next week, worked out the menu and the wines we'd serve. As usual, I'd do the cooking and Carol would help with the prep work. But nothing could prepare us for our friends' reaction when we dropped the bombshell on them.

 # Chapter Thirty-Nine
Coda

After a week of discussion with Carol and preparation for our announcement dinner, Saturday night finally came. My friends began to arrive pretty much on time, between seven and 7:30. All except for Sherry and Bill. We had a few hors d'oeuvres set out but dinner would be ready promptly at eight.

With everything that went on that week, I had no time to get together with Sherry to let her know in person exactly what Carol and I had ultimately decided. In truth, nothing had really been finalized until just the night before. I'd asked Sherry and Bill to get there earlier than everyone else because I wanted to tell them the news before the others got there. At 7:45, they still hadn't arrived. I was getting a little apprehensive– had they gotten into a car accident? A huge fight? Dinner and my big announcement was only 15 minutes away.

I was looking my watch when John, my electrical contractor buddy, came up to me and said, "Stop checking that damn watch. The food ain't gonna cook any quicker."

But I wasn't in the mood to joke. "Actually, I'm concerned that Sherry and Bill aren't here yet. I don't want to start without them," I told John, gravely.

"The hell with them. I'm starving and I can't wait to hear this big news of yours. I bet Bill's late because he's servicing one of his bimbo clients," John quipped with a wink and a smile.

Damn, I thought, does everyone know about that sleaze bucket?

"Yeah, you're probably right, John," I agreed. Then I excused myself and removed the roast from the oven to get it ready to serve. After I sliced it and covered it to keep it warm, I put the finishing touches on the garlic mashed potatoes and added a bit more soy sauce to the string beans. It looked great but I was still a bit bummed because I was really hoping to talk to Sherry privately before I served dinner.

Finally, she and Bill arrived, with Sherry looking a bit sheepish. "Sorry we're late," she apologized. "Bill had to work longer than he thought."

"I was finishing up a job," he added, guiltily, avoiding my gaze. *Yeah, right!* But I stopped myself before I said something I might regret. John caught my eye, smiled and shrugged his shoulders as if to say, *What can I tell you?*

I assured Sherry that it was no big deal, grinned nervously, then asked everyone to take a seat at the table. I was still disappointed that I didn't have the opportunity to talk to her before everyone else got there. I know she wouldn't be happy getting the news this way. I was also really pissed off at Bill for this thoughtless move, being late because of his extra-curricular activities.

"Dinner is being served," I said in a pinched, nasal voice like a proper British butler. Everyone must have been starving because they came to the table immediately Sherry sat directly across from me. I set the food on the table to oohs and aahs. I must admit the table looked—and smelled—great. The compliments about the delicious aroma played right into my delicate ego. I loved to cook but really enjoyed it most when I saw others enjoy a meal I'd prepared.

As I walked around the table, filling everyone's glasses with a hearty red wine, I joked with them, trying to ease my nervousness about what I had to say. I went back to my place at the head of my table, lifted my glass and thanked everyone for joining Carol and me. "As you may know, I have an announcement I'd like to make," I began. "I've asked all of you here tonight because I received final word on a wonderful opportunity and I wanted to share the news with all of you. It's an opportunity I'm going to take..."

Looking around, I noticed the apprehension on the faces of my guests, Sherry's in particular. Without hesitation, I jumped right into it. "I've taken a new job," I said. "This is the chance of a lifetime for me and there was no way I could turn it down. I wanted you all to celebrate with me."

I was now rushing through the words like a buzz saw. It was almost like I was hoping it wouldn't register with Sherry until I could talk to her privately, later. But I knew that wasn't possible. I knew my words were sinking in deeply, cutting her to the core. Which is why, coward that I am, I decided to tell her in front of a crowd.

I took a deep breath and continued, "Carol and I will be moving to Yellowstone National Park, where I've been invited to photograph the wildlife through the seasons." There were whispers and grumbles at the table but I plowed ahead. "This will take me several years. I have to leave in a week. Carol will be getting our things in order here and will join me once I get set up. We'll be living in a cabin on the grounds and I'll even have a National Parks Service car to use."

I paused and cleared my throat, "We will miss all of you but we promise to keep in touch. And I will be coming back here to represent my gallery and to do shows. This is a unique opportunity to live my lifelong dream, so I'm going for it."

I spit it all out as quickly as possible, with little hesitation or stopping to answer questions, avoiding details and keeping it as short as possible. "Now, let's eat. Dinner is getting cold," I said. I started the ball rolling by passing around the platter of roast beef, avoiding looking at Sherry.

The reception was mixed. Although almost everyone was happy for me, some expressed their fears of losing touch and missing our friendship. I was moved by their words because I never thought people would miss us...well, maybe Carol, but not me.

I raised my glass and asked everyone to join me in a toast. All but one did— Sherry. When I saw the wounded surprise on her face, I realized that I'd made a huge mistake...I should have told her about this sooner. But I really had no idea whether Carol would be joining me until just that morning. By then, I was so busy getting ready for the dinner party, I didn't have the time to meet with her—and I didn't want to tell her over the phone. That would have been too cold, too impersonal. But now I could see that telling her in front of a group of people was just as bad. In truth, there was no good way to tell Sherry. I knew she would be upset, no matter what.

I studied her blank expression as I passed the bowl of string beans. Her eyes dropped as she barely took a sip of her wine. My heart fell along with her eyes. This was worse than I thought. Words couldn't explain my pained emotions at that moment. Although everything was prepared perfectly, I could barely choke down the meal.

Suddenly, I felt a stabbing pain in my left shin—the heel of Sherry's shoe striking it like a dagger. It took all of my strength not to yell out. Although I knew my announcement might (okay, *would*!) bother Sherry, I didn't see how I could avoid it. If I put it off until after dinner, Carol would have gotten suspicious since we'd spent all day planning how we were going to break the news to our friends. And if I said I wanted to wait until Sherry and Bill got there, Carol may have put two and two together. Besides, everyone else would have pressed me for the news anyway. I was in a no-win situation.

I think everyone else enjoyed the dinner. The conversation was certainly animated as questions flew back and forth. Some couldn't believe how I could just pick up and leave like this. The guts it took to make such a big move impressed others. I explained that since our kids were grown and in college, what better time to realize a life- long dream. Of mine at least. I got the feeling that Carol was just doing it to placate me. And if the truth be told, I wasn't 100% convinced that she was going to go through with it and meet me out in Yellowstone once I got settled.

After coffee and dessert, everyone went downstairs to the family room for after- dinner drinks and more conversation. I lingered upstairs after Carol and the others went down ahead of me. So did Sherry. This was the first chance I had to talk to her alone, so I approached her before she could go down to the den with everyone else. But before I could say a word, Sherry stung me with her sharp tongue and cutting words. "I guess I don't matter in your life," she snapped.

"I thought you'd be happy for me..." I began. But the second the words came out of my mouth, I realized how selfish and thoughtless my actions seemed to her. Still, this was a once-in-a-lifetime opportunity to realize a dream. "I'm sorry," I told her. "I would have said something sooner but I didn't have all the details until just this morning. I was going to talk to you when you got here earlier but you guys were late."

"Damn you. I can't believe you're doing this," she whispered sadly, with a touch of anger thrown in for good measure.

"Can you meet me tomorrow morning?" I pleaded. "The place where we met by the river in the park?"

"When I leave tonight, it will be the last time ever you see me," Sherry said through tears and gritted teeth. "You had to know when you planned this dinner, what was happening. And don't you dare tell me you didn't."

"Please don't do this, Sherry," I begged. "I couldn't chance taking you aside to tell you sooner. Everything fell into place this morning. I feel awful about this but I swear we will be together again someday soon."

"Don't. Please don't say anything. We're finished," she insisted.

"I can't believe you're acting like this. I thought you'd be happy for me." "Happy?"

"Until a few hours ago, I thought I'd be commuting. I didn't dream for a second that Carol would agree to relocate." Nothing, silence. "Really, you've got to believe me. Please, just meet me there at eight tomorrow morning."

"Have fun," was her short, painful reply before she went downstairs to join the others. Very soon after, Sherry and Bill left. "I have a terrible headache," she explained to Carol, as they hugged goodbye. "It came on soon after I got here." Sherry didn't even look at me when she left.

The next morning, I headed up to my rock, not expecting to see Sherry. I sat there for almost two hours, sad and in pain, wondering what I had done, when all of a sudden, there she was. My heart raced with anticipation. I went over to kiss her but she turned her head away. "No, please don't," she insisted.

I took her into my arms but she resisted and tried to push me away. I held fast and wouldn't let her. "Please let me explain," I told her, my voice cracking with emotion. "This is something I've wanted all my life. I will find a way to be together again. They told me I could hire an assistant who'd get a house as well."

"Perfect...you, me *and* your wife," Sherry snapped.

"How different would it be than what we're doing now?" I tried to convince her. "Think about it, you'd be perfect for the job. I already told them about you and they said it was my choice entirely. I was hoping you would come out and be my assistant, be by my side in this wonderful, magical part of the country. We'll have a great life there."

"Oh, I see...I tell Bill I'm going out to be your assistant in some far off land. That will go over real well," she said.

"Don't you see, you won't need Bill anymore. Or if you decide you still want to be with him, you can fly out here and be my contact person between New York and Wyoming," I suggested.

Sherry didn't answer me so I let it go. Maybe she was considering it and I didn't want to put her under any pressure. But I was pretty sure I already knew her answer. Maybe I just didn't want to hear it just then.

I held Sherry tight until I felt her give way. She practically melted in my arms and began to cry. I did too. The pain of this move was much more than I had anticipated. My secret hope was that Carol would stay in Westchester with the kids (who were nearby, in college) and her job. Then I could convince everyone that Sherry would be my best choice as an assistant and liaison between New York and the galleries out west. Nothing in my dream plan ended up working out the way I thought it would. In fact, I couldn't have been more wrong. But I was committed and I couldn't turn back now. I was torn up inside and so was Sherry. "When do you leave?" she asked.

"I fly out Friday morning," I told her and she started to cry harder and hug me even tighter. My heart sunk into my hiking boots and my stomach ached. We held each other close as I tried to console her but there was nothing left to say or do except walk slowly back to our cars.

"Can we have one last date this Thursday?" Sherry asked, looking at me through red-rimmed eyes.

"I was hoping you'd want to meet," I admitted. "I'm subletting the studio to another photographer. He's coming by to pick up the keys at three. Any time after that will be good."

It was a long, difficult week as I thought and rethought about my decision. Was it worth attaining my dream only to lose my soul mate? But would I really lose Sherry? We'd lived so many past lives together, I hoped that this would just be a little blip in our long history. I hoped I could get her to think the same way so our separation would be less painful.

Thursday finally arrived. At 4:30, Sherry walked into my studio for the last time. She looked up at me as she approached me, grabbed me and pulled me close to her, tears streaming down her face. We kissed soulfully and both dropped to the couch. That night, we made love for hours, like never before. One act morphed into the next. We rose and fell, climaxed and recovered, then started it all over again. We spent much of our time talking, laughing and reminiscing, and avoiding the inevitable, but our short time together was running out. The hour has finally come for us to say our good-byes.

Sherry and I stood facing each other, fully dressed now, gazing into each other's eyes. Again, we flew together like two magnets connecting, the energy from within sizzling between us. Slowly our bodies separated, but not our hearts. I looked deep into Sherry's inky brown eyes and noticed new tears forming in them. My heart started breaking all over again. I told myself silently, *Be a man. Be strong for the both of you. Do what you have to do.* It took all my strength to walk her to the door, relishing the feel of her hand in mine. She grabbed me once again, pulling me against her in a kiss. Then we parted, but only because we had to.

As I walked Sherry to her car, I tried to kiss her one last time but she stopped me, turning away. She climbed into her car, started it and pulled away without another word. I stood there watching, as she drove off. The emptiness was crushing as her car quickly disappeared down the road. I never expected to feel like this. I foolishly had unrealistic expectations about so many things. Where the hell was my head? Once again, Sherry and I were pried apart, as we had been so many times before, in so many lives.

On Friday morning, after a sleepless night, I arrived at JFK Airport early. And in style, because my friend James was nice enough to offer to take me in his limo. (I left my car at home for Carol and the kids to use while I was out west.) I relished the thought of being alone for this trip to give myself time to reflect upon what was happening. The time spent, as it turned out, was tedious, empty and sorrowful.

I checked my bags at the curb, said good-bye to James and asked how much I owed him for the ride. He just gave me a hug and refused to take a cent for his trouble.

The walk to the gate seemed especially long, like a walk down death row. It took forever to embark upon the flight to my new world. When the announcement to board finally came, my heart sunk and my emotions ran roughshod over me. My legs could hardly carry me down the gangway. I felt a deep pit in my stomach as I boarded my flight. The emptiness was so overwhelming that I almost ran off the plane, back to what was now becoming my previous life. But I knew that backpedaling wasn't possible—it wasn't even an option. I'd made my bed and now I had to sleep in it. Alone.

I found my seat and buckled up just as the flight attendant anchored the door shut, trapping me. The airplane was about to rush me away from everything I had, everything I knew, everything I loved. The engines revved to a loud high-pitched whine as the plane slowly moved backward, then taxied to the runway, where we sat for several moments, as if to taunt me, torture me, rubbing in my foolish, thoughtless act.

Abruptly, the engines cut into high gear, thrust us forward and we were under way with a powerful suddenness that drove me back against my seat. I could feel the G-force pushing on my chest. (Or was it the pain of leaving Sherry?) As we lifted off and climbed into the clear, blue sky, I felt my heart leap from my chest. It was as though my soul were being yanked away from me in the jet's backwash. Airborne and climbing toward our altitude, I watched out the window as New York moved swiftly into the distance and away. Somewhere down there was Sherry.

What have I done? Why have I done this? I thought. What was it in me that needed to screw things up when everything was perfect?

I sat quietly reflecting upon my dreams, my choices, my decisions. I refused to look away from the cold, scratched plastic tray on the seat in front of me. I just wanted to be alone. I needed to avoid contact with anyone, everyone.

As I peered out the window, I noticed a reflection...a very sad man looked back at me. I saw unspeakable pain in his face, his lips quivering as tears began to flow slowly from his eyes, down his cheeks. He looked like exactly what he was—a soulless man with a broken heart, headed to a new life he thought he wanted. Who was he? Jeremiah? Robert? Or Jarred? Damned if I knew, but I was going to find out.

About The Author

Mr. Buchanan is married to Janice, they have two children a NYC elementary special education school teacher & a NYC police officer.

Reared in Westchester County, New York, Bob currently lives in Yorktown, New York. He graduated from Valhalla High School in 1968. During his varied interesting life's journey, He was a carpenter & taxidermist before joining the Greenburgh Police Department. He served as a decorated patrolman for ten years, before leaving to pursue a career as a commercial photographer. While still a police officer he opened Bob Buchanan Photography, creating award-winning photographs for many small and fortune 500 clients.

At the present time, Bob expanded to producing several of his own TV pilots and worked as an Associate Producer of two Indy films. Bob has published two art photography volumes that focuses on the special beauty of women over forty titled, "Real Woman, 40 and Beyond, that won the 2011 NY Book Fest top award for the photography / art category. His other photography volume "My Old Toy Box, Imagination Not Included, is photographs and commentary taking the reader to simpler happier days of their childhood.

Bob opened himself up as a Medium Caulbearer, something he has had all his life, but until recently hid from. His popularity as a medium has grown both nationwide and internationally. It is now Bob realizes those past lives in the book were visions from the other side.

www.ingramcontent.com/pod-product-compliance
Lightning Source LLC
Chambersburg PA
CBHW022218010726
47493CB00002B/512